Cassandra's Daughter

Also by Vickie Oddino

Clara's Journal: And the Story of Two Pandemics
nonfiction

Cassandra's Daughter

by
Vickie Oddino

Dobson St. Publishing
Chicago, IL

Copyright © 2022 Vickie Oddino

All rights reserved. No part of this book may be reproduced or used in any manner without the prior written permission of the copyright owner, except for the use of brief quotations in a book review. To request permission, contact the publisher at info@dobsonstpublishing.com

Paperback ISBN: 978-1-7369203-3-6
ebook ISBN: 978-1-7369203-4-3

Library of Congress Control Number: 2022915873

First paperback edition October 2022

Cover design by ebooklaunch.com

Dobson St. Publishers
Chicago, IL
www.dobsonstpublishing.com

This book is dedicated to Emily and James,
to whom I have bequeathed the power to tell my story.

"The past is never dead. It's not even past."

Requiem for a Nun
William Faulkner

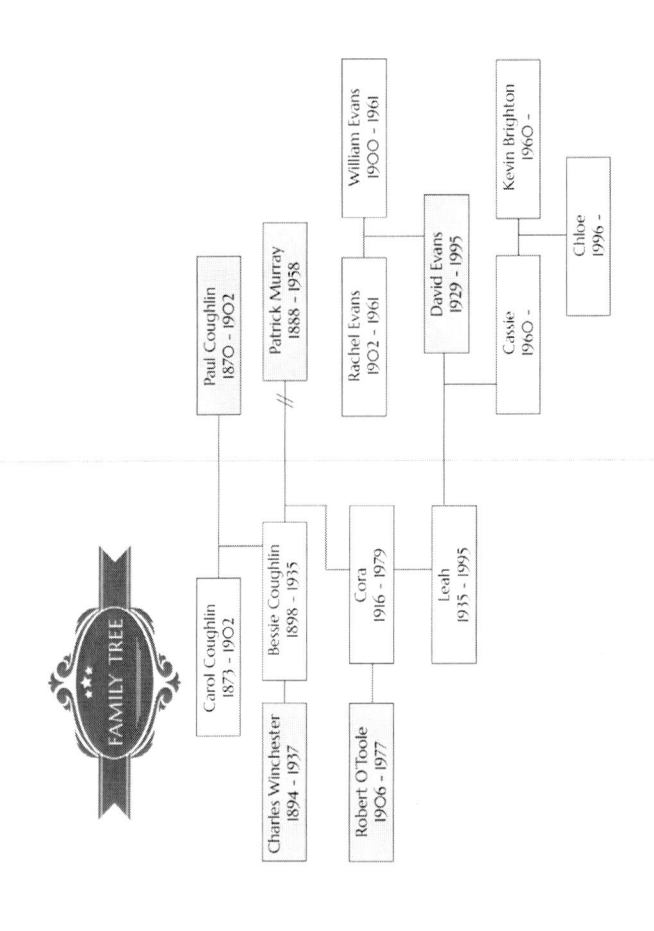

Prologue

April 2000

"Augustus Abner McGuire."
"Helen C. Moran."
"Captain Thomas Tillet."

When I am in a cemetery, I make sure to call out the names as I pass the headstones.

"Clarence Leary."

I've heard it said that we die twice. The first when our heart takes its final beat. The second when someone utters our name for the very last time.

"Penelope Brown."

"We will never forget!" we promise the dead. Until no one is left behind to remember.

"Sylvia Grace Smith."

I work to bring back to life as many as I can. It's an act of defiance against God. But it's never enough.

I'm overcome with helplessness when confronted with the starving who have been dumped unceremoniously into a mass grave in Skibbereen or the innocents incinerated into nothingness at Birkenau. Or with those buried in a Gullah cemetery, at rest under the words "Unknown Grave" scratched with a dull blade into makeshift tombstones. I can't save them.

So I concentrate on those I can save.

"Margaret Cooney."

As I wind my way through the grounds, incomplete stories stir under my feet. Stories of tenderness, of loathing. Of exuberant joy and intolerable despair. Stories of undaunted courage. Stories of cruel misfortune. Stories of shame and of suffering.

Those who now slumber here took great care to craft the stories they shared with the world, confident that these cold stones would forever stand sentry over the truth left untold.

I pass burial site after burial site, and my imagination fills in the blanks. I relive the heartbreak of a mother who buried her baby, a baby that gave up on this world in less than a day. I mourn the devastation of a family wiped out in a matter of weeks to an unnamed, deadly epidemic. According to the dates on the crosses clustered together, the son went first, then an infant, the mother, the daughter, and finally the father. What unimaginable agony for the father. Did he also succumb to the same disease? Or was it the torment of witnessing his entire family die, one by one? I experience the tragedy of a young Union drummer boy fatally injured at the Battle of Antietam, his body abandoned on the field to the mercy of looters and animals after survivors scatter in frightened defeat.

But it's time that wins. Time is always the victor. Limestone weathers, concrete crumbles, wood disintegrates, rivers swallow lands, sands bury towns. And stories collapse.

Yes. Stories collapse. For we can't let them rest. Instead, we incautiously wrest those stories from the grave and then brutally dismember, interrogate, and ultimately reconstruct them to suit us, to heal us. There's no safety in death.

But today is different. Today I visit Oakdale Cemetery.

I hurry through winding, overgrown trails. The glow on the horizon shifts from a deep orange to a pale splash of coral as the landscape anticipates the sun's arrival. The display of colors builds to a crescendo, and I quicken my step.

I am not here today to wander, to imagine, or to save lives.

I am here to see my mother.

Part I

Chapter 1

August 1921

The rumors were true. Patrick had been meeting some woman at cheap hotels and seedy bars, nearly daily. Bessie knew they were true because she went to the All Star Motor Court, one of the rumored hotels, to see for herself. And she brought her young daughter Cora. Even though she was only five, she should know the truth about her father.

Bessie didn't create a scene or even bother to confront him. It was unnecessary. As soon as he left for work, she packed one bag for herself and one for Cora, and they left him, hand in hand. A team. She didn't come all this way from Ireland to smell of sardines, but she would do so again because she certainly didn't come all this way to endure a rotten, cheating husband. They returned to India Street, deep in the Irish neighborhood of Munjoy Hill in Portland, Maine, and moved into one of the available rooms at the McCarthy's that was recently left vacant by a border who left to get married. Once settled, Bessie returned to work at the sardine cannery.

This was her second time landing at the McCarthy home. The first time was in 1914. Bessie had been only sixteen when she stood at the rail of the RMS Lapland as it prepared to depart from Queenstown Port in County Cork. Below, an electrified crowd of people gathered at the edge of the water, waving goodbye and calling out to those who stood all around her. The energy was so infectious that she waved back, beaming. It didn't matter that they were all strangers.

The harbor was teeming with boats: tug boats spewing black smoke out of their stacks, sailing vessels carrying teams of men scrambling on the decks, lone men rowing about in small wooden boats, and boats the likes of which Bessie had never seen before milling about.

She scanned the crowd onshore, in awe at the commotion that she had just navigated through in order to board the ship. Somehow she had wound her way around the throngs of people, making her way past dockworkers stacking baggage to load, past postmen pulling mailbags off train cars that had just railed in from all over Ireland, and past families sharing heartbreaking farewells. Before reaching the ship, her eye momentarily caught the milky eyes of an old woman frantically searching the crowd of passengers already at the rail above her. One of her hands tightly gripped the arm of an old man, whose disfigured back left him hunched over, and her other hand covered her mouth, her eyes darting back and forth across the ship's length. Bessie's stomach clenched; she was reminded of the look in her own nana's face back in Skibbereen when she had said goodbye, both understanding that it was likely the last time they would see each other.

She managed to find her way to the gangplank, and she hesitated at the bottom, taking in the scene. But the impatient young man behind her yelled, "Let's go! Move it!" So she did, following the crowd until she found herself at the railing.

The view was breathtaking. St. Coleman's Cathedral towered over the colorful buildings that lined the esplanade: the reds, the greens, the blues, and the oranges. As far as she could see, there was continuous movement. It was a stark contrast to the town she just left, which always felt stagnant, like it was full of death. Her parents died when she was young. She didn't remember either of them. Her nana said they died from a weakness in the Coughlin family line, a weakness that her nana managed to escape and that she grew up determined to also escape. Skibbereen had been disproportionately devastated during an Gorta Mor, and the Coughlins had performed their civic duty by sacrificing untold numbers to starvation in the name of Ireland.

A chilly breeze blew through Bessie's hair, and she pulled her coat a bit tighter around her, but enough sun had pushed its way through the clouds that one could call it a sunny day. She took a deep breath, drawing in the smells of sweat and smoke and fish. A handful of seagulls screeched as they circled the deck. And then the boat whistle: two long blasts that sent Bessie's hands up to cover her ears. Some passengers yelled out in excitement at the sound; others laughed. And one little boy shrieked in terror at the noise before collapsing into tears.

Men down on the dock pushed people aside, untying ropes and tossing them up to others on the ship who were waiting to catch them and reel them in. And then, barely perceptible at first, the ship pulled away. People on board rushed to the back rail so they could continue to wave to their loved ones until they vanished from sight. But Bessie stayed put. She grasped the charm hanging on a little chain around her neck between her thumb and forefinger. Her nana had given it to her before she left. She told Bessie to wear it as a reminder to stay strong.

As the ship pulled out of Cork Harbor, Bessie turned her back to Queenstown and walked to the front of the ship. They were headed for open ocean. It was hard to imagine that on the other side of that vast expanse was New York and a new future.

Only a few people stood at the front. It seemed that more people longed to look back at what they were leaving rather than look forward to where they were going. But Bessie was finished looking back. Her family had been looking back for generations. Yet as she gazed out into the unknown, a flutter of doubt ran through her body.

"No," she said out loud in an attempt to remind herself. "This is what I am meant to do."

A gentleman standing near her thought she might be speaking to him: "Excuse me, Miss?"

She smiled. "Oh, nothing. Just excited to get to America."

"As am I," he smiled back at her. "As am I."

And they both turned back to their futures.

Her future would take her from Ellis Island to Portland, Maine, where in her first years in her new country she lived with the McCarthy's. But now, returning to India Street felt like she was doing exactly what she had come to America to avoid: looking backward.

"Ow. Mamaí. That hurts," the little voice squeaked out of her young daughter. Bessie hadn't realized how tightly she was squeezing Cora's hand.

It was then that she heard the unmistakable voice of Mrs. McCarthy call out, "Bessie!"

On the front porch, the woman Bessie had grown to love as family pushed herself up off a rocking chair. This was the woman who upon her arrival had found Bessie work at a sardine factory and who had introduced her to the same Patrick that she was now escaping. Cora dropped her mother's hand and raced ahead, disappearing in the older woman's bosom. Mrs. McCarthy only let go of Cora when Bessie caught up, and heartbroken at what had happened with Patrick, she pulled Bessie into a warm embrace.

Once the two women let go of each other, Mrs. McCarthy, whose family was also from Skibbereen, hurried them into the home that she used as a lodging house for other Irish immigrants seeking work and a place to live. She took Bessie and little Cora to the room she had set up for them.

"Cora," Mrs. McCarthy said, "why don't you unpack your bag. You can use the bottom drawer in the dresser there against the wall. And let me talk to your mother for a minute."

Cora did as she was told, and the two women joined Mr. McCarthy in the parlor.

"I'm so sorry to be back here like this," Bessie apologized.

"Oh stop it. Right now. You are always welcome here, and you know it," Mrs. McCarthy scolded.

Mr. McCarthy chimed in, "I am just sick at that bastard."

"Mr. McCarthy!" His wife feigned shock at his language.

"Well, he is. And I feel responsible. We are the ones who introduced you two," he said.

Bessie paused before speaking. "Don't apologize. I have Cora because you introduced me to that ... well, he's right. To that bastard."

Mrs. McCarthy snorted when she was trying to gasp in shock, and the three of them broke out into laughter.

"Yes, you do," Mrs. McCarthy agreed. "And that young lady has the fight of your granda Sean inside her. I just know it. He wasn't going to lie down and let an Gorta Mor take him down with the rest of the family. He was strong, like you and Cora. Remember when Cora was born? I didn't think she was going to make it. I didn't know if *you* were going to make it. But she kicked and screamed and fought her way to this life."

Bessie knew that to be true. But she wasn't so sure if she herself still felt like fighting for this life.

Cora pulled the few things her mother had packed for her out of her bag: two cotton dresses, a cardigan and a pull-over sweater, a pair of stockings and a pair of socks, brown lace-up leather shoes (she was wearing her Mary Janes), and pajamas. But her mother told her she could also bring two special items, but only two, she stressed. Cora struggled with the decision as she carefully searched for something she couldn't live without. She decided on a large hair bow. It was so much more fun than wearing a dumb hat. And her baby doll, her Bábóg.

Now here in their new home, she placed everything in the bottom dresser drawer except Bábóg; they needed to have a talk.

"We're going to love it here. That's what Mamaí said. Mrs. McCarthy is going to take good care of us, so don't you worry," she assured Bábóg.

Cora didn't feel as confident the night before. Tucked behind a hedge, five-year-old Cora crouched down next to her mother and peered through the branches of a large bush. Her mother had woken her up and told her that they were going on an adventure. Cora was always up for an adventure. The two of them set out in the dark of night, ducking behind buildings and prowling alleyways.

"What is it?" Cora whispered, struggling to see the target of their evening expedition.

Her mother sharply shushed her, the index finger of one hand at her lips and of the other pointed through the bush toward a plain building on a street populated with others just like it. Streetlights illuminated most of the area but not where her mom pointed. That particular door was shadowed in darkness. Then it swung open, and momentarily, the light from inside revealed the faces of two men stepping out into the street.

Cora wondered who they were. And why they were here spying on them. But her mother hadn't said a word. The night air was cool, even for August, and when Cora involuntarily shivered, she tucked herself under her mother's arm for its warmth. The two sat crouched like that for an uncomfortably long time until another man approached the building and knocked on the next door over, a door better lit. When a woman answered, her features were unclear, but the man was spotlighted. Cora watched restlessly as the man turned back to scan the street. And then she saw it.

"Daidí!" Cora said under her breath. She assumed they were here to surprise him, so she moved to pounce out at him. But her mother stopped her cold. Her father glanced around once more, and Cora thought he had spotted them. Then a woman answered the door and threw her arms around his neck. He wrapped his arm around her waist and pulled her in close before disappearing behind the closed door.

"Didn't he see us?" Cora asked. "He'll be so surprised to see us!"

"No. We need to get home. We will be going to the McCarthy's in the morning, so think about what you want to take with you." She took Cora by the hand, and the two of them retraced their route back home in silence.

Cora didn't understand.

The next day, as directed, Cora picked out a few things to take with her. When they finished packing, she grabbed the bouncy sponge ball her dad had given her.

"I said only two, and you already picked the bow and your baby doll," Bessie reminded her daughter. So after some consideration, Cora dropped the ball.

Then the two of them journeyed to the other side of town. The McCarthys were like family. Cora struggled to keep up with her mother, who was dragging her along by the hand. Cora was just about to issue the usual complaints: "My feet hurt," "I'm tired," "Are we almost there?" when up ahead Cora saw Mrs. McCarthy rocking on the front porch. When Mrs. McCarthy saw the two approaching, she pushed herself up out of the chair to greet them. Cora dropped her mother's hand and ran to the woman who was like a grandma to her. Mrs. McCarthy swallowed Cora into her arms and squeezed tight. When she let go, she embraced Bessie.

Chapter 1

Cora clung to Bábóg as she wondered why they came to the McCarthys with suitcases and without Daidí. She tugged on her mother's dress, breaking up the long welcome between the two women and was then taken to the new room she would share with her mother.

When her mother was finished talking with Mrs. McCarthy, she came to get Cora to help with the dinner preparations. At home, Cora's job was to set the table, so her mother insisted she take up that job at the McCarthy's as well. But when Cora looked at the dining table, she let out an involuntary whine. The table was so big

"Hush up," her mother scolded. "You can do this. You just have to set more places, that's all. Here, start with the placemats." Her mom pointed to the stack of placemats in the pantry. She had barely finished when the other tenants appeared in the dining room, hungry for Mrs. McCarthy's cooking.

For Cora, the dinner was overwhelming. The table full of adults told stories she didn't understand and whispered secrets to each other before breaking out in riotous laughter. And she was still unclear as to why they had come here to stay without her father. But no one seem interested in that topic. Once everyone was finished eating, Cora helped clear the table. Her mother then sent her upstairs to get ready for bed. It had been a long, emotional day.

Cora did as she was told and changed into her pajamas. Then as she was tucking Bábóg into bed, her mother opened the bedroom door.

"Cor? I'm going to clean myself up a bit," her mother explained as she removed her necklace, wristwatch, and ring, leaving them on top of the dresser. "Then I think it's time for both of us to get some rest, she continued. "I'll be right back."

Her mother closed the door behind her, and Cora's curiosity got the better of her. She wanted to see her mother's jewelry. She had never seen her mother take her necklace or her ring off. She reached up to the top of the dresser. She hadn't ever paid either much attention. The ring was a plain gold band, but she wouldn't have been able to describe the charm dangling from the necklace in any detail if she had been asked to. But now she had a chance to hold that silver charm in her hand. She draped it around her neck to see what it would look like on her. She took it over to Bábóg and held it up to her neck.

"You look beautiful!" she complimented her baby doll.

Footsteps. Mamaí was coming back! Cora jumped up and returned the necklace to the dresser just as Bessie opened the door.

"Your turn, Cora," she instructed.

When finished in the bathroom, Cora bounced back into the room, and her mother was sitting on the edge of the bed removing her slippers; she crawled over her mother to plop down on the side of the bed closest to the wall, the side she had declared was "her side."

What a treat! Cora never got to sleep in the same bed as her mom. She curled under her mother's arm and reached over to feel if the necklace was back around her mother's neck. She was comforted it was.

"Where'd you get this, Mamaí?" she asked, stroking the silver charm. "What is it?"

"My necklace? My grandmother gave it to me. When I left Ireland to come to America."

"Your grandmother? Who's your grandmother?"

"I guess I haven't told you about her, have I? You would have loved her. She certainly loved me. And she would have loved you too. She was the only one who encouraged me to come to America, the only one who believed I was strong enough to actually do it. She gave me this cláirseach as a going-away gift."

"A what?" Cora had never heard the foreign-sounding word.

"A cláirseach. A harp. It was created by the Celtic goddess Canola," Bessie explained. "Do you want to hear a story about her?"

"Yes!" Cora answered.

Cora and Bessie stretched out on the bed, facing each other.

Bessie began. "One day, Canola was very upset after arguing with the man she loved, so she took a walk along the beach, hoping the ocean and the sand would give her strength during this time of hardship and heartbreak."

"And what happened?" Cora interrupted.

"When she got to the beach, the most beautiful music surrounded her. It was so lovely that she went off in search of its source and, would you believe it? She came upon the body of a giant whale that had washed up on the shore and died on the beach."

"A dead whale? Ewww." Cora scrunched up her face in disgust.

"But that's just it. It wasn't terrible. The music was created by the wind blowing through the remains of that same dead whale. And the music comforted Canola. You see, the music represented life, life that was borne out of death. It was so beautiful that Canola designed the Celtic harp to recreate the music she heard that day. This harp." Bessie held the charm in her hand.

Cora reached over and ran her fingers over the winged woman whose back served as the pillar of the harp.

"Is this Canola?"

"There are many stories about this lady. Some say she is an angel. Some say she is Erin, Ireland herself. I think she looks like a merrow."

"What's a merrow?"

"A merrow? Oh, a merrow is a very special creature. An Irish sea-fairy, much like a mermaid."

Cora had always loved her mother's stories. And she had been lucky enough to frequently be the audience to her stories, whether about the children in Lir or about the little white cat and the princess.

"Can you tell me about merrows?" Cora tucked herself back into her mother's arm in preparation for this new story.

"Of course! My nana told me all about them. Merrows have been around for a very long time. Sailors have reported hearing merrow music rising from the ocean. Some have even claimed to have seen merrows dancing upon the waves. Can you imagine seeing that? That would be something, wouldn't it? When I sailed to America from Ireland, I looked out on the sea in search of a merrow, but I never saw one. But if you ever did see one, you wouldn't want to treat it badly," she cautioned.

"I would never treat a merrow badly," Cora protested.

"Of course you wouldn't. But in the past, some people have treated them badly. They may be beautiful, and they can calm a storm at sea simply with their song. But they can also cause a dangerous storm if they are provoked."

Cora's eyes grew big.

"But most importantly, a merrow has a rebellious spirt and hungers for freedom." Bessie paused. "Like us, Cora."

Cora let go of the harp and rested her head back on her pillow.

"So my nana gave me this necklace when I left for America," Bessie continued explaining to her daughter. "No one from our village could understand why I needed to leave. No one in our family ever left Skibbereen. But Nana understood. She knew that a great new life awaited me here. And you know what? She probably knew that you would be here with me."

Bessie rubbed the pendant between her fingers. "I wear this to remind me that I have the power to create any life I want out of the ashes. And so can you," she concluded. Bessie unclasped the necklace. Cora lifted her head so that her mother could put the chain around her neck. "We both will have a new start here."

Bessie flipped the charm around so that the lady of the harp was face up as it lay on Cora's chest. Cora then vowed to forever wear the necklace with the magic harp. She rested her hand over it, and the two were soon asleep.

Chapter 2

July 1927

Cora quickly adjusted to life on Munjoy Hill. And over the years, as her mother improved her sewing skills and became a sought-after seamstress, Cora developed a love for creating new outfits with the bits and pieces of fabric and trim that she found lying around. Once she found a discarded lido hat, glued dried flowers to it, and wore it proudly to a neighborhood picnic. Another time when the McCarthys hosted a dinner for out-of-town friends, Cora made an appearance wearing her striped bathing suit, galoshes, outrageous costume jewelry, and her mother's elbow-high white gloves that stretched all the way up to her shoulders. Even when neighbors stopped by for a cup of tea and some gossip, Cora could be counted on to appear in some ridiculous outfit, whether in her bloomers and a blouse or wrapped in a sheet as a makeshift dress. She always received the reaction she sought: laughter and love.

Today, she grabbed her favorite dress from the closet. Two years ago, she had picked out the pattern from one of the catalogues that are always piled up on a side table in the front hall. And she asked her mother to make it for her ninth birthday. Her mother suggested the bright blue fabric because it drew out the blue in Cora's eyes. But today, the same dress was a muddy grey, thanks to hours in the sun and her mother's constant, and rough, washing.

She pulled the faded dress over her head, and she nearly stuck her hand through the hole near the elbow on the right sleeve. A few days ago she had tripped on an unseen rock and slid down a dirt trail, resulting in the tear. And her mother had long ago quit wrestling with the pleats. She dug around her mother's sewing box and found a green ribbon, which she used as a belt to eliminate the drop waist. The white pointed collar no longer lay flat; instead it poked her in the chin. So she rummaged through the sewing box for a safety pin to secure the collar to the front of her dress. Once the pin had done its job, Cora tore out of her room and out the front door.

"Bye Mom! Bye Mrs. McCarthy!" Cora yelled as the door slammed behind her.

She didn't wait for a response. She felt certain that today, as she felt about every day, held an adventure, and she was anxious to see what it might be.

She jogged down the front porch steps to the sidewalk, contemplating her choices for the afternoon, when whistles and laughter wound their way up the street. The neighborhood gang of boys was headed her direction. They found pleasure in frightening feral cats and little girls. And it was easy for them to do, strutting down the middle of the road, swinging chains, wielding pocket knives, and hurling rocks at fleeing targets.

She ran back up the steps, hoping to hide inside until they were gone, when she heard, "Cora! Wait."

Cora stopped, her hand on the door handle, surprised to hear her name coming from the group. Jimmy K., a mop of dirty blond hair bouncing atop his head, raced out in front of the other boys until he stood facing Cora at the foot of her walkway. He flashed her a little side grin as he brushed his hand across his forehead to push the hair back out of his eyes.

Jimmy K.'s family had lived next door since long before Cora and her mother moved in with the McCarthys. A number of years back, tragedy befell Jimmy K.'s family when his sister, who had been Cora's age, drowned in a nearby lake. Jimmy K's parents had since lived as if in a fog. Which meant Jimmy K. was, for the most part, on his own. His parents simply had nothing left for him, for all of their dreams and hopes settled at the bottom of the lake, never drudged up, not even when the Coast Guard recovered the body. Not even when the entire town came out to pay their respects. Not even when the little girl was laid to rest in a small church cemetery, safeguarded by a handful of Civil War veterans.

Jimmy K., on the other hand, was determined to survive his sister's death. His interest in Cora came from the guilt of not being able to protect his sister, for he was with her at the lake that day. He shifted his attentions to where he might be able to rectify his failure. And he found that in Cora. Only two years older, he behaved as if he were placed in her life to protect her as only a big brother can.

He continued up the walk to where she stood on the steps, leaving the rest of the boys down at the curb to watch.

"What you doin' with them boys, Jimmy K.? They're not nice," Cora scolded.

"Oh, they're fine, Cora. Don't mind them. They're not as tough as they look," he assured her.

He shot them his best attempt at a threatening glare, and they immediately quit fiddling around. And like that, the five menacing boys from whom she had wanted to run a moment ago faded from her view. They had transformed into five ordinary boys, not much older than she. One earnestly picked his nose, wiping the booger he found on the boy next to him, which was greeted with high-pitched squeals. The smallest of the group jumped on the back of another, wrestling him to the ground before bouncing right back up to yell "I win!" The defeated boy wiped his tears with the back of his sleeve. And a pudgy boy was distracted by a butterfly and chased it about.

With a newfound bravery, Cora faced Jimmy K., hands on hips.

"What'a ya calling me like that for? What'a ya want?" she demanded, striking a posture so that the other boys would know she was someone to contend with.

"Fine. Never mind. I wanted to make sure you were ok. Over at the market, your mom said you fell down and tore up your arm."

"Aw, I'm fine. It's nothing. I just tripped, that's all." Cora twisted around for a better view of her right forearm, decorated with red streaks that ran up and down like bloodied rivers, converging and meandering. Cora picked at the dried blood, flicking fragments onto the ground.

A chorus of protests sang out from the curb: "Oh man. Jimmy, let's get outta here. I don't wanna watch that." "You're sick!" "You better not hit me with one of those!"

Jimmy K. waved his hand at the boys, like a conductor signaling for a decrescendo, and they were left silent and gap-mouthed while awaiting their next order.

"All right then. Be more careful, Cora," he said with affection.

"Let's go to the tracks!" the smallest of the group, Wrestler Boy, called out. The rest wholeheartedly agreed. And they were off, alternately pushing, tripping, and pummeling each other as they ran.

When the boys disappeared around a corner, Cora knew she had found today's adventure. She had never been to the tracks, and she wasn't about to miss whatever might await her. She didn't have time to run back in and get shoes; the boys would get too far ahead. But by this point in the summer, her feet had toughened up enough that the pebbles she sometimes stepped on or the tree roots she stubbed her toe on went largely unnoticed. So she dashed off to follow them.

She ran as fast as she could, her skirt flying from one side to the other. But she maintained just enough distance so they wouldn't spot her and send her home. She tucked behind the red brick house on one corner only to peek out in time to see them race each other down the middle of the road. She crouched behind porches or a row of bushes. It was great fun. She imagined that she was on the African plain, a lioness tracking her prey. Luckily, the boys were single-minded, and they never did look back.

They turned left towards the river. She raced to the corner where they had disappeared, but she slowed as she rounded it in case they had stopped in the dirt field she knew was right there. But they were gone.

Now she had to play detective, relying on clues to find the boys. But she didn't have to wait long. Down at the next corner, a shoe came flying out from nowhere and landed in the middle of the intersection. Soon followed Crying Boy, one shoe on and one shoe off. He grabbed the wayward shoe and ran to the right. The chase was back on.

Chapter 2

When Cora turned right down the next street, she could see the group crossing Fore Street. They heckled people as they crossed, taunting drivers as they walked in front of cars and whistling at women of any age. Booger Boy grabbed a doll right out of a little girl's arms and swung it above his head as if he were going to launch it into the street. When her mother cursed him, he laughed, threw the doll at her instead, and ran to catch up to the others. Safely at a distance from the angry mother, he stuck his tongue out.

A couple of trucks rattled by, blocking Cora's view. After the trucks passed, the boys had disappeared from her sight. But she was not discouraged. At the next break in traffic, Cora darted across the street and slammed into the fence that cordoned off the tracks, both hands clutching the wires. She stuck her nose through one of the diamond-shaped openings and searched for the boys, but it was difficult to see through the thick brush on the other side of the fence. By now they would have made their way down into the ravine toward the tracks, she thought, frustrated.

Then she spotted them. She glanced around but saw no way to slip through the fence, and the barbed wire crawling along the top kept her from climbing over. She ran along the fence in the direction the boys were moving.

"Jimmy K.!" Cora yelled. She waved frantically and then straightened up to greet his shock at seeing her. He ran back up to the fence, leaving the others at the tracks.

"What are you doing, Cora? You shouldn't be here."

"I want to come to the tracks too."

Jimmy K. took a quick inventory of his surroundings. "All right. There's a hole in the fence down by that old oak you can crawl through. You just need to stay close to me. You understand?"

She nodded, contrite.

He pointed to a spot about twenty feet down and jogged along the inside of the fence to the opening.

She picked up a long stick, a perfect one for dragging along the fence: click, click, click. When she reached the hole, she threw the stick behind her, pausing to admire the distance it flew. Then without warning, she threw her legs through the hole, catching her dress on an exposed corner of the damaged fence. When she stood up on the other side, her dress was hiked up above her waist, exposing her knickers. Jimmy K. shielded his eyes, but Cora wasn't embarrassed. She was immersed in the anticipation of exploring the tracks.

"Let's pretend we're spies tracking soldiers who've deserted the fight! Think we'll find one hiding down here?" she wondered out loud as she wriggled around to release the hold the fence had on her.

Jimmy K. closed his eyes and felt around for the source of the problem. He gripped the dress and pulled, only to hear the material rip. His eyes flew open, the torn material between his fingers and no longer attached to Cora's dress.

"I'm sorry. I'm so sorry."

"Stop!" she protested, swatting his hand. She didn't want him fussing over her. Leaving him behind, she ran down the hill to the tracks to meet up with the other boys.

"I'm telling you, Cora. You'd better keep up with us. We're not waiting for you," Wrestler Boy warned her.

"I'll keep up. Don't worry about me," she assured him.

The group took off single file down the middle of the tracks, Jimmy K. bringing up the rear as any good leader would. As they neared The Portland Rail Company, multiple railroad sidings split off the main track, some storing empty train cars and others leading to warehouses. But the group stayed the course on the main track.

Before long, the enthusiasm of running wore them down, and they collectively slowed to a meandering stroll. Cora followed their lead, throwing ballast and startling chipmunks.

"Where we goin'?" Cora asked no one in particular.

"A tunnel," Butterfly Boy informed her, skipping backwards as he navigated the ties between the tracks. "Yeah, a long, dark, scary tunnel. You might be too scared for that Cora. Who knows what we might find in there." He wiggled his fingers in her face, trying to frighten her with the image. "Maybe we'll find a bear. Or pirates. Or maybe there's a dead man in there! Ooo-ooo-oo."

"I'm not scared," she protested. But just to be sure, she glanced over at Jimmy K. He smiled and slightly nodded to reassure her that she had no reason to take Butterfly Boy's taunts seriously.

Chapter 2

Cora hopped onto one of the metal tracks, tackling the thin rail as a new gymnast tackles the balance beam, each step landing squarely on its center, until a charge shot through the air, breaking her concentration.

The boys froze mid-step. Jimmy K. slowly raised a finger to his lips to quiet everyone, and he shot out his arm, motioning to the group to slow down. Like a soldier directing his troops away from the enemy, he motioned for them to back up into a set of bushes beyond the ballast on the side of the track. They obeyed, having learned long ago to trust Jimmy K.'s instincts. Cora, however, was not quite as trusting, so she performed her dismount and peered down the tracks, curious about what had interrupted their fun. Jimmy K. grabbed her arm and pulled her behind the bushes.

"What are you doin'?" she protested, spinning around to face him. Then it suddenly dawned on her. This was part of the game. "You see one of them deserters?!" She was wide-eyed with excitement.

"Quiet, Cora. I mean it," he hissed. She was taken aback by the seriousness of his demand and shut her mouth. Then she heard the voices. They came from a sidetrack where five or six boxcars stood empty. Jimmy K. pulled her down. Cora grunted as she fought against his strength. But he just tightened his grip, his fingers covering the bumps and valleys of scabs from Cora's previous fall.

"You're hurting me," she gritted through her teeth. But she wasn't going to be able to wriggle out of his grip, so she resigned herself to temporary defeat.

Cora crouched down next to Jimmy K. and peered through the branches of the bush. She scratched at the neck of her dress. She had no idea what they were supposed to be looking at. Jimmy K. continued to hold her with one hand and pointed through the bush and down the track with the other. Cora shuddered; her body reacted to the memory of another bush just like this.

She followed his finger until her eyes landed on two men, one in an elegant striped three-piece suit and a felt hat with a bright blue ribbon circling the crown. She had never seen such a colorful hat. All of Mr. McCarthy's hats had either a boring old black or grey ribbon. Cora thought this man was way too fancy to be in the squalor of a railyard. And just as she thought it, the man brushed something unwanted off the arm of his suit. Another man unloaded unmarked crates from one of the boxcars, a gun visible in a holster around his waist. The man with the colorful felt hat pulled a bottle from one of the boxes, opened it, and hoisted it to his lips, spilling liquid from the corners of his mouth. He extended his hand, and a third man in shirt sleeves and trousers held up with suspenders handed him a wad of cash. He held a gun in his other hand. The three men shook hands before the businessman crossed over a sidetrack and into the back of a black town car.

When the men disappeared, the boys exhaled in unison.

"You shouldn't have brought her here, Jimmy," Booger Boy said.

"I was quiet. I did what you said, didn't I, Jimmy K.?" She pleaded for his approval.

He nodded.

"What were those men doing? What were they talking about? Who were they?" Her imagination took off. "Were they thieves? Escaped prisoners? Fugitives?"

"We're getting out of here," Jimmy K. announced.

The boys stepped out from behind the row of bushes, and without a word, they all raced each other back to the hole in the fence, Cora right behind them.

Jimmy K. insisted they first take Cora home, and once there, he walked her to the front door.

"Sorry I let you come with us today, Cora. Didn't mean to scare you like that. You should never follow us again. You hear me?"

"You din't scare me at all. You boys were scared. Not me. Can't we go back tomorrow?"

"No, we aren't going tomorrow, Cora. Go on, get on inside, will ya?" He looked her in the eye to let her know he was serious, and then he turned on his heel and rejoined his crew.

Chapter 3

June 1929

In addition to her job at the cannery, Bessie had taken on periodic work as a seamstress. She gained a reputation as being both efficient and talented, so her name quickly spread across the town. She tracked the latest clothing trends and ensured that her clients stayed up-to-date, so it didn't take long for her to be able to eke out a living sewing. Thankfully, she was able to leave the cannery behind. So when Charles Winchester, a prominent local dentist, needed a suit tailored for an upcoming wedding, it was no surprise that he contacted Bessie.

With her sewing box in tow, Bessie arrived at Mr. Winchester's house in the West End neighborhood of Congress Street, an area a noticeable step up from Munjoy Hill. Bessie unlatched the large iron gate at the street and slipped through. She glanced around, admiring the colorful flowers lining each side of the walkway. When she reached the front door, she lifted the heavy ring hanging from a lion's mouth and used it to knock three times. Mr. Winchester opened the door immediately, greeting her with a smile and suit in hand.

Bessie heart pounded in her chest.

"You must be Mr. Winchester? Nice to meet you. I'm Bessie. I'm here to take measurements."

He didn't respond. He just smiled at her.

"For your suit," she added. "You needed your suit altered? Is that right?" Feeling flustered was new to Bessie.

"That's right. Yes, that's right," he replied, and he stepped back and motioned her inside.

He closed the front door and led Bessie to the parlor. She glanced around the room. It bore no resemblance to the McCarthy's home, which was an unintended tribute to the Victorian era: the dark floral wallpaper, the heavy burgundy drapes, the overstuffed furniture. Multiple framed photos, a variety of vases, and other assorted knick-knacks covered every flat surface.

In contrast, Mr. Winchester's home was so modern. Even futuristic. The unusual floor looked like a mosaic with paths of green and pink circling the perimeter of the room and geometric designs dancing across the center.

"Ah, I see you've noticed the floor. You like that? It's terrazzo. It was this floor that finally convinced me to buy this house a few years ago. Beautiful, isn't it?"

It most certainly was beautiful. And the furniture was sleek and clean, mostly made of leather with shiny brass accents. She ran her hand across the back of an asymmetrical green chair that had only one arm rest; the back was shaped like a scallop shell. Its partner chair was its mirror image.

"Those chairs were the first two pieces I bought for this room. I actually ordered them from New York," he said. Then he held out the suit he had been carrying and said, "Here's the suit I need altered."

"Oh no, not yet," she let him know. "I first need to take your measurements."

She placed her sewing box on an ottoman and opened it to retrieve her measuring tape. Instead, the box flipped and dropped to the floor, spilling its contents and causing a loud racket. Mr. Winchester tossed his suit onto the sofa and then dropped to the floor, and the two of them crawled about, scooping up the needles, thread, scissors, and pins that had scattered all over.

When they finished collecting all of her supplies, Bessie unrolled her tape measure and smiled.

"*Now* I'm ready," she let Mr. Winchester know.

"Of course. Of course. Do whatever you want to me." To Bessie's

Chapter 3

surprise, he laughed out loud. "Well, that's not exactly what I meant," he corrected himself. "Maybe not *any*thing." He chuckled and walked to the center of the room. With arms outstretched, he added with a wink, "I meant take any measurements you'd like."

Bessie couldn't keep herself from smiling at him before she encircled his chest with the measuring tape. She could feel his chest expand and contract as he breathed in and out.

"Forty-three inches," Bessie stated as she wrote the number in the little leather notebook that she carried around for such matters.

His arms still outstretched, she next bent over to measure his waist, unexpectedly self-conscious at the intimacy of the task despite measuring people's waists nearly every day.

"Excuse me." A woman's voice interrupted them.

Bessie dropped her arms and backed away. A middle-aged woman stood in the doorway, clearly hesitant to interrupt the scene. She wore a modest black dress, and her hair was pulled back into a tight braid. Was this his wife?

"Yes, Mrs. Wilson? What can I do for you?" he asked. That answered that. This was not his wife.

"I've finished with the kitchen. If you don't need anything else, then I will be going for the day."

"Of course, of course. Thank you. Please, go on home and enjoy your family."

"Also I left a letter on your desk from your sister-in-law with news about your children."

"That's great. Thank you."

"My pleasure. And I will see you in the morning."

Mrs. Wilson then opened the front hall closet to retrieve her jacket and hat, and she let herself out.

Bessie recorded his waist measurement, and desperate to make small talk to distract from the uncomfortable measurement of his inseam, she asked, "You have children?"

"No, uh. I mean yes. Yes. I have two children."

Bessie moved behind him to measure his arm length.

"You do? I have a daughter myself. She's thirteen. How old are yours?" Bessie continued.

"Three and one, but they no longer live here. They're in Michigan. With my sister-in-law," he explained as she measured his upper arm.

"I see," Bessie responded, confused. But it was none of her business, so she let it go and jotted down his arm measurements.

"I do miss them, you know. I didn't want them to leave. But my wife passed away," he confessed.

Bessie regretting bringing it up. She had no idea what to say.

"Honestly, I don't usually talk about it. It was a year ago. She died giving birth to my son. Our son," he corrected himself.

"I am so sorry Mr. Winchester. I didn't mean to pry."

"No, no. You didn't pry at all," he insisted. "At first, my sister-in-law stayed here to help with my two-year-old daughter and the baby. But she couldn't stay forever. She has her own family back in Michigan. I suggested we hire a nurse, and she even interviewed a few. But she claimed that none was sufficient for the job. So she thought it best to take them both back to Michigan with her. I really don't know what else I could have done. I have my own practice that requires my full attention. I'm sure it was the best decision."

"I'm sure you did what was best for the children," she agreed, uncomfortable with the conversation. "I have one more measurement to take: your neck. Would you mind sitting down so I can get that?"

"Of course, of course," he said, and he took a seat.

"Does your daughter need a dentist? My practice is in the Deering neighborhood. Winchester Children's Dentistry. I'd be happy to take her on as a patient," he offered.

"Thank you. Maybe." Bessie was fairly certain she could not afford him. And as she glanced around the room, she concluded that his practice had proven to be a very profitable distraction from the fate of his wife and two children.

"I can't raise them here, but I do send money every month to pay for their upbringing," he said. Bessie sensed a note of defensiveness.

"And Mrs. Wilson?" Bessie asked.

"She helps me out here. I can't even run this household by myself!" he laughed.

Bessie jotted down his neck measurement before slipping her notebook and measuring tape back into her sewing box.

Chapter 3

"Thank you for your patience, Mr. Winchester. I have all the measurements I need," Bessie told him.

"I'm sure you didn't want to hear all that," he apologized with a wave of the hand. He skipped a beat before continuing. "And please, call me Charles. So when do you think you can have the suit ready for me? Did I tell you I need it a week from Saturday?"

"Yes, you did tell me. I can have it for you by Wednesday if you'd like," she promised. "And please don't worry. I can't imagine how difficult it must be to have your children living so far away. I do hope you will be able to see them soon."

"I appreciate that. And Wednesday would be perfect. I look forward to seeing you. To seeing your work," he clarified.

She picked up the suit from the sofa, and he led her to the door, his hand guiding her on the small of her back. His hand was warm, and the warmth spread outward across and around her body.

When he closed the door behind her, Bessie paused. Poor man, she thought. And handsome. An afterthought.

She finished altering the suit by the next Wednesday, and before she headed back to Congress Street, she spent a little more time choosing her dress. She spent a little more time rubbing out the scuff marks on her best leather shoes. She spent a little more effort on the braid she twisted into a small bun at the nape of her neck. She glanced in the mirror and smoothed down any stray hairs around her ears and forehead. She pulled a small tube of lipstick out of her day bag, applied the color to her pursed lips, and used the tip of her pinky finger to straighten the line on her bottom lip. When Bessie stepped back, pleased with her image, she spotted Cora in the reflection. She spun around and embraced her, laughing.

"I didn't see you there, my dear. You snuck up on me. I've got to run now," Bessie said as she let go of Cora and picked up the finished suit. "I need to take this suit back to my customer. You be good. I'll be back soon."

A smiling Bessie floated downstairs and out the front door.

Chapter 4

August 1929

Bessie was finally ready to introduce her daughter and the McCarthys to Mr. Charles Winchester. The new couple had spent the past two months enjoying the Portland nightlife. And with him, Bessie felt the transformation she longed for. She even chopped off her hair into a stylish bob. The radio in her bedroom that had sat silent for years came alive, now broadcasting lively jazz tunes. Bessie bounced around the room, often pulling Cora into an impromptu dance. Sometimes the two of them let the music direct them, and their spasms would spill out into the hallway or down the stairs to the parlor.

Bessie hoped Cora would take to Charles easily. Not that it mattered. *She* had taken to him. But it would make all of this easier if Cora did as well. The two of them had lived at the McCarthy's for seven years now. As much as she appreciated their generosity, she was anxious to set up her own household. And what a house he had. And what a car too! A brand new burgundy Nash, with mohair seats. Bessie didn't know much about automobiles, but she did know that the car was beautiful.

The Sunday dinners Mrs. McCarthy prepared were legendary. People constantly moved in and out of the house on India Street, and many frequently returned on Sundays for one of Mrs. McCarthy's home-cooked meals. Bessie's plan was that Cora and the McCarthys could meet Charles during one of these Sunday dinners.

On this night, Mr. and Mrs. McCarthy, Mr. McCarthy's father, Bessie, and Cora would be joined by a previous tenant and his new wife, and the family of Mrs. McCarthy's cousin, the Cooneys, including her two girls who were close to Cora's age. With Charles, that would make eleven diners. This would be a Sunday dinner bigger than usual.

Mrs. McCarthy and Bessie spent the entire day in the kitchen. Charles would be a good match, they had both concluded. So they wanted everything to be perfect.

Charles was the last to arrive, and when the knock came on the door, the Cooney twins raced to answer it, dragging Cora with them. Charles blew into the McCarthy house like a strong wind, a bottle of Club Whiskey tucked under his arm. Mr. McCarthy pushed his way through the girls to properly greet his guest. And after a firm handshake, Charles presented his host with the bottle. Mr. McCarthy nodded his head in approval. Few could get the real McCoy during these times. Impressive. Charles removed his boater hat and placed it on the hat stand at the front door before turning to the little girl who looked like a miniature Bessie.

"You must be Cora," he declared.

Cora nodded her head.

"Well you are just as beautiful as your mother!" He unbuttoned his navy blazer and pulled out a small package. He bent down to eye level and handed her the brightly colored package. Enchanted, she politely accepted it.

"Go ahead. Open it. It's for you," he encouraged.

Cora tore open the paper, and inside was a Princess Mary mesh bag. The Cooney girls squealed. It was beautiful, the most beautiful gift Cora had ever received. She clutched it to her chest and thanked the stranger who she was told loved her mother.

"Dinner's ready," Mrs. McCarthy called from the kitchen. Charles had arrived just in time. The rest of the introductions were made, and the group disbursed to take their seats around the table.

"Everyone, please help yourself," Mrs. McCarthy invited as she picked up and passed the baked ham to get things started. Soon, all of the dishes were being passed around.

"We are so glad you could join us tonight, Charles. We love our

Bessie and sure would like to get to know you better," Mrs. McCarthy said as she scooped a spoonful of carrots and peas onto her plate.

"I look forward to getting to know you too," Charles replied. "I know how important you are to Bes. So ask me anything."

What followed was a barrage of questions from all of the dinner guests, not just from Mrs. McCarthy: Where were you born? Who are your parents? Where do you live? Where do you work?

But it didn't take long before Charles turned the conversation around and was the one asking the questions.

"So how did the two of you meet?" he asked his host and hostess as he helped himself to seconds. And before she knew it, Mrs. McCarthy was transported to Clonakilty, County Cork, and immersed in the love story of her and Mr. McCarthy.

After the Cooneys shared the story of their courtship, and the girls started to squirm restlessly in their seats, Mrs. McCarthy told her guests to wait one minute, and she dashed into the kitchen.

When she returned, she announced, "Here is Bessie's famous pineapple upside-down cake. And everyone simply must have a slice!" Bessie didn't really have a famous pineapple upside-down cake. But Mrs. McCarthy thought tonight would be as good a night as any to declare that she did.

Once everyone had cleaned their plates and complemented Bessie on her baking skills, Mr. McCarthy suggested, "Gentlemen, let's retire to the parlor, shall we?"

"Would you like us to help clean up, Mrs. McCarthy?" Charles asked as all the men stood up from the table.

"No, no, no. Don't be silly. These girls can help me. Ladies, why don't you join the men," Mrs. McCarthy insisted, "and we will join you in a few minutes." Cora and the Cooney twins all groaned. "Let's go girls," Mrs. McCarthy laughed. "Help me clear this table."

The rest of the adults took seats in the parlor, and the elderly Mr. McCarthy offered the men the cigars he saved for occasions such as this. Charles and Mr. Cooney thanked him, but Mr. McCarthy opted for his pipe, his usual after-dinner indulgence.

When they finished clearing the table, the three girls raced past the parlor and filed upstairs. They were uninterested in any boring adult talk.

Mrs. McCarthy then joined the others in the parlor. Before she had a chance to sit down, Charles placed his cigar in the ashtray, stood up, and took her hand.

"Would you care to dance?" he asked the surprised woman who hadn't danced since before World War I.

"Oh no, I can't dance," she playfully protested.

"Come on, Bessie. Let's show 'em how it's done." Charles took off his blazer and hung it across the back of his chair. Bessie jumped up to join him.

"Can you find us some dancing music on the radio, Bes?" he asked. "We're going to teach you the Charleston," he explained to the men and women in the room.

The McCarthys weren't the dancing type. They rarely even listened to music. An unstoppable force, Charles cleared the center of the parlor, pushing tables back against the wall and moving chairs to the entryway while Bessie took charge of the radio and sought a station playing the latest hot jazz.

"That'll work, Bes. It's Ben Bernie. Turn it up!"

When they heard the music, Cora and the Cooney girls scrambled back down the stairs and into the parlor. This was the music Bessie sometimes played on the radio in their bedroom.

"What's going on?" Cora asked.

"We're dancing!" Charles said, and he and Bessie were soon wildly swinging their arms and twisting their legs in the middle of the room. Mrs. McCarthy pulled her husband out of the chair where he was enjoying his pipe, and the two of them attempted to replicate the dancing that was lighting up their parlor. It didn't take long for the others to join them in a frenzied imitation of the couple. Cora and the Cooney girls joined in, bouncing around the room, kicking and spinning and ultimately falling in a pile on the floor laughing. Even the elderly Mr. McCarthy involuntarily tapped his foot to the rhythm of the unfamiliar music.

After a few more songs, even Bessie and Charles collapsed, and the Cooneys announced it was time to get the girls home and to bed. The girls protested until Charles switched off the radio, indicating the end of the fun. Once the Cooneys and the other couple said their goodbyes,

Chapter 4

Charles complimented Mrs. McCarthy on the delicious dinner, thanked the elderly Mr. McCarthy for the cigar, and praised Cora for her enthusiastic dancing. Mr. McCarthy gave Charles a hearty handshake and invited him over again soon.

"Cora," Mrs. McCarthy called, "why don't you come with me to the kitchen, and you can help me finish cleaning things up." She glanced back at Bessie and gave her a little wink and a little privacy. And Bessie walked Charles out to the street.

A few minutes later, the front door closed, and Bessie breezed back into the kitchen, grabbing Mrs. McCarthy by each hand.

"Tell me. Isn't he fantastic? I think I love him!" Bessie spilled out.

"Shhhh. Come on, Bessie." Mrs. McCarthy pulled her back into the parlor, leaving Cora behind to put away the rest of the dishes.

Chapter 5

June 1930

Cora had never given much thought to her hair and could rarely be bothered to pull a comb through it. Earlier in the year, her mother convinced her to cut hers into a simple bob too. After all, the new style would require very little maintenance.

But recently, she found herself combing it out and smoothing it down more often. And she even sometimes added extra pins to gain more control over it. On this day, she had desperately wanted to recreate the finger waves she saw on so many fashionable Portland women. So as soon as she woke up, she carefully pinned back the hair on the left side of her head, leaving the right side to hang loose. Her mother was always trying different hairstyles, so after wetting down the loose hair, Cora helped herself to the clips and gels on her dresser and got to work, carefully following the directions she found in a magazine promising "Fabulous Finger Waves in Three Easy Steps!"

Before she rejoined the guests, she stopped to look herself over in the entryway mirror at Charles's house, which she kept forgetting was now their house too. The waves weren't perfect, but she was satisfied Not bad for a first attempt, she thought. She pinched her cheeks to add a bit of color and then stepped back to take in the dress that her mother had made for her to wear on this day, the day her mother married Charles. The dress was made from a pastel green satin, panels of lace intermixing with satin on the drop waist skirt. The top half was a bit boxy, but she loved how the skirt swirled when she twisted her hips back and forth. Cora felt so grown up. She looked forward to the day she might find a man who loved her as much as Charles loved her mother.

Cora had liked Charles the first night she met him, but she had rarely seen him since then. Mostly, he and her mother went out to celebrate one thing or another. Cora missed having her mother to herself. But the fact that the woman who loved to giggle and imagine and explore had reappeared after years of somber seriousness made up for spending less time with her. However, as nice as he seemed, Cora wasn't sure she was ready for the adjustment of moving into Charles's stylish house. In the mirror, however, she saw a young woman who might more easily make the transition.

The guests gathered in the back yard under a tent Charles rented for the occasion. Cora didn't know most of the people invited, so she hesitated before returning to the scene where all the chairs and tables had been pushed aside and strangers danced, oblivious to anything but the unbounded joy of the moment.

As Cora glanced at her reflection one last time before returning to the party, Jimmy K. walked in through the front door. Cora's heart surprised her by skipping a beat. He donned a blue serge suit for the occasion, his wild blond hair tamed with a bit of Brilliantine, a razor-straight part slightly off-center. He tugged on the collar around his neck. She knew he was much more comfortable wearing a vest and trousers and running around with his friends.

"Look at you. And that hair!" Cora teased as she reached up to touch the greasy hairdo.

"Don't touch." He grabbed her hand. But then he promptly dropped it, and they were locked in an awkward silence.

"You look nice," he finally said.

As her mind searched for a response she was comfortable with, his blush deepened. And she found that she enjoyed his blushing.

Boom! The front door flew open, startling Cora. Jimmy K. groaned. It was the neighborhood boys, Butterfly Boy and his gang. Jimmy K. had grown away from the boys since that day at the train tracks, but these boys hadn't changed a bit.

"Oh ho ho! Lookey wat we got here fellas!" Booger Boy, aka Milford (Cora laughed out loud the first time she heard his actual name), slowed down to encircle and examine Jimmy K. "You look mighty fine today, I'd say! You wouldn't be getting all dolled up for this here Cora now, would you?"

The boys all strutted in the doorway to surround Jimmy K. and to laugh at his carefully Brilliatine'd hair. Then they turned their attention to Cora.

"Whadda ya think about Jimmy K., Cora?"

"Lookin' pretty good, huh?"

"How about that hair?"

Laughter punctuated the interrogation.

Cora froze.

"Time for cake!" Mrs. McCarthy had come searching for Cora and thankfully interrupted the uncomfortable silence. "You don't want to miss that."

The boys were officially done with Jimmy K. and Cora. They scrambled off like little toddlers at their first birthday party.

Jimmy K. was back on solid footing. "Come on, Cora. Let's go get some cake. I sure do hope it's chocolate."

"I can tell you that you're in luck today. It most certainly is chocolate." she assured him.

Chapter 6

July 1933

Cora fairly quickly adapted to life on Congress Street, and her mother had no problem making the adjustment. But they continued to visit India Street as often as they could. So when it came time for the annual street party, Cora and her mother spent the morning making potato salad. Cora diced the boiled potatoes while Bessie chopped the hard boiled eggs. Cora appreciated this time with her mother. She just finished up high school, graduating only a couple of weeks ago, and she had focused on finding a job.

Bessie dumped the eggs into a large bowl of celery and onions. "You done with the potatoes?" she asked Cora.

"I am," Cora answered, putting the knife down and dumping the potatoes into the bowl. "Are we done? Can I go finish getting ready?"

Bessie laughed as she poured the dressing into the bowl. "Yes, go, go. And hurry up. We need to leave soon."

Cora untied her apron, threw it over a chair, and ran up the stairs to her room. She loved the Fourth of July. She stepped in front of the full-length mirror and double-checked the high-waisted pants that she had slipped on earlier. Yes, she was happy with them. It was a new style for her; normally she wore dresses, but she loved how playful, and maybe even a little mischievous, she felt in these flowy pants. She had let her hair grow out, and the curls cascaded right below her shoulders. As she smoothed down the stray hairs, her mother called up to her.

"We need to go, Cora. Come get this container of the cookies we made last night."

Cora raced back down, and her mom handed her the cookies. She then picked up the potato salad, and the two left to make their way to Munjoy Hill. Charles had an emergency patient who he agreed to meet at his office. He would catch up with them later.

The block where the McCarthys lived was shut off to traffic, so all of the neighbors had gathered in the street. Cora and Bessie weaved through the crowd, greeting friends along the way, to find the long table where they added their dishes to the cornucopia of food.

Just as Cora pulled the top off the container of cookies, a hand reached from behind her and grabbed one. She knew exactly whose hand it was, and she gave it a playful slap as she scolded its owner. Then she spun around to face Jimmy K., who already had the cookie in his mouth and a smile on his face.

"Shame on you! These are for later," Cora teased.

"Aw, come on. I want to make sure I get one before they're all gone," he protested, wiping the crumbs from his face with the back of his hand. "That's pretty good!"

"Thank you," Cora curtsied in jest.

"Come with me," Jimmy K. said as he grabbed her hand to lead her away. "Remember Milford? He's a great saxophonist, and he started a swing band. They're setting up in front of my house. Let's go see how they sound."

Cora wanted to hear them too. He dropped her hand as soon as they stepped away from the food table, and they navigated the crowds that socialized up and down the block. As they approached Jimmy K.'s house, they could hear the music, and a little dance floor had opened up around the band.

"Oooo, I know this song!" Cora declared as they reached the dancers. Soon she was swaying and singing along: "Walk right in, sit right down. Daddy let your mind roll on …"

Jimmy K. let out a nervous laugh. She stopped and smiled up at him. "Don't you know this song?" she asked.

"Of course I do. But I'm not going to sing it. But by all means, you go ahead. Keep singing," he said, lightly elbowing her as encouragement.

A couple pushed their way between them, and soon they were engaged in a complicated dance right in front of them. They were obviously practiced dancers, and Cora enjoyed watching them. Jimmy K. quickly added, "I'm not dancing. I have no idea how to do any of that." Cora didn't either, but she did think it might be fun to try.

"Walk right in, sit right down. Baby let your hair hang down …" she softly sang as the song winded down.

The band announced they were taking a quick break, and Milford put down his sax before running over to Jimmy K.

"How'd we sound?" he asked with an infectious enthusiasm.

Jimmy K. and Milford then engaged in a conversation about the band that Cora excused herself from. She went on to enjoy a day of pleasantries with her mother's friends and the McCarthy's neighbors, of feasting on barbeque, and of games and entertainment. As dusk set in, Cora and the kids from the Munjoy Hill area raced over to the Promenade to catch the fireworks display that was about to start.

"I got a job," Cora confessed to Jimmy K. as they followed the crowd to the waterfront.

"You did? That's great. You found that so fast. You just graduated. I know people who have been looking for work for months."

"Charles helped me."

"Still, you had to interview for it, right? You got the job because you had a great interview. Besides, you deserve it."

Cora giggled, "Yes, of course. I went to an interview."

"So what's the job?"

"At Casco Bay Iron Works. The switchboard."

"That's fantastic, Cora." In a spontaneous display of enthusiasm, Jimmy K. picked her up and swung her around. "Congratulations!"

"Put me down!" Cora screeched in laughter.

He did, and she smiled up at him, smoothing down her hair. "I spent a lot of time on this hair," she protested, knowing he would take the scolding more seriously than she meant it. So she reached up and mussed up his head of floppy curls before jogging off to secure the perfect spot for viewing the fireworks.

Chapter 7

May 1934

For months, Cora had been transferring Mr. Gene Peterson's calls to the company president, Mr. Longfellow. And then by chance, she actually met the man whose calls she had been answering. At the end of her shift one day, Cora opened the door to the stairwell as two men in suits were coming down from the third floor. She typically took the stairs, but Casco Bay Iron Works had recently installed an electric elevator, and Cora didn't feel comfortable riding it. It broke down repeatedly, and she had a paralyzing fear of being inside when it broke down. And judging by the traffic in the stairwell, it must have broken down yet again. She hesitated in order to let them pass. She noticed one of the men was wearing almond toe oxfords, and she smiled to herself. Her mother, who always had an ability to recognize the new styles before they became mainstream, had only last week been trying to convince Charles that he needed to trade in his box toes for almond toes. Inevitably, Bessie would one day soon bring home the shoes she thought he ought to wear.

The two men continued their conversation, which had something to do with a federal bank, bulls and bears. And horses? She wasn't sure. But one of them mentioned imports. But they stopped their conversation and gestured for Cora to go down before them. When they all reached the first floor, the man with the fashionable shoes opened the door to the building's lobby for her. She walked through the door and said, "Thank you." Before she got out of earshot, one of the men said his goodbyes: "I appreciate your input today, Gene." Cora stopped, and the man continued. "I will have those reports for you tomorrow afternoon. In the meantime, have a great night."

Cora turned around, curious. The two shook hands, and the one named Gene walked straight towards Cora. This is where her youth served her; she reacted with a complete lack of self-consciousness.

"Are you Mr. Gene Peterson?" The words were out before she had a chance to think twice about asking.

"Why, yes I am. And who would you be? Have we met?"

"I'm Cora Coughlin. I work on the switchboard. I have spoken with you several times."

"Nice to meet you, Cora." He extended his hand, and Cora extended hers to meet it. He held on to her hand longer than she expected as she blushed, lowered her chin, and responded, "Nice to meet you also."

Mr. Peterson pulled his hand back and took a half step away from her to take her in, from top to bottom. Cora found herself unable to think of anything to say to the handsome man in front of her. But he relieved her of having to come up with anything.

"Aren't you a beautiful young lady. And you must be more ambitious than to be satisfied with a career at the switchboard. Am I right? I'm sure you won't be there for long. What do you hope to do? Work as a secretary? A bookkeeper?"

The question caught Cora off guard. She hadn't really given much thought to the rest of her life. She had only taken this job because the family could use the money. The economy was slowing business down for everybody, even for Mr. Charles Winchester, dentist to the children of Portland.

"I'm not sure. I am enjoying the switchboard right now." She felt herself wanting to impress Mr. Peterson, and she wasn't at all satisfied with that answer.

"Well, you'll figure that out. I need to run. I have a dinner meeting I need to get to." He placed his hand on her upper arm and let her know, "I'll talk to you again soon!"

Chapter 7

Then he bowed his head, slipped on his hat, and disappeared out onto the city street.

Cora didn't immediately follow him out but found a dark corner in the building's lobby out of the main line of foot traffic. She wanted him far enough ahead of her so that they wouldn't run into each other again outside. But she also didn't want to see any of the other women from the switchboard. She wanted to savor this moment in private. Her cheeks hurt from the smile that wouldn't quit. And meeting him gave her a newfound eagerness about going in for work.

Typically, her days at work often blended together. Daily, she hung her jacket on her assigned hook in the coatroom, took the second seat from the left in front of the switchboard, slipped on the headset, adjusted the microphone, and waited for a call. When a call came in, she always answered, "Casco Bay Iron Works. How may I connect you?" Then she would put the phone plug into the appropriate jack to connect the call, disconnecting it when the call was completed. She would do it again. And again. Until it was time to remove her jacket from the coatroom and go home. The routine never changed.

Until the day a man from the mailroom, a package wedged under his arm, called out, "Cora Coughlin?"

The women glanced around, puzzled. Mail was never delivered to the switchboard.

"Yes," Cora self-consciously responded.

"I have a package for you," he paused for effect. "From Mr. Gene Peterson." He let loose a smirk and made sure the whole room saw it.

Cora's world stopped. The world also stopped for the rest of the women in the room, most in mid-call.

Determined to come off as nonchalant, Cora accepted the package and thanked the young man. He left, but not before he shared a knowing look with the others in the room, all who sat agape. An involuntary rush of heat ran up Cora's back. She was certain the flush on her cheeks was visible to all.

This would be the book Mr. Peterson had promised he would send her. But truthfully, she never expected he would actually follow through. This was an extravagance she wasn't accustomed to. Her hand was drawn to the Irish charm hanging around her neck, and her fingers ran over the mermaid and the strings of the harp.

The women teased her before returning to their work.

"A package from Gene Peterson?"

"He's a smooth one!"

"Looks like someone is dizzy with Mr. Peterson."

"Cora! Ooh-la-la"

A bout of laughter followed the last comment.

"Cindy, could you take my calls for a couple minutes?" Cora asked. "I need to run to the ladies' room."

"Of course, Cora," Cindy agreed, winking at the other women.

Cora raced out of the room. She grasped the package close to her chest and made her way down the hall to the ladies' room. She wasn't even aware she wore a huge smile until someone coming the other direction toward her commented, "You must be having a very good day, young lady."

Yes, she was.

She slipped into the bathroom and tucked into a stall. Her name was written across the front of the package. Had he written her name himself? Or had he asked his secretary to address it? She ran her fingers across the lettering and concluded that yes, he must have written it himself: Cora Coughlin. It was beautiful.

She flipped the package over and pulled off the brown paper. It was a brand new, hardback copy of *Light in August*.

Gene Peterson called for Mr. Longfellow several times a week. Whatever their business together, it required frequent communication, and recently it seemed more frequent than usual. On one of his calls, he had asked her if she enjoyed reading Faulkner. She had never even heard of Faulkner. She could read, but she was not well read. He told her he would take care of that. She pulled the book up close and rested her nose on the cover. She inhaled sharply, drawing the scent in for as long as she could. Then she opened the book, right in the middle, and read:

> A man will talk about how he'd like to escape from living folks. But it's the dead folks that do him the damage. It's the dead ones that lie quiet in one place and don't try to hold him, that he can't escape from.

She had no idea what that meant. But she was intoxicated. She

Chapter 7

tenderly closed the book and again drew it to her chest, embracing it as if it were Gene Peterson himself pushed up against her. Her entire body tingled in a way she had never experienced. She wrapped the book back up in the brown paper before returning to her duties at the switchboard.

"Casco Bay Iron Works. How may I connect you?"

"Do I have the pleasure of speaking with Cora?" asked the caller.

Cora's free hand touched her reddened cheek. Despite her repeated attempts to remain unaffected, she failed to stifle the smile that rose to her lips whenever he called.

"Yes, this is Cora."

"Well hello, young lady. Did you receive the book I sent over for you?" the caller asked.

A tightening fluttered inside her.

"Good morning, Mr. Peterson. Yes, I did. The book is simply beautiful. That was very generous of you," she told him.

"I'm glad to hear that."

"Would you like me to connect you to Mr. Longfellow?" was her comeback in the face of nervousness.

After running into her in the stairwell, Mr. Peterson had been engaging her like this. When Cora answered his calls, he took the time to ask a question or two that would give him a little insight into the type of girl she was. She was flattered. She revealed that she had an adventurous streak and a vivid imagination but that she didn't have much opportunity to exercise those instincts anymore. She enjoyed reading, but she wasn't interested in the dental books that filled her stepfather's library. And spending her own money on a book would have been wildly indulgent.

So Mr. Peterson indulged her.

Cora spent the next few evenings working her way through the book. It was a difficult read; she had never read anything like it.

Finally, after a painfully long five days, he called.

"Hello, Mr. Peterson. It's Cora." She glanced around to see if anyone noticed the change in her voice.

"Hello there, young lady. Have you had a chance to finish that book I sent you? *Light in August*? I probably should have sent you a less controversial book. I just happen to be a Faulkner fan."

"No, it's fine. I did finish it. I loved it."

The truth was that she was shocked by what she read. Shocked by the sex, by the unmarried pregnant teenager, by the violence, and the murder! It gave her a chance to climb into a world that even her imagination could never have conjured up. A world that made her life appear so naïvely simple. The conclusion she drew from the book was that her life was small and easy. And see longed for something bigger. Not that she wanted to experience the pain and suffering depicted.

"You weren't shocked?" he asked.

"No! No." She immediately regretted the excited protest that only served to reveal her actual shock at what she read.

"Ah, you were a bit shocked. Nothing to be embarrassed about. I probably should have considered that possibility before sending it."

"Maybe a little surprised," Cora coyly responded. "But I'm glad I read it, even if I do have a few questions about it."

"Questions? What kind of questions?"

"Well, yes," she said, again glancing around at her co-workers. "Like why did Brown turn Christmas into the police?"

Mr. Peterson laughed, not at her but as a compliment to her enthusiasm and her innocence.

"Tell you what. I need to speak with Longfellow. We have some business that needs to be addressed immediately. But are you free Saturday morning? We could take up this conversation then."

"Saturday?" Could she make this happen? She ran through the logistics. "Yes, that should be fine."

"Great. I'm staying at the Lafayette Hotel, right downtown. Why don't you meet me in the lobby. At 11:30?"

"Yes, I can do that. Thank you, Mr. Peterson. Let me put you through to Mr. Longfellow, and I will see you Saturday."

She had four days until Saturday. She used that time to read *Light in August* again, staying up later than she should have to finish it a second time. She wanted to make a good impression. She wanted to ask the right questions, the questions that would convince Mr. Peterson that she was both intelligent and introspective.

Chapter 8

June 1934

It was finally Saturday, the best kind of Saturday. The sun illuminated the city, feathery clouds drifted across the sky, and the humidity was kept at bay. Cora slipped on her nicest day dress, the one with the blue stripes and butterfly sleeves. The fabric was as close as her mother could find to that of her favorite old worn-out blue dress. But she could never replicate that dress, just as Cora could never replicate the days running about on Munjoy Hill in her bare feet.

Her mother often worked on Saturdays, and today was no exception. Cora snuck in Bessie's room and pilfered a tube of lipstick from her mother's cosmetic bag, and she now carefully applied it as she had watched her mother do hundreds of times, using the tip of her pinky finger to straighten the line on her bottom lip.

Cora opened her bedroom door. She heard her stepfather clattering about in the kitchen.

"I'm going out!" Cora yelled as she opened the front door.

It wasn't that she wanted to avoid Charles. Meeting Charles was one of the best things to happen to her and her mom. He obviously loved her mother, and he took good care of them both. Yes, she would even say that she loved Charles too. But today, she didn't want anything slowing her down.

"One minute," came the reply. Cora assumed the rest of the

sentence would include some chore he needed her to complete or a question about where she was going, but she was able to shut the door behind her before he got the words out.

Each morning during the week, women emerged from their homes and apartments and joined Cora in a silent pilgrimage. They didn't interact, for they each lived inside their own heads, in their own worlds, fighting their own battles as they made their way downtown until they would split off in multiple directions.

But on Saturdays, including this particular Saturday, no one was out on the street other than a few kids throwing around a baseball and arguing about who would be the next Babe Ruth. The adults of Portland, preoccupied with paying their bills and struggling to keep their businesses open, had forgotten how to play and rarely left their homes or found time to laugh.

Cora, however, felt as carefree as a kid again and skipped out to the street. She brought the mesh bag that Charles had given her the first day they met all those years ago, a day filled with laughter and dancing. Now it rarely left her closet.

Since meeting Mr. Peterson, Cora felt as though the whole world had changed. And now, here she was, walking on air on her way to the Lafayette Hotel.

"Cora!" The call surprised her.

Jimmy K. jogged across the street to meet her. He was beaming. "Cora! Wait for me!"

Cora's heart sank. He was working the loading dock at Porteus Department Store, which was right down the street from Charles's house on Congress Street. So on those days when his shift ended near the time Cora would be getting home, he had gotten into the habit of stopping by to say hello to the family before heading home. But he didn't work on Saturdays.

She enjoyed Jimmy K. He was a sweet boy. She didn't have the heart to ignore him.

"What are you doing downtown?" Cora asked him, her voice tinged with annoyance.

"I was at Maine General. Didn't you hear? My grandmamma fell. They're taking care of her. My mom said I should go visit since I wasn't working today. Hey, where you going all dressed up like that?" he asked.

"Something for work." She purposely left it vague. "I'm late. I really have to go."

"I can walk with you for a bit. Then I gotta get back home. Why you gotta go to work on a Saturday?" He walked by her side, rubbing his dirty hands on his pants.

"It's a special event." Cora didn't want to have this conversation.

"I hardly ever see you anymore. Sometimes I think maybe you're avoiding me," he teased. "I'm just kidding around. Maybe I could take you to a movie tomorrow afternoon. What da' ya think? *The Thin Man* is playing at the Strand."

Being with Jimmy K. wasn't as easy as it used to be. He acted nervous around her, which then made her nervous. He stumbled over his words. His cheeks flushed when their eyes met. He sometimes placed his hand on her arm when he spoke. And once he even reached up and brushed her hair back off her face.

A sadness swept over her. There may have been a time when she would have considered the possibility of a life with Jimmy K. But now, at the prospect of Mr. Gene Peterson, the possibility of a future with Jimmy K. evaporated. He was a sweet kid. And that was just it. When Cora conjured up an image of her future with Mr. Peterson, or rather, with Gene, a life with Jimmy K. just couldn't measure up. She giggled at the idea of calling him Gene. And a wave of warmth ran through her body. Gene was established, sophisticated, worldly. And successful. Thinking about him made her feel grown up.

The more she fantasized about Mr. Peterson, the more she avoided Jimmy K. But there was no avoiding him now.

"So what do you think? You want to?"

What had he said to her? She had stopped listening.

"I'm sorry. I need to go. But I'll talk to you later," she dismissed him while turning away and quickening her pace.

"That's ok. We can go to a movie any time. See you soon!"

Cora waited a moment but then allowed herself to check if he had left. She turned back and caught a glimpse of him sprinting away. But right before he turned a corner and disappeared, he saw her watching and threw his hand up in the air to wave goodbye. She acknowledged him with a slight nod, wishing she had just kept walking.

She picked up the pace, and in a few blocks she stood outside the Lafayette Hotel. She entered the lobby with a confidence she didn't feel and glanced around for Mr. Peterson.

There he was. She broke into a smile. And it was met with an equally big smile from him.

He took her hand and lifted it to his lips. "Come. I have a suite upstairs. We can have lunch there and discuss the book."

Cora was mesmerized and followed without answering. He did not let go of her hand as he led her to the staircase. Electricity coursed through her veins. It was the only way she could describe it. Even though the feeling frightened her, it felt too good to succumb to the fear. She followed his lead, doing her best to come across as if this were all completely natural for her.

He pulled the key out of his pocket and unlocked the door to the suite. He pushed it open and gestured for her to enter first; Cora melted at the gentlemanly consideration. Upon entering the room, she involuntarily gasped at the extravagance. She did her best to come across as nonchalant, but her inexperience was transparent.

"You like my room? I stay here whenever I'm in Portland. They take good care of me."

"Yes, it's beautiful. Do you come here often? To Portland?"

"I'm here often enough. Come. Sit." He motioned toward a table set up in the middle of the living area. "I hope you don't mind, but I ordered lunch." He held out her chair. "Do you like salmon?"

"Oh yes. Yes, I do." Truth be told, she had never had salmon.

Mr. Peterson pulled out Cora's chair. She stepped in front of it, ran her hands down the back of her skirt to smooth it, and bent to sit. Mr. Peterson pushed the seat in just right so that no adjustments needed to be made once she sat down. Before taking his own seat, he removed the lid from her plate, revealing a filet of salmon, rice, and a mixture of steaming fresh vegetables.

"Thank you, Mr. Peterson. It smells delicious."

"Please. Don't call me that. Call me Gene. You make me feel old when you call me Mr. Peterson."

"All right. Gene. Thank you."

Chapter 8

Eager to discuss the book, she placed it on the table. She pulled out a sheet of paper folded inside its cover where she had taken notes and had listed some questions.

"Put that away. We can do that later. Let's enjoy lunch first. I'd like to learn a little more about you," he directed.

Feeling foolish about her rush to discuss the book, she placed both it and her paper on the floor. She picked up the fork resting on the side of her plate and broke into the pink flesh in front of her. She slowly brought it to her mouth, and once she pulled the fork out, she paused. Cora closed her eyes as the blend of flavors explored her taste buds. She swallowed and opened her eyes. Mr. Peterson, or rather Gene, was staring at her.

Cora squirmed uncomfortably and coyly averted her eyes. But she could feel his eyes bore through her. When she glanced back up at him, his eyes looked black. She had never seen black eyes, and she tried to remember if they had looked black when he greeted her in the lobby.

Before she could decide, he left his seat and walked over to help her out of hers. They had each taken only one bite of the food. But she stood up. It was as if she had lost control of her own body. He pulled her to him and tenderly kissed her. Her body responded, and she collapsed into him. She had never been kissed before. And now she couldn't get enough of it. She didn't allow herself to contemplate the appropriateness of what she was doing. She dissolved into herself and fully experienced the feeling of this man kissing her.

He unexpectedly pulled back and reached down to pick her up. She let out a little squeak when she landed in his arms, and she nestled her head into his chest, much like a little girl would when falling asleep in her father's arms. He carried her to the door to the bedroom that had been left ajar. He kicked it open and tossed her down on the bed.

That didn't feel very playful. Her heart started racing.

"Mr. Peterson? I mean, Gene?" She wanted to appeal to the gentleman that she knew he was.

He did not respond. Instead, he unzipped his pants and dropped them to the floor in one quick movement. Cora bolted up to a sitting position and backed away from him, pushing against the headboard. But there was nowhere to go. He grabbed her legs and pulled them toward him so that her body flopped back down on the bed.

"Mr. Peterson. What are you ... ?" Her voice clamped shut when he lifted her dress and pulled at the satiny tap pants underneath.

She had fantasized about him taking her in his arms, pulling her in tight, and pressing his lips to hers in a kiss that would leave her weak in the knees. She had imagined how that first kiss would play out, how it would feel. She imagined that they would hold hands and walk around town and through Deering Oaks Park. He would tell her he loved her and lean down to give her a soft, tender kiss, right there in front of everyone. Her entire body had tingled at the thought.

But she didn't imagine this. He was hard and rough with her. Why? Even though she still hoped that he might fall in love with her, her body fought against the assault. Something was wrong. He climbed on top of her, propping himself above her with one hand and struggling to gain access with the other. When she yelled out and kicked at him, he put his full body down on her and covered her mouth. She tossed her head about, trying to free her voice, but it was stuck in her chest where his weight bore down.

Her arms were free, so she pushed up against his shoulders. But her efforts had no impact. With her small frame, she didn't stand a chance. So she changed her strategy and quit fighting. Instead, she relaxed her body. He loosened his hand from her mouth.

"What are you doing?" she asked innocently. "Stop. You're hurting me." It hadn't occurred to her that he might not be concerned about hurting her.

"Quiet," he ordered

He tossed her undergarments aside, and she lay on the bed, exposed. He moved one hand to hold both of her arms above her head, and with the other, he pulled her hips toward him.

"No. No. No." Her voice escalated in fear but not in volume.

Ignoring her cries, he grabbed himself and pushed between her legs. She struggled against his hold and twisted her hips in a feeble attempt to ward off the inevitable.

She withdrew her mind from the room and retraced the steps that put her in this position. It started that day she ran into him in the stairwell, and then there were the calls. How did they turn personal?

Chapter 8

What had he said that made her dream about the next time he would call? And what would she tell her mother? No. She would not tell her mother. She would tell no one.

Then he found her, and she was immediately brought back to the moment. She screamed out at being ripped apart. Mr. Peterson ignored her scream and pushed hard against her. Then began the rhythmical push and pull; pain seared through her body with each thrust. And the moans that came from him. They were otherworldly.

She couldn't stop him, that was clear, but he was not going to destroy her. With that decision, the pain stopped. She shut everything down and waited. At some point, he rolled off of her and onto his back. She closed her legs and pulled her arms, now free from his grip, down to her sides. He mumbled something, but she heard only her heartbeat thumping in her ears.

When he regained control, he stood up, pulled his pants up from his ankles, and tossed her the panties he had ripped off her.

"Here. Put these on. But first clean yourself up in the bathroom. Through that door on the right."

Dutifully, she did as she was told. She picked up the silk underwear that she had carefully chosen to wear today, not because she expected anyone to see it but because it made her feel sophisticated. She didn't notice her necklace tangled in the sheets; the clasp had broken. She closed herself in the bathroom, where she slipped on her panties and examined herself in the mirror. She gazed deep into her own eyes, searching for recognition. She ran the index fingers of both hands under those same eyes to remove the smudged mascara. Her mother's lipstick bled out beyond her lips. She took a tissue and rubbed it off.

She wanted to go home.

He was finishing the last bites of his salmon. His mouth full, he gestured for her to come take her seat and finish up her meal as well. He didn't pull her chair out this time.

"No thank you," she squeaked out in barely a whisper.

When she picked up her handbag from the floor, she caught a glimpse of his coat and hat, both tossed onto the small couch in the sitting area. A wave of recognition rode through her body. The hat. The blue band around the hat. Cora suddenly remembered. He was one of the men from the tracks on the day she followed Jimmy K. and the boys. He was up to no good that day. And he had been up to no good today. She may not have been scared then, but she realized that she needed to be scared today. She needed to leave, and she could never speak of this.

As the door closed behind her, two words escaped the room: "Your book." Cora no longer cared about the book. She sprinted down the steps and only slowed once she hit the lobby, where she strolled casually towards the front entrance, head held high. She would make sure that no one would ever suspect what had happened in room 205. Unable to find her voice, she nodded politely to the doorman as he held the door open for her. Once outside, the sun clicked onto her like a spotlight. She let out an involuntary cry.

"Excuse me. Ma'am?" the doorman cautiously approached. "Is everything all right?"

No. No, nothing is right, she thought. But she didn't acknowledge the doorman's question.

Once she made her way home, she paused at the front door of the house, bracing for what she might find on the other side. Her mother was likely out working. But Charles was certain to be home. She pushed open the door and as noiselessly as possible, stepped into the foyer.

"You look nice today, Cora. Where were you, all gussied up?"

He meant well, but Cora could not have a conversation with him right now. She walked right past him and upstairs into the bathroom. She turned on the warm water to fill the tub before she pulled off her dress and stepped out of her panties. They were stained with blood. That may have scared most girls, but nothing scared her anymore. In fact, she had expected to see more blood.

For the first time, her naked body made her uncomfortable. And ashamed. She intuitively reached up to the base of her neck and sighed in defeat when she discovered that her necklace was gone. She lowered herself into the filled bathtub, took in a deep breath, and dropped under the surface, welcoming the loss of sensation that the water offered her.

She held her breath for as long as she could, but eventually her body craved oxygen more than it craved escape. She had hoped to emerge from the water a different woman than the one who went under.

She sought change that would manifest in her bones and between her legs. This wasn't to be.

Five months later, she could no longer hide the truth that grew in her belly.

Chapter 9

November 1934

Cora knew at some point she would have to acknowledge what was happening to her body. But she wasn't ready to do so yet. Besides, she had so far found it easy to disguise her ever-growing belly. Her mother was rarely home; she was either out working or searching for work. And Charles mostly stayed away from Cora, only interacting when Cora initiated. So if Cora pulled back, Charles permitted her retreat.

Mr. Peterson's calls continued to come through the switchboard. Life had continued unchanged for him. Cora had successfully mastered a voice devoid of emotion, and she put it into play each time she received his calls. There were no more idle chats. She simply connected him to Mr. Longfellow.

He would never know about the baby. That was an easy decision. But it meant coming to work early and leaving late to avoid any possibility of running into him again in the stairwell should he be in town and at the building for a meeting.

No one noticed her changing body because the further along she got in her pregnancy, the further she folded into herself.

She moved through the days with an air of indifference. Most people felt the instinct to leave her alone. Neighbors who used to engage her in conversation when they crossed her path avoided her.

On one cold November day, Cora came home late from work and was surprised to find both her mother and stepfather on the sofa in the parlor, engaged in what appeared to be a serious discussion.

"What can we do, Charles? If people can't afford to get their children's teeth …" Bessie stopped mid-sentence when she heard the front door close, and she turned her attention to Cora.

"What are you doing home so late?" Bessie asked.

"I'm really tired. One of the girls came in late for her shift, so I had to stay to cover her calls. I just want to go lie down for a bit."

Cora threw her coat on a chair and turned to retreat to her room until called for dinner.

"Cora," her mother said. "Please. Don't leave your coat there."

She turned back to grab the coat. Fatal mistake. Her mother gasped. Cora froze. She had been exposed.

"Cora. Come here. Let me see you," her mother directed. Cora grabbed the coat from the chair and clutched it in front of her as her mother stood to meet her. She steeled herself for what she anticipated was to come. Her mother snatched the coat out of Cora's arms, exposing Cora's protruding stomach.

"Oh Cora." For the first time, Cora heard defeat in her mother's voice. "What have you done? Tell me you aren't. You can't be."

Cora couldn't find a way to admit to the woman standing in front of her that she indeed was pregnant.

"When? Who? How could this have happened?" Her mother's disappointed voice cut right through Cora.

The two stared at each other in a tense standoff.

"What's going on?" The confused voice from her stepfather, who was still sitting on the sofa, broke the silence.

"She's pregnant," Bessie admitted to her husband, who without hesitation, shifted the conversation to damage control.

"No. No. We are not doing this." He stood up. "We are not. You absolutely cannot keep that baby."

"Charles, stop," Bessie responded, turning her back to Cora and grabbing Charles's hand.

"Bes, we cannot let this happen. Do you know what it will mean to my business?"

Chapter 9

While her mother worked to calm her husband, Cora retreated to her room and collapsed on her bed, expecting tears to release themselves. But they didn't. No one would ever learn how she had been hurt. Of that she was sure. Nothing good could come from revealing what Mr. Gale Peterson had done to her. Her mother would be devastated. She couldn't pile that information on top of the news of the pregnancy. But also, that man was powerful in this town, even feared by some. She had recently noticed that the newspapers periodically published stories about him, some of which were not very flattering.

Who was she kidding? She may not have understood what she had seen years ago on the tracks, but she now understood that Jimmy K. had been only trying to protect her. He'd always tried to protect her. But unfortunately, he didn't have that kind of power. Evil had found her anyway. She did not see how she could ever face Jimmy K. again.

She pulled the blanket over her head and turned on her side. Now that she didn't have to hide her pregnancy, her body allowed itself to relax into sleep. Her mother never came to get her for dinner, so she slept soundly through the night. When she woke early the next day, she was not only well rested, but she was at peace. She braced herself for the storm brewing downstairs, where her stepfather would most likely be sitting at the table with a predictable cup of coffee and a poached egg. When she walked into the breakfast room, her mother was coming out of the kitchen, wiping her hands on a dish towel.

"Before you leave for work, we need to talk. Go ahead. Sit down," Bessie motioned to her daughter. Cora took a seat at the table, folded her hands in her lap, and waited.

Then Bessie disappeared into the kitchen, quickly returning with Cora's poached egg.

"We found a place that will take care of this for us," she informed Cora as she placed the egg in front of her and took a seat at the table.

"For us? How is this about *us*? And what do you mean, 'take care of?'" she questioned with an attitude that surprised even her.

"New York City," her mother continued, ignoring Cora's tone. "You can stay there for the remainder of your pregnancy. The baby will go up for adoption. We will tell people that you went to stay with a cousin of Charles's in New York who has a newborn and two older children. You will be going because she needs your help with domestic duties. She'll be a distant cousin. We'll call her, what did we decide Charles? What will be her name?"

"Julia," Charles answered. "She'll be my cousin Julia. That will make it more believable. And we all have to stick to the same story."

"Julia. That's it," her mother said. Then she turned back to Cora and added, "And once you have recovered and are strong enough, we will welcome you back with open arms. Maybe you will even be able to get your job back at the switchboard."

They had obviously spent the night creating the official version of the story that would be told and retold to family and friends. How far her mother had come, Cora thought, from a mother refusing to hide the truth from her five-year-old about the very adult and destructive activities her father was engaged in to a mother conspiring to hide her daughter's disgrace from the world. She was hiding it even from herself, Cora realized. Her mother had never even bothered to ask how she might feel about the father or about the coming baby.

"Here is the address of St. Anne's Maternity Hospital. It is run by the Catholic Church and a group of sisters. They're expecting you. You're to ask for, let's see." She glanced at the paper in her hand to find the name. "Sister … Here it is. Sister Rosella." She slid the piece of paper across the table.

Cora didn't reach for it. She just let it sit in front of her.

"You will be leaving tomorrow morning. You'll take the 8:30 AM train to Grand Central Terminal," her mother continued.

The early departure was obviously on purpose. There'd be a smaller chance of a neighbor witnessing her exodus. Cora was to leave before the sun cast its rays upon the shame that had descended on their home.

"Cora. Do you understand?"

"I understand," she coldly conceded.

Cora understood that she must leave for her mother's sake, and she would do so willingly.

"I hope you understand Cora, her stepfather interjected. "There simply is no choice in the matter. I have a reputation to uphold. News of this could negatively impact my practice."

"I understand," Cora repeated, and without taking a bite of the breakfast prepared for her, she picked up the address and left for work, where after putting in a full day, she asked for a meeting with her manager. She informed him that this would be her last day.

"Could you please mail my last paycheck to this address?" she asked as she handed him the address on Congress Street.

"Is there any way we can get you to change your mind? We really need you. Did something happen that made you want to stop working here?" The manager wasn't going to let her leave without pushback.

Cora didn't explain herself, but she also made sure that he understood to stop asking what had happened and that he would not be able to change her mind. She felt guilty about walking out, but that guilt was tempered with the knowledge that she would never again have to speak to Mr. Peterson.

The next morning, Cora snapped closed the clips on the small overnight case she had packed. Downstairs, she walked past her mother to pull her warmest winter coat off the rack in the foyer. As she stretched the coat over her protruding stomach and struggled with the buttons, her mother stood sentry at the front door.

"Excuse me," Cora said when she was ready to leave. She would never say it, but she yearned to be taken into her mother's arms, like when she was a little girl.

"I'm sorry about this, Cora," her mother said.

Cora looked her in the eye before she crossed the threshold alone to the outside. Then she heard the click, sending a shiver through her body. Her mother had not taken her in her arms. Her mother had shut the door.

She bit her lip. She wasn't going to cry. Instead, she focused on the journey ahead of her. She chose to take side streets rather than take the more direct route to Union Station, a straight shot down Congress Street, in order to avoid any possibility of running into Jimmy K. (or anyone else she might know, for that matter), who could be on his way to work downtown. The hurt she would cause him if he saw her in this condition was more than she could bear. She had done everything she could to avoid him since they ran into each other that day she met Mr. Peterson at the hotel.

She felt a touch of sadness thinking about Jimmy K. He only

wanted to keep trouble from reaching her, and he did manage to shelter her from any ugliness in the neighborhood. He would be heartbroken if he knew what had happened to her. He already failed his little sister. Failing two would have broken him, she decided. It was better for Cora to rebuke his increasing advances and to disappear. And any possibility of a relationship after she gave birth was impossible, she concluded. He deserved better.

By the time she arrived at the train station, it was bustling with people buying tickets, bidding farewell to loved ones, and rushing to catch trains. Cora spotted a sign directing her to the ticket booth and got in line.

She tightened her hand around the money in her pocket that was meant for the train ticket. And the remainder in her purse was meant for the Sisters of Charitable Works, the group that ran what her mother described as the place for "friendless, unwed mothers."

It was her turn. "One way. To New York's Grand Central Terminal," she told the teller.

"Track 6. 8:30 AM. A dollar twenty-five," came the terse reply.

Cora placed the money on the counter, and a disembodied hand snatched it and then slid a ticket towards her.

"Next."

The short, balding man who was next in line was out of patience. As soon as Cora picked up the ticket, he pushed Cora aside and saddled up to the counter and demanded a refund for a train he missed. Cora hadn't had a chance to ask where she could find Track 6.

People dashed about in every direction in a choreographed chaos. Cora waited for a break in the crowd to jump in. It was like jumping into a game of double Dutch, where the timing had to be perfect in order to flawlessly join in the dance of the ropes. Otherwise, ropes and player came crashing down. Once Cora found an opening, she clumsily jumped in and was whisked off.

A sign pointed the way to Tracks 3-6, and she followed the line of people moving in the direction of the arrow. Travelers peeled off for tracks 3, 4, and then 5. That left Track 6 at the end of the hall. Cora found an open bench in the waiting room and tucked her case underneath it before she sat down for the half-hour wait.

Chapter 9

She felt the baby settle down just as she did. She'd been so consumed with hiding the pregnancy that she hadn't acknowledged the very real baby at the center of this scandal. But now that the secret had been revealed, it freed Cora to consider the little person growing inside her. She didn't see that she had a choice; her mother certainly hadn't offered one. But now, for the first time, she wondered if she would have wanted to keep the baby had she been given a choice. And for a brief moment as she imagined holding her own baby, the very real baby that she felt moving inside her, she felt comfort in the possibility of keeping her. For the first time she took possession of the life that grew inside her. But just as quickly, the image was replaced with the visage of Mr. Gene Peterson. And she shuddered.

No. She could never support a baby. And her mother, or at the very least her stepfather, would never approve.

As the baby settled, Cora imagined her mother composing the story for the people in the neighborhood, for the friends who called on her, for her clients. For Charles's clients. And for Jimmy K., who would soon come calling on her. The actual story would never be told. After all, wasn't that the point of being sent away? Hide her. Take the baby. Erase the entire incident from her history.

The baby moved again, a little spasm, a kick. Cora took her gloves off and gently placed her hands on each side of her belly. When the baby quieted, she pulled her coat back over the bump. She reflexively checked for the money in her right pocket. It was still there.

Sitting across from her was an older woman clutching her purse on her lap and glaring at her. When the woman finally broke her stare, she moved her gaze to Cora's left hand. Cora glanced down. She, obviously pregnant, had no wedding ring. The woman's expression was not communicating the understanding of an older woman sharing an intimate moment with a younger woman. No, her tight-jawed expression telegraphed a hard contempt. This greying woman was not an ally. She was the enemy. Cora made the move to put her gloves back on but then changed her mind.

Mrs. Armstid, Cora thought and smiled. The character from *Light in August* with the cold, hard, irascible face. She had had to look up the word "irascible." What was it again? Angry, irritable? Yes. This woman saw Cora just as Mrs. Armstid saw Lena Grove. But Lena felt no shame about her condition as she travelled in search of her baby's father, a man who had abandoned her. Lena didn't let it bother her. She was resilient, and she held her head up high.

Cora wondered how many more enemies she would encounter on this trip.

"Next stop. Grand Central Terminal. That's Grand Central, New York," the conductor announced as he walked through the train car before disappearing out the back to repeat the announcement for the passengers in the next car. People began to stir: stretching their legs, closing books, folding newspapers, pulling bags out from under seats, lining up at the door.

When the train came to a stop, Cora buttoned up her coat, collected her case, waited her turn, and disembarked. She was immediately swept into the wave of passengers shuffling down the platform. At its end, they all funneled through an opening that led to the Main Concourse, and passengers darted off, left and right. The bedlam that reigned at Grand Central made Portland's station seem like a quaint country village stop. Cora slowed to take in the enormity of the room. A woman who wasn't paying attention bumped into her from behind and dropped her purse. Cora apologized and labored to bend down to pick it up for her.

"Don't touch my purse," the woman sneered as she retrieved it herself. A sharp pain shot through Cora's lower back and stopped her cold. She no longer discerned individual people, only blurs whizzing past her. She held her breath as she waited for the pain to subside, oblivious to the hordes streaming around her like a river flows unperturbed around a fallen tree. But as quickly as the pain seized her body, it retreated.

She needed to leave the station and get outside. The surge of people crashing toward the exit pushed her along and out into the sharp, crisp air. Then in an instant, the crowd dispersed, leaving her to navigate the strange city alone. In Portland, she was a big city girl living in a nice home downtown and working at a large company. But here, she felt like an out-of-place, small-town rube.

New York City assaulted her senses. The stench of the trash

flooding the street clogged her nose. Automobiles making little progress in a jerky parade competed with streetcars for space. They swerved recklessly and blared a jarring combination of horns. All the while, native New Yorkers comfortably wandered into the chaos of the street whenever they felt the need to cross to the other side. Businessmen who wore the same wool coat that her stepfather wore weren't hustling off to work but instead lounged on curbs and along storefronts, smoking pipes and kicking aside trash. But upon a closer look, she noticed something different in these men. They all wore caps, something no businessman would dare don at the office. The patches on their coats, the scuffs on their shoes, the frayed sleeves. These men were out of work.

It was only four o'clock, but skyscrapers blocked any light coming from the sun, giving the illusion of a moonless night down at street level. It was such a stark contrast to Portland, where only the Chapman building, the tallest at twelve stories, towered over the city.

Cora retrieved from her pocket the slip of paper where her mother had written the address of St. Anne's Maternity Hospital. She had checked a map before leaving Portland, but now here, in the shadows of building after building, she was disoriented and unsure about which way to go. A mother struggling to corral her three boys, all who appeared to be under the age of six or seven, paused in front of her. Cora missed the exasperation that had forced the mother to regroup.

"Excuse me, ma'am? Could you tell me where Lexington Avenue is?" Cora's voice was so soft that the woman wasn't even sure if Cora was talking to her.

"What?" came the curt reply.

"Lexington Avenue? Could you please tell me which direction Lexington is?"

"Do I look like I have any idea? Hey, Jimmy! You come back here! Right now." And while dragging one boy with each hand, the woman ran off after Jimmy, who had broken free.

Jimmy. Cora cringed as Jimmy K. leapt back into her consciousness. He would never forgive her for disappearing like this. But she had no choice. It was her turn to protect him.

A policeman, the seams of his uniform stretched to their limit under his weight, chewed on a stubborn thumbnail as he strolled his beat and approached Cora.

"Your first time here? Yuh thinkin' yuh gonna try an' make it big here in the ol' Big Apple? Yea?" he asked.

Cora didn't understand him.

"Are yuh lost, or what?" he followed up.

"Lost, I suppose," Cora said, grateful for someone who might be able to help her. "Where can I find Lexington Avenue?"

"Two blocks that a'way." The cop pointed her in the right direction, then shrugged, and continued on his beat.

Once Cora reached Lexington Avenue, she checked the address again and turned left. St. Anne's was about a mile up the street. She could find her way from here, so she allowed herself to soak in the sights. And she quickly realized that the economic downturn in Maine was nothing compared to the desperation she now witnessed.

On the other side of Lexington, a line of people three or four wide curved around onto a side street. There must have been hundreds waiting. What could possibly be so popular as to attract this kind of crowd? She finally spotted the front of the line, where a sign on the building read "St. Peter's Mission." Under the sign, a group of women stood at a table scooping what she supposed was soup into bowls, one for each person as they reached the entrance. An elderly woman wearing a tattered overcoat with fur around the collar shuffled away with a bag of food.

Yes, Cora's family had been struggling, but this was suffering she had not realized existed. If things didn't improve, is this how Maine would look?

She continued toward St. Anne's.

A fire popped in a metal trash can in a narrow empty lot that jutted off to her left. The flames shot up the lumber that extended beyond the top of the can and licked at the hands that hovered above.

At the pop, three boys, not much younger than Cora, jumped back from the flames, but as soon as the fire settled back down, they reformed their circle surrounding it, rubbing their cold hands together in an attempt to find feeling in their fingers again. Right beyond them, a line of makeshift shelters had been constructed against a brick wall. A couple of men sat on stools; one was lighting a cigarette and the other was running his hand along the spine of a scrawny cat seeking handouts.

The shacks were hobbled together using doors, crates, 2x4s, tarps, sheet metal. These were the shanties that were popping up all over the country as more and more people lost their jobs and were booted out of their homes. With nowhere to go, they had no choice but to get creative.

A chamber pot sat perched on a little table at the far end. One shanty even had a stove pipe poking up out of a hole in what appeared to be a front door being used as a roof. Could they actually have a wood stove in there? Cora also spotted a pram. Babies were living this way. And a broom. She wondered at the futility of sweeping dirt. Above a tarp that covered the opening of one of the shanties, someone had hung a painting, the dull orange and reds catching Cora's attention. The painting depicted a scene of two women at a table inside a Chinese restaurant. The dead eyes of one of the women looked right at her. It sent shivers down Cora's spine. It was a deadness she saw more and more often and sometimes even felt herself.

"Hey. Whatcha lookin' at?"

The boys had spotted her. She didn't mean to gawk. Embarrassed, she turned and hurried up Lexington.

Fifteen minutes later, there it was: the five-story, red brick building, its facade indistinguishable from the dozens of storefronts and apartment buildings she'd already walked past. The only differentiating feature was the St. Anne's Maternity Hospital sign hanging above the door, perpendicular to the building.

Cora knocked. The door opened, and a hand motioned her in out of the cold. Cora reflexively pulled her coat tighter around her. She forgot; she needn't hide here.

"What's your name, Sweetie? Were we expecting you?" Louisa asked as she quickly closed the door.

"Cora. Cora Coughlin." The inside of the building was very dimly lit, and it took Cora a moment for her eyes to adjust.

"Yes, I see your name right here," Louisa said as she read from a list on a clipboard hanging beside the front door.

Cora had assumed she would be greeted by a harsh, elderly nun. Instead, Louisa wasn't wearing a habit. And she was far from elderly even though the lines around her eyes seemed deeper than they should have been.

"I was told to ask for Sister Rosella. My mother arranged for me to come here to deliver my baby," Cora explained, inadvertently calling it "my baby."

"It's nice to meet you, Cora. I'm Louisa. Come into the parlor. Let's sit for a minute and get to know one another away from that darn draft blowing in through the cracks in this front door."

Cora followed Louisa, who had a noticeable limp, as she made her way across the hall to a couple of chairs in the front parlor. Louisa offered one to Cora while she took the other seat, grimacing as she rubbed her leg.

"Are you all right?" Cora asked.

"Yes, I'll be fine. My leg acts up sometimes, and the pain typically heightens in the cold, especially as the day progresses," Louisa explained. "And yes, Sister Rosella is in charge here, but she is supervising in the kitchen right now; I'll introduce you to her later. So where are you from, Cora?"

"Portland," came the response.

"Oh, Portland! I've never been there. I really don't know anything about Maine. I'm afraid I've never travelled outside of New York," Louisa admitted.

Cora relaxed, feeling that she found the face of a friend.

"I had never been outside of Portland until I came here. And New York is so different."

Soon, the two chatted like best friends, Cora romanticizing life in a smaller town and Louisa glamourizing life in a big city. Not that Cora had felt particularly enamored with Portland before she arrived in New York. And not that Louisa had done much exploring of the largest city in the country since arriving at St. Anne's. But for a few minutes, Cora was just an ordinary girl making friends.

At the sound of a bell, Cora was jolted back to reality, and Louisa jumped up. "We really need to get you set up. We have a bed ready for you upstairs. Is this all you have? This one case?"

Cora nodded. "Yes, just the one."

"Let's get you checked in. Sister Abigail is the dorm supervisor and is stationed up on the third floor. She'll have some paperwork for you,"

Chapter 9

Louisa said and directed Cora to the staircase. "I have to get back to work down here." Louisa embraced her in a little hug. Cora didn't expect it and flinched, so Louisa let go quickly.

As she climbed the stairs, Cora wondered where all of the girls were. And the babies. The building was so quiet. When she reached the landing for the third floor, she found Sister Abigail at an old wobbly desk with a stack of papers in front of her. Here was the elderly nun. Sister Abigail pointed to the only chair facing her. Cora obediently took a seat.

"Name?" Sister Abigail's hand rested on the stack of papers at the ready. Only then did she raise her eyes to see who would be providing the answer.

A pasty, cadaverous face scrutinized Cora from inside an immaculate, white coif. A skinny, sharp nose jutted out from the center, a pair of wire glasses resting at the bridge. Two vacant eyes sat behind them. There were no discernable lips, but at her mouth, a web of lines darted out in all directions, like someone hammered an icepick into a frozen pond. A starched black veil draped down the nun's back, and a long tunic concealed any evidence of a female figure underneath.

"Cora. Cora Coughlin," Cora replied.

"Cora Coughlin," the sister grumbled, flipping through the stack. She jerked out the form with Cora's name, and then scanned the document while she held out her trembling hand: "Donation?"

"Oh yes." Cora pulled out the money her mother had directed her to give to the sisters.

"Due date?"

Cora knew exactly when the baby was due, for she knew the exact moment she got pregnant. "The baby is due in March."

"This form says you're from Portland. Is that where you will live after the birth?"

"Yes. That's where my family is." But did she even have a family anymore? Would her mother ever forgive her?

"And the father of the baby? Is he in Portland?"

"He's dead." Cora had not planned on saying that. She didn't expect to be asked about the father. But just as well. That would end any further questions about that.

"Of course he's dead." Sister Abigail sneered at Cora. Cora knew Sister Abigail didn't believe her. But she wasn't concerned. Wasn't this entire institution all about deception?

"Sign here." Sister Abigail held out a pen to Cora.

"What am I signing?" she dared to ask.

"You aren't keeping this baby. Am I right?"

"No. No, I'm not."

"Then sign here. It gives away your rights to St. Anne's."

Cora signed on the line at the bottom of the paper.

"You are boarding in Room 303," Sister Abigail said as she picked up the wooden cane that had been resting against the desk and pointed it as if it were a long gnarled finger toward Room 303.

"Your sheets are in there." She swung the cane around behind her and tapped on a cupboard. Cora pulled down a bag of clean sheets.

"Go make your bed, and then complete your intake in the kitchen. You'll be given your chore schedule. You are expected to complete all of your chores while here. You are expected to earn your keep."

The speech was given from rote memory.

Cora opened the door to Room 303. The rectangular room that was painted grey, as far as she could tell in the dim light, had the feel of a hospital. The headboards of four beds lined the far wall, and the other two stuck out awkwardly, one from each side wall. Only one had no sheets. The last bed to the left on the outside wall would be her home for the next few months.

She was curious about her roommates. Curious about the girl who slept with the well-worn teddy bear lovingly tucked in. Or the girl whose hand-made quilt sat folded at the end of her bed. Who was the girl who had so many loved ones that she had a large pile of letters stacked on the floor? Or the girl determined to record her experience here in the journal tossed haphazardly on her bed? What about the girl with a framed photo of a middle-aged man and woman posing on the front porch of a house? In this simple room, Cora would spend the most intimate time of her life with five women she had never met.

She made her bed, tucking the top sheet under the thin mattress and pulling the case over the pillow. She placed her bag under the bed and realized that she had not brought anything to personalize her space.

Chapter 9

When Cora returned to the hallway, Sister Abigail was completely engrossed in shuffling through papers and didn't bother to acknowledge her as she passed the table to go downstairs to find the kitchen.

Chapter 10

January 1935

The bell rang throughout the building, alerting residents to the beginning of another long day. They learned very quickly that while here their time was not their own. There were chores to be completed, prayers to be recited, penance to be begged for, sisters to appease. And bells to obey.

But the day was never so long as the night. Some of the girls softly cried in bed. Most were still children themselves, and they missed their families. Some yearned for their mother's pot roast or their father's ambitious attempts at conquering Mozart at the upright piano in the parlor. Others cried because they had nowhere to go when they would be released from here. Or they were haunted by specters of abuse or neglect. Or maybe they were simply lonely.

Cora saw nothing to cry about. She had decided to trust her mother. They had been through too much together. She didn't believe her mother could have completely closed the door on her. She would certainly be waiting for her when she came back home, and they would pretend none of this ever happened.

The bell rang a second time, signaling residents to proceed to the dining hall for breakfast. Immediately. Stragglers would receive extra chores. This threat usually sent the weary girls into double time. Cora pulled on a light sweater and retrieved her shoes from under the bed as the rest of the girls scrambled to get dressed and down to the first floor.

The dining hall presented all the joy of a dark cave, a large wood-paneled cave. The purpose of the room shifted throughout the day, but the gloom always remained. Sometimes it served as a group counseling meeting place, where girls placed their chairs in a large circle to be lectured at by the sisters or by a visiting priest about straightening out their wayward paths. Other times, the dining hall transformed into an all-purpose room for immediate families of the pregnant girls; for donors seeking reassurance that their donations were put to good use; and for higher ups in the church hierarchy, intent on keeping the Sisters of Charitable Works in line.

When the room served as the dining space, four long rows of tables ran the length of the room. Each girl picked up a folding chair from a stack right inside the doorway and placed it at one of the tables. When the meal was finished, each girl returned her chair to the stack.

"Hurry up, Cora!" the little redhead scolded as she raced past Cora on the second floor platform while holding the hand of a young girl who must have been all but 13 years old. The two could have easily been mistaken for a couple of schoolgirls skipping off to French lessons and giggling about a kiss stolen in a dark hallway.

Cora let four or five others pass her by on the stairs. She learned exactly how to navigate the dining room, and it meant she needed to arrive last, but not late. That way, when she picked up her chair, only one empty spot at a table would remain, and she would slide her chair in next to a girl she hadn't yet met. The empty spot was never in the same place two days in a row. Too many girls coming and going. And with relationships constantly shifting, the configurations of who sat where constantly changed.

"I'm Cora. What's your name?" she asked the young girl who had just arrived the night before as she pulled up a chair in the empty slot next to her. Her eyes were bloodshot and swollen. Cora assured her she would be safe here. At the end of the meal, the frightened girl left the table stronger and less alone.

After breakfast, Cora was on kitchen duty, which involved washing dishes and preparing bottles for the always-hungry babies. Sister Rosella kept the girls working long days, leaving them isolated and exhausted, with little time for chitchatting among themselves other than during meals. They were responsible for sweeping, mopping, cleaning windows, and doing the laundry, the majority of which involved washing dirty diapers. The pregnant women might go a week without clean clothes, but the babies, who were the actual product of St. Anne's, always wore clean diapers.

She was drying dishes when Louisa handed her an envelope. Cora wiped her hands on her dress and took it from her, surprised. She never received any mail. And she didn't recognize the writing across the front of the envelope. Louisa picked up the dish towel and told Cora that she would finish the dishes for her, that she could go ahead and take it to her room to read.

Sitting on her bed, Cora inspected the envelope, trying to imagine who might have written her at this address. This was not her mother's careful handwriting. Then it hit her: the only other possibility was her stepfather Charles.

With that realization, she tore it open, nearly ripping its contents in the process. She unfolded the paper inside. The date across the top was January 5, 1935, three weeks ago.

She had a bad feeling. Why would he be writing to her? Why hadn't her mother sent a letter?

"Dear Cora," it began.

> I write to you with a broken heart. I can hardly bear to give you this news, but give it I must. On December 21, we lost your mother. It was sudden and unexpected. She was tragically hit by a car right in front of our house. The driver lost control. The *Portland Press Herald* ran a real nice article about your mom.
>
> I would like to apologize for the delay in writing you with this information, but the anxiety of facing the future without her has had me irrevocably grief-stricken. And to compound my distress, conditions have gotten considerably worse here in Portland. Many businesses have shuttered their storefronts, and more and more often, I see people I used to do business with waiting for assistance outside the First Parish Church.
>
> It is a grim situation, and I do not see any relief in sight.
>
> Unfortunately, my practice has been steadily losing

business. Many no longer have the disposable income to care for their children's teeth as they should. As a result, my plans are now settled. I have put the house up for sale and am moving to Michigan to stay with my sister-in-law and to reunite with my children, where I hope to again practice dentistry. I will be leaving Maine in the morning.

Always remember how much your mother loved you, and I want you to know how proud she was of you in the face of your condition.

I remain confident that once you return to Portland, you will find great happiness and success. I have enclosed ten dollars to help you get started. I wish I could afford to enclose more, but that's all I can spare right now.

Now I must finish. There is much work to be done.

Be prudent and take care of yourself.

With great affection,

Charles

The floor dropped out from underneath her. For a moment, she floated untethered. Until she came crashing down. She couldn't sit still and got up to pace the room. It momentarily quieted the storm raging in her head.

After a few minutes, she stopped at her bed to pick up the envelope. No return address. No indication of where he might be staying. No way of ever reaching him again.

She was incredulous. His children? What children? She had never heard about any children. Had he abandoned his children to be with her and her mother? And a sister-in-law? Had he been married before? Had her mother known?

The baby kicked, hard. Cora gasped at the sharp pain. An errant foot pushed up right under her ribs. The assault caught her off guard. She pushed back until the foot retreated and the pain subsided.

Cora dropped the letter into the wastebasket by her bed and then dropped her head into her hands. This isn't the way it was supposed to go. The plan was to start over with Mamaí by her side. After all, they had done it before; they could do it again.

A lump caught in her throat.

Chapter 10

While at St. Anne's, Cora had spent many sleepless nights imagining her future, and her vision never considered the possibility that her mom was not in Portland, alive, and ready to welcome her home with open arms and a forgiving heart.

Cora lay down on the bed, positioning her pillow under her head and curling up into a fetal position.

She had even perfected the conversation they would have on her first night home. She would confess to going to the Lafayette Hotel and to what Mr. Peterson had done to her. Her mamaí would pull her deep into her arms as Cora rested her face under her chin, taking in the woody smell of her hair. Her mother would have forgiven everything, and she would have apologized for her harsh treatment.

A chill ran across Cora's back. She pulled herself further under the blanket, pulling her legs up tight until they hit her protruding stomach.

She remembered the days when she and her mother would marvel at a line of ants snaking its way around a patch of dirt before disappearing down an ant hill. Or the time they stumbled upon a family of skunks and ran away squealing when one lifted its tail, preparing to spray. They balanced on logs that had fallen across creeks. They plucked wildflowers from their beds and created colorful bouquets. Bessie caught Cora as she jumped out of trees, and they raced imaginary competitors. Cora planned on reminding her mother of those days and begging for a return to them.

But maybe that was the point, she thought. You can't go back to those days, can you? The truth of that reality sank deeper as it washed over her. And wrapped up in that reality was the knowledge that she would never see her mother again.

She didn't move until she was able to accept the news. Really accept the news. She was alone. And completely on her own.

Then the rumbling began, a rolling across her belly that reminded her that she wasn't actually alone. She placed her hand so she could feel the waves. The baby soon found a comfortable position and quieted.

Cora had no idea how long she lay in her bed, but by the time she returned to the kitchen, Louisa had long ago finished the dishes. Cora wanted to apologize for not finishing them herself, so she began her search. She spotted Louisa when she poked her head in the parlor;

Louisa was speaking with prospective parents, and not wanting to interrupt, Cora quickly pulled back. After all, the sisters insisted that any adopting parents would never cross paths with the girls who made their adoptions possible through their sacrifice. But Louisa caught a glimpse of Cora before she disappeared and politely excused herself.

Cora plopped down on the staircase as soon as she felt her legs buckling. Louisa sat down next to her and put her arm around her.

"What happened, Cora? What was in that letter?"

"Come on, move! How am I supposed to get these towels upstairs?" The harsh voice startled both of them. It was the resident, an angry girl, assigned to laundry duty. She glared at the two, waiting for someone to move. Louisa got up and let her pass. Once she was out of earshot, she tried again.

"Cora. You're scaring me. What happened?" she pleaded.

In silence, Cora shook. Louisa sat with her until Cora let out a huge sigh, tears making their way down her face and dripping onto her lap.

"It's my mother," she finally revealed. "She's gone."

"Oh, Cora."

"I have no one. I have no family. I have nowhere to go."

Louisa gasped and shook her head, eyes squeezed shut.

"Louisa!" It was Sister Abigail calling her from the door of the parlor. "We are not done in here. I need you back. Now."

"I'm coming," she told Sister Abigail. "Cora, I need to go. Why don't you go back upstairs and rest a bit. I'll talk to you later."

She helped Cora stand up, the growing baby making it a struggle for her to do so alone. But then Louisa unexpectedly sat back down.

"Are you ok?" Cora asked, noting that the color had drained from Louisa's face.

"Yes, I'm fine." Louisa responded, distracted. "It's just that I hadn't thought about my own mother in such a long time."

Chapter 11

February 1935

"That German girl? She has the face of a horse. How did she convince someone to slip it into her? Not that I'm surprised he promptly disappeared," Sister Abigail's voice trailed off, but the clacking of her knitting needles continued.

The staff of St. Anne's resided on the fifth floor, and each staff member had her own room, as modest as it was. The small sitting area at the top of the stairs often served as a gathering place after the building quieted at night. The staff took turns on the overnight shift. One of them would stay awake all night in case of an emergency with either one of the girls or one of the babies.

When she first arrived at St. Anne's some ten years ago, Louisa had kept to herself. She had been a walking corpse. She wandered in off the street with a painful limp. She couldn't lift her right leg high enough to make a complete step and sometimes it was easier to let that foot drag along the ground. She was greeted by the director of St. Anne's Maternity Hospital at the time, Sister Margaret, who had agreed to provide her with room and board in exchange for a hard day's work for as long as she wanted.

Sister Margaret encouraged Louisa to sit with the sisters at the end of the night so that she could get to know them better. But Louisa quickly found that she had little in common with any of them. For one, she was much younger. Still a teenager. To her young eyes, the sisters seemed unimaginably old. She also was shocked to find that even though St. Anne's promised its girls and its clients confidentiality, the staff gossiped ruthlessly. But she quickly learned that the gossip was central to the culture. The staff turned over dozens of times, but the titillating as well as the mundane gossip remained.

"That Italian that showed up yesterday? Her uncle was the one defrocked last year. The one living with that floozy. No surprise she ended up here, is it? The whole family is corrupt," Sister Rosella added, trumping Sister Abigail's gossip about the German girl.

"Hold on." The knitting needles stopped. "Are you talking about Father Francesco? That girl is *his* niece? Why should I be surprised?" And she returned to her knitting.

"Yes, that's him. Same with that girl she attached herself to. The redhead. Her father's in Sing Sing. I can only imagine what he did. We'd better watch her closely."

But Sister Abigail wasn't to be outdone. She had dug out Cora's letter from the garbage. And she shared its contents with the pious busybodies of the fifth floor.

"Cora's mother died. She got a letter from her stepfather, and he abandoned her for his original family. He has two other children! This is why getting involved with a man who already has a family is always a grave mistake," she warned, concentrating on a buttonhole. But then she stopped her knitting and looked up at her captive audience.

"But you can't trust any man, can you?" she added before returning to the sweater she was knitting. "After all, Cora's fiancé went and died on her, leaving her pregnant. Hmph."

Louisa clutched the fabric that stretched across her chest and ached for Cora. She knew her mother had died, but she didn't know about her fiancé or her stepfather. Cora had not shared that information. However, this was exactly the kind of information that Louisa counted on. And why she continued to sit with the sisters.

Since Louisa came to St. Anne's, she had greeted hundreds of young ladies just like Cora as they walked through these doors, only for them to disappear a few months later. Louisa did everything she could to avoid letting the girls all blend together, to no longer see Marie, who got pregnant right before her boyfriend's family moved to California. Or Elizabeth, who had an affair with a married man who had no intention of leaving his wife. Or Helen, who found herself pregnant after leaving her abusive husband. Or Cora. The sisters had become immune to the sufferings of these girls and long ago stopped hearing their stories.

Sister Abigail quit tackling the buttonhole and wound the loose yarn around the ball before dropping the project into the basket by her chair. She announced that she was retiring. The rest of the sisters also said their good nights and disappeared into their respective rooms.

Louisa was on overnight duty, so she made her way down to the nursery. By the time she gently opened the door, her eyes had adjusted to the darkness. A baby girl had been born last week, and she did not seem to be taking to this life very well.

"Hello, little Immie," Louisa whispered as she picked her up. She knew she shouldn't give her a name. Doing so was against the prevailing philosophy of St. Anne's. But simply coming to see Immie at night was also against policy. The sisters dictated a strict schedule of feeding, of holding, of changing diapers, and of sleeping. They would have vehemently disapproved of Louisa's interruption of the prescribed nighttime schedule.

She carried Immie to the rocking chair in the front corner of the room. She felt a bit heavier tonight. And she seemed more alert. Maybe her visits were helping her thrive. She liked to think so. It was the least she could do. Finding a home for a scrawny baby was unlikely. While she cradled the baby snuggly against her body and stroked her soft downy hair, Louisa thought about the best way to approach Cora while Immie fell back asleep.

When the church bells struck one o'clock, the noise startled Immie, her whole body jerking to the unexpected sound. It was time to put her back in her crib. Louisa laid her down carefully, and the little girl fell right back to sleep. She kissed her lightly on the forehead and then climbed the stairs to the desk on third floor landing to spend the rest of her shift.

The next day, Louisa slept until lunch and then made her way to the kitchen to help prepare the meal. When the bell rang, indicating that the girls should begin their march to the dining hall, Louisa positioned herself at the bottom of the stairs. As expected, Cora was one of the last to come down.

"Can we talk, Cora?" Louisa asked.

"Sure. What do you need? You need help in the kitchen?" Cora offered, ever helpful.

"No, no. Nothing like that. I want to see how you're feeling."

"I'm feeling fine. The baby has definitely been more active though," Cora said as she placed one hand on her swollen belly. "That makes it harder to get a good night's sleep, but it's fine. Thanks for checking in with me though."

The Cora from yesterday on the stairs was gone. She acted as if she had never gotten that letter from home, as if she had not just heard that her mother had died, as if nothing had changed.

Cora slipped out from under Louisa's arm and reached down to grab a chair for the dining room. Louisa wanted Cora to be honest. She wanted to shake the truth out of her self-imposed cocoon, the cocoon she understood so well because she herself lived there too.

"I know you told me about your mother, but I understand that your fiancé also died," Louisa blurted out. And it worked. Cora reacted. She dropped the chair back in the pile. She was caught off guard. But that was all Louisa needed. An opening.

"Come on. Let's talk." Louisa led Cora by the elbow to the parlor.

The two women sat on the love seat; Louisa took hold of the hand that rested on Cora's thigh.

"Your fiancé died?"

"Yes," Cora said.

"I would love to hear about him," Louisa pressed on. "When were you supposed to get married? Did you tell him you were pregnant before he died?"

"There's really nothing to tell." Cora was not going to expand.

Louisa changed the topic. "Again, I'm so sorry to hear about your mother. Were the two of you close?"

"We used to be. But no, we weren't close," Cora assured her.

Louisa read the pain in her hesitation and squeezed her hand. "I'm so sorry. She abandoned you here, didn't she?"

"No," Cora protested a bit too quickly. "She would have welcomed me back. She loved me."

Clearly, Cora had no plans to share more about her mother. "I understand you're planning on giving up your baby for adoption. You don't have to do that, you know. Especially now that you have no family. The baby could be your family."

Louisa hoped that the seed would take hold. Cora hadn't been abused or promiscuous. She had been in love. She had been engaged, or so Louisa wanted to believe. And unfortunately, the man she loved died before they could build a life together. Louisa couldn't imagine that Cora wanted to be rid of the only piece of him, the piece that was inside her. She was certain Cora would regret giving away this baby.

Louisa continued. "You could even tell people that you had gotten married and that he died before the baby was born. You could be a grieving widow. No one would have to know the truth, and nobody would harshly judge a widow left with a child."

Cora shrugged her shoulders nonchalantly.

It was then that Louisa recognized the falsity of the story. After all, she was familiar with the crafting of such stories: "My name is Louisa. My parents were killed when our fishing boat sank." No, she wasn't just familiar with the craft of storytelling—she was an expert.

"What is going on here, Louisa?" Sister Rosella appeared, putting an end to the conversation.

Cora jumped up and left to join the others in the dining hall for dinner. Louisa simply brushed right past Sister Rosella and made her way to the kitchen. She was done being concerned with what Sister Rosella might have to say about anything.

Chapter 12

March 1935

The stabbing pain catapulted Cora straight up in bed. It took her half a second to decide whether the pain was part of a violent dream or the attack of an assailant who had been hovering over her sleeping body.

Another stabbing pain ran through her body. Now wide awake, she realized what it was. She was sitting in a puddle.

She didn't want to frighten the sleeping girls, so she stifled the scream that had formed when another pain rolled through her body. She breathed deeply, doing her best to ignore the assault, courtesy of a baby ready to thrust itself into this cold night.

She admitted to herself that she was scared. No. Terrified would be more accurate. The sisters here failed to prepare the girls for what would be coming. Instead, her education came from listening to the wails of other girls in labor. Cora had seen them writhe in pain waiting for the doctor. She heard the frightened questions spill from their lips as they disappeared into the delivery room, for the girls were ignorant about what was happening to them and to their bodies. She felt their cries in her bones. Their cries for the babies that never took a breath, leaving their mothers with nothing to show for nine months of hiding in shame. Their cries for the healthy babies that were stripped from their bodies, removed before they could touch them, smell them, feel them, hear them. No sensory contact between mother and baby was permitted. Their cries. The cries of both mother and child.

She wondered how any of them reconciled their losses after they left here. Perhaps they simply brushed this time from their minds and from their hearts. That was the whole idea, right? To brush away these unfortunate circumstances? To pretend none of this ever happened?

The cold night air drifted into Room 303 through gaps in the windows, leaving goosebumps up and down Cora's arms. She needed help. She pulled her covers off in one fell swoop. An uncontrolled yelp escaped before she could swallow it. She lurched forward as another pain seared through her. She endured the pain through clenched teeth and squeezed her eyes so tightly that tears spilled out the sides, like water rushing out of a dam that could no longer withstand the pressure.

Surely, she would die. She couldn't imagine such pain was survivable. Something must be wrong.

A recurring vision of her death had repeatedly visited her in dreams that now felt all too real. In them, she floated on her back in a calm sea with nothing but blue sky above. Little waves slowly bobbed her body up and down, and the rolling seduced her into a relaxed, blissful state. But then the waves increased, throwing her body about. In her dream, she wasn't afraid. She relaxed into the water, letting it toss her as cloud cover expanded overhead. The frantic cries of a baby filled the air. The cries would shake her from her bliss and deliver her into chaos. She found herself fighting to stay above water, choking and spitting as waves crashed down on her. She took one last breath before an unseen force pulled her under, and the baby's cries grew more and more distant.

"My baby," she cried out.

She stretched her arms up to reach her baby as her body sank deeper and deeper. Eventually, the cries stopped. And Cora shot up to the surface, gasping for air. And it was at this moment that she awoke. Every time.

Another wave of pain rolled through her and landed on her back. A sharp intake of air was the only outward sign she released. All the girls in the room were still asleep.

She needed to get to Sister Abigail, who should still be sitting outside their door, before the next onslaught of pain. In that moment of

Chapter 12

relief, she rushed to the door, conscious enough to remember to lift up on the knob slightly to keep it from squeaking and waking anyone up, a routine all the girls agreed upon during any middle-of-the-night trips to the bathroom.

Just as she made it out the door, she fell to her knees and shouted out. She was deep inside of herself, lost from reality and now simply fighting to survive.

Sister Abigail was not at the desk.

Cora managed to stand up, but she put one hand on the desk for balance and the other under her tightened belly. She concentrated solely on her breathing. In and out. In and out.

Sister Abigail climbed the stairs to her desk, precariously carrying a cup of hot tea. Cora was resting both hands and her forehead on the top of the desk.

"What are you doing out here? Get to bed!" came the scalding voice as her cane clattered on the last few stairs.

Cora attempted to stand up straight, but as she pushed her weight off of the desk, her hand slipped and a file filled with handwritten notes slid onto the floor. The papers landed at Sister Abagail's feet.

"No. No! NO!" Sister Abigail escalated her protests as the papers flew. She slammed her teacup down, liquid fleeing the cup at the shock and soaking the few papers that managed to stay on the desk. Her body had stiffened from her years of life and years of disuse. The best she could do was to transform her cane into a makeshift broom and sweep the papers aside before Cora could read what they contained. As she swept, she furiously mumbled something about the gall of this girl rummaging through her papers when she stepped away, about the ingratitude of the girls, about being sick and tired of all of it.

Cora's mind slipped from her as her body transferred all its resources to the delivery of this baby.

"Help," Cora whispered as both arms encircled her stomach. Sister Abigail ignored the insolent girl and continued pushing the papers on the floor around.

"Please. I need help." This time, it was a desperate, animalistic cry. Sister Abigail froze.

"You're having your baby?" She spit the rhetorical question at Cora, saliva droplets spilling out of her mouth and dripping down her chin.

Cora replied by doubling over and again holding the desk for balance. Her body wanted to drop, so she followed its command and allowed her knees to collapse. She squatted and rocked through the contraction, wailing in a rhythmic song.

Sister Abigail watched, beads of sweat taking a rocky voyage down the nooks and crannies of her angry face.

"No. This isn't happening," Sister Abigail insisted. But when Cora yelled out again, she told Cora to stay put, an absurd instruction.

In an effort to take her mind from her body, Cora focused on the slow, rhythmic clank of the cane hitting each step as Sister Abigail ascended the stairs to find help.

Finally, the clicking stopped and a silence followed as Sister Abigail paused to catch her breath. Then her voice travelled down two flights of stairs. "Louisa! Get out here." Sister Abigail pounded on Louisa's door. "Cora's having her baby. Right now."

"I'm coming," Louisa replied, and Cora could hear her door open and close. She felt better knowing Louisa was on her way.

Soon, another door knocking.

"Ginny. Ginny," Louisa yelled, knocking more and more aggressively. "We need you. It's your chance to deliver your first St. Anne's baby. We have a girl about to deliver. Ginny!"

Another pain hit Cora. She tuned out all noises and voices to get through it. She didn't notice when Louisa and Ginny arrived at her side.

"Is Dr. Barter on his way?" Ginny tentatively asked Louisa when they reached Cora where she labored in the hallway.

"No, he's not coming" she told her. "No one was due for two more weeks, so he went to the Hamptons with his new wife. You are on your own here, Ginny."

"Oh god!" Ginny screeched, an unseen force pulling her back.

As the wave of pain temporarily washed from Cora, a wave of concern took its place at hearing Ginny's reaction.

"What do you mean, 'Oh god'?" Louisa asked as she faced her.

Ginny whimpered. "No, I can't! I can't! I don't know what to do! What would I do??"

"Do what you always do," Louisa countered. "Come on. We need to get her downstairs."

"I've never done this before! Dr. Barter hasn't had a chance to teach me yet."

Another contraction. "My baby, my baby," Cora deliriously repeated to the shocked witnesses that had been drawn from their warm beds to the unearthly sounds in the hall.

Cora squeezed Louisa's arm, repeating, "My baby, my baby."

"Yes. Your baby, Cora," Louisa cooed, trying to calm her.

In the meantime, Ginny hugged the wall on the third floor landing, trying to dissolve into it.

"Ginny, get over here. We need to take Cora to the delivery room," Louisa ordered. Ginny reluctantly let go of the wall and took one step towards Louisa.

"And the rest of you, go back to bed. Cora is fine. She'll be fine," Louisa assured the frightened girls huddled in their doorways.

Louisa stood on Cora's right and Ginny on her left as a wheezing Sister Abigail finally made it back down to the third floor. She held the banister with one hand and waved her cane with the other, demanding as if she were in charge of this situation, "Get her out of here!" Louisa and Ginny each grabbed one of Cora's arms with her outside hand and placed her other hand under her armpit.

"Ready?" Louisa confirmed with Ginny. "One, two, three."

The two women worked to lift Cora to her feet. Cora was helpless at this point, the two quickly discovered, and she was unable to stand on her own. Ginny collapsed under Cora's weight and dropped the expectant mother back to the floor.

"Get Freddy to help me with her," Louisa directed Ginny, who ran off at once. "And you," she directed Sister Abigail without regard for her position at St. Anne's, "go get the delivery room ready." Slack-jawed, Sister Abigail obeyed.

While they waited, Louisa ran her hand in circles across Cora's back while Cora squirmed in pain on the cold floor.

Ginny soon returned with Freddy, who she found mopping the floor in the kitchen. The janitor helped Louisa hold Cora up, and they gently guided her down the stairs. They took it slowly, one step at a time. Then another contraction came on. Cora was nearly out of her mind, humming wildly. Freddy and Louisa struggled to hold her on the step while she rode through the wave of pain. Cora wrestled her arms from them and ran her hands frantically over her protruded stomach as if possessed by a maniacal spirit. And the two held her shoulders. When Cora quieted and nodded, they resumed descending the staircase.

Once in the delivery room, Freddy helped Louisa lift Cora onto the bed while Sister Abigail sat slumped over in a chair, panting like a dog. Cora fought with all the strength she could find. She didn't want to lie down; she was more comfortable standing at this point. But Freddy and Louisa made sure she lost that fight.

As soon as she was in bed, Freddy begged off, "Gotta get back to my cleanin'."

By now, Cora was shaking uncontrollably.

"Something's wrong with her. Something's terribly wrong," Ginny screeched, unwilling to come within five feet of the patient.

Louisa shushed her. "Don't listen to her, Cora. Nothing is wrong. You're going to do great. We'll all do this together." Cora rolled onto her side and gripped the bed railing.

A moment later, Cora let out a shriek that shook the room. She rolled on her back and pulled her knees to her chest.

"Stop it!" Ginny shouted at the girl on the bed while covering her ears. Then she saw blood between Cora's legs. And she let out a shriek that rivaled Cora's. In a full-on retreat, Ginny ran out. No one tried to stop her. She was simply collateral damage.

Sister Abigail made her way over to the patient and stood by Louisa's side. She also saw the blood. The crown of the baby's head soon emerged.

"It's coming! C'mon Cora! You're doing great. You can do this. Keep pushing, Cora," Louisa encouraged as she gently swept Cora's hair out of her eyes.

The next shriek came from between Cora's legs. Thrashing about on the table was a newborn covered in a yellowish cream. And in blood.

Part II

Chapter 13

March 1935

She maneuvered into place, ready to launch a surprise offensive. It was early, but she was ready, driven by a hunger for life she didn't comprehend but couldn't fight.

The travel from womb to world is never easy, for mother or baby. Ignorant and naïve, the baby squeezed through the birth canal head first, jolted by starts and stops. Cora's last push expelled her forever from that cradle of peace and protection into a world that offers neither.

The new life landed on the table between Cora's legs with a flop, like a fish that leaps out of the lake in a celebratory dance only to find itself helpless on the deck of a boat. It was an all-out assault on the senses: the hard bed with no give to soften the blow, the stench of blood and amniotic fluid that filled both nostrils before they had a chance to take in their first breath of air, the bright lights that slammed the sensitive eyes closed, the blast of cold air that enveloped tender skin, the emotional sobs of Cora ringing in her ears.

The baby shrieked at it all. She was unprepared for the world that greeted her.

The women in the room recoiled at the sound. But the noise also propelled them to launch a response, causing the baby to instinctually withdraw and cry with wild abandon. Louisa jumped in to cut the umbilical cord. Just as she fastened the clamp, Sister Abigail picked up the frightened newborn, which was unfortunate. She grabbed it by one leg and one arm. She was not going to let this baby win.

This was life.

"Shut this child up," Sister Abigail railed at no one in particular, except perhaps to God himself as she shuffled cautiously, without her cane over to the box that served as a temporary bassinet and dumped the newborn into it.

Louisa pulled a rag out from a cupboard and dipped it in a bucket of water. She went to work removing all evidence of the battle this baby just fought. Once cleaned up, the baby's milky skin glowed, and a full head of fine black hair glistened. Louisa noticed a spot she missed. She picked up the rag and ran it down the side of the shocked new face. But at her temple, a deep purple bruise could not be wiped away. Louisa then wrapped a dry blanket around the chilled newborn before presenting the stunned mother with her daughter.

Cora turned her head away, and the sudden movement caused the baby to startle, a natural response to the unexpected in this new world. Louisa nearly dropped her. When she adjusted her grip on the baby, Louisa returned her to the makeshift bassinet just as Freddie arrived to begin the cleanup of the carnage.

Still groggy, Cora glanced around the room. It took a moment to find her bearings. She grasped at pieces of memories. Then a painful aching between her legs broke through.

She remembered. Her hands dropped to her stomach. Where yesterday it felt like a tight ball, it was now fleshy, yielding to her touch. As hard as she worked to keep her eyes open, her lids lowered, and she was back asleep.

The next time she woke, the fog in her mind had lifted. She had given birth to her baby. She now lay in the small recovery room set apart from the other residents. She winced as she struggled to push herself up.

Louisa poked her head in the door and then rushed to Cora's side to convince her to lie back down. Cora didn't have the strength to fight Louisa or her own body's desire to collapse. Soon she was again asleep.

The next time she woke, Louisa was at her bedside, her hand on her forehead checking her temperature.

"How are you feeling?" Louisa asked in a gentle whisper.

Cora searched for her voice, but she found it was more work than she had the energy for.

"I'm going to get you some broth. We were able to reach Dr. Barter this morning, and he's on his way back. He should be here tonight. In the meantime, you need to gain your strength back. And I will be right back to bring you your daughter." With that, she disappeared.

Her daughter? Cora was confused. The sisters never allowed the girls to spend time with their babies.

A memory clattered about her head: a desperate plea. A woman's voice, frantic. Inconsolable. What was so urgent?

Then it hit her. That voice was her own. Had she actually called out for her baby? Or was that a dream? She had no way to support a child. She wasn't even sure how she was going to support herself now that her mother was gone and that she had no way to contact Charles. She had no idea what to do with a baby. No. That voice couldn't have been hers. Could it?

A faint cry became increasingly louder as it moved down the hall towards her. Cora's body responded. Her belly tightened in a sharp cramp, and her breasts ached as they released droplets of liquid that she would discover her baby naturally craved and that her own body instinctively supplied.

"Cora, this is your daughter." Louisa placed the baby into her arms. Cora initially winced, unaccustomed to the vulnerability confronting her unapologetically.

"I have a daughter?" Cora questioned. She pulled down the corner of the blanket that covered her daughter's chin and took in her little face. "I have a daughter," she confirmed.

"What do you think you're doing?" Sister Abigail screeched as she appeared in the doorway from seemingly nowhere.

Cora flinched. The baby cried out. Louisa rushed to Cora's bedside to block Sister Abigail from reaching the baby.

"Leave her alone!" Louisa snarled.

Cora's eyes filled with tears. She had never heard Louisa speak any way but kindly.

"I saw you in the hallway with that baby, and I just knew you were headed here. You know that the girls are not to see the babies. You *know* that." Sister Abigail hobbled over to the bed, relying on her cane to keep her upright. She used her free arm to push Louisa aside. But Louisa had youth and conviction on her side and didn't budge.

"Turn over that child right now," the red-faced sister demanded, pounding her cane on the floor to punctuate her words.

But Louisa was ready for combat.

"This baby needs her mother," she declared but then paused. "No, that isn't it at all. No. This mother needs her baby."

The infant squirmed in Cora's arms and burrowed into her chest. Sister Abigail's rebukes faded, and Cora untied the top of her nightgown, offering her breast. The baby continued burrowing until landing on what it sought with the same instinct that made Cora offer it to her.

"Oh!" Cora let out an involuntary gasp at the same moment that the baby latched on and began to suckle.

Sister Abigail saw the baby at the breast and, forced to concede, spit out, "Louisa, you are done here. The archdiocese will be hearing about this!" And despite the fire and fury in her voice, the sister and her cane could only manage to totter out in retreat.

Victorious, Louisa waited for the sister to leave the room before attending to Cora, whose eyes were wide as saucers and imploring Louisa for guidance.

"Cora, the two of you are beautiful together," Louisa assured her as she sat down on the edge of the bed.

"I can't. You don't understand." That was all Cora managed to squeak out before a prickly lump travelled up her throat and landed at the curve in the back of her mouth. This baby, all of it, was supposed to be a secret. The baby pulled off the breast and nestled into the crook of her arm and then released a deep sigh.

"Ah, see that, Cora? That baby is right where she wants to be."

"I don't ever want to be reminded of him," Cora whispered.

Louisa doubled over as if punched. And the baby howled.

Cora immediately regretted her words.

She lifted the crying baby up for Louisa to take as if she were passing off a live grenade. Once Louisa took her, Cora rolled over on her side, turning her back to Louisa. Louisa stood for a moment, the baby fussing in her arms, before she backed out of the room.

"Don't worry, little one," Cora heard Louisa coo to the baby right before she left the room. "She loves you."

Cora rolled onto her back in an attempt to ease the pressure on her swollen breasts.

Chapter 14

April 1935

On Cora's last night at St. Anne's, she was on dinner dishwashing duty, her last chore during her stay. After Louisa checked that all of the dishes had been cleared from the dining hall, she walked right past the other girls in the kitchen and straight to Cora. She took Cora's hand and said loud enough for everyone to hear, "Cora, I want to make sure to say goodbye before you leave tomorrow. If I don't see you again, best of luck."

Louisa slipped a note into Cora's hand and nodded at her, signaling that she should go along with this ruse, so Cora dropped the note into her pocket and said, "Thank you." She then picked up the next plate in the stack and scrubbed off the dried peas.

Despite Sister Abigail's protestations, St. Anne's needed Louisa, especially since Ginny had packed up and disappeared. A board meeting and a stern talking to later, Louisa no longer had to worry about being thrown to the street.

The note Louisa passed Cora read, "Please meet me in the chapel tonight. I have something important to share with you before you leave. I'll be there at midnight." She could only hope that Cora would be willing to meet with her. It was a rendezvous that would be just as important to Louisa as she hoped it would be to Cora.

Once all of the sisters had retired to their rooms for the night,

Louisa slipped into the chapel. She had been taking late night trips to the chapel since her first night at St. Anne's. When she showed up at their doorstep those many years ago, Sister Margaret, who ran the place back then, took her to the chapel as part of her guided tour of the building. The room was more of an ambitious storage room than an actual chapel.

On the far end of the room, a wooden crucifix hung at the center of the dirty white plaster wall. To the right stood a simple lectern for visiting priests to lean on as they admonished sinners who sat in the six pews facing them.

"Some of the very first sisters here at St. Anne's created this little chapel. It isn't fancy, but God lives here. You know, it doesn't have to be fancy to be a House of God. And you can come here any time you want," Sister Margaret assured her.

She then pushed a button right inside the door of the chapel, and two stained glass window boxes, one on each side of the room, revealed themselves in what should have been a bright brilliance. But the illumination was muted and dull. Neglect had left a layer of dirt and dust that dimmed the light. On the left wall was a customary clichéd portrait in glass of the Virgin Mary holding the baby Jesus in her lap. Mary's red robe had faded to a pale maroon and both figures were draped in dingy shawls that had presumably once been white. Sister Margaret swept off a cobweb in the corner by the Christ child's feet with a brush of her hand. It wasn't a sight that spurred inspiration.

"I come here every morning," she continued, "to reconnect with God and with our mission. Some of the girls that come through our doors have suffered terribly, and I worry about the babies sometimes. But I can always come here and speak to God; and He assures me that all of this is part of His plan. We are truly doing God's work here."

But Louisa had stopped listening. She was taking in the window opposite the Virgin Mary.

"We truly are doing His work," Sister Margaret again said before noticing that Louisa was distracted. "Isn't that beautiful? So unusual for a chapel, isn't it?" she boasted.

Louisa was drawn to the window. She ran her fingers along the glass, letting them cross over the bridges of lead to touch each pane.

Chapter 14

"Sister Teresa, she isn't here anymore, but she found that window and brought it in. No idea where she would have found a stained glass window. Seems odd, doesn't it? Who finds a stained glass window? Maybe it was in her family. I don't know. But she was one of those women you know not to ask too many questions of. You know what I mean, right? She would reveal what she wanted to reveal. But don't misunderstand. It's not that I think there was something untoward about how she acquired the window. I certainly don't want to imply that. Sister Teresa was most certainly pious. Very pious. But some of the ladies here didn't want to put that window in the chapel, because, well, it isn't exactly religious." She whispered the last part of this sentence as if revealing an institutional secret.

"Some thought we should have stained glass depicting a parable of Jesus," she continued. "But we don't have the kind of money required to purchase that kind of thing. That other one over there, the one with Mary and baby Jesus? Isn't it beautiful? That was a donation from the archdiocese for our grand opening. So without funds to buy another for this wall, how could we refuse Sister Teresa's gift? We needed something to dress up this gloomy room, right?" Sister Margaret let out a hearty laugh at this.

Louisa examined the waves that graced the unusual window. The thin lines of lead meandered across the pane. They didn't seek the shortest path across, but they curved around, reaching the top and dropping to deep depths. They carelessly intersected with each other, never slowing, as if an unseen voice beaconed them as they danced across the surface. The black lead, arching and swelling, contracting and spreading, created spaces between the lines in unpredictable shapes. Some with smooth edges and others with abrupt, jagged corners, no two spaces the same.

And the colors. Louisa squinted as her eyes passed over the window, removing her peripheral vision to better focus on the play of colors. The colors stirred something in her body. She closed her eyes to place the reaction she was having. Her chest. A tingling sensation deep in her chest, moving about haphazardly. Until it came to rest over her heart. She opened her eyes and relaxed her focus. The black lines separating the glass disappeared, and the colors blended together. Blues and greens, sometimes marbling with white. Different shades flowing into each other, creating one continuous movement. It was alive. No, that didn't quite capture it. It was life.

"Louisa?" a voice interrupted.

It was Sister Margaret. And just like that, the physical reaction, and the spiritual reaction, that Louisa experienced in front of this stained glass in an obscure room in yet another institution buried among the crowded, anonymous buildings of New York City was yanked from her.

Louisa cleared her throat. "Yes. Sorry."

Sister Margaret turned off the lights and shut the door to the chapel before leading Louisa upstairs to her new room.

It was this same stained glass window that Louisa wanted to share with both Cora and her baby. Louisa grabbed two chairs from the dining hall pile and placed them so that they were facing the stained glass window that spoke to her. The house cat that the sisters had brought in last month to keep an epidemic of mice at bay had darted into the chapel as soon as Louisa opened the door. It padded around the corners of the room, hunting for the source of the scritching behind the floorboards. Louisa left the cat to do its work and went to the nursery to retrieve Cora's daughter. Then she took a seat in one of the chairs and lost herself to the splash of crashing waves in the glass while she gently cradled the little one tightly against her body, indulging in the feel of new life.

Louisa was rarely moved in this place anymore. She had been at St. Anne's long enough that it was difficult to resist viewing the pregnant women coming in and out as merely faceless bodies. Or resist seeing the babies merely as the end product. Louisa was ashamed to admit that she had once believed she was better than the women toiling away in factories, that she had a nobler profession, of a spiritual rather than an earthly nature. But as she walked through the rows of cribs in the nursery, she realized that she was just like those in the garment factories only a few miles away, impersonally moving merchandise. It was a startling realization.

She lost herself in the glass in front of her.

When she was a little girl on Long Island, Louisa spent many summer days with her mum at the beach at Telawana Park. The ocean

Chapter 14

mesmerized her and invigorated her at the same time. Apparently what happened when she was 14 hadn't changed the draw the ocean and the waves had on her.

A tear dropped onto the little girl's head, a baptism of sorts. A baptism into this wounded world.

Soon enough, the bells of a distant cathedral signaled midnight. Soon after, Cora poked her head into the room. Louisa patted the empty chair next to hers, and Cora took a seat. The cat rubbed up against Cora's legs, and she bent to run her hand down its back. Satisfied, the cat wandered off.

Louisa had not said anything since Cora arrived, so Cora finally asked, "What are we doing here?"

Louisa braced herself for her confession, the confession of a story that had gone untold until tonight. She hoped that Cora might feel compelled to confess as well, and the two might find some healing in the sharing.

But first, Louisa told Cora, "You're going to be a great mom."

"How can you possibly know that? I don't even have a place to go when I leave here tomorrow."

"You might not be ready to hear it, but this baby needs you. I can feel it in my bones."

Cora squirmed in her chair. "Why are you telling me this?"

Louisa stood up to hand Cora her little girl, and Cora involuntarily took the baby in her arms. The baby rooted around for the breast and grew increasingly frustrated when it was not presented. Uncomfortable, Cora pulled her robe closed and held the baby away from her body as she felt milk dripping from her breasts.

"The baby's hungry, Cora. Hold her tight. I'll be right back."

Louisa disappeared. This time, she came back with a bottle. She held the nipple of a bottle to the newborn's mouth, and the baby latched on immediately. Louisa took Cora's free hand and wrapped it around the bottle so that she could feed her baby herself.

Cora and the baby soon fell into a rhythm.

Louisa began. "Before I came to St. Anne's, I was Florence."

Chapter 15

March 1924

He occasionally brought home prostitutes and fucked them with an anger that frightened even the most hardened woman of the night. And when he was finished with them, they scrambled, clutching their clothes and promising to keep quiet. Girls left with black eyes, broken fingers, cigarette burns down their backs, and bruised bodies. Sometimes he threw a bootlegged bottle of gin at one of his girls as her trembling hand grasped the doorknob in a futile attempt at escape. She would jump at the sound of crashing glass; he would laugh. Inciting fear was his most effective tool in his attempt to prove his superiority. And before the girl was even out the door, Florence's mother would be on her hands and knees cleaning up the pieces.

It hadn't always been like this, but her mother was incapable of stemming the evil that took possession of the household. The more her father drank, the more his paranoia grew that the two women in his house were conspiring against him. But he needn't have worried. Florence's mother, also named Florence, after her own mother and grandmother, followed a long line of Nicolo women who would never have dared to stand up to, let alone conspire against, their husbands. As a result, with each generation the men who showed up to marry Nicolo women increasingly pushed the limits, like little boys testing their teachers and mothers. The Nicolo women increasingly failed such tests.

And in the family tradition, Florence took her mother's lead. She adapted to the constant changes in their circumstances as a dutiful river adapts to the ever-changing paths carved by the waters that came before. She dropped out of school in the middle of sixth grade when the three of them moved from Long Island to a two-room tenement in Manhattan, but in those days, children stopped attending school for all sorts of reasons. Nothing suspicious or unusual about that.

In 1924, a late-season blizzard paralyzed Manhattan. George spent the day inside drinking. George. The name the whores spit out when they begged for his mercy. Florence couldn't bring herself to call him Father anymore. She spent the day under a quilt mending a tear in a shirt, and her mother quietly peeled potatoes in the crowded, dank corner at the sink next to the stove. Florence heard the peeler drop to the floor. When she looked up from her sewing, George was standing above her. He normally paid her no attention.

"Come here, girl," he hissed at her as he unsteadily shifted his weight back and forth.

She froze.

He fiddled with the chewed-up toothpick dangling from his lips and then threw it across the room. He straightened up and repeated himself. "I said, 'Come here, girl.'"

Her mother picked up the peeler and continued her work at the sink while Florence kept her eyes on his hands. One of them reached for her arm.

Suddenly, her mother swung around and screeched, "Let her go! Leave her alone!"

It was the first time, and as it turned out the only time, that Florence had heard strength in her mother's voice. It caught her off guard, a fatal mistake that would change the course of Florence's life. The hesitation allowed her father to grab her upper arm before she had a chance to jerk it back.

Her mother ran behind the chair and pulled on Florence's shoulders from behind. But with his free arm, he backhanded her right off her feet and across the floor.

Florence dropped the shirt, ready to fight back, only to have him drag her, kicking and scratching, to the sleeping room the three of them shared. He kicked aside the flattened bedroll that Florence slept on and threw her down on his and her mother's mattress.

"Take your clothes off," he ordered. Florence changed her strategy. She wouldn't be able to fight him off. He was too strong and too full of the courage he had been drinking all day. So she did as he asked. He unbuckled his belt, and for a moment, she was grateful that all she might receive was a whipping with the buckle end. It was wishful thinking. He unzipped his pants as she removed her top, folded it, and placed it on the floor. But that was as far as she got. He pushed her on her back, used one hand to hold her down, and lifted her skirt with the other.

He brought women in here all the time. And when he did, Florence usually scrambled out and down to the street. He beat them and tortured them, but truthfully, Florence had failed to understand the climax of the abuse they endured until that day.

A searing pain ripped her body in two. His belt buckle dug into her inner thigh, scratching up and down as he moved in and out. She screamed as he thrust into her, again and again, his grunts coordinated with her cries until he fell into a state of spasms. He collapsed on top of her, all his weight bearing down as the place between her legs wailed at its betrayal.

He nuzzled her hair, and his nose briefly brushed her ear. He brought his lips up, and she could smell the stale cigarettes and whiskey on his breath. Her stomach clenched as she willed herself to not react. He whispered from a place far away.

"You are beautiful. Ummmm. Flooo-reee-nce." He stretched her name into a three-syllable slur. "You always been beautiful. That's why I married you. Mmmmm. Yes, my pretty girl."

Then he pulled out of her raw, bloodied body, zipped up his pants, and left the room, but not before spit out, "Whore. Remember, you owe me. I saved you. Me! Heh, you damn'd quiff!" In his drunkenness, he actually believed he was assaulting his wife, not his daughter.

At first, Florence considered herself lucky. He didn't slap her. He didn't pull swatches of her hair out. He didn't punch her. He didn't cut her with a broken beer bottle. He had left her unscathed. Or so she liked to think.

When the bedroom door opened, she caught a glimpse of her

mother in the same chair that George had dragged Florence out of, hunched over and wailing.

The front door slammed shut.

Florence sat up on the mattress, but quickly dropped back down from the heightened pain that he had inflicted. Instead, she rolled off. When she finally stood up, her underwear circled one ankle. She kicked it aside. Her torn skirt fell to the floor. Florence paid it no mind and walked naked from the bedroom. With a confident sense of purpose, she stood in front of her mother, silent. Her strength swelled as she disconnected from her body. Let her mother stand witness to the blood and semen flowing down her legs. Let her clean it up off of the floor. Florence stood this way until the throbbing, the stinging, the raw tenderness, and the sharp daggers piercing inside her slowly dulled.

She left for the bathroom they shared with the other tenants. She filled a pitcher with cold water and then stepped into the tub to pour the water over her. The mixture of her father's fluids and of her own washed from her legs and swirled around the drain, only to effortlessly disappear. She wiped herself off with a rag. She filled the pitcher once again. This time she brought it back for her mother to erase the evidence that Florence had let drip at her feet, including the trail she left from the bedroom. She tossed the rag into her mother's lap.

But her mother didn't move. So Florence dropped down on her own hands and knees, bowing before the woman who had given birth to her, took the rag, dipped it in the water, and scrubbed clean her father's crime. Upon finishing, Florence stood up to inspect the job she did.

Only then did her mother uncurl herself from the chair and drift into the bedroom, closing the door behind her. Only then did Florence allow herself to break down. But she didn't cry at what her father had done. She cried because she had cleaned up her father's mess for him. She had become officially complicit.

Chapter 16

June 1924

It had been three months, and George hadn't returned. In that time, Florence and her mother had rarely spoken beyond brief courtesies. Her mother rarely left the bedroom. Florence assumed that her mother was grateful that George was gone, and perhaps George, horrified by his own behavior, was gone for good this time.

Initially, Florence possessed blind rage at her mother for leaving her vulnerable to George's assaults. Over time, however, the anger dampened to a quiet pity at her mother's powerlessness.

But her mother let it slip one day: "Do you think your father will be back soon?"

It wasn't until after the question was uttered that her mother realized what she had revealed to Florence. She wanted him back. Her mother gasped at the confession, both hands covering her mouth to stop any more words from spilling out. She couldn't function without him. Florence didn't have the courage to tell her mother that she couldn't function with him either. His presence was immaterial.

One morning, her mother summoned Florence to join her in the bedroom. When Florence entered, her mother fell to her knees in supplication to a God she did not know. Florence's anger was tempered although it lingered near the surface. She kneeled beside her mother, curling her arm around her shoulders and pulling her in close. She squeezed her mother to still the flow of shame and guilt that now tumbled out of the destroyed woman. Florence understood from a very early age that her mother wasn't well. But she also loved her, much like a child loves a bird with a broken wing. Florence rocked her mother, slowing her own breathing in hopes to slow down the convulsions jerking through her mother's body. After a few minutes, her mother pulled her heavy head up from her hands and gazed at Florence.

"You can't have that baby. You can't. I'm telling you. You cannot have that baby." Her mother's voice was accompanied by the quiver that had become a constant.

Her mother had recognized the signs. And as much as Florence willed herself not to be pregnant, she had her own suspicions.

Every moment of her mother's disappointing life had manifested itself in her physically. She may have been only 35, but her spindly legs could barely support the body that was folding in on itself as it retreated further and further from life. It gave her the appearance of Old Lady Winslow, the eighty-year-old who lived downstairs. Old Lady Winslow may have been able to take care of herself and even do her own shopping, but her chest permanently faced the ground as the hump on her back grew larger and larger. Yet she was steadier on her feet than Florence's mother.

With Florence's help, she pushed herself up on those unsteady feet, and during her unsteady journey around the room, she tripped over imaginary obstacles, or she leaned against a wall to regain her balance. All the while, she cursed the fate of her daughter coming up pregnant.

After circling the room, she came to rest and collapsed in a corner, mumbling repeatedly that something needed to be done. Florence wondered if the mumblings at this point even had anything to do with her or if her mother was somewhere else entirely.

Florence didn't want to have this baby. Florence didn't want to be pregnant. Florence didn't want to be taken into her father's bed. She didn't want any of this. The place of pity for her weak mother crumbled as fury soared to replace it. He was an evil man. But her mother was just as evil. She gave him the freedom to commit evil. She was, Florence now understood, a worse kind of evil. An evil that knowingly serves others up for suffering so that it doesn't suffer alone.

Chapter 16

But Florence refused to give her mother the benefit of a reaction to her hysteria, so she choked down her anger and left the bedroom. She took a seat in the same chair where her mother sat as audience to her husband's act that put her in this condition. Where was her mother's fight then?

Let her suffer this, Florence thought. But she quickly realized that it was not her mother's suffering she should be concerned about. Her mother had perfected suffering, and this event was simply an opportunity for her to sharpen her skills. It was her own suffering she should have been concerned about.

Her mother paced in front of Florence. "I'm so sorry. I'm sorry, Flo. I can't get it together. We need help, and I don't know who can help us. We need help."

She flinched at the intimacy of the nickname. Flo. Had her mother ever called her that before? She had a faint memory of it. It must have been long ago, probably before the accident. She was too young to remember it, but she had heard all about it; her mother repeated the story to make sure that George never forgot.

George worked in Long Island City, in one of those factories lining the waterfront. Her mother hadn't worked in a factory, so Florence wasn't exactly sure how the two met. But she was suspicious that it wasn't under the most innocent of circumstances.

Right after they married and when her mother was pregnant, George got sloppy at work. Had he been drinking back then too? Florence wondered about that. A rotating shaft grabbed hold of his shirt sleeve. He lost his thumb and forefinger. And his hand was forever deformed. That was the end of George's working days.

Those in the know, and George was in the know, had no problem finding bootlegged liquor in those years. And now he could spend his days seeking any moonshine he could get his hands on. Like so many men down on their luck, as he drank more and more of the tainted booze, his eyesight, and eventually his mind, continued to deteriorate.

It wasn't long before the downward spiral landed them here, in a tenement in the city. Florence couldn't understand how they ended up in a two-room apartment, what many would consider a luxury for a family with only one child. Other families had as many as seven people living in two rooms. Florence wondered what special favors her mother might be offering for the luxury.

The parlor also served as the kitchen. The sink and wood-burning stove stood against the back wall, and the cupboards overflowed with mismatched and chipped dishes. The room was an odd collection of tables and chairs that had carved deep scratches and grooves on the rough wooden floors. Lace curtains, browned from exposure to the ever-present smoke from the stove that burned all winter, hung from the only window, which was barely a window. It faced an airshaft, so the sun never made it to the interior of the room. And the stench outside meant the window was usually closed. Another window had been installed in the wall between the parlor and the bedroom, meant to give the interior room some natural light, which didn't exist in this apartment. A clothesline hung across the room, usually drying her father's undershirts and a pair of his pants.

And here, Florence lived with a shell of a mother. No, shell was too kind. And not accurate. She certainly wasn't empty. She was filled with bitterness and panic.

Her mother stopped pacing. "I'll be back," she announced. She had found a purpose, a reason to live. That reason turned out to be a desire to kill.

Her mother smoothed out her skirt, grabbed her jacket, and walked out the door.

Florence slumped to the floor. No, she thought. She was not going to turn into her mother. She fought gravity with everything she had and forced herself to stand up. And while she tried to make sense of what was happening, she didn't realize that she began to follow the same path around the room that her mother had already forged.

When an hour later the door flew open with the directive, "Take this. Now. Take it!" Florence didn't at first recognize the authoritative command as coming from her mother. Where had *this* woman been all these years?

She was presented with a vial. Florence instinctively reached out for the vial, but before she took it from her mother, she caught herself and closed her hand into a fist. She wouldn't be commanded to take the vial.

"This will take care of that baby. I told you. You cannot have that baby. It's not going to happen," her mother reminded her.

"What do you mean 'take care of the baby'?" Florence naturally placed her hand over her growing womb. Wouldn't she be taking care of the baby?

"It'll get rid of it. You're not keeping that baby. Here. Take this right now, and that baby'll be gone." She grabbed Florence's upper arm and shook her. "I've tried a lot of things, but this one will work. Take it." She jerked the vial at her.

Florence took the vial and rolled it between her fingers, inspecting the liquid swirling inside.

"It's either this, or I swear I'll take that baby from you myself." Hysteria found her mother's voice. Florence balked. Something her mother said caught Leah's attention, and she couldn't move past it.

"Wait a minute," Florence interrupted. "Just wait. What do you mean you've tried lots of things?"

"You think you were my only baby?" Any strength or courage Florence might have caught a glimpse of in her mother vanished and was replaced with cruelty. "You think you were special or something? Your father found me Sadie long ago. No, you were just the only one who survived, that's all."

The words punched so hard that Florence lost her breath. She had always wondered why she didn't have a brother or a sister, and sometimes she imagined that at one time she did have loving siblings but that her father had killed them all. She was wrong about that. Her mother had killed them all. And now her mother wanted to kill this child. The vial slipped from Florence's hand with this realization, and the sound of the shattering glass shocked her mother into silence.

But not for long.

"What the hell did you just do? *God* damn it. God *damn* it."

This time, her mother used more than words. Her hand let loose, and she slapped Florence across the face. Then she stormed out, slamming the door behind her.

Florence tasted blood. She ran a finger across her bottom lip; it was wet and swollen. She used her sleeve to wipe off the blood and sucked on the cut. Then all she could do was wait for her mother to return, for she had no doubt that she would indeed return. There was no escaping what her mother wanted her to do. As her mother didn't have the strength to stand up to George, Florence didn't have the strength to stand up to her mother. And as George knew this about her mother, her mother knew this about Florence. Besides, the reality was that Florence was revolted at the idea of giving birth to her father's child. She retrieved the rarely-used broom from behind the stove and swept up the tiny glass shards as best she could.

When she finished, she collapsed in the only place she could escape: the upholstered Chesterfield next to the window that overlooked the airshaft. She had no idea where the chair had come from, whether it had been left there by a previous tenant or if it had been retrieved after being discarded in an alley. It didn't fit in. It still exuded an elegance, at least at some earlier date, that none of the junk collected in the apartment possessed.

Florence could escape in this chair. She didn't notice how much the rust colored flowers had faded or how the fabric on the arms was threadbare. The cord trim on the seat cushion hung down to the floor, unraveling at the end. And one of the springs in the seat cushion was collapsed, so Florence would sink deep into it when she sat down.

But nothing could beat the padded back of that chair as it enveloped her in a warm hug. Florence was curled up in its embrace when she heard footsteps on the staircase. The doorknob turned. Florence's heart pounded. While she had been waiting, she had decided that she would confront her mother and inform her that this would be her last day living in this apartment. She had no idea where she would go, but she wasn't concerned about that. She had to escape this. She also had resigned herself to do whatever was asked of her.

It didn't take long for her to realize that that she should have taken whatever had been in that vial.

The front door blew open, and her mother burst in, her eyes wild. She was on top of Florence so fast that Florence didn't see the woman who had come in with her. She lowered her head and gripped the arms of the chair. Her mother was so close that Florence could feel her breath as it spit at her.

"You're going to listen and do exactly what I tell you," her mother growled through her teeth. "You hear me? You HEAR?"

Florence barely nodded. But it was enough.

Her mother retreated to the bedroom, which is when a red glow appeared in the shadow of the corner. Florence looked up to better see what was there. A specter emerged, taking a drag on a hand-rolled cigarette. Florence recoiled, pulling her legs up into the chair with her. She couldn't make out any features through the smoke being exhaled. A woman emerged and stood directly in front of Florence. She flicked her cigarette to the floor. Her face resembled an ancient plot of land, covered in deep etched river beds long ago gone dry. Only one round, watery, ghostly eye stared back at her. The other was hidden behind a pink slash.

Her mother had brought the Devil, Florence realized, horrified.

"Get on the floor," the raspy voice commanded.

Her mother had spread out a stained sheet on the floor where the Devil pointed.

Florence did as she was told.

"You'll do everything Sadie tells you to do. You hear me? Do you?" Her mother was hysterical. But she needn't worry. Florence had already committed to whatever curse her mother had for her.

Sadie handed Florence a flask that she pulled from the leather bag slung over her shoulder.

"Drink," she was instructed.

Florence did as she was told.

The liquid set her on fire as soon as it hit her split lip. She swallowed the fluid in one gulp, which spread the burning down her throat. Against her will, she choked and coughed. Sadie took her own swig from the flask before she tucked it back into her bag. She closed her cloudy eye and flailed her hand about as if conducting Satan's orchestra. Her mother understood the language and pushed Florence down on her back.

"Pull up your dress," her mother translated.

Florence did as she was told.

In one swift motion, her mother reached under her dress and pulled off her undergarments.

"Don't move," Sadie barked.

Florence did as she was told.

The tears that had been pooling on her lower lids from the burning drink squeezed out and flowed from the outer corners of her eyes down into her hair.

Sadie invaded the space between her legs, and Florence's body flinched, leading Sadie to nod to her mother, who kneeled at Florence's head and held her down, one hand on her shoulder and the other pressing down on her forehead.

"Spread your legs, girl. How am I to get in there? Spread 'em," Sadie ordered.

Florence couldn't release the tension that gripped her lower body. "Come on. You gotta let me in there. Drink." Sadie passed the flask to her mother, who poured another shot down Florence's throat. At least this time she was prepared for the fire. Then her mother resumed her position as imprisoner, holding her down while Sadie pushed apart her legs. This time, Florence's breathing slowed, and she relaxed as the liquid spread a welcomed warmth through her body.

The noise that came next from Florence's lips was brought to the surface from the bowels of the earth, a cry buried deep in the souls of generations of women. But neither her mother, who knew the sound well, for she had made it herself, nor Sadie, who had heard it countless times, responded. The fire erupted between her legs. Sadie had been waiting for the moment Florence would relax, and when that moment came, she shoved a catheter up inside of her. Florence howled, out of her mind. Then, blessedly, she lost consciousness.

When she came to, Sadie was gone, and her mother sat in the Chesterfield by the apartment's lone window staring at the wall outside. Florence still lay on the floor on the now bloodied sheet. She lived through the pain of when her father had climbed on top of her, but she wasn't sure she could live through this. Her father may have raped her, but her mother was a killer. She wasn't sure which shocked her more.

The apartment was dark when she made it back to her bedroll, a feat she didn't know she was capable of. All night, she wandered in and out of sleep, her thinking murkier each time she woke. By the time the sun rose, she was burning hot and drenched in sweat. She groaned in pain and was surprised to find that her mother was at her side with her hand on her forehead.

Chapter 16

"Shit. Shit! You burning up. Shit. Whada I do? What am I gonna do? Shit."

Florence's mind was a mass of confusion. She couldn't tell the difference between sleep or consciousness, between dream or reality. Between yesterday or last year. But sleep was easier than staying awake, so she drifted off quickly after each brief moment of awareness. Each time she woke, her mother was at her side, and each time, it surprised her. Sometimes she recognized her, and other times she was a stranger.

"Mama?"

She hadn't called her that since she was a little girl. And when her plea for "Mama" landed on her mother, it nearly knocked her down.

"Yes, it's me," she answered.

"Am I going to die?" Another plea.

"You've had a rough time of it, but you're going to be fine."

And that was all Florence had the energy for, and she was soon back asleep.

The next time she awoke, her mother was gone. Florence's head was clearer now. She tried to make sense of time, and any memory of her mother tending to her were erased when she realized that the sheets she was lying on were sticky with blood and smelled of urine. She was no longer sweating, but she could feel the cool wetness of the sheets under her. She wanted to sit up, but she didn't have the strength. Her hands went to her belly, which was growling with hunger. And as soon as she touched herself, she knew. The life that had once been inside her had been extinguished. And then she remembered.

Her mother walked in with a bowl of soup. Florence took it and sipped at it until the liquid was gone.

This scene was repeated until Florence could sit, then stand, and eventually move around on her own. The two women now shared a shameful secret, one of such trauma and heartbreak, of death and near death, that most women would have been drawn closer. But Florence never felt more disconnected from the stranger she called Mother. They never discussed what happened on the floor of that apartment.

For the next few days, they developed a regular, if unremarkable, routine. Florence forgot about her plan to leave this life behind, leave her mother behind. She could only access the resources necessary to survive, minute by minute. She hadn't even the energy to decide if she wanted to survive at all. Instead, every morning she walked the city in search of work, but work proved to be hard to find. Her mother's hands bled at night from washing dishes during the day for anyone willing to pay. One evening, the two sat down for a meager meal of cornbread and milk that the woman who lived two floors below them gifted her mother as a thank you for quietly introducing her to Sadie. Business must have been good.

A barely perceptible creak outside their door stopped them mid-bite. It wasn't as if noises in the halls were nonexistent. People came and went from their apartments, visitors wandered, neighbors bolted and unbolted their doors, breezes blew through windows left open. But with the instinct of antelope in the Serengeti, the two women sensed danger. They jumped to their feet. The front door slammed open onto the wall behind it, sending wooden slivers across the room. In the doorframe stood Florence's father. His eyes were crazed with anger. He stumbled into the room, revealing that he had been drinking and increasing the level of danger he posed.

"What have you done with my baby?" he slurred as he slammed his hand on the table where they sat. Neither woman said anything. Once he regained his balance, his fist punched the table, sending the bowls to the floor. Florence's mother cowered, and Florence mimicked her mother's posture.

"Did you hear me? What the hell have you done?"

How could he have possibly found out that not only had Florence been pregnant but that the baby was now gone?

"That's right," he challenged them both, as if he could read their minds. "You think I don't know people around here? You think people don't talk?"

His sudden concern, and anger, made no sense to Florence. Why would he care? He had no interest in any babies. They had wanted Florence to have ended up a bloody mess on the bed too. Her train of thought came to a screeching halt. He's the one who brought Sadie to the house for her mother.

"Sadie." The name escaped her lips as the realization hit her. Sadie's allegiance was to him, not to her or to her mother. She may have betrayed him by treating his daughter without his knowledge for a few bucks, but she was able to pay him back by confessing that she had attended to Florence.

Just another woman, complicit.

Chapter 17

July 1924

Her body hit the water with a slap. She landed on her back, and the stinging from the impact was quickly eclipsed by the shock of the ice cold water. Florence was under water, her body a tight knot, her mind and body involuntarily shut down to anything but survival.

Her head slammed onto the rocky ocean floor, but she managed to hold her breath. After flailing about and scratching up her legs and arms as the current dragged her back and forth, she pulled the useless limbs into her body to remain small. She then flipped around, head over heels, side over side. She wouldn't be able to hold her breath much longer. When she unexpectedly bobbed up above the surface, she gasped at the air, only to be greeted by another wave crashing down on her and driving her under again. The rough floor scraped her back, and she immediately put her hands down at each side to stabilize herself. She no longer tumbled, but her body was sucked out to sea, dragging her and all of the water surrounding her, about ten feet out. Then it pushed her violently back toward shore.

But the sea wasn't finished with her. The current slammed her into a piling under the pier. The impact knocked the breath she was holding out into the ocean. She clawed at the swirling waters, searching for something to grasp onto, something to steady herself. Her left side scraped against the piling yet again as she was sucked under and thrown about under the pier. Another wave sucked back from the shore, and the water under her became shallow enough that she planted her legs in the sand. But then the next wave overtook it and crashed along the pier toward her. She grabbed hold of one of the posts and squeezed.

She scanned the water's turbulent surface; the relentless waves crashed onto the shore. Her lower body was alternatively pulled in and then pushed out into open ocean. But she held tight, ignoring the splinters from the worn wood sliding into her arms as the ocean thrashed her about. She would learn of that later and spend hours, days meticulously pulling out the evidence of this horror.

Stomps echoed above her on the pier. Her father. She loosened her grip to slip further under the water. She had to make sure he didn't see her right under him. And he didn't. He stepped uneasily off the end of the pier onto the sand and checked the ocean for evidence of his handiwork. His hands rested on his hips, satisfied. Then he stumbled and fell to his knees; the liquor made it harder to navigate the soft sand but easier to justify disposing of his daughter.

Her father had been furious with them both. Since his return, the three of them lived like strangers, rarely interacting and only surviving. Her mother had insisted that she got rid of the baby to protect Florence, not to protect George. As if it mattered. Perhaps that was noble. Funny thing about life. How do you measure that? It didn't feel like protection. It certainly didn't protect her from her father's wrath or from the scars that he inflicted. And it didn't protect her from this day at the beach.

On the sand, George cursed and struggled to stand as Florence tracked him. If he looked her way, she would shimmy down the pole to hide. She knew she couldn't let go. That would be certain death. Fortunately, the concentration required to balance himself on his feet monopolized all of her father's mental energy. It took him multiple tries, but on the third, he managed to get up on his feet, his arms thrown out to the side to maintain his balance. He stood motionless until he was confident he would remain on his feet. Then he stumbled off in search of his next drink; Florence was confident that he had already blacked out what he had done.

Florence waited until he wandered out of sight and then gasped for air in a stubborn, unwanted, fight for survival at any cost. The body involuntarily battles for life, no matter how ugly, abused, torturous, or painful that life is. So her body fought hard, and Florence couldn't will it to quit the fight. A cramp locked up her left calf. She arched back in pain but swallowed the scream. She needed to get out of this water if she wanted to survive.

But there it was. Did she want to survive this?

Before she found the answer, something brushed against her legs. She jerked her knees up to her chest, frantically scouring the swirling grey waters. She saw nothing. But her imagination created all sorts of phantasms: a shark, an eel, a piranha. The further her mind took her under the surface, the tighter she hugged the wooden lifesaver. Then someone, something, grabbed her foot. She let out a scream. All concern about being discovered disappeared, and she screamed until whatever grabbed her slipped away. And right in front of her, a body, face down, bobbed to the surface, caught up in the current under the pier. Florence immediately recognized the dress. Her mother.

Then as quickly as the current brought her mother to her, it dragged her out to sea. There was no life in her to fight for. The shock of seeing her mother float away drove her from the water. When the next wave receded, she gained a foothold on the momentarily shallow ocean floor and ran with an inhuman strength. Once safely on shore, the searing pain of the cramp in her calf knocked her down. Collapsed on the sand, she kneaded the fist-sized ball, digging her fingers into its center, working to break it up. Finally, the knot reduced to the size of a pebble. And although it was sore, it was a relief from the earlier stabbing pain. Florence tried to stand up, but that pebble exploded, and she was on the sand again, clutching at her leg.

A bump on her shoulder throbbed, but that pain faded as the pain of her left eye came to the forefront. Florence ran her hand across her face, her fingers now covered in blood, salt water, and sand. A drop of blood mixed with salt water dripped down her cheek and landed on her top lip. Her tongue licked it off, and her mouth spit it out.

The beach was empty. No one to help her, but also no one to ask questions. The clouds watching her fight for life dissipated, and the sun pushed its way through, blanketing Florence with warmth to calm the shivering. She made an effort to relax, lowering her shoulders, unclenching her toes, and loosening her jaw.

It was low tide; the ocean had calmed. The waves smoothly lapped at the shore. Sitting in the sand, Florence folded her legs under her and searched the horizon. She couldn't find a sign of her mother's body and acknowledged that the ocean would not be giving it up.

But this was best. Her mother was now free. She had been a prisoner of her own making for far too long. And as inmates who find themselves released often find a way back behind bars, her mother would not have been able to find freedom any other way.

The ocean offered a different fate to Florence.

The laughs of a woman and the squeals of a little girl and her brother came bounding down the beach. They wore matching striped bathing suits, both dressed like miniature sailors. The girl's suit differed only in the bow pinned to her chest. Both were swinging colorful tin pails decorated with lively summer beach scenes as they made their way to the perfect spot.

The two flopped on the sand and commenced digging. They came to build sand castles. The mother pulled out a towel from the beach bag slung over her shoulder and flopped down next to them. The children raced to the water's edge and filled their pails with wet sand. Their mother brushed away the loose hair blowing around her face and then lifted both hands to secure it back into a clip.

As she smoothed the sides, she spotted a woman approaching. She watched the young woman and when the state of Florence came into focus, she jumped to her feet.

"Are you all right? Are you hurt?" the woman asked.

Florence blankly replied, "My name is Louisa. My parents were killed when our fishing boat sank."

The woman stared in stunned silence and then ordered, "Kids, pack your things."

The two children were covered in sand, and one of them was sitting in a hole. They didn't move.

"Let's go. We need to help this lady. Pack up!" The mother implored of her kids.

Florence couldn't remember the last time someone wanted to help

Chapter 17

her. "Thank you," she managed to get out before she crumbled at the feet of the two children.

Florence woke to a band of women staring down at her.

"Miss? Miss? Is it Louise? Or Louisa? Can you hear me? Louisa?" The women sprayed her with questions.

Who are they talking to? Who is Louisa?

"Yes?" Florence, or rather Louisa, whispered.

"Yes, honey. You're fine," the woman who was checking Louisa's blood pressure assured her. "You're here at St. Cecelia Hospital. Do you remember what happened?"

She had expected to emerge from the water a changed woman. She had expected to live from this point forward as if the past had never happened, as if her past did not actually belong to her. But she couldn't shed it that easily. The best she could do was discard her name. She was now Louisa.

"I don't know. I don't remember what happened," Louisa said, daring the nurse to challenge the obvious lie.

A man in a white lab coat entered the room. The doctor, she presumed. The women stepped back as he approached, as if he were Moses parting the Red Sea. He stood at her feet and observed her. It made Louisa uncomfortable.

"You're lucky to be alive. And you're lucky to have been brought here. Not everyone is as sympathetic about these things as we are," he finally said.

There it is again, Louisa thought. Lucky. And sympathetic about what things? What were they talking about?

"Thank you?" she replied in a manner that was more of a question than a declaration of appreciation.

"I want to examine you once again, to make sure you're healing well." Then he helped himself to the place between her legs.

Louisa tightened up.

"Don't worry. I'll just be a second. Whoever did this to you really butchered you. You'll never have children, but at least you'll live. Many women are not that lucky."

Lucky? She certainly didn't feel lucky.

He continued. "But the bleeding's stopped, so that's a good sign. We'll monitor you for a couple of days, make sure this infection is under control. That's what'll kill you."

She couldn't believe she had survived. She couldn't believe the world was still working so hard to kill her. She still had to convince herself the fight against death was worth winning.

Two weeks later, Louisa was discharged from the hospital. Before sending her on her way, one of the nurses offered Louisa the name and address of a local organization: The Sisters of Charitable Works.

She stuffed the address in her pocket. She had nowhere to go, but she just wasn't sure about this. Florence had never even set foot in a church before. She was raised to believe that no church would accept them. They weren't good enough. People at churches were judgmental, exercising the power to pick and choose who was blessed with salvation and who burned in hell, her mother had preached. Florence never questioned this truth.

She knew that her great-grandmamma, a woman her mother had never met, denounced the Catholic Church back in Ireland for a slight the local priest had made against her family. What that slight was, no one had remembered for generations. But she passed the animus against the church down to all of her descendants. That animus would die right here, she decided. Everything from her past would. Maybe Florence had never faced the church. But Louisa would.

The Sisters of Charitable Works operated a maternity hospital for unwed mothers in Manhattan, and recently a position opened for someone to clean, do laundry, and complete other chores. The sisters had been discussing the need when Louisa serendipitously showed up at their front door. The warm welcome she received from the sisters was a pleasant surprise.

The sisters filled her stomach, bought her a train ticket to Union Station, and scribbled the address of St. Anne's Maternity Hospital, 891 Lexington Avenue, on a piece of paper. They walked her to the
door leading outside into the rain and bid her farewell. And good luck.

Chapter 18

April 1935

When Louisa finished her story, the only sound in the room was the rhythmic breathing of the sleeping baby. The cat had tired of hunting and was curled up under Louisa's chair.

"You're the first person I've told that to." Louisa stared straight ahead. "I promised myself that I would never tell that story. I promised myself that Florence was forever dead and that I, Louisa, had been reborn out of the shattered remains of Florence. But I've realized that Florence isn't dead. She continues to live and breathe in every cell of my body. I've spent years denying her existence, only to have her haunt me in a desperation to be recognized."

The two women sat in silence. Louisa felt relieved to have so explicitly acknowledged what happened to her.

Louisa whispered, "You don't have to tell me anything. But I want you to know that you can. You may even find that you feel better after the telling."

Louisa fiddled with something around her neck. Cora caught a glimpse of the charm hanging from her necklace.

"What's that on your necklace?"

Louisa held out the charm.

"This was given to me by my mother."

"May I see it? Please?"

Louisa unclasped the necklace and let the pendant rest in the palm of Cora's hand.

"My mother gave me the same harp. She wanted it to remind me that at any time, I have the ability to rise from the ashes. But I lost it," Cora said.

As soon as she said it, she realized that wasn't the truth.

"Or rather," she corrected herself, "it was taken from me."

The next morning, at the front door of St. Anne's, Louisa tightly hugged Cora, who stood stiff and straight. When she let go, she kissed the baby and took a moment to take in the little girl's smell.

"Have you decided on a name yet," she asked Cora.

"No," was Cora's one-word response.

"Don't waste any more time, Cora. That baby needs a name. Promise me you will take care of that today, will you?"

"Yes," Cora robotically responded.

Louisa opened the front door, and both Cora and the baby squinted against the bright sunshine that greeted them. After bidding farewell to the new mother and child, Louisa closed the door. She worried that Cora might not be able to love her little girl. She worried that maybe she shouldn't have encouraged Cora to keep her baby. But all she could do at this point was pray that the love of this little blessing would prove strong enough to break open the shell Cora had grown around her heart. Louisa sensed that it was a shell recently installed, so she hoped it was still penetrable.

In a last-minute decision, Louisa dropped her harp necklace into Cora's coat pocket without telling her. Louisa no longer needed it. But she felt strongly that Cora did. She didn't want to present it to her as a gift. She wanted Cora to discover it on her own.

She then climbed the stairs to the room she had called home for a decade. She packed her meager belongings in an overnight bag and carried it down, past Sister Abigail at her desk on the third floor, past the pregnant girls lingering on the stairway, past the chapel, past the dining hall, and to the front door.

"Louisa," a voice sternly called as she opened the door onto the street. "Where do you think you are going?"

Chapter 18

Sister Rosella stood with her arms crossed. Louisa giggled at the sight. Yes, she giggled. She couldn't remember the last time she had giggled. Louisa was a grown woman, and Sister Rosella wanted to scold her like an errant child right now?

"My name is Florence," she responded. And she walked out, closing that door behind her.

Chapter 19

May 1935

When Cora stepped outside of St. Anne's, she actually needed a moment for her eyes to adjust. She hadn't ventured out in months. It had been so easy to hide away inside St. Anne's, ignorant of any life outside. But she couldn't hide away forever. She picked up her suitcase and crossed the threshold out into the city. Then she retraced her steps back to Union Station to catch a train back to Maine. It was a default choice. She simply didn't know where else to go. Nothing much had changed since she had first walked down Lexington Avenue, except that scarves, hats, and makeshift fires were no longer necessary to fend off the bitter cold. But the lines for food, the men on the curbs, the expressionless faces passing her by all remained. She felt invisible here. Everyone looked past each other, immersed in their own troubles. She would be glad to get back to Portland, and she decided that she would be glad that her mother and stepfather would not be there to greet her. She would have probably been thrown out of the home anyway if she had shown up at the front door with this baby. That wasn't how the story they told was supposed to end. No, it was better this way.

Cora had hoped to stay untouched by her four months at St. Anne's. But she had definitely been touched. She was now responsible for another life. She tried to see the baby as a blank slate, but instead it was a constant reminder of her own misplaced trust. She knew it wasn't the baby's fault, and she didn't blame it. However, she couldn't get past blaming herself.

By the time Cora made her way through Union Station and to the track where she would be catching her train, her arm was cramping up from the weight of the baby. People were already boarding. She found a seat and settled in, cradling the dozing baby. She slipped her free hand into her pocket to check the address of the church in Portland that Louisa found that would help her acclimate to her new life.

She felt something unexpected and pulled it out, surprised to find Louisa's Irish harp necklace. She smiled. Louisa must have slipped it in her pocket when she hugged her. She folded it back into the tissue and returned it to her pocket, not sure how to react.

Is it possible for someone to give back to me what had been taken by someone else? she wondered.

Both Cora and the baby slept for most of the train ride. When the conductor announced their arrival in Portland, Cora picked up her bag and walked confidently from the train station in the direction of the address that Louisa had given her.

She found the church easily, and she found that the benevolent sisters were dedicated to helping her get reestablished into the community. They secured her a job at the prestigious Chase Hotel in downtown Portland as a hostess. They also provided her with a reference so that she and the baby could move into a duplex within walking distance of the hotel. They would live with a long-standing member of the congregation, Mrs. Olivari, a widow herself, living off her husband's veteran's benefits. The deal that they agreed upon was that Cora would assist with cleaning and shopping, tasks the older woman found difficult to complete, and Mrs. Olivari would care for Leah while Cora worked.

As Cora made her way to her new home, the baby began to cry and squirm. Cora continued walking, explaining to the baby, "I'm hungry too. Nothing I can do about it right now." She was irritated. Everything seemed to be happening so fast. And her arm was burning under the fussy baby.

Finally, she spotted the duplex. She double-checked the address, dropped her bag, and gently knocked on the door on the left. It wasn't hot out, but sweat began to drip down the sides of Cora's face. She really needed to put this baby down.

"Oh yes! You're here!" Cora heard a woman's voice exclaim from inside the apartment. But the door didn't open right away. Cora stood there as she heard rustling, grunts, squeaky springs, and finally footsteps. And then the door slowly opened. On the other side was a huge, toothy smile attached to a plump woman wiping her hands on an apron. She was a custom-made grandmother.

"Come in, come in, come in, le mie bellezze," she insisted in a thick Italian accent.

Mrs. Olivari immediately took the baby from Cora's arm, enveloping her in her bosom and rubbing her nose on the baby's forehead. She invited Cora into the apartment and then set the baby down in the new bassinet that she had purchased as a gift for her new roommates. Cora closed the front door and dropped her suitcase before plopping down in a chair.

"Oh my dear. You are tired, are you not? Come. I made some dinner. Let me show you to your room, and then you can have a bite to eat. Do you have food for the baby?" Mrs. Olivari asked as she made her way to the door that led to what had been set up as Cora's bedroom.

"Yes, the nuns packed up some formula for me to take." Cora got back up and followed the tottering woman with her suitcase.

"Great," Mrs. Olivari responded. "Come see your room. I think you'll be happy here." She was eager to tell Cora about everything in her new room: the dresser from the old country, the photo of her deceased husband, and the afghan she had knit when her own baby was born, the one who now lived with her husband and their children in New York. Her oldest grandson was stationed here in Portland, in the Navy, she explained, ruffling her feathers a bit. But they were interrupted by cries coming from the front room. Mrs. Olivari lit up and waddled out.

Cora opened her suitcase and arranged the few items she had brought with her in the dresser. Thankfully, the church had a collection of donated baby clothes and allowed Cora to choose a couple of outfits to bring with her.

When Cora finished unpacking and returned to the front room, spaghetti was boiling on the stove, and the smell of a simmering tomato sauce wafted through the room. Mrs. Olivari was playing peek-a-boo.

"What is the name of this gorgeous little bambina?" she asked while covering her eyes, pretending to hide from the baby.

Cora didn't answer.

The old woman uncovered her eyes and looked over at Cora. She asked again, "What's her name?"

Her name. Cora hadn't given her a name. A name would provide the world with a way to identify her. And by becoming a part of the world, others would now have an opportunity to love her, but they would also have the opportunity to destroy her. However, Cora knew it had to be done.

"Her name is Leah."

Chapter 20

August 1941

Cora, Leah, and Mrs. Olivari (or Nana Oli, as Leah liked to call her) had developed an easy routine. Nana Oli spent her days caring for Leah, and Cora continued to work at the Messe's Bistro, housed on the ground floor of The Chase Hotel.

Cora usually worked the night shift. Lunch customers were primarily serious businessmen solidifying important deals over baked ham or tomato soup. Cora found them insufferably humorless, even when she attempted to lighten things up with a round of Stingers. It never seemed to make a difference. She preferred the dinner shift. It was busier and, therefore, more profitable, but it also was filled with livelier customers out to celebrate, whether a birthday, an anniversary, or just each other.

Cora was grateful for Nana Oli. She probably didn't make this clear often enough. But she never felt completely comfortable around her. Nana Oli and Leah were very close, so sometimes Cora felt like an intruder. When she saw Leah curled up with Nana Oli, her heart ached for her own mother. She missed her. And she missed the carefree life before Leah. It wasn't that she blamed Leah for where life had taken her. It wasn't Leah's fault. It was the choice she made to go to the Lafayette Hotel that changed everything.

Cora didn't become fearful of going out alone; she didn't become fearful of men. She didn't blame the entire population of men. No. She blamed herself. For misjudging a man who cared nothing for her. For losing control of the situation. Or rather for not taking control of the situation herself.

She accepted that there were some things she couldn't control: her mother's death, Charles's abandonment, Leah's birth. But shouldn't she have been able to stop Mr. Peterson? She had been so naïve. But that was behind her.

No, she didn't blame Leah; she blamed herself. However, when she looked at Leah, she didn't see the face of Gene Peterson. She didn't see the man who betrayed her. Who violated her. No. When she looked at Leah, she saw herself and her inability to stop him. Her inability to disarm him. Her inability to control the situation.

Her tight grip on Leah came not from a desire to protect her from the world or to ensure that someone like Mr. Peterson would never get his hands on her. No, it came from her commitment to rewrite history and gain control of that fateful day. And Leah was the only means she saw to do so.

One dinner shift, Cora volunteered to stay after hours to serve a table of ten who were visiting from out of town and were in no hurry to break up the party. When she came home later than usual, she found Mrs. Olivari reading to Leah from a book of *Just So* stories, a favorite that Mrs. Olivari used to read to her own children. The two of them were waiting for Cora on the couch in the front room, Leah's head in Mrs. Olivari's lap.

It was awfully late for either of them to still be awake.

"Mamma?" Leah squeaked out when the front door opened, struggling to sit up to greet her mother.

"What are you still doing awake?" Cora scolded as she closed the door behind her.

It wasn't unusual for Mrs. Olivari to wait up for Cora, passing the time by knitting an afghan or a sweater. Other times, Cora came home to a small group of women in a half circle around the radio, listening to *The Shadow*, whose narrator competed with the clicking of knitting needles and the gleeful gossip. Cora had never been much interested in what the radio had to offer.

Chapter 20

But usually Leah was already asleep when she came home from a late shift at the restaurant.

"Mrs. Olivari, We've talked about this before," Cora reminded her. "Leah's on a schedule. And I need you to abide by it. It's very important that I know where she is and what she is doing. And that means she is getting her sleep, even when I'm not here."

"Yes, I know, but …"

"I'm much more comfortable if I know that the routine at home is being followed."

Leah interrupted them by jumping off the couch and rushing to Cora, arms outstretched. She caught her mother off guard, and Cora instinctively flinched, so Leah hesitated and stepped back. But then Cora placed her hand on Leah's shoulder, giving Leah an opening to wrap her arms around her mother's legs.

Leah confessed, "I don't feel well, Mamma. I have a headache. And Nana Oli says I have a fever. Right Nana Oli?"

"Si, LeeLee." Mrs. Olivari scooted herself up to the edge of the couch and then rocked until she was able to push herself up to retrieve Leah from her mother's side. "Ok. Your mamma's home. Time for bed. Come on, andiamo." She took Leah's hand and pulled her away.

Leah struggled against her. "You'll come say good night?" she asked her mother. "And tuck me in?"

"Yes, I will," Cora responded, distracted by folding up the blanket that had been sprawled across the couch.

"Go, Lee. Your mamma needs to talk to me."

Leah obeyed and disappeared into the bedroom.

"What do you think about our Leah?" Mrs. Olivari asked.

"No, no," Cora dismissed the concern as she fluffed the cushions on the couch. "She'll be fine. You can take her to the clinic tomorrow. I'll leave money for you."

"Ok. But I'm worried. There are a few cases of polio around here. You know the Cotters, no? On Chapel? Their little bambino got polio. He's wearing those leg braces now. Maybe forever! And the Hamiltons? On Oxford? Two of their little ones have polio. They're both at the hospital. Been there four days. Now Mrs. Hamilton might have it." Tears welled up in Mrs. Olivari's eyes.

"Yes, I know. I heard about the Hamiltons. But no. Leah doesn't have polio. And she won't get it either. She can't. I don't have time for that. And I can't afford to miss any work. She's going to be fine."

"Mamma? Did you forget? Aren't you coming?" Leah peeked around the corner at the two women.

"No, no. I'm coming," she told Leah. "And take her in tomorrow," she told Mrs. Olivari.

The next day, the doctor examined Leah and judging from her symptoms was fairly confident she had not contracted polio. He prescribed three days of rest and observation. If her fever didn't break or if she complained of neck and back stiffness, they should bring her in for a follow-up appointment. But Leah was to isolate until the doctor cleared her; only Mrs. Olivari would interact with her. Cora would sleep in the living room. She simply didn't have time for polio. She couldn't miss work, and she couldn't risk possibly infecting anyone at the restaurant if Leah indeed had contracted polio.

For the next three days, Nana Oli made Leah soup, read to her, placed cold washcloths on her forehead, sang her songs, and napped by her side. Three days later, Leah was symptom-free. And Leah would never forget Nana Oli fussing over her when she was sick and ensuring she recovered.

Chapter 21

December 1941

Cora had been working a double shift at the hotel when a sailor tore in searching for his commander. He spotted the officer at a table near the kitchen. He frantically wound his way through the room and out of breath, stood erect at the side of the table. He rendered a salute, awaiting permission to interrupt the commander and two other officers mid-bite. Most of the patrons paused their own meals in curiosity.

"Sir. You've been ordered back to the ship immediately," the private recited, still in a hard salute.

The three men at the table grumbled in protest. They hadn't finished lunch. Or their drinks.

"The Japanese, Sir," the sailor continued. "The Japanese have attacked Pearl Harbor. You have been ordered back to the ship."

The three men jumped up, dropping their napkins to the floor, and broke into a jog.

Word blazed through the room. Shock and fear emptied the place in record time. Patrons abandoned each other as well as their food, their half-emptied drinks, and their lives as they knew them.

The manager of Messe's Bistro, Leon Mercier, was a first-generation French Canadian who far surpassed his parents' expectations of his success in the United States. He closed the restaurant so that he and his staff could go home to find out what this meant for their loved ones in the military and for the city. Cora rushed home simply because that was what everyone did. No one she knew served in the military, other than her regulars at Messe's Bistro. But she had kept a professional distance from them. At home, Leah and Mrs. Olivari were glued to the radio. When Cora walked in the door, Leah jumped up and down and pelted her mother with questions.

"Who are the Japs? Where are the pearls? Why do they want to kill us? Are they coming here?"

Cora waved at her to hush up as she pulled over a chair to sit next to the older woman in front of the radio. She could feel the tension radiating from Mrs. Olivari, whose grandson was still stationed here in Portland. He would now most likely be deployed to fight in the Pacific. The radio returned to regular programming, promising updates when they came available. Cora turned it off as Leah belted her with even more questions.

"What happened? Are you going back to work, Mamma? Are we going to be killed? Do I have school tomorrow?"

Cora was annoyed with the incessant questions. She didn't have the answers. And Cora could see that Nana Oli was losing the battle of keeping it together. Her eyes began to tear.

"No answer. Niente," Nana Oli hadn't been able to get any news about her grandson.

"Let's try again. And Leah, go to our room. Maybe you can read for a bit. Nana Oli and I need to talk."

"But Mamma, are the Japs going to come here to Portland to get us?" Leah sounded terrified.

"No, LeeLee," Nana Oli interrupted. "Do not worry. Our brave soldiers will protect us."

Leah walked right past her mother to give Nana Oli a hug and then closed herself in the bedroom.

Right then, the phone rang. It was Nana Oli's daughter. She had heard from her son in Portland, and yes, he would be deployed to the Pacific as soon as possible. That was all she knew.

Nana Oli began the Lord's Prayer. "Padre Nostro, che sei nei cieli." Cora could hear Nana Oli's daughter on the other end of the line join in, and together the two of them continued, "Sia santificato il tuo nome."

Cora signaled that she was going out. She wanted to see what was happening on the streets of Portland with this news.

Nana Oli nodded her head. "Venga il tuo regno, Sia fatta."

Cora shut the door behind her. And as expected, she was greeted with chaos. It appeared that everyone else in town had the same idea as she did. People had streamed out of their houses and gathered outside despite the cold. Restless, like Cora, they sought information but also confirmation that things were under control. The people of Portland were unable to find either in those first hours.

The next day, Leah, Nana Oli, and Cora gathered around the radio with millions of others to hear President Roosevelt address the nation. Obviously, the country was now at war. Nana Oli turned on the radio and struggled to tune into a station that had the clearest reception. Then at 12:30 PM the president's voice bellowed out:

> Mr. Vice President, and Mr. Speaker, and Members of the Senate and House of Representatives: Yesterday, December 7, 1941—a date which will live in infamy—the United States of America was suddenly and deliberately attacked by naval and air forces of the Empire of Japan.

The speech ended with Roosevelt's appeal to Congress to officially declare war. When he finished speaking, Cora switched off the radio.

"With all of the preparations, Leah, you won't be going to school this week. And the restaurant is also closed. So you're going to stay as close to home as possible until things calm down. This is very important. Understand?" Cora asked.

"Yes!" a seven-year-old Leah said as she jumped up, not sensing the gravity of the President's message and ready to play. "A *whole* week? What should we do?"

"You're going to make sure Nana Oli has everything she needs. And I need to go out and see what I can do to help at the restaurant. They're using it as an information center. I'll stop to get groceries on the way home. We should probably stock up."

Cora gave Nana Oli a hug, and said, "Don't worry. He'll come home safely. He'll be a hero for fighting the people who did this to us," referring to the grandson who weighed heavily on Nana Oli's heart.

Chapter 22

September 1944

Three years after Pearl Harbor, most in Portland would agree that the servicemen as well as the laborers who came from all over the country to build the Liberty ships in their shipyards changed the town for the better.

Portland was full of life: the traffic in the Bay, the crowds downtown, the smokestacks spewing black smoke. Despite the fact that the United States was losing soldiers overseas every day and despite the fact that many of those boys had ties to Portland, citizens of the city found comfort and pride in their patriotic work supporting "the cause." Yes, it was an exciting time to be in Portland.

Leah thought Nana Oli was the most patriotic person she knew. She and Leah would read books at night that glorified the Allies and their noble cause for democracy and ensured the defeat of the Nazis and the Japs. Leah couldn't understand why there were such horrible people in this world, people so full of hatred.

One day, the *Press Herald* had been left tossed on the kitchen table, and Leah caught a glimpse of a cartoon. She loved cartoons and picked it up to get a closer look. She was worried about Annie after Daddy Warbucks died a few weeks ago and thought she would sneak a peek before she and Nana Oli sat together for their daily reading of *Little Orphan Annie*. Leah's heart broke for Annie. Even though he had been sick, she was shocked at his death.

When she unfolded the paper, she gasped. Looking back at her was a large head with thick round glasses, pointy bright white teeth, and a knife at a soldier's throat, blood dripping from the blade. The man wore a hat with a sun on the front. Leah didn't know what it meant, but she found it scary and dropped the paper back on the table right as Nana Oli returned to the room.

"Ready to read today's *Little Orphan Annie*?" she asked. When Leah didn't answer right away, she followed up, "Tutto ok?"

Leah pointed to the newspaper. "What's that?"

Nana Oli picked it up and shook her head. "That's no cartoon for little girls. It's about war. But we can see what Annie and the Junior Commandos are doing."

The two snuggled together with the newspaper on the sofa in the front room. Nana Oli found the comic and began reading until Leah interrupted the story when Sandy, Annie's dog, showed up in a panel.

"I lo-uh-u-ve this dog! He's so cuuuuute!" Leah squealed, her hands cradling her cheeks. "I wish I could have a pet just like him!"

It was only two weeks later that Leah's wish slipped right through her hands. She attended Schools at War meetings after school; she and her classmates had volunteered to sell war stamps and bonds to help with the war effort. While walking home, she passed a group of boys roughhousing in front of a building a few doors down from their duplex. She sped up and kept her head down, hoping to avoid drawing their attention. Then she was jolted by a guttural yowl that did not come from one of the boys. A tabby kitten was arched and puffed up while it dodged pebbles kicking up dust and clunking on the wall behind it.

"Stop it!" Leah yelled without thinking. The boys froze mid-throw, and all turned to her at once. "Leave that cat alone!" she demanded.

At the break in the onslaught, the brown kitty hobbled away down the sidewalk. Leah was astonished it had only three legs. She raced over to snatch it up in her arms.

"This is *my* kitty," she told her stunned audience as she picked up the cat and walked off, the boys yelling insults that she ignored.

"You poor baby. Those terrible boys. I'm sorry they were being so mean to you. You want to come home with me? Can I call you Sandy?

You can be my Sandy." The kitten thanked her by breaking out into an involuntary purr.

As she turned up the walk to the duplex, she realized that she had a problem. Her mother would never let her keep this cat. She wasn't even sure Nana Oli would take her side on this one. Before she opened the front door, she tucked the scrawny kitten under her shirt. Fortunately, Nana Oli was back in the kitchen.

Leah called out, "I'm home," and then raced to her room and closed the door.

"Ow!" She pulled the kitty out and dropped it on the bed so she could examine the wound on her stomach. "Why'd you do that? Bad kitty," she scolded.

But it was only a little puncture from a claw. She scooped it up and rubbed her face along its side. Then she set out to inspect its leg. Or rather, its missing leg. She nervously ran her hand to the spot where the leg should have been, afraid of what it might feel like. But it wasn't as scary as she thought it would be. It was just a little stump of a leg that ended way too soon.

"Oh you poor baby! What happened to you? Does it hurt?" Leah cried. "I'm going to take care of you, don't you worry. I don't care what anyone says."

"Leah!" Nana Oli called from outside the door. "Come help me in the kitchen."

"Right now?"

"Yes! Right now. Certo! Now."

Nana Oli opened the door to speak with Leah directly. Startled, the three-legged kitten leaped out of Leah's arms and hobbled as fast as it could out of the room.

"Dio mio! What was that??" Nana Oli screeched, not sure of exactly what she saw.

Leah followed it out, explaining, "It's a kitten. I saved it, and I'm going to take care of it."

"No. That rat must go!" Nana Oli informed Leah.

"Cat. It's a *cat*," Leah objected, racing around the apartment trying to catch the wayward animal.

"Cat, rat. No, no, no. It cannot stay here. It must go. And it will go before your mamma gets home."

Leah was now on her hands and knees, peeking under the sofa where the kitten had hidden.

"Come here, little one. Come on. I'm going to take care of you. Don't listen to Nana Oli. She will grow to love you too. Come on out," Leah begged.

She reached her hand under the sofa to try to pull the cat out. But the cat hissed and took a swipe at her. Then as it ran out from its hiding place, Nana Oli opened the front door, and the kitten escaped and immediately disappeared. Leah popped up and ran outside, only to learn that the three-legged kitten was a lot faster than she would have thought when it had escape on its mind.

"Sandy? Kitty? Come back! Where are you?" she cried desperately.

Finally giving up, she went back inside and fell into a waiting Nana Oli's arms. "That kitty needed me," she got out between sobs. "Didn't you see it was missing a leg??" But the realization that perhaps it didn't need her, and in fact didn't want her, left her dismayed.

Chapter 23

December 1944

"Hey boys. Let's get that door closed! You're letting all the heat outside," Cora teased the group of sailors taking their time coming into the restaurant and thus welcoming the cold and snow to drift in while they dawdled. They immediately hustled in, and Cora led them to their regular dinner table while they worked to get back on her good side, apologizing for their slow entrance.

She didn't bother bringing them menus. Instead, she rested her hand on the shoulder of the man whose back was to her and asked the table of five, "The usual?" And they all nodded.

"Yeah, I figured as much. You boys aren't much interested in trying anything new, are you? All about sticking to the routine?"

"No, not at all. We just want to keep things easy for you, Cora," one sailor assured her.

"Wouldn't want you to have to work any harder than necessary, now would we?" another interjected.

"Right. Ok, boys. Whatever you say. I'll be right back with your drinks," she said as she winked at the young man who sat at the far end of the table before sashaying off.

Cora was now the lead waitress at Messe's Bistro. She made more money than most, for she had perfected the ability to anticipate the customers' needs before they were even aware they needed anything. Customers regularly asked for her, none aware that she had a daughter hidden at home with an elderly widow.

When she came back balancing a tray of cold beers, Bernie, the sailor from Nebraska who had only recently arrived in Portland, made a proposition: "Cora, I've got two tickets to the symphony on Saturday. What do you think? Will you allow me the privilege of escorting you?"

Immediately, the others commenced with taunts and whistles.

She placed the last beer in front of Bernie. With one hand on her hip and the other holding the tray down at her side, she challenged him, "Ah, Bernard. You trying again, are you? What makes you think I'm going to say yes this time?"

"You never know. I might have grown on you!" was his retort.

The hecklers at the table joined in on the humiliation:

"Give it up, buddy."

"She ain't ever gonna say yes."

"No, you just keep trying, Bern."

"Why do you think she would change her mind? You haven't even grown on us yet!"

The last quip resulted in beer-spitting, table-pounding laughter.

Cora left with a twirl, only to glance back to let them know with a wave of her hand, "I'll be back in a few with your food!"

At the next table over was Corporal Curtis of the USS Denebola, her best customer. He often entertained visiting naval officers at Messe's and insisted that Cora wait on he and his guests, not only because of her service, but also because Cora expertly danced on the line in her interactions with men so that they felt both attractive and appreciated. The women she worked with didn't necessarily feel as enamored with Cora, but she didn't care. What she cared about was counting her tips.

Leon had Cora to thank for much of the success he enjoyed at Messe's Bistro, a place where he promised the sailors stationed in Maine good food, good service, and good times. He regularly booked live entertainment, making the restaurant a good place to escape the news from the varied fronts, which was rarely good. Even when the Allies made progress, the citizens of Portland were keenly aware of the numbers who were killed, even in victory, and oftentimes they

Chapter 23

recognized a name on the list of those killed in action as someone who had lived on their streets at one time or another.

By mid-December, Messe's Bistro was drenched in Christmas. Ever since Leon had spent a Christmas with his wife and two boys in New York City six years ago, he asked Cora to imitate the Macy's Christmas scenes in the two restaurant windows facing the street.

In 1944, the theme for the window decorations was "Always Our Heroes." One of the two windows was dedicated to the sailors in the US Navy stationed in Casco Bay and the other was to those men in the Army Coast Artillery Corps defending Portland Harbor. Leon provided Cora with a generous budget, hoping she could outdo what she had put together the year before. The crowds of people that the windows attracted made December, despite the foul weather, continually one of their most profitable months.

Cora put the final touches on the US Navy window display and then carried an extra teddy bear and nutcracker that she didn't end up using to the back office. There she found Leon fiddling with the radio, turning knobs and adjusting the antenna as he fought the static that punctuated the news from the Pacific.

"Everything ok? Is there news?" Cora asked.

"A typhoon. In the Pacific. The Third Fleet is in the Pacific," he responded as crackles from the radio punctuated his words. "My son. My son is in the Third Fleet."

"Oh, Leon. Here, let me see if I can help you," she offered, taking over the knobs as Leon's head dropped into his hands.

Cora found a signal: "... Typhoon Cobra has ... the US Navy off the Philippines ..." It was staticky, but they could make out some of the report. "... the worst natural disaster to hit the Navy ... three destroyers ... and the Third Fleet ... casualties estimated to be in the hundreds ... The USS Monaghan, the USS Spence ... and the ... USS ..."

"The USS what?? What was the third?" Leon shouted at the radio as he jumped up from his chair. They had lost the signal.

"Leon," Cora interrupted. "Go home; be with your wife. Maybe you can get better service on your radio there. I can take care of everything here tonight. And if I hear anything, I'll send someone to you right away."

Leon's eyes were bloodshot and coated in tears that had not yet been shed. Cora was his most important employee, but she knew little about his family. She had been unaware that he even had a son serving in the Pacific.

Right then, his wife appeared at the doorway. Leon got up to meet her, and she dropped into his arms. She had gotten word. Their son was gone. What a waste, Cora thought. Their son didn't die fighting for freedom or protecting his loved ones. He died from someone's incompetence at forecasting the weather. Cora could only shake her head at the news.

She left the two grieving parents, giving them privacy in their pain.

Leon, however, wasn't comfortable indulging in that pain, so he didn't stay home for long, returning to the restaurant even before his son's body was returned and the funeral was held.

"What are you doing here?" Cora asked Leon when he appeared in the kitchen a week later. "You are supposed to be home."

"I can't sit around any longer," Leon explained. "My wife won't talk to me. She just knits. Day and night. Socks, mufflers, mittens. For the troops, she says. I can't sit by and watch her knit and knit for someone else's son."

"Cora! Your order's up. It's gonna get cold," the chef yelled.

"Go on," Leon told her. "Don't worry about me. We don't want that food getting cold."

Cora grabbed the dish from the window and dashed off into the dining room, and she dashed back just as fast.

"I have an idea," Leah told Leon. "How about we put your wife's knitting to good use." She had his attention. "The Navy is always requesting donations. Socks and such. Why don't we host a donation drive? Here at Messe's? Your wife can feel like she's doing something useful. And it would be great for the restaurant too."

Leon hesitated.

"What do you think, Leon?" Cora asked, hopeful he would agree. "We could use the private dining room as a meeting place for volunteers. They could work after the lunch rush and before dinner to package and wrap donations to be sent to the Pacific. Dinner could be on the house. The price of admission would be a donation. People

Chapter 23

could bring socks, blankets, books, or money for the troops."

He started to warm to the idea as she explained her vision, and by the time she was finished talking, he had offered to close down the restaurant one night for the volunteers and their best customers.

Cora and Leon's wife dove into the project and distributed flyers throughout town to announce the event. Doors would open at 5:00 PM sharp on December 30th.

When the day arrived, Leon locked the doors right after the lunch rush, and the transformation of the restaurant began.

The men pushed most of the tables out to line the perimeter of the room. They left a few scattered around the middle of the room so people could sit and enjoy the food the kitchen was busy preparing. Leon had been collecting boxes from food deliveries, and he stacked some under each table. Cora assigned volunteers to be posted at the tables on the left and right sides of the dining room to collect donations. A few older women from the Methodist church offered to wrap packages and sat at one of the two tables near the front that was piled with leftover Christmas wrapping paper donated by a few of the local stores. They weren't sure what all else people might bring, but they were prepared for it all. Cora even placed a cash box on a table near the front of the room so that Leon's wife could also collect any cash donations. Along the back wall was a line of tables that would hold the buffet. Leon led his kitchen crew in preparing hot food as a thank you for the hard work and for the donations that would made this night possible.

As they finished setting up, Cora rolled a coat rack just inside the front door, and she was pleased to see that outside, dozens of people had arrived early, arms laden with donations and bouncing in place to ward off the cold.

Inside, pent-up energy buzzed around the room as volunteers finished last minute preparations and took their positions at their assigned tables. The wait staff removed the lids from the serving dishes on the buffet table, and the room filled with the comforting aroma of a trio of warm soups, their famous homemade meatloaf, and buttery mashed potatoes.

Cora took one last glance around the room and smiled when Leon's wife approached her.

"Thank you. Thank you for thinking about our sons fighting this terrible fight," she said. "I know we can't help my boy anymore, but maybe we can help someone else's son. This work has been so helpful for me. I just can't believe he is never coming back." Her voice cracked. She gave Cora another squeeze and then took her post at the register.

Satisfied that everyone was ready, Cora flung open the doors, and the crowd rushed in to escape the cold. She quickly pulled the doors closed behind the first rush of people and began making the rounds, greeting regular customers and their families, people from the neighborhood, sailors she had served, and strangers alike. She scooped up a whining toddler into her arms. Mrs. Henrick's husband couldn't come tonight, and the struggling mother didn't have enough hands to hold onto the knitted blanket she had made and brought to donate as well as her five-year-old and the toddler. They were fairly new to town; her husband was the commander on the USS Alcor, which had only just arrived to Casco Bay in July. Cora had just quieted the little boy when a volunteer from the wrapping table interrupted her.

"Excuse me, Cora. Do you have a pair of scissors? I could have sworn I'd brought two pairs, but I can only find one in my bag."

"Yes, I have an extra pair. Let me get it for you."

Cora placed the boy back down on his wobbly feet, offered to take the blanket from Mrs. Henrick, and sought the box of extra supplies she had left at the maître d stand near the front door. She dug through the box and found the scissors. As she headed to the wrapping table, scissors in hand, she nearly bumped into a tall man in his early thirties wearing his army dress uniform. He had just entered the restaurant holding a bag of socks to donate. Cora's hand instinctively grasped at the base of her neck. But there was nothing there to grasp. For a moment, the world stopped. Until the soldier found his courage and broke the spell.

"Cora?"

It was Jimmy K.

The little girl pressed her nose and both of her hands against the window of the restaurant to get a better view of the Christmas scenes inside. A laughing Santa held out a gift for one of the animated sailors

Chapter 23

gathered around him. Loads of toys were piled high under a twirling Christmas tree. A train carrying stuffed animals spilling over the sides of its boxcars wound its way into her view and then out of sight. She stepped back from her imagination, leaving two handprints and a nose smudge on the window. Then she braced herself and walked through the front door.

Inside, the woman she came to see held a pair of scissors and stood face-to-face with a man that she didn't recognize. They weren't talking to each other, so the little girl slipped in between them and interrupted: "Mammina?"

Leah's voice shook. She had never done anything like this before; she had snuck out to go see her mom at the hotel. On the walk over, she imagined her mother's surprise at seeing her. She would scold her but then swoop her up in her arms. And then she would introduce her to all of her work friends.

Instead, Cora asked Leah, "Would you like to make a donation? Come with me. You can make your donation right over here." She guided the confused girl to a quiet corner without a word said to the confused man.

Her mother didn't seem angry or concerned. She simply asked, "What are you doing here?"

Leah quickly strategized.

"I don't feel well. Nana Oli's asleep. I didn't know what to do."

Cora looked at her daughter as though she were a stranger.

"Couldn't you just go to bed?"

"I can't sleep. Can I please stay here with you?"

Before Cora could answer, Corporal Curtis approached.

"And who is this young lady?" he asked, a twinkle in his eye.

"This is Leah. And she was just leaving," Cora responded, with one hand at Leah's back as she moved to lead her to the front door.

"Hello, young lady. Would you like to help us?" He bent down to talk to Leah eye-to-eye. "Could you help organize socks? We have an awful lot of them to send out to our troops overseas."

Leah looked to her mother for a signal on how she should respond.

"She's not feeling well," her mother answered for her.

"I'm so sorry to hear that. Come with me. This will make you feel better. I promise." He took her by the hand and winked at Cora. He grabbed a chair and placed it at a table with two young ladies who stopped what they were doing to greet the handsome officer.

"Good evening, ladies. Have you met Leah yet? She would like to help out our soldiers too. Do you think you could find something for her to do?" he asked.

"We certainly can. Who is this beauty? Is this your daughter, Officer?" one of the ladies teased.

"No, but she really wants to help our soldiers tonight. Can you put her to work?"

"We'd love to. How old are you, Sweetheart? Eight? Nine?" one of them asked.

"I'm almost ten," Leah proclaimed proudly.

"Wow. Almost ten?" Corporal Curtis acknowledged. "I have a daughter at home about your age. My daughter is eight. And you know, sometimes she doesn't feel well either. But if she were here tonight, helping our troops would make her feel better too. I'm sure of it. So you ready to help out, Leah?"

"Yes, I can do that. I think I might even be feeling a little better," Leah countered.

"I'm sure you'll feel better very quickly. Thank you ladies," he said.

The two ladies pulled up a chair between them and showed Leah how to sort socks. Leah wasn't watching. She instead kept an eye on her mother and the man who brought her to the table. She couldn't make out what they were saying, but she could see her mother giggling. Her mother whispered in his ear, and he placed his arm around her waist to pull her in close. Cora swatted his arm playfully and floated away. Then she disappeared in the crowd.

After only a few minutes, a completed pile of socks sat in front of Leah. The ladies directed her to put the stack in a box and then take it to the wrapping table. Leah obeyed.

Jimmy K. brought a donation that his mother had been working on for this event, and he privately hoped he might run into Cora. It had been years since he had last seen her. Back then, he would often run into her, especially on Sundays when she and her mother visited the

McCarthys. But when he hadn't seen her for a few weeks, he came up with an excuse to be on Congress Street so that he could check in on her. He didn't know why he was so nervous when he knocked on the front door, but his mouth had gone dry, and he swayed as he shifted his weight from one foot to the other.

Cora's mother, surprised to see him, answered and apologized. Cora wasn't there. She had unexpectedly left for New York to help out a relative in the city, a cousin of Charles's, she said. He was stunned.

"How long will she be gone?" he asked.

"Hard to say." Bessie clearly wasn't going to expand on that.

"Can I write to her? Can you give me her address?"

"No, that won't be possible. They will be moving around, travelling. But it's very nice to see you again, Jimmy K. You are looking so handsome. You sure have grown up! Tell your mother I say hello." And she shut the door.

That doesn't make any sense, he thought as he walked away. Why would Cora leave without even saying goodbye? But her mother obviously wasn't interested in giving him any more information.

Three months after Cora disappeared, Jimmy K. turned 21 and turned his future over to the army. He never heard from Cora again, and so he rarely returned to Portland. The scar of her abandonment ran deep, and it hardened a corner of his heart. But he met a woman while stationed at Fort Benning, and her love danced around the scar. Even if she could never soften it, he grew to love her dearly and asked her to be his wife. She gave him two sons who burst open other parts of his heart when they burst onto the scene. He would say he was a happy man.

But recently, his parents' health was failing, so he did his best to return as often as he could. On this latest trip, one of the boys from the neighborhood told him that Cora was working at Messe's. So before his leave ended, he made the decision to stop by the restaurant's event and drop off a donation.

The first thing he saw when he opened the door was Cora. He recognized her at once, and he did his best to suppress the smile that swept over his face. She was walking across his path, so he cut her off.

"Cora?"

Before she responded, a little girl slid between them.

"Mammina?"

And then Cora led the girl away. Uncomfortable, he glanced around to see if anyone noticed what had just happened. But the room was a coordinated chaos of people coming in and out, greeting friends and meeting strangers, laughing and sharing a tear. Jimmy K. moved further into the room, and an older gentleman in an overseas cap covered in pins and insignias from his service in World War I stopped him.

"Young man," he said, "what unit are you with?" He took Jimmy K.'s hand in both of his. Jimmy K. paid his respects to the veteran by answering his questions and thanking him for his service. Others also approached him, taking the opportunity to shake the hand of an active soldier. A woman took his donation, which he kindly appreciated.

After his donation bag was taken, he watched Cora approach a group at a wrapping table and introduce herself to a sober man in full navy dress blues.

"Hello, handsome," Jimmy K. overheard her say as she slipped into the empty chair next to the man. "I'm Cora. And you are?"

Jimmy K. balked and stepped back to watch the rest unfold from a few feet away.

The little girl that he had seen earlier walked right past him and straight to Cora. "Mamma, here are some more socks," she said.

"Robert, can you wrap those?" Cora asked the officer.

"I can certainly try," he laughed.

Robert took the socks from Leah, and he grabbed a sheet of wrapping paper.

The little girl stood for a second before she returned to the young ladies at the sock table, passing right by Jimmy K. once again.

He quickly did the math. Cora had abruptly left town without saying goodbye. Her mother told him that she would be gone indefinitely while she helped a relative in New York. He had been heartbroken at her sudden disappearance. He never forgave himself for not confessing how he had loved her. But he wasn't even sure when it happened, when she changed from the scrappy tomboy next door to the intriguing young woman whose presence caused flutters to swirl through his body. And she was gone before he had made sense of his feelings.

It never occurred to him that Cora's mother had lied. But the truth

Chapter 23

was now obvious. There had never been a cousin needing help in New York City.

She had Cora's blue eyes. And there was something in her gait. She didn't have the same swagger as her mother did, but she performed a little check-step every few feet that Jimmy K. never would have remembered but instantly recognized from his days running about the neighborhood with Cora.

Robert apologized for his poor gift-wrapping skills as he struggled with the socks that the little girl had just delivered. Cora completed her own mediocre attempt at wrapping socks and laughed when she put the package down next to Robert's wrapped gift.

"Well you're clearly not much better at this wrapping business than I am," he pointed out. And it was true. Cora managed to make hers sloppier than his.

Jimmy K. would forever love Cora, but he no longer recognized her. The spunky, curious girl had grown into a manipulative coward. She obviously had no intention of talking to him, and he wasn't going to fight for her attention.

It was time to leave.

Outside, Jimmy K. fought the impulse, but failed; he looked back through the window one last time, just as Cora's giggles overtook her, and she placed her hand on Robert's arm. Tiny snowflakes swirled around his head. The door opened again, and he jumped back so it wouldn't hit him. Music and laughter spilled outside while three people tumbled out of the restaurant, full of life. They brushed past Jimmy K. and disappeared around the next corner for whatever adventure awaited them. He knew what awaited him; he was headed to the front lines, shipping out to the Pacific in the morning.

He walked off in the opposite direction of the trio, defeated at the knowledge Cora hid the truth from him. But also full of regret that he had hid the truth of his feelings from her.

Chapter 24

April 1945

The wedding took place only a few months later, right before Robert O'Toole was deployed for another tour of duty in the U.S Atlantic Fleet. Cora had pushed for the quick marriage. Robert, having just turned 39 years old, had gotten used to the bachelor life, but ever since the donation drive at the hotel, Cora and the naval officer she met wrapping socks had spent as much of their free time together as they could. Sometimes it was just the two of them, but often they joined other naval officers and their dates.

"Lee?" Nana Oli peeked into the bedroom. "Time to wake up. Your mamma and Mr. O'Toole are getting ready to leave for the courthouse. Come say goodbye, and then we need to get everything ready for our guests."

Leah jumped out of the bed she shared with her mother and threw on a robe before pushing past Nana Oli. When she reached the front hall, Mr. O'Toole's hand was on the doorknob.

Were they going to leave without even saying goodbye?

"That doesn't look like a wedding dress," Leah said. Her mother wore a blue Victory suit, and Mr. O'Toole was dressed in his naval white dress uniform. Leah found out about the only wedding a few days earlier, so she didn't know the plans. She'd never been to a wedding, but she had seen pictures of brides. The bride always wore a white gown.

"Oh no. I'm too old to wear white," she laughed. "Besides, we're just going to the courthouse," she said as Robert pulled open the front door. She bid the two farewell before following Robert out the door.

Nana Oli assured Leah, "They won't be gone long." Then she turned to the task ahead of her. "I need your help to get ready. Go put on clothes. Hurry, hurry."

Leah ran off, and Nana Oli suddenly yelled out, "But not the dress for the party!"

When Leah returned to the kitchen, Nana Oli slipped an apron over her head and secured it by tying a bow in the back. Then she put Leah in charge of the fruit and walnut salad while she stirred her famous marinara sauce as it simmered in a pot, checked the meatloaf in the oven, assembled the ingredients for the green bean casserole, and kept Leah away from the carrot cake that would serve as the wedding cake. Leah quickly forgot her project as she watched Nana Oli dance around the room.

"Leah!" Nana Oli scolded, nearly tripping over her. The next exclamation came out in her native Italian, which Leah didn't understand. But then she continued, "We have much to do! We will make a buffet. I need you to stack the plates and put the silverware and napkins on the table. The guests will come soon."

Leah headed to the cabinet holding the silverware and got to work.

A knock on the front door and a voice calling "Hello?" soon interrupted them. The first guest had arrived. Leah abandoned the silverware and raced to her room to change clothes, leaving Nana Oli to answer the door. Leah wasn't sure what she was supposed to wear. Her mother hadn't gotten her a new dress for the party, so she would wear one of her dresses from last spring. She slipped one over her head. It was a bit short. After all, she had grown since last year. But she could still get it buttoned up properly.

By the time she emerged, Mr. Mercier from the restaurant and his wife were sitting in the living room. And Mr. O'Toole's friend from the Navy, judging by his uniform, was removing the jacket from a young woman; she was very giggly, Leah noted. The neighbor from downstairs was handing Nana Oli a can of ground coffee.

Leah watched as the adults introduced themselves and engaged in the small talk that adults always seemed to do. They all had brought presents and had stacked them in a pile on the coffee table.

Oh no. She hadn't gotten her mom a present. But she had an idea. No one had yet noticed her, so she slowly backed herself into her room, but at that moment, Nana Oli brought the bowl of spaghetti out to the dining room table and spotted her trying to sneak out.

"LeeLee, bring the salad from the kitchen?" Nana Oli asked.

When Leah placed it on the table, Nana Oli announced to the guests, "Eat! Take a plate. Our newlyweds will be home soon, presto!"

Leah took that opportunity to retreat to her room and to come up with a gift.

It wasn't long before Cora and Mr. O'Toole appeared at the door, and the room erupted into applause and cheers. Leah heard the commotion and left her room to join the party. Her mother was spinning around, lavishing hugs on anyone within arm's length. Leah was just out of range, watching on the sidelines. Nana Oli took Leah's hand to lead her into her mother's orbit.

"Wait! I have to get something from the bedroom," Leah remembered. She let go of Nana Oli's hand and ran off. She quickly returned, a piece of paper flapping in her hand. She showed it to Nana Oli first.

"Beautiful, LeeLee," Nana Oli told her. "Tell me about your picture." Then she broke out in laughter. "That fat one behind you? That's me?"

Leah laughed. "Yes, and see? You're holding my hand. And that's mom holding hands with Mr. O'Toole. See, I drew her blue suit?"

"Si! Why is she so big? She's bigger than Mr. O'Toole! And that's a salute, no?"

"Because he's in the Navy."

"Your mamma and her husband look very happy in your picture, no? They will love it. Come. Give your mamma a big hug on her wedding day," Nana Oli directed Leah back to her mother.

"Here's Leah." Nana Oli interrupted Cora before someone else grabbed her attention.

"Look what I made for you!" Leah pulled out the picture from behind her back as if to say, "ta-da!"

As Cora reached for the picture, her husband swooped in, put his arm around his new wife, and pulled her in for a kiss on the cheek. Leah let go of the paper, thinking her mother had a hold of it, but instead, it fell to the floor as Cora giggled into her new husband's neck. Leah dropped to her knees to retrieve it before one of the newlyweds inadvertently stepped on it.

When she stood back up, Cora instructed Leah, "Be sure to hug your new daddy."

Leah froze. Was he her daddy? It never occurred to her that he would now be her "daddy." She had really only thought of him as Mr. O'Toole. But that led to wondering about her real dad. Who was he? His identity was a mystery that had lingered right under the surface but had as yet remained unexplored. She stood frozen as new questions darted around her head.

Nana Oli pushed Leah towards Mr. O'Toole, her "new daddy." Leah pushed back against her but not strongly enough, and she ended up stumbling forward.

"If he's my new daddy, what happened to my old daddy?" Leah wondered out loud. As soon as the words spilled out, she understood that asking had been a mistake she wouldn't repeat.

The blood drained from Cora's face. Leah was taken aback. For the first time, she witnessed her mother lose her composure. But Cora was quick to recover.

"There's no 'old' daddy, Leah. And there's no 'new' daddy. Robert is your father. There is nothing more to say about it."

"Go LeeLee. Give them a hug," Nana Oli encouraged.

The new family stood in an awkward triangle. Mr. O'Toole had one arm around Cora's waist, and he placed the other hand on Leah's shoulder. Cora's arm draped over Mr. O'Toole's shoulders, she was slightly taller with her heels on, and she placed her other hand on Leah's back, patting it lightly.

"Ok. Everyone wants cake, no?" Nana Oli announced as she whisked Leah away from the couple. She left Leah to guard the cake while she trotted off to the kitchen in search of a knife.

Leah glanced around. No one was paying attention. So she slid her finger across the icing of the cake and put it in her mouth. Then she retreated to the bedroom, picture in hand. And she never brought up the subject of her father again.

Cora didn't often find herself at a loss for words, but when Leah asked about her father, she was indeed at a loss for words.

She had stored any memory of Leah's actual father so far away that she was jolted by the reminder. But she didn't want Robert to see her react. He only once asked her about Leah's father, asking in the form of a question about what happened to her first husband. Cora simply replied, without correcting him about the husband part, that he had died before Leah was born and that it was too distressing to discuss. He respected her wishes and never brought it up again. But Leah had never asked about her father before.

It had been nearly eleven years, and Cora had managed to wipe him from her mind. She had nearly convinced herself that a man was not involved in Leah's birth at all. It was quite remarkable, actually. Cora had made the decision when she moved into Mrs. Olivari's apartment with the baby that she would never discuss what happened or reveal who he was.

Cora did not appreciate any question about the father of her child. It was nobody's business, not even Leah's. And she would not allow it to come up again. Robert was Leah's father. That was all anyone needed to know.

After the celebration died down, Nana Oli lightly knocked on the bedroom door. Leah hadn't come back out to the party.

"Lee? Can we talk?"

Leah opened the door, and Nana Oli asked if she could sit with her on the bed.

"I leave tonight, LeeLee. My mimma and her husband will be here soon. I'm going to live with them in New York. In the city!"

Leah was dumbfounded. She couldn't imagine life without her.

"Why? Why are you leaving?" She began to cry.

"Tesora. I can't stay. There's no room for me. Now you'll have the room to yourself, no?"

"I don't want this room to myself," she protested.

"But you're a big girl. You don't need me. And I miss my daughter. You can visit me in New York, no? Wouldn't you like that? We can plan it, yes?"

Leah gasped. Nana Oli asked her to sit forward, and she slowly rubbed her back in circles until Leah calmed down and her breathing slowed. Then Nana Oli took the distraught girl into her arms, kissed her on the head, and promised that she would be back to visit her soon. When she left, she closed the bedroom door and Leah listened to her footsteps recede. The three of them had lived here together for as long as Leah could remember. She picked up the picture she had drawn for her mother and decided she would keep it for herself. She folded it in half so that only she and Nana Oli were visible, and she tucked it under her pillow.

She lay awake, thinking of the nights cozying up to Nana Oli with a good book. Leah loved how she always smelled like a freshly opened box of Ivory soap. And Nana Oli had perfected the read-aloud, complete with individual character voices and histrionic scenes. Leah's favorite had been *The Moffats*. Like the children in the book, she had no father, but she liked to imagine, like the children in the book, that she had a house full of siblings and a life of exciting adventures.

She heard the car pull up. She heard Nana Oli's daughter help her with her bags and into the car. She heard the car drive off. Only then did her mother come into the bedroom.

"Did Nana Oli tell you that this is now your bedroom? All by yourself! So let me just get a few things. I'll be sleeping in Nana Oli's room from now on. I'll get the rest of my things out of here tomorrow. I will see you in the morning. Good night."

And she was gone. She hadn't given Leah a chance to respond. To any of it.

The next morning, Nana Oli wasn't in the kitchen baking her famous scones or browning breakfast hash. Instead, her mother was pulling eggs out of the refrigerator.

"I don't understand. Why did Nana Oli leave?" Leah asked.

"With Robert moving in, there's no room for her to continue living here," Cora said while breaking eggs into a bowl. "And besides, you're old enough to take care of yourself now. Aren't you? You don't need

Chapter 24

her anymore. Her daughter took her back to New York City to live with them. It'll be good for her to spend this time with her own family. I'm sure she'll come back to visit."

Mr. O'Toole entered the kitchen, still buttoning his shirt. "Leah, you do understand that Mrs. Olivari isn't part of this family, right? Believe me, this is better for her, to be with her real family." He walked over to the stove where her mother had just poured the eggs into a skillet and gave her a kiss. This didn't make sense to Leah because Mr. O'Toole wasn't part of their family either.

Cora insisted that Leah call him "Dad." And Leah obeyed, but doing so never felt right, so she avoided addressing him at all.

More and more often, she wondered about her real father. Had he ever lived with them? Had her mother married him? Had he held her in his arms when she was born? Had he loved her mother? Had he abandoned them?

She didn't know the answers to these questions, but she could make up stories. Sometimes Leah imagined that her father was a crook. That led to dramatic stories that played out in her imagination of robbing banks, of mafia hits, of police chases. But more often, she imagined him as a hardworking, loving gentleman who dearly loved his daughter. Her mother had snatched her from him and ran off, leaving no forwarding address. He would spend the rest of his life in a relentless quest, searching for his beloved daughter. It sounded so romantic.

Chapter 25

August 1950

Leah gripped her bag in front of her with both hands. In it, she had stuffed everything she would need for the next four days as she and her mother travelled from San Diego, where Robert had been stationed for the past ten months, to Norfolk, their new home. Robert wasn't coming with them by train; he would be following up in a few weeks. But, her mother explained, they couldn't wait for Robert because Leah needed to enroll in her new school.

They had ridden countless trains in the past five years as Cora chased her husband from city to city, not only in the United States but also in Europe when he was stationed in England and Germany. Victory over the enemy apparently didn't mean a Navy officer's job was done.

The Navy had supplied their transportation to the train station, and when the two of them were dropped off at the curb, a porter greeted them, offering to transport their trunks for the cross-country trip. Cora pulled out some bills from her pocketbook and slipped them into the porter's hand.

"Now you promise me that you will take good care of those trunks, right? We want to be sure they make it all the way to Norfolk." She smiled to let him know she was teasing him.

"Yes ma'am. I promise," he replied with a tip of the hat. "Have a pleasant journey."

Leah didn't understand her mother's need to talk to every person they came in contact with. What was the point? They would never see that porter again. And then they were swallowed up by the activity inside the station. Her mother seemed to know exactly how to navigate the place: where to purchase tickets, where to locate a restroom, where to find the gate. As far as Leah knew, her mother had never been here before, yet she walked around as if she had a personal familiarity with the place.

Leah tried to stick close to her mother's side, but she struggled to keep up. Her mother walked with purpose through the station, around the crowds of people, and down hallways. They turned a corner just as the gateman announced, "Line up and pull out your tickets. We will begin boarding."

"Perfect timing!" Cora said, more to herself than to anyone in particular. She showed the gateman their tickets, and he waved them through, wishing them safe travels. They walked down the length of the sleek, shiny train, and at one point, Cora reached up to run her had along the side of the train. She walked briskly, staying one foot ahead of the crowd.

"Mamma, can you slow down?" Leah's voice was barely a squeak.

Cora turned around and now walking backward asked her daughter, "What? What did you say?"

Leah hesitated, giving her mother the opportunity to turn back around and resume her quick pace. "Hurry, Leah. We want to be one of the first on board and get settled before the train leaves the station."

So Leah picked up her pace. Cora glanced at her ticket and approached the next porter they saw.

"Good morning, sir. I believe this is our car," she greeted the gentleman. He confirmed that she was correct and told them their berth would be through the third door on the left. He held out his hand to Cora to steady her as she stepped up on the stool and then into the car. Leah walked right past the porter and followed her mother in search of their living quarters for the next few days.

When they found their berth, they quickly unpacked the small bags they brought for the trip. Just as they finished, the porter made the final call: "All Aboard!" And then the train was underway, the wheels screeching under the weight of its load. Once the train was out of the station and had reached its cruising speed, the mother and daughter duo ventured to the dining car. Cora ordered them each a bacon, lettuce, and tomato sandwich and ordered herself her requisite hot tea, a habit she picked up while they lived in London.

Leah took a sip from a glass of milk. "How long do you think we will live in Norfolk?" she tentatively asked her mother.

"I have no idea, but I am sure Norfolk will be great. Robert should arrive in three weeks, and by then we should have our house all set up and ready for him," Cora replied.

"Am I going to start school as soon as we get there?" Leah asked, closing her eyes as she rubbed both temples.

"You'll start school next week, when everyone starts." That was the end of that conversation.

Leah hated to admit that she dreaded having to attend yet another school. She stared out the window as the Southern California desert rolled by. It would be fine, she decided. She had grown pretty good at making friends quickly. The problem was that they never stuck. She always moved away before those relationships developed any permanency. She had been to four schools in the last five years. And now this would be her fifth.

After finishing the rest of their lunch in silence, Leah mentioned that she wasn't feeling well; the food wasn't agreeing with her.

The waiter approached from nowhere and motioning to her half-eaten sandwich asked Leah, "Are you finished with this, young lady?"

"Yes, thank you," she replied. As he reached down to pick it up, she explained further. "I'm not feeling well. My stomach is upset, so I should probably go lie down for a bit. At least until it settles down." Then she addressed her mother. "Don't you think? Should I lie down?"

Her mother told the waiter that he could also remove her plate, and when he excused himself, she agreed with Leah. "Yes, that is probably best. I am going to go to the lounge. Maybe I'll write a letter to Robert. Or play some cards"

The two stood up from the table. Cora set off to the lounge car, and Leah returned to their berth, where the first thing she did was to close the curtain over the window to create as much darkness as possible. She seemed to be feeling unwell an awful lot. If it wasn't a stomachache, it was a headache, a swollen throat, or congestion. And it seemed to be happening more often.

Chapter 26

June 1952

The graduation ceremony dragged on. Leah sat on the stage in the school's gymnasium among a sea of caps and gowns. She was one of 256 students graduating from Ulysses S. Grant High School. She had only been attending the school since January. That was when her stepfather officially retired from a career with the Navy, and the three of them committed to finally putting down roots on the South Side of Chicago. They bought a house near Mr. O'Toole's family, the same family that had disowned their son "because of me," Leah never forgot. She never met them, but being so close made their absence just that much more obvious.

"Charles. Matthews."

The announcement of some students' names were accompanied by huge roars that erupted from the crowd as extended family cheered the accomplishment of not only the student but of the entire family.

"Cynthia. Marie. McDonald."

Leah scanned the audience for the two who came to witness her graduation. For years, it had been just the three of them. She also had never met anyone in her mother's family. What had happened to them? Did her mother even have her own mother? She never mentioned one. A father? A baby sister? Maybe an older brother? Leah couldn't imagine that her mother had ever been a child. She could only imagine that she had sprung forth like Athena, full-grown in a complete suit of armor."

"Michael. John. Nelson."

Leah made friends easily, and boys formed a line to date her, drawn to her sleek black hair, milky smooth skin, and Irish blue eyes. She appreciated the attention. But her mother held her tight, reining in any sense of exploration her daughter might develop.

"Jacob. James. Nottingham."

Since the three of them typically stayed in one place for such a short time, little opportunity was available to form deeper connections. So Leah lived in a perpetual honeymoon. When she met someone who caught her eye, she would play out the relationship in her head. She could imagine the first kiss, holding hands at a movie, maybe even an engagement! She entertained herself sifting through the possibilities. And while she had mastered the art of first impressions, she had never been tested beyond that, for as she said goodbye to one set of friends or to one smitten boy, she introduced herself to a brand new set of friends and another smitten boy.

"Leah. Anne. O'Toole."

She crossed the stage, accepting the diploma from a principal who registered nothing as he handed her the rolled-up paper. She shook his hand, searched for her mother in the audience, and found her chatting absently with Mr. O'Toole. Then she returned to her seat as she felt another headache coming on.

Chapter 27

April 1959

Leah easily found a job downtown as a secretary for Prudential Bank. In her first week on the job, a young loan officer on her floor invited her to the Italian Village in the Loop. He had recently moved to Chicago from Kansas City and had made it a goal to find all the best restaurants in the city. She gladly accepted.

At 5:00 on Friday, Leah made a quick trip to the ladies' room to freshen up before Pete was to stop by her desk and the two of them could walk over to the restaurant together. He held the door open for her; she slipped her arm into his. They ordered martinis—she felt so grown up—and he let her have a bite of his veal marsala. They had a few more dates, but then Pete tried to dig a bit deeper, get a little closer, do more than hold hands.

"You keep asking about me, Leah, but what are your dreams? What do you love to do when you aren't at work?" he asked. "Do you hope to have a family? How many kids do you want?" he probed further. But she managed to steer the conversation in such a way that she never directly answered the questions.

He walked her to the door of her apartment building. He dropped her hand and turned to face her, pulling her in close. He placed his other hand just under her chin so he could tilt her head up and properly kiss her. But Leah pulled back. Despite the fact that he was loads of fun.

And he was certainly popular around the office, a "real catch," according to the gossip of the secretarial pool.

Leah wasn't quite sure why, but she soon found herself busy on nights he wanted to see her. She wasn't available to talk when he called. She had too much work to catch up on. It didn't take him long to find someone more enthusiastic about spending time with him. And he quickly found that woman on the fourth floor.

A few weeks later, Henry visited the office. Henry was handsome. He was a salesman hoping to land a contract to supply Prudential with his company's paper products. That day, he had an early meeting with Leah's boss, who happened to be running late. So Leah captivated him in the small talk she had perfected. On the way out, he invited her to lunch. She left her sandwich in the drawer and agreed to meet him at noon at a Jewish deli he said she simply must try.

"There's something about you, Leah. I can't quite put my finger on it. But I really would love to get to know you. It seems like you're hiding something. Like you've been terribly hurt. Tell me about your parents, about growing up in Maine," he casually asked as he tangled with a pastrami on rye, sauce dripping between his fingers and onto the plate.

"Oh, I don't want to bother you with any of that," she responded.

And she didn't. The next time her boss had an appointment with Henry listed on his calendar, she made sure to step away from her desk on an "errand."

Cora knew all about her daughter's dating life. Leah called her nearly every day. She had gotten into a routine where she would call right at the beginning of her lunch break. It took Cora a few weeks to realize that the calls had become daily. That seemed a lot. Sometimes she didn't answer. Talking to her daughter brought her down; Leah managed to make even good news exhausting.

The night before Leah moved out of their home into her own apartment a few years ago, Cora and Robert treated her to a fancy dinner at a steakhouse in the neighborhood as their send off. The next day, the movers showed up at the house. Leah took her bedroom set with her, but she would have to furnish the rest of her place herself.

After the truck was loaded, Cora and Robert walked her out to the street to say their goodbyes.

"My phone won't be hooked up until Tuesday, so I can't call you this weekend," Leah warned her mother.

"That's fine," her mother answered.

"Oh wait!" Leah suddenly interjected. "Do you mind if I take the aspirin bottle in the medicine cabinet? I forgot to ask earlier."

"No, of course. Go get it."

Leah dropped her bag to the ground and then ran back to fetch the aspirin. Cora and Robert waited at the curb for her to return.

When she did, Robert placed his hand on her shoulder. "You better hurry if you don't want to miss that train. And congratulations on getting your first apartment. You'll love it."

Leah leaned in to give her mother a hug. Cora moved into her arms, and Leah grabbed her tightly. Cora's body stiffened, but Leah didn't let go. Cora could not remember the last time the two of them shared a hug. She did her best to relax into it, but her body wouldn't allow it. Instead Cora backed her way out of Leah's arms. Leah obediently let go and stepped back. Cora certainly loved her daughter. She just wasn't accustomed to showing it, especially physically.

"Bye, Leah!" Robert broke the standoff.

Leah picked up her bag and then walked off to catch the train and follow the truck into the city.

As Cora and Robert waved goodbye from the curb in front of the house, a lightness washed over Cora's body. She wriggled her hips and stretched out her arms. She found herself throwing back her shoulders. And then she laughed.

"What's so funny?" her husband asked as she balanced on the curb, cautiously placing one foot in front of the other in the direction her daughter just left to catch the train.

"I'm not sure," she responded, smiling as she got up on her toes and spun around before making her way back to Robert.

Leah also met David at work. He was an accountant at a large public accounting firm and lived in a small apartment north of Lincoln Park. He spent more nights in hotels than in the sparse apartment. Still a relatively new CPA, he frequently travelled throughout the Midwest, whether for a warehouse audit in Omaha or a hardware chain audit in Peoria. He had spent little time in the city until he was assigned to the team auditing Prudential.

She noticed him early on. She flirted, she pulled back, she played coy, she teased. She had mastered that game. But he still didn't ask her out on a date. She asked around the office whether or not anyone knew if he was already going steady with someone. No one was quite sure. It seemed that no one really knew much about him. That intrigued Leah. She would find out.

The next time she saw him, she approached him, determined to get a date out of the encounter. They were in the cafeteria on the first floor, and he had just ordered himself a black coffee.

"Hello, David," she said as she slinked up next to him.

"Oh yes, hello, Leah," he replied as he pulled out a pocketful of change and dug around for a dime to hand the cashier.

"Are you in the office tomorrow too?" she asked.

"Yes, yes, I will be here every day this week," he said and then lightly blew on the hot coffee before taking a sip.

"Great! Let's go to lunch tomorrow. Pick out a place, and I'll make a reservation," she suggested with a huge smile.

"I don't really know this area," he admitted. "Why don't you pick out what you like and let me know."

"I can do that," she said. She decided on an American bistro. The menu was varied enough that certainly he could find something he would like there.

And so began a polite courtship, one where Leah was not pushed to talk about her childhood.

Chapter 28

June 1959

The only one of his siblings to not yet have married, David rarely spoke of his family, but when he did, he relied on strings of clichés and vague adjectives. To Leah, it hardly seemed possible that his family consisted of real people, actual flesh and blood. But that allowed Leah the freedom to build elaborate structures around his generic modifiers. Of course, eventually David's parents insisted he bring her to Wisconsin to meet the entire family.

After a four-hour drive up north, David turned onto the farm's dirt driveway. Two nondescript, mongrel dogs bounded out of nowhere to greet them. Complete with matted coats and paws caked in mud, they nipped at the tires and yelped, announcing the arrival of visitors. No need for a doorbell, a locked entry, or a doorman here.

Leah pulled down the sun visor mirror, smoothed her hair, and checked her lipstick as the car kicked up rocks. She took a deep breath to calm her nerves. She was concerned she wouldn't measure up.

As they rounded the curve in the driveway to the back of the modest, two-story farmhouse, the screen door flew open, nearly ripping off its hinges. A woman wiping her hands on a checkerboard apron scrambled out, echoing the excitement of the dogs leaping in the air. It wasn't clear if the dogs had learned to mimic her energy or if she took her cues from the ebullient dogs. Either way, it was a welcome the likes of which Leah had never experienced. This was David's mother, Rachel. No sooner had the screen door slammed back against the metal frame than it bounced open again. A gentleman in work pants, work boots, and a button-down shirt calmly crossed its threshold and stopped to survey the scene before descending the three steps to the ground. This was David's father, William.

As Leah opened the car door, the fresh air filled her lungs. She stepped out of the car, dogs scrambling at her feet, tails whipping at her legs, tongues wagging in out-of-breath excitement. And before she stood completely up, she was in Rachel's arms. Leah's concern about being good enough for their son evaporated. She had come home, home to a place she had never been, home to people she had never met. It was an odd sensation.

David stepped out from behind the wheel to shake his father's hand in the formal manner that would make his superiors at the firm proud. A strong handshake conveyed everything that needed to be said. It was evident that David respected his father. But Leah sensed a bridge between them that had never been crossed.

Rachel was full of life, yet she managed to maintain the decorum of a sturdy farm woman. She had mastered the reserved exterior, but she treated herself to moments of unbounded joy. Anyone in her presence could see it shine from her like an internal flashlight.

She took her son's face in her hands and stood on her toes to give him a quick kiss on the cheek. He leaned down to meet her. Leah watched David's awkwardness. He appeared to be unaccustomed to a warm welcome. That seemed strange, since Leah could only imagine that every homecoming was met with equal enthusiasm.

Leah slipped her hand into David's and ignored it when a moment later he discarded it. They all walked to the house and up into the kitchen. David could fetch the bags later.

Inside, a small mudroom housed work boots in various stages of wear and tear as well as jackets suitable for all kinds of weather. Past that, the kitchen was simple, covered in a red and ochre toile wallpaper featuring scenes of an idyllic country life. A small enamel top table and four metal kitchen chairs, seats covered in red vinyl, dominated the room. A few plates dried in a rack, and a stack of bowls soaked in soapy water in the sink. They had caught Rachel mid-dishwashing. The group made its way through the kitchen and into the living room.

In an instant, the future Leah longed for presented itself. It wasn't that she desired the creaky steps or the mismatched curtains. Or the threadbare carpet. Or even the sink with the rust stain circling the drain. This house possessed a warmth that allowed her to relax into herself. She was enough here.

Just when she allowed herself to settle into that warmth, David announced: "I need to run to town." Leah was caught off guard. William didn't react. Rachel gave a little flick of her hand in his direction but said nothing. When Leah was ready to ask where he was going, he was already gone. She heard the trunk of the car slam shut. David had retrieved her suitcase from the car and placed it in the mudroom.

The engine roared to a start and the tires skidded along the rocks as David pulled away.

Rachel pulled Leah in close. "He's probably just going over to the cemetery," she casually revealed. "He usually does when he is home."

"The cemetery? Why the cemetery?"

"To visit Catherine's grave."

"Catherine? Who's that?"

"David didn't tell you about Catherine? Oh Leah, I'm sorry. He should have told you about her. They were engaged to be married, and only two weeks before the wedding, she wasn't feeling well. No one thought much of it, but three days later, she passed. It was quite sudden. And shocking. To this day, we aren't sure what happened to her."

Leah was stunned. Rachel did not mention how long ago this might have been, and Leah wasn't sure she wanted to ask. Instead, an awkward silence followed.

"Come on," Rachel changed the subject. "Let me show you where you will be sleeping."

"Thank you, Mrs. Evans," Leah said.

"Oh please. That is much too formal. Call me Rachel."

A warmth travelled up Leah's body and rested on her chest.

She followed Rachel up the staircase, treading carefully on the uneven steps. At the top, Rachel pulled a string that lit up a bulb screwed into the ceiling to illuminate the small upstairs hallway and three closed doors. Rachel opened the first one to the left.

"Here you go. You'll stay here. This is David's sister's room, so it's filled with all of her awards. Most from when she was in 4H. Did you do 4H, Sweetie?"

Leah had no idea what 4H was. She wished she had done 4H.

"That's ok. You probably didn't have 4H where you grew up. Hope this will suit you. Why don't you fetch your suitcase—I think David left it downstairs—and unpack?"

Leah followed her back down the stairs to retrieve her abandoned suitcase. She felt the familiar throbbing in her head. "I think I'm going to lie down for a bit. I feel a headache coming on," she explained as she picked up her bag.

"Oh honey, don't worry about it. I'll finish the dishes and start dinner. Feel free to freshen up and lie down. The bathroom's across the hall from your room. Come on down whenever you're ready."

"Thank you. I will," Leah replied.

Leah climbed back up the stairs to her assigned room. She sat down on the bed, imagining what it must have been like to have grown up here and to have shared secrets with girlfriends in this room. Leah examined a shelf that held a handful of trophies for horseback riding, a bowl full of 4H member pins, patches, and a leadership pin, plus a bulletin board covered in county fair ribbons and even two from the state fair. David's sister's specialty had apparently been sheep.

Leah emptied her suitcase into the bottom dresser drawer that Rachel had cleaned out for her. On top of the dresser, she pushed aside a framed picture of what she assumed must have been David's sister and a high school boyfriend to make room for her prescriptions, including the one she would take for the migraine she felt coming on.

Leah worried that the pollen up here, or the ragweed or whatever other allergen existed in Wisconsin, might trigger a reaction. Perhaps an asthma attack. Her doctor wasn't convinced it would be an issue, but he knew this patient well. He had already treated her for migraines and other allergies as well as a number of unspecified ailments. A pill usually solved whatever the problem. Sometimes the office visit alone cured her. Luckily, most doctors were eager to provide solutions. So when she left their offices, she felt better about her condition, about herself, and

Chapter 28

about life. And as a bonus, doctors asked nothing of her in return.

Once she finished unpacking, she lay down on top of the bedspread. She must have managed to doze off for a bit, for when she opened her eyes, the sun was dipping just below the horizon. She crossed the hall to the bathroom and rinsed her face. Then she paused briefly at the top of the stairs before she tiptoed down. She needn't have bothered with the tiptoeing. The creaking of the steps disclosed her impending arrival.

"In here, Leah," Rachel called from the kitchen, where she prepared a freshly killed chicken from their coop for dinner.

"Can I help you?" Leah asked wide-eyed.

"Why sure you can," came the enthusiastic reply. "How about you tackle that pile of potatoes right there." Rachel pointed to a pile waiting to be rinsed and peeled.

A mutual affection grew between the two of them over the preparation of fried chicken, boiled potatoes, and the spinach picked from Rachel's well-tended garden.

As Leah finished setting the kitchen table, the screen door outside the mudroom slammed shut, and William entered. "Dinner smells great," he noted, nodding to Leah before going upstairs to clean up.

Soon after, the thud of shoes dropping on the mudroom floor announced David's return. Rachel wiped her hands on her apron and greeted him with the same warm hug as she had earlier.

"Smells good," he said as he passed right by Leah and took his suitcase upstairs.

"I'm going to wash up for dinner," Leah told Rachel, and she followed David upstairs.

He was unpacking his suitcase in the room where he had slept as a teenager. They weren't married, so out of respect for his parents, they would not be sleeping in the same room. She glanced around. She couldn't tell a lot about his childhood from this room. The walls were bare. The top of the dresser was empty. A shelf held a lamp and nothing else. A plain navy blue bedspread and a white and blue pillow lay atop the bed.

"So was this your bedroom?"

"Yes," He opened a dresser drawer and dropped a pile of folded clothes from his suitcase into it.

"Is this how your room looked when you lived here? Or did your parents clean it out after you left?" she asked. She knew he was a simple man, and his room indicated he always had been.

"No, it's the same," he said as he pulled out his toiletry kit.

Leah sensed that she shouldn't ask where he had been. And he certainly didn't seem interested in offering up that information.

"I got a bit of a headache while you were gone." It was the best she could do at broaching the subject of his disappearance. "So I took a nap," she added. He continued placing items in the dresser.

"I'm going to wash up for dinner. I'll meet you downstairs," she told him.

Dinner was filled with conversation catching up on family and local news and learning as much as they could about Leah.

After dinner, Leah helped Rachel clear the table and wash the dishes. Standing at the sink, something caught Leah's attention out the kitchen window.

"Are those lightning bugs?"

"Well, we call them fireflies, but yes, they are," Rachel said as she wiped down the counter with the dish towel.

"They remind me of growing up in Maine. I always wanted to collect a jar of them and keep them in my room, like a nightlight. Isn't that silly? But my mother and I shared a room, and she would never allow that," Leah laughed.

"Really? So you've never caught a firefly? We need to change that right now. Come with me," Rachel instructed.

Rachel grabbed a canning jar from the pantry, and Leah followed her through the mudroom. Rachel flipped off the back porch light and went outside. Then she demonstrated how to catch one. First, stand perfectly still with hands up ready for one that flies close by. When one gets close, she instructed, gently cup it in both hands and drop it in the jar, quickly returning the top before it flies away.

After successfully catching three, Rachel encouraged Leah to try. The first few dodged her hands as she tried to catch them. But then she caught one and squealed with delight. She dropped it in the jar and was eager to try again. When they had ten fireflies between them, they were satisfied with their haul and returned to the house where William and David shared an after-dinner drink in the living room.

Leah placed the jar on the coffee table so they could watch the flashing lights as they continued the dinner conversation.

The next day David's sister and brother drove their families out to the farm to meet Leah. Turns out that David was the youngest of the group by eight years. Either David must have been a surprise, or Rachel suffered a lot of heartbreak in the years before his birth.

David stood in the shadows, more observant than participatory. He attracted little notice from his family or from Leah, who herself was preoccupied with absorbing all of the warmth and stability that his family exuded.

Chapter 29

September 1959

Three months after the visit to Wisconsin, Leah announced her engagement. She delivered the news to her own mother on one of their daily calls. She struggled to get the words out. Most of their conversations consisted of filler. She gossiped about a neighbor's children, discussed doctor visits, complained about the weather. Leah's news seemed so personal. So she nervously procrastinated until the call was winding down.

"I'm getting married," Leah announced unceremoniously. "David and I want to keep it small. Keep it simple. So we have an appointment at the courthouse next weekend."

"So you aren't having guests? Just you two? Is that really what you want to do?" her mother asked.

"David explained it to me. We can save a lot of money if we do this. Then we'll have enough to buy our own house. Wouldn't that be great? If we could get a house? Besides, didn't you and Robert get married in a courthouse?"

Yes, that's exactly what I did, Cora thought. She didn't regret the small civil ceremony. Not at all. But that was different. It was war time. She was much older. She already had a child. She had just assumed that Leah would want a more formal wedding. That's what most young people wanted.

Cora hung up and actually felt a bit lost. Robert was in Annapolis doing some consulting for the Navy, which meant she was alone in the house for three days. She couldn't remember the last time she had been alone for this long. She had always kept Leah close, and then when Robert retired and Leah moved out, the husband and wife team spent nearly all of their time together.

She was happy with life. She was thankful to have found Robert. They understood each other and didn't require deep conversations about their relationship or about the future. Or even about the past, for that matter.

The phone call with Leah had stirred a sensation that, without Robert there to tap it down, rose from a deeply buried place. This emotion had escaped one other time. When Leah was nine. Before Robert. Leah had heard some kids in the neighborhood talking about going to the circus. When Cora came home from working a lunch shift that day, Leah greeted her at the door and begged her to take her to the circus on Friday.

Cora didn't have the money for something like that. And she was scheduled to work the day the circus was to be in town. But Leah continued asking. It had been raining, and Cora hung her raincoat on the coat rack before making her way back to the kitchen to get a glass of water. Leah followed her.

"The circus is here Saturday too." The tone of voice surprised Cora, and she stopped in her tracks. When she turned around, Leah stood with her hands on her hips. Her eyes were black. A vision jumped up from deep inside Cora's bones. She gasped as if someone had sucked the air from her lungs.

Leah stormed off before Cora recovered.

Nana Oli was already in the kitchen putting clean dishes into the cupboard. She quietly interrupted Cora's thoughts. "I can take her if you'd like. I wouldn't mind going to the circus," she offered.

Cora resumed breathing, and the feeling left as fast as it came. But she had already said no, and she wasn't going to change her mind now.

But today, Nana Oli was not there to distract her thoughts. The house was quiet, and Robert's absence left a vacuum. And vacuums

Chapter 29

demand to be filled. She thought about Leah. She didn't understand her daughter. Cora could have planned a tremendous event to celebrate her marriage. She loved to entertain, after all.

But this way was probably better. Everything always seemed to be too much for Leah. And the stress of a wedding would probably trigger her asthma. Or whatever current issue she was dealing with. Cora couldn't keep track. And didn't try.

Brrrring. Brrrring.

The phone interrupted her thoughts. It was Robert. He had gotten settled into his hotel and was checking in. She forgot to tell him about Leah's news.

Once Leah hung up with her mother, she dialed David's parents to share the news with them.

"We're getting married," Leah blurted out as soon as her future mother-in-law answered.

A squeal came from the other end of the phone. Leah's cheeks hurt from smiling.

"We want to be there! When will the wedding be?"

"We're just going to go to the courthouse," Leah explained. Hearing the disappointment in Rachel's voice made Leah question their decision. She would have loved for his parents to have joined the celebration.

Instead, when the day arrived, a justice of the peace performed the ceremony, and a court clerk and a court officer served as witnesses.

"We are gathered here today in the presence of these witnesses to join David Evans and Leah O'Toole in marriage," the justice began the standard civil service package

Leah's nose itched. She did everything she could to avoid scratching it, but she was making all kinds of strange faces in an attempt to stop the itching. Was it the flowers? She hadn't considered that. Maybe she was allergic to the bouquet of white chrysanthemums she had tied together to carry during the ceremony. She let go with one hand and scratched the side of her nose, hoping to relieve herself of the distraction. It didn't work.

But she was pleased with her dress. It wasn't fancy, but she bought it in the spirit of spending very little on this wedding. The simple knee-length, off-white dress had a slight flare below the sash that was tied delicately around her waist. She swished her hips just ever so slightly to enjoy the movement in her skirt.

"Leah O'Toole." The sound of her name pulled her out of her thoughts. She was about to ask, "Yes?" but the justice continued before she had a chance to respond.

"Do you take David Evans to be your lawfully wedded husband? To have and to hold from this day forward? For better or for worse, for richer or poorer, in sickness and in health, to love and to cherish, until death do you part?" she was asked.

"I do," Leah replied.

"Do you have rings to exchange?"

"Yes, yes we do," Leah answered. The court clerk had been holding the rings and now handed them to Leah and David.

"David, put the ring on Leah's finger and repeat after me. "With this ring …"

David repeated as instructed, and so did Leah. And that was it.

"By the authority vested in my by the state of Illinois, I now pronounce you husband and wife. You may kiss the bride."

They were married. As the court clerk leaned in to her for a congratulatory hug, Leah again second-guessed her decision to not invite David's parents or her own parents. But the important thing was that they were married. As they walked out of the courthouse, she continued to get more congested. She worried that she might be allergic to the flowers after all.

"One minute," she told David, leaving him on the steps out front. She ran back inside to find the court clerk. She would give her the flowers as a thank you for being so nice to her today. At first, the clerk refused the gift. It was too important of a day for Leah, she explained, to give away her flowers.

Then Leah drew her in close with a whisper: "I actually think I'm allergic! My nose is so itchy. I've never had chrysanthemums before, so I didn't realize it. Really, I want you to have them. I'll feel better soon."

How could the clerk refuse? So she happily accepted them.

Chapter 30

February 1960

It came as no surprise when soon after the wedding Leah found herself pregnant. She had already missed two periods when she scheduled a doctor's appointment for confirmation. She hadn't yet mentioned anything to David. They hadn't actually discussed children. It never occurred to Leah that it needed to be discussed. Wasn't it a given? But now that it was a real possibility, she grew nervous about how he might respond.

The doctor promised a nurse would call her with the results. On the bus home, Leah placed her hand over her abdomen and imagined a baby growing inside her. She already knew what the results would be. She had mentioned to David that she had been feeling nauseous while he was at work and that sometimes she felt so sick she actually had climbed back in bed after he left in the morning. But he never asked too many questions and didn't seem to consider the possibility that she might be pregnant.

When she stepped off the bus, she took her time walking the two blocks to their house. She had given up her job when she got married, so she used her time to tidy the house that they had moved into right after the wedding. She did the laundry and had dinner ready for when David came home. She didn't yet have friends in the new neighborhood, so the gaps in her day grew longer. David hadn't made clear to her what was required of a junior accountant in a big accounting firm. A few successful years there, and he could control his professional future, he said. But she didn't anticipate the heavy cost of getting to that point. A junior accountant, at least an ambitious one, can never refuse an assignment. And every accountant at the firm was ambitious.

When David came home from work that night, she had his favorite dinner waiting for him: minute steak. He had simple tastes. She greeted him at the door, he gave her a cursory kiss, and he dropped his jacket and hat on a chair. He wordlessly walked to the head of the table and took a seat.

He was clearly tired. It must have been another long day. He was hungry and didn't feel like talking. But Leah had important news.

"I'm pregnant," she bluntly stated. It wasn't how she planned to tell him, but she was brimming with the news. She anxiously waited for his response. She knew he hadn't expected this announcement.

"Fantastic," he responded.

"Are you happy?"

"Very."

"I'm due in August."

"That's perfect. Not during tax season."

"Oh. I hadn't thought about that. But yes, that's true."

Leah hopped over to her husband, threw her arms around his neck, and leaned in to kiss his cheek. He accepted her kiss before popping a bite-sized pile of mashed potatoes into his mouth. Leah returned to her seat and cut into her steak, satisfied that he was pleased.

Chapter 31

August 1960

Leah dropped to the floor, writhing in pain, with no audience to her agony. She pulled herself into the fetal position, curling her arms around her protruded belly until the sharp pains subsided. She needed to call David. He would be at the office. He had requested an assignment with a local client to ensure he would be in town when the time came.

"David." It was all she could manage before howling in pain.

"Leah, Leah? What's going on?" Still no answer, only moans. "Are you there? Leah."

"Please, help me."

"I'll call your mother to drive you to the hospital. I'll meet you there. It will take me too long to get home."

Within an hour, Cora pulled the car right up to the hospital's emergency room door. A candy striper rushed out with a wheelchair, helped Leah out of the car, and whisked her off. As soon as the passenger side door was pushed shut, Cora pulled away from the curb and drove back home.

Her mother's disappearance went unnoticed by Leah. She was distracted by the fear of what was to come as she was wheeled into the hospital. She had been frightened she wouldn't make it in time, she explained to the overworked candy striper as she pushed Leah through the hallways to a large room where she would remain until she was close to delivery. Five patient beds lined each side of the room, with space left between them for nurses and doctors to examine each woman's progress as they completed their rounds.

Leah felt she was in good hands here. The bleached walls, the sterilized sheets, the fluorescent lights, the metal nightstands—the signs of a professional institution—all gave her a confidence she couldn't manifest at home. Another labor pain gathered, but she didn't panic now that she was here. At home, the pain was compounded by the fear of giving birth alone.

The first three beds to the right were occupied, so Leah was assigned to Bed 4. The young girl pushed the wheelchair right up to the bed and left her there. Throughout the day, Bed 5 and then one by one, Beds 6-10 on the other side of the room would be filled, only to circle back to Bed 1 once it had been vacated. Clearly, the baby business was a good one.

A nurse arrived and pulled a hospital gown down from a shelf above Bed 4 and tossed it on the bed.

"Let me get you out of this wheelchair. I need it for another patient," the nurse ordered. "And you should put on the gown."

The nurse then put her hand under one elbow to guide Leah from the chair to the bed. And just as fast, the nurse and the chair were gone. Leah was left to change into the hospital gown herself.

Another wave overtook her. She curled into herself to ride it out. When the pain subsided, she picked up the thin piece of cotton that had been tossed on her bed. Was she supposed to undress in front of all these strangers? She scanned the room nervously, but she discovered that no one paid her any attention. The three women already in labor grappled within their own living hell, and other women were being wheeled to their own beds, one of them possibly in the chair that had just been ripped out from under her. She only had a couple of minutes before the next pain would come on, so she quickly removed her clothes and put on the gown, buttoning it up to her neck and straightening the rounded collar. She tucked her bag under the bed and tucked herself under the sheet. She then pulled the blanket folded at the foot of the bed up to her chin.

Chapter 31

That was the moment a doctor and his team appeared at her side. But this wasn't a doctor she recognized.

"The nurse will give you an injection. You should feel much better," said the stranger. The intensity of the labor pains was increasing, and Leah was terrified of what was to come. She welcomed the injection if it would lessen the cramping.

"You know about my allergy to penicillin, right?" Leah asked.

It wasn't a concern, the doctor told her. Penicillin was not part of the cocktail today.

A nurse swooped out from behind the doctor, pointing a huge needle at the ceiling, much like a cop sweeping out from behind a corner with his gun at high ready. She stepped forward as the doctor peeled off to issue the same directive about the injection to the woman in Bed 5, who was now in her own flimsy gown and struggling to pull up her blanket.

The nurse aimed the needle at Leah's thigh. Leah clenched her hands into fists in anticipation of it slicing into her flesh. But the procedure was stopped by a wild shriek that bounced off the ceiling and the walls.

Frantic cries followed: "What's happening? Help me!"

The nurse at Leah's side marched to the next bed over, Bed 3, needle still erect. She put her free hand on the shoulder of the crying woman and instructed her as if she were scolding a young child, "You're having a baby. Quiet. You're going to be fine. You're having a baby."

Leah's eyes were saucers. She had been so consumed with fears about what this day would hold for her that she failed to recognize what these other women were enduring. The woman next to her was writhing uncontrollably and moaning hauntingly while strapped to the bed frame by restraints on both arms and both legs.

The shot entered her thigh effortlessly, but the pinch made Leah flinch. She wasn't expecting it.

"What was that?" she cried out reflexively.

"Something to help you have this baby without all the pain. You're going to be fine," the nurse replied with a wave of the hand before moving on.

The sight of the woman in Bed 3 agitated Leah. But then another contraction came on. She gritted her teeth in preparation. But a series of howls jolted her outside of her own pain. The room was an immediate flurry of activity.

"Bed Number 2," someone called out. "Delivery room."

Three nurses advanced to Bed 2, where a woman in a white blindfold thrashed back and forth as she yelled, "I can't do it. I need help!" The nurses whisked the bed, and the patient, out of the room.

That woman was in agony. The nurse said there would be no pain. Hadn't she also been given the shot? A young nurse again assured the woman in Bed 3, who continued to question "What's happening?" to no one in particular, that she was just having a baby.

Leah called out, frightened. But her voice was absorbed in the cacophony of vocalized pain that filled the room. She called out again, louder. Still no one responded. So she leaned out and tugged on a nurse's uniform as she passed by. The nurse spun around, indignant at the violation.

"Hey! Why aren't you restrained?" It was a rhetorical question.

"What's wrong with these women? Why isn't the shot working?" Leah frantically shrieked.

"The shot *is* working. They're fine. They won't remember any of this. Don't worry, you'll be there soon too," she told Leah. "Hey! Mary!" she hollered to another nurse in the room. "We need to put this one in restraints. She is about to go under."

Leah fought to keep her eyes open while her insides cramped up; she couldn't remember why she had even lain down in this bed.

Her left arm was pulled down to her side. Her right arm was pulled down too. If only the cramping would ease up. She lifted her knees to her chest, hoping to relieve some of the pressure, but as soon as she found relief, someone grabbed both legs, straightened them out, and held them down.

The room was spinning, and Leah sank into blackness.

The delivery room had been cleared out after the unfortunate birth of a stillborn boy. It would be a nurse's job to break the news to the mother once the medication wore off. The doctor had other deliveries to perform. But he did take the time to step outside for a smoke while the nurses sterilized the room for whomever the next patient might be.

The lead delivery nurse nervously poked her head out the door to interrupt him, knowing he might snap at her for doing so. "Doctor? Excuse me. The patient from Bed 4 is ready. They are wheeling her into delivery right now."

He took a drag off the cigarette and held it up to inspect it. He hadn't even finished half of it. He determined they could wait. The smoke spilled out of his wide-opened mouth. He needed this smoke. It had been a long day with few breaks. He had to clear his mind, especially after that stillbirth. Not that he blamed himself. He felt no guilt about it at all. It wasn't his fault. But it did mean dealing with more paperwork and possibly speaking with the parents. When a birth went well, parents rarely considered a conversation with the attending doctor. But when things went poorly, they demanded answers. He was grateful that the lead delivery nurse had perfected her speech for such patients, making it increasingly unnecessary for him to interact with them at all.

Inside the delivery room, one of the younger nurses panicked. "Where's the doctor? She is going to have this baby any minute."

Leah thrashed about on the delivery table despite being strapped down, arms to the sides of the bed and legs to the stirrups, to avoid injuring herself. Before the use of restraints, women sometimes came out of the delivery room with scratches on their faces or bruises across their chests. Understandably, the husbands might ask about what appeared to be a violent birth. But they rarely complained outright. Popular culture dictated that giving birth ought to be accompanied by strong medication and was strictly between a woman and her doctor. No husband would dare presume to attend the birth or to question the procedure. But the restraints conveniently eliminated any appearance of a difficult birth.

Leah grew particularly agitated all of the sudden, so a nurse found a cloth to tie around her head that would cover her eyes and ears. Hopefully, dampening any stimuli would calm her down.

"Seriously, this baby is on its way!" a nurse yelled.

"Quick, close her legs," another one directed.

Another nurse unstrapped Leah's legs from the stirrups; the two held her legs crossed over each other. And they waited. The nurse who was visibly nervous was new to labor and delivery. Sweat beaded on her forehead as she worked to stop Leah's leg from thrashing about. She wasn't particularly strong, and Leah had the ferocity of a grizzly.

Finally, the doctor arrived.

"Let's go. Put her back in the stirrups." The nurses snapped to and promptly had her in position and ready for the doctor.

"First step, an episiotomy," the doctor announced to the room unnecessarily. He liked to put on a show. He positioned himself on the stool that was pre-adjusted to the exact height he required to perform his work, and he rolled himself between Leah's legs.

He made the incision quickly, like the pro that he was.

Leah moaned like a cat in heat.

"Give her another injection," he ordered.

One of the attending nurses was prepared for such an instruction and did as she was asked. Leah quieted down, her moans transforming to white noise, a droning hum.

He rolled back a bit to admire his work. The episiotomy was perfect. He rolled in close so he could check her cervix. Perfect. He asked one of the nurses to position herself by Leah's chest in case he needed her to apply fundal pressure should the baby not surrender peacefully to being removed from the birth canal.

"Forceps."

"Forceps," a nurse replied as she handed over the forceps.

The doctor took one half of the forceps and inserted it up against the right uterine wall. Once that was in place, he took the other half and inserted it against the left uterine wall.

"Ready." He locked the forceps in place. The most difficult job of the nurse positioned at Leah's chest was anticipating the exact moment the doctor wasn't making enough progress and required fundal pressure from above. She couldn't move a moment earlier, thus underestimating his abilities, nor a moment later, or they could be entering dangerous territory for the baby. But she had worked with this doctor long enough that she could assess exactly when to apply the pressure.

She spotted the twitch of the eyebrow that told her to push. She climbed atop Leah, leveraged herself with the bed railings, and pushed

Chapter 31

toward the doctor and his forceps.

"There we go. Here it comes. Just a little more," the doctor narrated as he tugged on the lethargic baby. It was an art form. He wriggled the baby out of the birth canal and onto the table.

A nurse slid over, cut the umbilical cord, and picked up the baby, wiping out its eyes and nostrils, clearing out its mouth, and waiting for a sign of life. In the meantime, the doctor reached inside Leah to remove the placenta.

"Ah! There it is!" the doctor exclaimed when the baby took its first, silent breath. Now the nurse could retreat with the baby to the nursery for weighing, measuring, and examining.

The last step, sewing Leah back up. The doctor whistled while he repaired the cut, adding an extra husband stitch before leaving the nurses to finish up. He exited the room for another cigarette to await the next patient.

"Leah, you need to wake up. You've been lying here for six hours. Let's get moving now."

Groggy and disoriented, Leah swam in pain.

"You have a baby girl. Here she is!" A nurse cradled a baby swaddled in a hospital-issued blanket and tilted her towards Leah so she could see her.

"A baby girl?" Leah asked.

She studied the baby in the nurse's arm. Something seemed wrong. What was that swooping red line down across her eyelid, down around her cheek, and up by her ear? And her head? It came to a point. Whose head is shaped like a point?

"Yes. Meet your baby girl. Isn't your daughter amazing? Everyone adores her in the nursery. She is so quiet and compliant," the nurse said as she held out the newborn.

Leah stared, wide-eyed. She pushed herself up for a better view and winced in pain. The nurse used her free hand to put a pillow behind Leah to prop her up a bit.

"Would you like to hold her?"

"Yes?" Leah was unsure. Her wrists were sore. She rubbed them before taking the baby. The nurse tried to show her how to hold the little girl so that the baby would be comfortable.

"You hold her just like that. No, no, honey. Move your arm here. Yes, and your hand over here. There! I'll be right back. I have to check on another patient real quick."

Leah pulled the blanket back from her baby's face. A bruise revealed itself on the cheek opposite the one with the mysterious red line. Even though the baby's eyes were open, she appeared to be asleep. Her left arm pressed up against Leah's body, but her right arm dropped limply. Her legs hung down from her hand, lifeless and boneless.

"Are you all right?" Leah sincerely asked.

The baby sighed and then returned to her slow, labored breathing.

"Isn't she wonderful?" The nurse had returned.

"Is she all right? Her breathing is so heavy, and she has no …" Leah wrestled to find the word. "… no, *life* in her."

The nurse laughed as she took the baby from Leah. "Oh no, honey. She's fine. The medicine needs to leave her system, like it does yours too. By the time you are feeling like your old self again, she will be a bundle of energy." And before Leah could say anything else, the two disappeared from the room.

Part III

Chapter 32

September 1960

Leah and her new daughter were released from the hospital after four days of mostly sleeping. Four days when all of their needs were attended to.

David pulled the car into the roundabout at the hospital exit to wait. As a nurse wheeled his wife and daughter to the car, he was busy perusing the front page of the *Wall Street Journal*. A knock on the passenger side window pulled him up from an article about the success of Sputnik. A cheerful nurse smiled into the car. He folded the paper back up, put it under his seat, and climbed out to meet them.

The nurse made some idle chitchat, and David soon realized the nurse expected him to transfer the two patients from the wheelchair to the car himself. He first picked up the tightly swaddled baby. His new-father awkwardness was evident, for he held her like he was holding a log to toss in the fireplace.

The nurse's idle chat transformed to harsh warnings: "Hold her head. You don't want her head snapping back." David obeyed, cupping one hand under the infant's head and placing the other below her torso, and he set her down in the bassinet in the backseat.

Leah struggled to stand. But the nurse put her hand on Leah's shoulder and held her down. "Wait until your husband can help you. Remember, you just had a baby."

David opened the front passenger door and dropped a starter bag of supplies that the hospital provided onto the car floor. He held out his hand for Leah to grab and pulled her up until she was standing. He helped spin her around so she could back into the passenger seat. Once she was settled inside, he closed the door. He jogged to his side, started up the engine, and drove off.

Once home, he helped Leah out of the car and let her hang on to his arm as they plodded up the sidewalk to the front door. He left her there and jogged back to the car for the starter bag of supplies. He placed that next to Leah on the front porch, and then he returned for the new baby. As he struggled with the bassinet up the sidewalk, the phone rang on the other side of the front door.

"I'll get that," David offered. He typically never answered the phone; the calls were never for him, he liked to point out. He set down the bassinet, asked Leah to move aside, and fiddled with the keys to get the door unlocked. Once inside, he disappeared down the hall, leaving Leah and the baby on the front porch. But the phone continued to ring. It was as if the ring moved to a frequency outside of David's hearing range, and he had forgotten he offered to answer it. Leah struggled to pull the bassinet across the threshold, grunting in pain. She closed the front door behind her, left the baby in the hall, and picked up the phone extension in the living room.

"Hello?"

"You're home!"

It was her mother, who had yet to meet her granddaughter. After dropping Leah off, she had not returned to the hospital in those four days. But now, she wanted to come by.

"Great, we'll be over in an hour. Kiss the baby for me!"

And she hung up.

"That was my mother. They're coming now," Leah called out, still unclear where David had disappeared to.

Leah left the baby in the bassinet by the front door and withdrew to the bathroom, which was next to David's office. That same office would double as the baby's room. When she walked by, she saw him digging through some papers on his desk, but she said nothing.

After a few minutes, Leah left the bathroom with a shower cap still covering her hair and disappeared into the bedroom. And right as the knock came on the front door, Leah emerged, hair perfectly coifed in a makeshift beehive and dressed in a flattering black dress, black pumps, and a string of pearls. No one would have guessed that she had given birth four days earlier.

Leah went to answer the door. The baby was sleeping soundly, still in the bassinet in the front hall and blocking the door.

"David!" she yelled. "Can you come move this bassinet?"

David showed up at her side, picked up the bassinet and baby, and placed it in the living room. Leah then opened the door, and Cora filled the space. Robert was right behind her. He shook David's hand, and David offered Robert his signature Manhattan. The two made their way to the kitchen to retrieve the Canadian Club whiskey that Robert favored and Leah always kept stocked specifically for him. Cora reached down for the sleeping baby, plucked her from the bassinet, and showered her with kisses. An unexpected pain in Leah's chest dimmed the dull pain still throbbing between her legs.

"Let me take a picture of the two of you," Cora offered. "Where's your camera?"

Leah opened a drawer in a side table next to the couch, pulled out her camera, and dug around in the back of the drawer for a spare flash bulb. The men emerged from the kitchen, each with a fresh Manhattan in his hand.

"Here, hold the baby," Cora instructed Leah, "and give me the camera. Go sit on the couch with her. Robert, let me have a sip of that."

David offered to make her one, but she declined, satisfied with a sip before getting to the business of capturing the moment on film.

Leah sat down on the edge of the couch, ramrod straight. She positioned the baby, still swaddled and falling back to sleep, in the crook of her arm as she was taught by the nurses. She placed her other hand on her waist, fanning her elbow out to the side. She angled her knees slightly to the right. She was undeniably beautiful, and she had perfected the pose as if she had had professional training. She smiled for the camera, her eyes flat.

"Say cheese," her mother ordered, peering through the viewfinder, finger positioned over the shutter-release button.

Leah smiled without saying "cheese." Cora pushed down.

Pop. At the sound of the flash, a jolt shot through the baby. Leah was unprepared, and the baby nearly rolled right out of her arms. To stop the fall, Leah grabbed her, causing her to let out a whimper.

"Oh baby," Cora put the camera down on the coffee table. "I'll go make a bottle. Come with me, David. Show me where everything is." And David followed Cora into the kitchen. David had absolutely no idea what they would need for a bottle, he admitted. They had just gotten home from the hospital and hadn't fed her yet.

"Check in the hospital bag. They sent some supplies home," Leah said, still struggling with the squirming baby. Her mother bounced back out and found the bag of supplies sitting outside by the front door, right where David had left it. Then she bounced back to the kitchen to make a bottle. All the while, the new grandfather silently sipped on his drink.

After a few minutes, her mother handed Leah the warm bottle, which Leah placed near the baby's mouth. To her relieved surprise, the baby took the nipple and sucked, putting an end to the whimpers.

"Why did you drop me off at the hospital and then leave me there alone? You never even came to visit." This wasn't how Leah had wanted to bring up this topic. She had considered how to ask this question for the past four days. She had even rehearsed exactly what she would say. But this wasn't what she had practiced.

"Labor lasts hours, sometimes days. And they weren't going to let me anywhere near you anyway. I saw no reason to sit in a cold, uncomfortable waiting room all day. I knew someone would call when it was all over. And I was right, wasn't I? David called."

Leah had no response to that.

David enjoyed another drink. Pictures were taken of Cora and the baby; Cora, Robert, and the baby; David, Leah, and the baby; and Cora, Leah and the baby. Finally, Cora was satisfied with all of the combinations caught for posterity. Then the new grandparents bid the new family goodbye.

Leah dropped the baby into her crib and then dug into the supply bag she had brought with her to the baby's room. She felt around, pulled out a bottle of pain medication the doctor had prescribed, and retreated to the bedroom.

Chapter 32

Once outside of Leah's, Robert held open the car door for Cora, and she slipped in, tucking in her skirt to make sure it didn't get caught as he closed the door for her.

As he pulled away from the curb, Cora looked over at his profile. She loved him dearly. She smiled. Their lives were simple. What more could she ask for?

"I'm worried about that baby," she admitted in a moment of vulnerability she rarely allowed herself. But holding that baby moved her heart in a way she didn't expect.

"Why?" he asked, keeping his eyes on the road.

"It's Leah. It's like she's never held a baby before."

"Well, has she?"

"I don't know. But it's not that hard though, is it?"

And the baby? She seems asleep? I don't know. Do you think something is wrong with her?"

"Oh, I don't know. Babies sleep, right?" Robert tried to diminish her concern. "But Leah seemed upset you didn't come to the hospital," he added.

"I don't know what that was about. Truly. They wouldn't have let me in. She was well taken care of."

"Do you hear yourself?" Robert laughed as he put on the blinker and glanced back to check that no one was in his blind spot. The two of them rarely discussed Leah. "I know she doesn't care much about me," he admitted, "but you're all she has. Her father died before she was born. David's parents live out of town. I know she would never ask you to be there. But it was more important than you realized."

"Please. It isn't like she had an abusive father or was abandoned when she was young or anything. She was always well taken care of," Cora told him.

It was a story Cora had perfected back at St. Anne's. Leah's father had tragically died while Cora was pregnant. Even Robert had accepted that story. After Robert came into her life, people just assumed he was Leah's father, so she stopped having to respond to questions about her past. Leah had brought up the question of her own father only once, at the wedding. Cora didn't answer her. She had no intention of ever answering that question. But she needn't worry. Leah never brought the topic up again.

    Cora reached over and put her hand on Robert's thigh. He smiled at her and then placed his own hand on top of hers, where it remained for the rest of the drive.

Chapter 33

October 1960

David's family was eager to get their hands on the new baby. Rachel loved babies, which was no surprise to Leah. So after a couple of weeks, once Leah had completely healed and felt she had the energy, David and Leah drove north to the farm to introduce the baby to his family. *Her* family, she reminded herself.

She and David finally chose a name for the baby, something that took longer than it should have, not because of wild disagreements or a lack of possibilities. They just didn't make a decision. But they eventually settled on Cassandra, which they shortened to Cassie.

Rachel was outside before David shut off the car's engine.

"Let me see that baby! Where is she?" She scurried around the car like a ground squirrel, peering through windows until she spotted the baby in the back seat. She popped open the back door and scooped up the baby in her arms, purring at her as she walked back to the house.

Leah jogged to catch up to Rachel and the baby. David grabbed the suitcases from the trunk and followed them all to the house. Inside, William awaited the presentation of his granddaughter. And his wife didn't disappoint. She playfully bit the baby's little fat leg before plopping her down in William's lap. Leah worried that maybe she was being a bit rough, but the baby broke out into a smile.

"David! Did you see that? She smiled!" Leah glanced around; David wasn't in the room. He had missed it.

Cassie knocked off Grandpa's glasses with a stray arm, and William let out a hearty laugh. Pretty soon, Rachel and Leah joined in the laughter. Grandma sat on the arm of the chair and leaned down to smother the baby in kisses.

Suddenly, Rachel jumped up. "Let me find you some food. You must be famished after your drive." Leah followed Rachel to the kitchen while William played with Cassie.

They spent only two nights at the farm. David had work Monday. During the quick trip, David's sister and brother, with their spouses and kids, made the drive out on Saturday to meet the new addition. Cassie was the center of attention. The women fought for a chance to indulge the beautiful, docile child. Leah watched, amazed, as Cassie attracted their love like a magnet.

"Don't you just love being a mom?" her sister-in-law Nellie gushed.

"What? Oh yes! I do," Leah stammered.

"I know. Life really changes, doesn't it? When our little Claire was born, I completely fell in love. With her. With being a mom. With all of it. I couldn't wait to have another one. I know it's a bit early to ask, but do you think you'll have another?"

Leah had a ready answer to the question she hadn't really considered. "I don't know about that. This has all been so difficult. With David working so much and travelling so often. And the baby never seems to sleep. I am simply exhausted all the time. It makes it really difficult when I get a headache. You know that I suffer from really bad headaches, right? Did you know that?" Leah ran right past the questions. "Migraines. And I have terrible asthma too; it makes it very difficult when a baby has to be changed and fed and bathed. Thankfully, she doesn't demand much attention."

"I'm so sorry. I had no idea you get migraines. I once had a neighbor who would get migraines, and I remember how they put her completely out of commission, sometimes for days. I can't imagine how you do it, Leah." Nellie reached for Leah's hands and squeezed them in a show of sympathy.

On Sunday, Leah settled into the passenger seat for the drive home. She thought about how well the introduction of Cassie to the family had

Chapter 33

gone. She was the perfect grandbaby, a grandbaby only she, Leah, had been able to gift them. She held tightly to a roll of film. The last picture on the roll was of Mom holding Cassie and sitting next to Dad. Leah planned on getting prints for the entire family on Monday and maybe even an enlargement to frame for Rachel.

As the car pulled out the long driveway, Leah was overflowing with love for David's family.

Chapter 34

April 1961

Graduation was only a couple months away. But right now, Jack Nelson was concerned only with tonight. He was finally 18. No longer a minor, the milestone gave him a sense of empowerment that he hadn't earned. An adult. A man. He puffed out his chest. Yeah. That's right. A man. The fact that it was a Sunday, a school night, wasn't going to dampen tonight's celebration.

Jack had been holed up in his room for the past hour. He checked the mirror one last time, slicked back his hair, and jogged down the steps to the living room where his predictable, bumpkin parents sat in silence watching *The Ed Sullivan Show*. He grabbed his jacket off the back of a chair and the car key off the hook next to the front door. The door slammed behind him before his mother had a chance to wish him a happy birthday or to ask where he might be celebrating. Or when he would be back.

Typical. She rarely spoke up in time to be heard by her son or her husband. She was used to standing idly by as they both moved in and out of the house, in and out of her life.

Standing outside on the front doorstep, Jack could hear his dad make a feeble attempt to care: "Where the hell's he goin'?" his father asked no one in particular when the slamming door jerked him out of his TV trance. He was predictably a step behind. He didn't expect an answer from Jack's mother. And she didn't give one.

Jack jumped into his dad's truck and peeled out. He wasn't interested in going to college. He had never been on that track, as the adults at school were happy to repeatedly remind him. But he sure was ready to leave Ashfield, soon-to-be population 231, down from the current 232, and out of that stifling, uptight house.

The house sat back, far from the dirt road connecting the town's farms, which meant a long driveway. Jack floored it, getting the truck to 40 before hitting the brakes at the end and sliding into a turn onto Route 148. He perfected the move long before the state issued him a driver license. He must have been thirteen. He chuckled at the memory of the first time he didn't end up in the ditch on the other side of the road. His dad celebrated the victory by popping open Jack's first beer.

Larry lived off this same road, and Jack's goal was to reach 100 mph before Larry's driveway. When he finally left this backward town, he would buy a truck where reaching 100 was no challenge. But today, he managed to hit 100 in his dad's pickup, yelled in triumph, and then slammed on the brakes to make his first stop.

Larry heard Jack hollering and was out the door and waiting outside by the time the truck pulled up to the house.

"Let's go! Come on!" Jack beckoned as he laid on the horn.

Larry's mom pushed open the screen door and waved, "Bye bye!"

"Oh good god," Jack mumbled under his breath. "Just shut the fuck up."

"Hello Jack," she yelled out. "Happy birthday. You boys be careful out there tonight."

"Thanks, Mrs. Hemstad. We will," Jack called back sarcastically. He stretched over to the broken passenger door and pulled on the handle before kicking it open so Larry could jump in.

Jack did a donut right there in front of the house before flying down the driveway into the dark. When he steered the truck back onto the road, the two boys stuck their heads out the windows, like dogs on a joy ride, and let out a war whoop.

They had four more to pick up. Three of them would sit in the front, and the other three would ride in the bed of the truck. Next stop was Danny.

Chapter 34

Danny was in charge of bringing the liquor. His parents kept ample supplies of alcohol in the house well beyond the liquor cabinet, including under their bed, in a cabinet at the back of the garage, and on top of the refrigerator. They had no idea what they even had or what they had already drunk. They would never miss a bottle of whiskey or two. Or even three. Jack didn't care what Danny brought as long as it was something that would light him up and make this night one for the record books.

A magnum of Wild Turkey landed in Jack's lap after Danny tossed it through the driver's side window. Jack unscrewed the top and poured the liquid down his throat as Larry and Danny shouted their approval, egging him on.

Jack dragged his sleeve across his mouth, his shirt soaking up the excess whiskey, and he handed the bottle to Larry, who was holding two more. Larry kicked the door open so Danny could slide in next to him, and they took off to pick up the other three, who one by one would vault up and into the bed of the truck.

The Sirens were at work, luring the boys to the abandoned Deere warehouse down in Farmington, where they could do whatever they wanted without any judgment pricks ruining their fun. That's all they wanted to do. Have fun. Let loose. Hang with each other. Hell, enjoy life. What was so bad about that?

Once the other three were in the back and passing around a bottle, Jack drove the truck down Route 56 and turned onto a dirt road marked Private Property. The chain link gate, topped with mangled razor wire, had long ago been knocked over. Jack sped onto the grounds with only his headlights to guide him in the pitch black darkness. A cloud-covered sky muted any light that might have come from the moon.

When the building came into view, the three leaped out of the back before the truck even stopped. Jack positioned the truck so that the headlights pointed at the opening left by a broken roll-up door, a spot where trucks used to back in to make deliveries. The three in the cab of the truck jumped out next and ran inside to join the others who were already in a pile on the floor in an impromptu wrestling match. The noises they made were reminiscent of hyenas celebrating a feast.

The boys took turns downing shots of Wild Turkey, pushing each other around, and hollering to hear their echoes reverberate. Jack leaned up against a table that was left behind despite extensive looting by locals after Deere deserted this location. He took another swig and nodded in satisfaction. This would be a good night.

With that, the drinking games began.

A couple of hours later, they had exhausted the alcohol. It was inevitable. Jack held the final bottle upside down, attempting to squeeze out one last drop. When he was confident there was no more to be had, he threw the bottle across the room, where it hit a wall and smashed into pieces. As it hit, he arched his back and let out a howl that would terrorize the wolves he imitated. The other five joined in the chorus, howling at the roof, pounding their feet, and then pounding each other. When they finished proclaiming their dominance, they raced each other to the truck; the last three would be stuck back in the bed.

They had driven these roads so many times that Jack could find his way home if he had been unconscious, which he nearly was. Turn left. Right. Floor it for the straightaway. Jack loved speed. The other boys were carrying on, arguing about the size of some girl's tits and about who had or hadn't seen said tits. But Jack blocked out their childish boasting, for he was now 18, and he stared at the speedometer, squinting to focus while his head bobbed. How fast was he going? 35? 40? What did that say? Should he speed things up a bit?

Silence slammed into him.

His head hurt. No, it didn't just hurt; the pain was excruciating. Jack couldn't make sense of it.

And what was that sound? Was that an animal? He opened his eyes, confused as to why his eyes had been closed. Next to him, Larry held his head, blood pouring through his fingers. And the windshield was shattered. That was when Jack realized that he wasn't sitting behind the steering wheel anymore. He was in the middle seat, and Larry was in the passenger seat. Where was Danny? Danny's door was open. Jack leaned over Larry to look out the door to where Danny had landed on his ass and sat stunned in the dirt.

Forgetting about the blood gushing from Larry's head, Jack laughed out loud at the absurdity of Danny on the ground. How the hell did he wind up there?

Chapter 34

"Shit," a voice outside in the blackness yelled.

"What the hell? Danny. Why are you on your ass?" Jack sneered at his friend.

"Shut the hell up, Jack. Get out here now. NOW."

Jack scooted over to the driver's side door, but he couldn't open it; it was completely smashed in.

"Move. Move!" Jack ordered Larry, irritated.

Larry, in shock and still holding his head, stumbled out the open passenger door. Danny stood up, brushing the dirt off his pants and shaking his head to stop the ringing in his ears.

"My leg!" one of the boys who had been in the back of the truck yelled, and he followed the cry with a terrifying scream. In the dark, Jack couldn't see where he was. But he didn't have time to find out.

"Jack! Get over here. I'm not kidding!"

Danny followed Jack to the driver's side of the car where the other two from the back of the truck stood in shock over the third, who was writhing in pain at their feet. But they were not paying attention to him. Jack searched their faces. What were they looking at?

He took a step closer. And then he saw it. Two people in the road. Lying next to a car with its front end completely gone. And the night couldn't have been any quieter. Or darker. Jack dropped to his knees, head in his hands.

The frightened yells of two men from a nearby farm arrived at the scene. They had heard the unmistakable sound of metal on metal. As the two men came upon the intersection, they saw the bodies in the road. The two were clearly dead.

"Oh God," one muttered.

The other ran back to the farmhouse to call the police.

"What the hell happened here?" the first demanded of the boys gathered there. "What the hell happened? Who was driving this truck? Which one of you?"

Jack went to stand up but couldn't catch his balance and fell back to his knees.

"Was it you? Were you the one driving? Good God. How much have you been drinking?"

Leah had just finished feeding Cassie when the phone rang. She placed Cassie in her crib so that she could jog back to the phone and answer before the person on the other end hung up.

"Hello?" she answered, out of breath.

"Leah, it's Nellie." It was David's sister in Wisconsin. She had never called Leah before. Leah often talked to her mother-in-law but had not yet created a habit of talking to Nellie regularly. Leah was thrilled. Maybe this would be an opening for them to get closer, to be like real sisters. She always wanted a sister.

"Oh! Hi. Good timing. I just finished feeding Cassie. How are you?" Leah stretched the phone cord out long so she could grab a chair. It was only then that she noticed that Nellie was crying.

Leah settled into her seat. "Nellie, what's the matter?" she asked, feeling grateful that she had called to confide in her.

"Is David there?" she struggled to ask.

"No, he's at work. Is everything ok?"

"Oh, that's right. He would be at work now," she realized.

"What's going on?"

"It's mom and dad," Nellie spilled out. Leah was concerned. She could hear the emotion on the other end of the line. "They …" Nellie was sobbing.

"They what, Nellie?" Now Leah was nervous.

"They were killed. Last night."

"Killed? What are you talking about?"

"An accident. A drunk driver." Nellie's voice broke. "Hit them and killed them both."

The news landed on Leah like a right hook, knocking her out cold.

"They were coming home from Aunt Carol's," Nellie continued, almost in a race to stay ahead of breaking down further. "Just driving home, and from nowhere, a pickup crossed through the intersection. The truck didn't have its headlights on. They have the boy—he's a boy, just 18—in custody."

Leah stopped listening. She couldn't take any more. As soon as she hung up, she collapsed in bed, helpless to deal with the shock. She faded in and out of consciousness. When awake, she played out all of the ways this could have been avoided.

Chapter 34

They had been visiting Rachel's sister, right? What if Rachel had indulged in one more slice of cake? Or had skipped cake altogether? What if they had delayed their departure because the men wanted to share a cigar? If the driver had had one less drink? Or had one more? Any of those minor decisions would have thrown off the timing. Trivial moments, yet just one of them would have changed everything. Or more accurately, would have changed nothing. It would have been another unremarkable day. Instead, nothing could be the same.

Hours later, the sun's rays stretched long across the bedroom. In the distance, a constant buzzing captured Leah's attention. She couldn't place what the sound was coming from, but her body tensed at the noise. Then a new sound entered her consciousness, a sound she recognized: her husband's key in the front door.

She heard his footsteps, and then he flipped on the light in the front hall. She had memorized his routine. He would drape his suit coat over the back of the chair in the living room before making his way to the back of the house.

She heard the low buzzing noise again. It worried her; she didn't know why. The buzzing grew louder when David opened the door to his home office across the hall, where the crib was set up. Leah could see that he turned on the light; the crack under her door went from black to illuminated. Then he quietly opened the bedroom door, lighting up the entire room. Leah wasn't ready to face him, so she pulled the covers over her head.

"Leah," he whispered. "The baby is crying."

That was the sound, she thought. She had spent the last eight months learning to decipher every one of that baby's cries. One cry might mean hunger, another a wet diaper. Her only job each day was to keep that cry at bay. But in that moment, she had become so disconnected that she didn't even recognize the sound she had been hearing as the cry of her own baby.

Then the phone rang.

"I can't get that," Leah whimpered through the tears.

David left Leah and the crying baby to answer the phone in the kitchen. Leah dragged herself out of bed to gather the baby. Turned out she needed a new diaper.

"Hello," Leah heard her husband's voice in the kitchen bump through three beats to get out the greeting.

No other sound came from the kitchen. Leah went through the motions of changing the baby's diaper while he was getting the news about his parents. She couldn't see his face, but she was well aware that he wouldn't show the emotion that she had spilt throughout the house. He would remain contained. Letting it go would have been too big of a mess. They wouldn't be able to clean that up by themselves. So he did his part by not contributing.

Leah heard the handset click back onto the wall mount. The light switched off. The front door closed.

She brought the baby to the darkened kitchen, made a bottle, and took the baby back to her own bed to feed her. They lay on their backs, side by side. When the bottle was empty, Leah placed it on the nightstand. Then the two fell asleep, the baby satiated, Leah empty.

When her husband eventually walked back into the bedroom, she wasn't sure where he had been or how long he had been gone. But while he was gone, he had made all the necessary decisions: "We are going to the farm first thing tomorrow. I'll pack a bag for us. I've already called Mike at work to let him know I won't be at the office for a few days."

She pushed herself up and swung her legs off the bed. She had to go to the bathroom. She couldn't wait any longer. Feeling dizzy, she sat there for a moment to prepare herself to stand up. Once she stood up, she disturbed the sleeping baby, so she returned her to the crib. Then she wandered into the bathroom. While there, she opened the medicine cabinet and ran a finger across the rows of pill bottles: Bayer, Alka-Seltzer, her inhaler, Anacin, Tylenol, antihistamine, Ativan. Every bottle had a story.

She sought comfort from this cabinet if she felt a scratch in her throat or a cold coming on. No, in actuality, she sought refuge here anytime she felt. Here, she could find a pill to numb the scratch, the cold, or the feeling.

She searched for one bottle in particular. She had been given the prescription months ago. After giving birth, she had difficulty sleeping and was exhausted. The doctor didn't hesitate to prescribe her Librium. He was convinced she wouldn't adequately care for her baby without it.

Chapter 34

There it was, the middle shelf, behind the aspirin and eardrops. She popped a Librium in her mouth and cupped her hands under the faucet to catch water to wash it down.

When she returned to bed, David was feigning sleep. She turned her back to him, pulled up the covers, and escaped.

Before they left for the farm the next morning, Leah called her mother. She was nervous to deliver the news of what had happened to David's parents. But she needed her mother to know how much pain she was in. So despite the nerves, she revealed her news as soon as Cora answered the phone.

"Rachel. And William. They were killed. By a drunk driver. Both of them." How would her mother take the news?

"Oh, poor David. How is he doing?" her mother responded.

"He's packing his bag. We are leaving for Wisconsin." Then Leah broke down in tears.

"I hope you can be there for your husband and his family. This is simply tragic, and they need you to be strong for them."

That wasn't what Leah wanted to hear from her mother. Why wasn't she worried about someone being there for her? Couldn't her mom hear how upset she was?

After a few moments of silence, David summoned her. "The car is loaded. You ready?"

"Yes," Leah responded before saying goodbye to her mother.

As they drove to the farm, Leah glanced at her husband, but his eyes never strayed from the road. She wouldn't find the comfort she sought from him. Her mother was worried about David, but Leah was too immersed in her own loss to consider its effect on anyone else. She rested her head against the window and closed her eyes.

When they arrived at the farm, the dogs chased the car down the driveway, but no one came from the house to greet them. David got the luggage, and Leah got the baby from the back seat, and they let themselves in the house. David nodded to the family gathered there and climbed the stairs with the suitcases. Nellie jumped up to greet the baby, who Leah gave up without complaint.

Chapter 35

May 1961

After Rachel and William's death, the days became indistinguishable. Leah woke up, made coffee for her husband, changed the baby's diaper. She put the baby in the playpen with a bottle, served her husband breakfast. He read the morning's *Tribune* as he nibbled on the food placed in front of him. He checked his watch and muttered that he needed to leave in precisely three minutes. He folded up the newspaper and gathered his briefcase, hat, and coat. He gave Leah a kiss on the cheek, and he left the house.

David had returned to work the day after the funeral. He worked a rigorous schedule; he had to if he ever expected to make partner. Leah had long ago quit expressing displeasure at his absence. She may as well have complained about the color of the grass. That's just how it was going to be.

She envied that David could escape by immersing himself in his work while she remained at home, obsessed with the seismic shift that had just taken place. But his accelerated withdrawal from her and into something productive, something tangible, served to accelerate his wife's downward spiral.

Each morning, as soon as the door closed behind him, Leah cleaned up his dishes and then sat down to make the daily call to her mother to repeat a conversation that consisted of nothing of note but that she had come to depend on.

The moment she hung up, she picked up the baby and sat down on the couch. She propped the baby up on a pillow to let her finish the bottle. And again, Leah broke down. It simply had become part of her daily routine. It didn't take long for the baby to spit out the bottle and join in, creating a chorus of cries. But not for long. Leah stopped and stared at the baby. The whole scene irritated her. Why couldn't she just have a moment?

The baby eventually tired, shifting from wailing to weeping to whimpering before finally falling asleep next to her mother. Leah picked her up off the couch and laid her in the crib in David's office. The baby fussed at the disruption. But once in the crib, her searching hand landed on her blankie, pulling it in close before falling back to sleep. It was worn thin in some places; stitches were pulled out in others. And the light blue had faded to a dingy grey.

Leah sighed as she watched. The blankie provided her with the security she needed to sleep soundly. Leah wanted to sleep soundly. So she sought the medicine cabinet. She found the bottle she wanted, opened it, and was relieved to find that she had only taken a few of the pills so far.

She then drifted off to the kitchen and filled up a large glass of tap water. She usually drank her water cold, and she debated whether to put ice cubes in the glass or if she should drink the water at room temperature straight out of the sink. She stood in front of the open freezer as she weighed her options. She finally elected to forgo the ice; fighting to remove a few cubes from the metal tray would be exhausting.

She walked back to the bedroom, pills and lukewarm water in hand. After placing the pill bottle and glass of water on the nightstand, she turned down the covers and flipped her pillow over before sitting down. Then she dumped the contents of the bottle and spread the pills out on the nightstand. She recalled a movie where the lead actress grabbed a handful of sleeping pills, threw them all in her mouth at once, and swigged down a gulp of water. She would have loved to have done that right now. It was so dramatic. And decisive. But she could never swallow them all at once. She couldn't even handle two at once. She'd probably choke if she tried that.

Chapter 35

She laughed out loud at the irony. Choking would do the job, but what a violent way to go, she worried. Her body would involuntarily fight like hell for oxygen despite her mind's desire to let life go. No, this way, her body would be forced to cooperate with what her mind longed for. She would work her way through them one by one.

Pick up pill, put in mouth, sip water, swallow.

Pick up pill, put in mouth, sip water, swallow.

Pick up pill, put in mouth, sip water, swallow.

Pick up pill, put in mouth, sip water, swallow.

She had a nice rhythm going. And she found pleasure in the repetitive motion.

Pick up pill, put in mouth, sip water, swallow.

Pick up pill, put in mouth, sip water, swallow.

Pick up pill …

The baby cried out, breaking Leah's concentration mid-pill picking. She froze. Silence met her. A terrifying thought followed. She couldn't just leave the baby in the crib until her husband came home. Or could she? Could a nine-month-old baby survive unattended in a crib?

This question puzzled her. She put down the pill she had been holding between her thumb and forefinger, and she pushed herself up off of the bed. She doubted this scenario was addressed by Dr. Spock. She would ask her mother. Her mother would know. She was convinced she could ask nonchalantly so as to not make her mother suspicious. She would make the call and then finish the few pills she had left after she hung up. It seemed a reasonable plan. She again drifted into the kitchen, and as she lifted her hand to remove the handset from its base, she lost her balance. Her body slammed into the wall, her head knocking the handset to the floor.

It took her a minute to remember why she was standing there. She rubbed her hip and realized that a huge purple and blue bruise would quickly overtake that spot. She bruised so easily. She rubbed her head. Did she hit her head too? She noticed the headset sitting on the floor, its cord snaking up the wall to its empty cradle.

Did she want to make a phone call? Who was she going to call? She bent down to pick up the receiver and winced at the pain in her hip.

Then everything went black.

The next thing Leah felt was cold. She couldn't stop shivering. She could feel the weight of blankets on top of her, but she couldn't stop shivering. What was going on? She couldn't form a complete thought to try to make sense of anything. Her eyes wouldn't open, and she struggled to catch her breath, but when she finally managed a deep breath, she audibly gasped. Her throat was screaming in pain.

She whimpered as she continued to shiver under the blanket. Then she felt a tug on her left hand. Her right hand instinctively reached for it. What was that? A tube?

And it hit her. Oh god.

"Oh god," she panicked. "Oh god."

She wanted to sit up but could barely lift her head. She fell back and then managed to open her eyes momentarily, long enough to see the fluorescent lights shining above her.

Where was David? Her mother? Her mother would be angry. She wanted her mother to feel guilty, to suffer, to appreciate her, to miss her, to love her. She couldn't help but think that maybe she would have gotten all of these things from her mother if she had actually succeeded.

What went wrong? She remembered taking the pills and saying goodbye to the baby. Well, not actually saying goodbye. But thinking about how she ought to say goodbye.

The baby. What had she done?

She couldn't handle the fallout. She squeezed her eyes shut and gave in to sleep.

The next time she briefly awoke, a nurse was securing a blood pressure cuff around her arm. Her breath was steady. Leah's body would not give up its craving for oxygen. In and out. In and out. In and out. She returned to sleep.

The next thing Leah remembered was hearing voices. Was she dreaming? Was she awake? She couldn't make out what the voices were saying. Was that David? Why was she so cold? She went to take a deep breath, but the burning in her throat stopped her short.

"Leah?"

Yes. That was David.

She blinked her eyes open. The lighting in the room was dimmed. A man stood next to David. Who was he?

Chapter 35

"Good morning, Leah. I'm Dr. Clark. I was just telling your husband that you are a very lucky woman."

She closed her eyes again. Lucky? Is that the right word?

The doctor continued talking to David. "She should recover from this. As I said, luckily, the sleeping pills she took were slow-releasing." He then lowered his voice because he didn't want Leah to hear what he was saying to her husband. But she wanted to know what he had to say, to understand what was happening. So she did her best to concentrate.

"Most women who attempt suicide," the doctor explained, "don't really want to kill themselves. It's a cry for help. You said you found her by the phone. Maybe as soon as she had taken the pills, she regretted it. So she tried to call someone. If she hadn't taken those slow-acting pills, that phone call, well, nothing would have saved her. She clearly did not want to die. She wanted someone's attention. Your attention, perhaps?"

Leah didn't hear a response from David. She turned her head away from the two men before opening her eyes and staring at the IV bag dripping fluids into her hand.

Dr. Clark continued. "The plan right now is to admit your wife to Lakeside Institute for mandatory observation. That's required of all patients who have …" His voice lowered again, but Leah knew what he was saying. "We may want her here at the hospital for a couple of days, but we'll transport her to Lakeside ourselves when she is well enough to check out of here. They will observe her for 72 hours and make a determination regarding the best treatment after that. They may recommend that she stay longer. You'll have to wait and see. Do you have any questions?"

David said no, he had no questions.

"Leah," the doctor addressed her, his voice raised again. "Do you have any questions? About your treatment? About next steps?"

She didn't answer. She was hungry. Could she starve herself? How long would that take?

The doctor left the room and closed the door behind him. David sat down in the chair next to the bed. Leah asked, her voice gravelly, "Where's my mother?"

"She's not here," David said.

"Is she coming?"

"I don't think she's planning to. She's watching the baby."

"What happened?" She knew what she had done, but she didn't know how she ended up in the hospital.

"I came home from work, and the house was dark. I could hear the baby crying in my office. I called you, but you didn't answer. I turned on the lights as I walked through the house calling your name. When I got to the kitchen, you were lying on the floor. It looked like you fell in the middle of a phone call. Who were you calling?"

Leah had no idea.

"I could see you were breathing, but it seemed like you were having trouble getting a breath. I thought maybe you had an asthma attack. The baby was still crying, but I thought I should get you to bed. I bent down and picked you up. And you were lifeless. I couldn't figure out what happened to you. But I carried you to the bedroom and laid you down on the bed."

Before he continued, he paused. Leah couldn't face him.

"I saw what you did. The pills were on the nightstand."

Leah lay on her back and with eyes closed said, "I'm hungry."

"I'll call a nurse."

He buzzed the nurse's desk, and soon a young, cheery woman bounced in wearing a huge grin.

"What can I get you?" she gently asked.

Leah stared at the ceiling.

David answered. "She wants something to eat."

"Oh good. I was told you've missed too many meals. You must be feeling better! I'll be right back," the nurse chirped.

Leah would eat whatever was brought. She conceded defeat.

Chapter 36

July 1961

At Lakeside, Leah existed in a space that's fuzzy, where it's difficult to distinguish between what is real and what are simply images conjured up from a cruel subconscious. A dutiful nurse administered a daily pill and a nightly sedative to keep her in that space. Patients sometimes hid pills under their tongues. The staff often suspected this, and those who were caught doing so quickly regretted their choice. But not Leah. She fantasized about never waking again, so she took any pills that were offered unquestioningly, grateful for the escape. But it was only temporary; morning was a stubborn foe.

But the longer her stay dragged on, the harder and harder it became to stay clear. The foggier her mind, the stronger the paranoia. And paranoia was a trait of the crazy. It was a vicious circle. More pills, more fog, more paranoia, more crazy, more pills.

When she first met her assigned psychiatrist, Dr. Pendergast, she was inclined to trust him implicitly. He would have her best interest at heart and would fix her so she could leave this place. When he asked how she was feeling, she told him as best she could.

"Is my husband having an affair?" she asked during one of their sessions. The question had been on her mind for a while.

"I have no idea," the doctor responded. "Why do you think he might be?"

"A woman is living at our house. I don't know who she is. He must be having an affair, don't you think?"

"Isn't the woman there to take care of your daughter? She's still a baby, you know. Your husband certainly can't stay home from work to take care of her while you're here, right?"

"That's true." The point gave Leah pause. She actually hadn't considered that.

She glanced around the room until she saw the requisite photo propped up on his desk of what appeared to be his wife and two towheaded little girls. The three stood at attention, spaced evenly apart, arms at their sides. They were arranged tallest to shortest and stood in front of a brick wall. Their house maybe? The shortest of the little girls appeared to be around five years old. She wore little clear plastic glasses. The other, standing in the middle, perhaps eight. The wife? She certainly wasn't beautiful. But she wasn't ugly either. Her nose was a bit big for her face. Her eyes a bit too far apart. But she had a thick head of hair that was parted off center and short enough that it framed her face just perfectly. The children's hair was not attended to with the same care. Someone had cut their bangs way too short, leaving them both with huge foreheads and what looked like a curtain valence across the top. Tangled waves hung down past their shoulders. Had they even combed their hair for this picture?

And the dresses? All the same. Even the wife. It was a dress more appropriate for a child than for a grown woman. It would have been a complicated pattern to have sown. The full skirt attached to the white and black spotted top that buttoned down the front. Two little pocket flaps matched the belts around their little waists and the rounded collars circling their graceful necks. The photo was black and white, so she couldn't be sure of the colors, but it must have been summer, for the dresses were sleeveless.

She leaned in to get a closer look at the people depicted in the photo. Depicted. That was an odd word. Or was it? Why did that word pop into her head? The presentation came across as staged and stilted. Was this even his family? He wasn't even in the photo.

"All right. Your time is up." Dr. Pendergast tossed his notebook onto his desk and stood up.

Chapter 36

Leah had escaped into the photo and had no idea how much time had passed.

"You need to return to your room," he said.

He rang up his secretary, who sat obediently at a desk right outside his closed door in her starched white shirt and pencil skirt, her hair in a tight bun.

"Yes, Doctor?" she inquired as she entered the office.

"We are done. Take her out of here."

"Yes, sir."

She was taken to her room, and she climbed in bed. She stared at the ceiling as her mind wandered back to the woman who moved into her home, replacing her as her baby's mother, as her husband's lover. Was it really possible? Sometimes her mind played tricks on her. She alternated between a conviction that her husband would never betray her to a visualization of the affair in living-color images that danced across her mind. On most nights, she drifted in and out of sleep. Each time she woke, she wasn't sure if she had actually witnessed this woman playfully flirting with her husband or if she had only dreamt of them curled up together on the living room couch, the couch Leah chose when they bought the house. The couch David said was too expensive. The couch that faced the fireplace and anchored the room, as Leah explained to her husband in her winning bid to spend the money. She spent her waking moments dismissing the possibility that David was having an affair, only to return to sleep and be taunted by the possibility.

Chapter 37

August 1961

Her panicked breathing was the only discernible sound. But something didn't feel right. She slowly opened her eyes, only to see a small group encircling her and holding its collective breath as the room pulsed with anticipation.

Where was she? The last thing she remembered was a pinch, a sting in her thigh. And Dr. Pendergast standing above her. Now, her frantic eyes darted back and forth, searching for an empathy that no one possessed. She couldn't move her arm, and she pulled and pulled. She couldn't move either arm. And when she realized that both of her legs were also strapped to the bed railings, panic set in. All four limbs struggled against their oppressors.

"Shhhh," a voice above her head spit at her. "Lie still."

The door opened, a slight squeak the only indication that someone had entered the room. The voice that just scolded her had a few words for this delinquent nurse.

"Annie. Good thing the doctor's not here. He never would have allowed your lack of preparation. Get over to the cart."

Annie showed up in Leah's peripheral vision, and the young nurse lowered her eyes before standing erect at her assigned spot. Leah noticed her freshly-applied lipstick. A peachy shade, one that complimented her fair skin. Leah knew a little about lipstick; it was an accessory her mother always wore whenever she left the house. But her face showed something else. She looked like a wounded dog, thought Leah. She felt an unexpected connection to her. She wanted to catch her eye, to let the nurse know that she understood, that they were comrades, but Annie never looked at her. Instead, she looked right past Leah to another nurse, and the two exchanged a barely perceptible grin.

What was going on? Leah pulled on her restrained arms.

But then the door to the examination room exploded open. No one moved. A man in a white lab coat flapping behind him like a superhero's cape swooped in and landed at the foot of the same table where Leah lay motionless.

He assessed the scene.

"Tell me everything is ready," the voice demanded.

The room's scold replied, "Yes, sir."

Leah felt the bile rising in her throat, and she swallowed hard. She had no idea what awaited her, but she knew to be terrified. How had this happened?

In unison, three nurses stepped toward the table. Leah held her breath, but she couldn't quiet her eyes. No one was willing to look at her. To do so might bring her to life. The fourth nurse, the one who had walked in late, rolled a cart over from a corner of the room, a broken wheel screeching through the silence.

How had she ended up here? The last thing Leah remembered was sitting in the common room. She often found herself there, alternating between watching the droning characters on the television set and finding escape through naps.

"Leah. You have an appointment scheduled today. Get up."

It was the doctor's secretary, balancing that bun like an errant ping pong ball that had landed on top of her head.

"Get to his office. Right now," the secretary demanded.

The lethargy Leah increasingly felt left her slow to respond. Sometimes her voice felt trapped inside her body, and it took a minute for it to escape. During those moments, Leah was acutely aware that she was expected to say something, and she got lost in a conscious wonder at her inability to do so.

"I said get up." The woman towered over Leah. "It's not up to you to decide when you see the doctor. It's not your decision."

By remaining silent, Leah risked punishment and having a note of admonishment placed in her file. The staff here could write anything about her they wanted. Their words carried all of the weight while hers carried none. She understood that her version of events, her experiences, and even her feelings were not stories anyone found interesting or worthy of record.

The secretary leaned out the door of the common room and into the hallway. "I need help in the common room!" she yelled.

Leah was still trying to construct her response to the interruption of her solitude. But it was too late. Three men arrived to put an end to whatever craziness they would find this time. But there was no craziness to be found. The men scanned the room, right past Leah, who still reclined on the couch.

"What's the problem?" one of the men asked.

"This patient needs to be in Dr. Pendergast's office right now. And she refuses to go," the secretary said.

One of the orderlies grabbed Leah's upper arm and pulled.

At first, Leah didn't fight back, but she didn't cooperate either. Like a small child, she went limp.

The orderly wasn't new to this. He pulled out the leather restraints from his back pocket. Like a caged animal, Leah surged from passive resistance to wild protest. The three men jumped on her. The secretary yelled for backup, as if more than three grown men were needed to restrain her. Leah fought like hell. No one would ignore her today.

Then there was the pinch in her thigh. And she woke up here.

"Four." The voice at her head jolted her back to the present.

"Three." Electrodes were placed securely on each temple. She jerked at the pressure.

"Two." The nurses surrounding her grabbed her arms and legs. Leah felt a surge of claustrophobia.

"One." Leah gasped.

The doctor flipped the switch, filling the room with a dull hum.

The violent convulsions started immediately.

… the taste of rubber …

… disembodied voices …

… heaviness …

The patient's eyes cracked open, and the milky orbs sought recognition as they filled with tears. The doctor stood at her feet, checked his watch for the time, and made a note on a clipboard. She didn't have the energy to keep her eyes open, so her eyelids dropped, and she wandered off.

… running water …

… clanging metal …

… cold, shivers …

Click. A door closed.

Back in her room and lying on the bed, the patient wanted to speak, to shout out. To question, to rebel. But she couldn't find her voice. Instead, she looked around and sought to communicate her confusion and her concern through her eyes. She sought for compassion, for some semblance of humanity. Then she saw someone at the side of her bed, reaching for her.

In her confusion, Leah whispered, "Mom?"

But no one was there.

Chapter 38

September 1961

"I would like to talk about how you are feeling, Leah. How are you feeling?" Dr. Pendergast asked, inspecting her with the curiosity of an academic studying a mouse navigating a maze.

She stared at him while she waited for the words he uttered to process. She needed a moment to drink them in, bounce them around, and make sense of the sounds. She needed a moment to think about an answer, balancing what she wanted to say with what he might want to hear, for she understood that he held her fate in his hands. She needed a moment to organize her words so that they would roll off her tongue with sincerity.

But the truth was, she felt nothing—and that was not the answer he wanted from her.

He fidgeted in his chair while he waited and while she searched for a time when she did feel something. Anything.

She remembered what feelings felt like. She did. Didn't she?

There was the day her mother married the man she could never bring herself to call "Dad." She had feelings that day.

The day Mrs. Olivari left without saying goodbye. Yes, she had feelings that day.

The day she met David's parents. She had been overcome by love for the first time in her life. Those were feelings.

But surely those weren't the only days.

The most intense feelings she had ever experienced were the ones that brought her here to Lakeside, the day her feelings became manifestations of hell itself.

"Leah." The doctor uncrossed his legs and planted both feet firmly on the ground as he leaned in. "How are you feeling?"

She had forgotten he was waiting for her. But her thinking was muddled and that wasn't compassion in his voice. She wanted to talk. She really did. But her voice was stuck in her throat. She did her best to get her thoughts together so that she could share them with Dr. Pendergast and be deemed "cured." Maybe then she could go home.

"Leah." The doctor leaned back in his chair. "I asked you how you are feeling."

Marvin Pendergast waited, impatiently, for Leah to respond, the minutes slowly ticking by. Today, he was in a particular hurry, anxious for his meeting with the hospital board to discuss the effectiveness of a new medication he had invested in that promised to be the latest weapon against anxiety suffered by young women. He had staked his career on this, and its success would change the course of his life.

"Leah. How are you feeling?" He uncrossed his legs and planted both feet firmly on the ground as he leaned in to try to interrupt her inner journey. But he got no response.

It was all so predictable once Leah had revealed her need for acceptance from her disapproving mother. He had written it down in her file: "approval-seeking daughter." And no wonder. Leah's mother, who lived only a half hour away, had yet to visit even once.

He was in familiar territory. The "approval-seeking daughter" was a topic where he felt he had some expertise. It was part of his research in grad school at Haynes University. One of his professors, Dr. George Cummings, wrote the bible on mother-daughter relationships. Marvin owned a well-worn, dog-eared copy of his book, proudly displayed on the shelf behind his desk. Chapter 8 specifically addressed the "approval-seeking daughter." According to Cummings, Leah would never obtain the approval she was seeking. It was virtually hopeless, an incurable condition, which gave him permission to fail with this patient.

It didn't take him long to decide that she had married her mother, a

Chapter 38

diagnosis he never shared with her. Freud began the scholarship on this subject when he stated that marital relationships repeat the patterns of our relationships with our parents. Thanks to much work that had been since completed on this topic, Marvin would guess that Leah received about as much attention from her husband as she did from her mother. One clue was that, according to the visitor log, her husband typically came to see his wife only once, occasionally twice, a week.

He repeated the question. "How are we feeling today?"

Seriously. Love, hate, fear, elation, embarrassment, anger, guilt. Anything will do, he silently pleaded.

Leah felt ready to answer.

"They were coming home from Ashfield. Can you imagine that?" Leah didn't pause for an answer. "What did they ever do to deserve that? Nothing. They never did anything to hurt anyone. They *loved* me. They loved *me*. I'll never forget the time they …"

She had never really talked about that day with anyone. Leah noticed he was writing things down.

"… the time they …" She tried to continue her story, but now she was distracted.

Was he listening to her?

"The time Rachel …"

She stopped talking. She'd forgotten what she wanted to say. But he didn't stop writing. A minute passed in silence, but his pen continued scratching across the paper.

Finally, he said, "Leah. You have done very well today." His eyes never left the paper. She longed to hear pride in his voice, but he sounded much the same as when he asked her if she would like a glass of water.

"We will need to continue this later," he said to end the session. "I'll call someone to walk you back to your room."

"Wait," she hesitated. "I wasn't finished."

"You'll need to finish the story at your next appointment. We can take it up where you left off. I've written it all down right here." He flipped through the paper on the legal pad he held.

Had he actually been listening? Perhaps she had been mistaken.

"Right here." He pointed aimlessly at the top page right before he tossed the pad on his desk. Then he stood to escort her out.

Leah glanced over at his nearly illegible handwriting. The top page was decorated with arrows, lines scratched out, a stray word jotted down here or there. Without reading any of it, Leah knew he had not written down her story. He made assumptions and drew conclusions. He determined what was important and what could be eliminated; entire sections were ignored or scratched out. He reduced it all to a bullet-point presentation. Any life that her story once held was not on that piece of paper. He had killed it.

Chapter 39

February 1962

The most difficult part about losing nine months is that no one else loses that time. Too much changes. A man who abandons his family, whether for booze, for a woman, for drugs, for any reason, cannot show up when his kids are all grown up to recover the lost time. It can't be done. The time lost inevitably sends people on different trajectories.

Leah's husband did visit her periodically, even if not as often as Leah would have liked. David's hand shook as he signed the discharge papers that committed him to providing Leah with a place to live and the support she would require to make the transition home.

The discharge nurse outlined the instructions for Leah's follow-up treatment: "She has two prescriptions we are going to send home with her. Here is the first three months' worth of both. You will need to bring her in for an appointment in two weeks and then every month after that. At least for a while. Here is an appointment card. We've already set those up through May with Dr. Pendergast. The dates are listed on the card."

But she wasn't following any of it. She was instead watching her husband, who appeared to her a stranger, nod robotically. But he certainly didn't seem to be listening

The nurse continued, "You'll want to make sure that she's not alone, at least for the immediate future. The transition is difficult for some, so we don't want her to have an opportunity to harm herself if she is initially struggling."

Leah continued to watch her husband, the voice of the nurse droning in the background. Her husband stared at his shoes.

"And here is a sheet that will give you all the necessary phone numbers: the Lakeside Institute general number, Dr. Pendergast's secretary, two pharmacies that we recommend, and the after-hours consult line," the nurse finished.

Leah was obviously nervous to go home, but she hadn't realized how nervous David was to have her home. During her lost time, the three of them, David, the baby, and the young nanny who had moved in to help out, had probably developed a comfortable routine, a comfortable life, without her.

The drive home was conducted mostly in silence. David spoke only once to inform Leah that her mother and Robert were at the house with Cassie. She didn't have the strength to respond. Her mother had not once, not a single time in her nine months at Lakeside, come to visit her.

David parked the car in front of their house. He removed Leah's small bag from the trunk while Leah remained in the passenger seat. She barely recognized the house. Had that planter been on the porch when she left?

"Aren't you coming?" David asked while he knocked on the passenger side window.

Life had marched on without her. The tulips that were just breaking through the ground when she left had bloomed and then withered, and now the bulbs lay slumbering under a thin layer of ice. While she was gone, a neighbor had announced her pregnancy to ecstatic first-time grandparents. The woman had converted their guest room to a nursery, been thrown a baby shower by the ladies in the bridge club, and given birth to the healthy baby boy, now napping in his crib. The elderly couple across the street had sold their house and moved in with their son and his wife, and a newly married couple had bought the house and planted a row of bushes where the lawn met the sidewalk.

No one had waited for Leah.

David opened the passenger door. "Come on. Let's go."

Chapter 39

Leah climbed out of the car and journeyed up the walkway to the front door. David opened the front door and motioned to Leah to enter before him. Was this a gentlemanly gesture, or was it a cruel directive to force her to face the disappointment of her mother? Inside, on the living room couch, her mother tickled Cassie. Robert must have been in another room.

Cora stopped mid-tickle to acknowledge Leah's entrance. "Well, look who's here!"

Cassie sat up and pulled her shirt down to cover her belly.

"See Cassie," Grandma Cora said. "I told you your mother would come back, that she would be home today. And look! There she is! Go on. Say hello."

She plopped Cassie onto her feet on the floor. She hadn't yet navigated walking when Leah was checked into the hospital, but there she stood, on her own. But she wasn't walking. Was something wrong with her?

Cassie didn't recognize her mother. And Leah didn't recognize her daughter. Cassie didn't recoil, but she didn't move towards her mother either. The woman who had been living there and caring for Cassie was gone, and as Leah glanced around the room, she saw no indication that another woman had ever been there. She was grateful for that. But her daughter was holding her arms up for her grandmother, not for her. Leah was confronted with the evidence that the time that passed while she was gone meant that she was now a stranger to her daughter.

"Go on," Cora encouraged Cassie. Cora remained on the couch, not getting up to greet Leah herself. Leah bent down to Cassie's level and held out her arms, willing her to fold into them. A good little girl, Cassie listened to her grandma and obediently toddled over, letting Leah take her in her arms. When Leah loosened her grip, Cassie again sought the familiarity of her grandma. Cora took her hand, and together the two of them approached Leah, who was still kneeling at Cassie's level.

"Give Cassie a minute, Leah. She hasn't seen you in a while. Who knows if she even remembers you?" her mother said.

Robert entered the room, drink in hand. "Right, Robert?" she asked him, laughing.

What was the funny part?

Leah looked up at her mother who was still holding Cassie's hand. She tried to remember if her mother had ever held her hand. She couldn't really remember her laughing either. Well, that wasn't entirely true. She remembered laughter with others, when she was at the hotel or with friends or with Robert. But did she and her mother ever just laugh, out of silliness?

Leah stood up. "I'm not feeling very well. David, could you put my bag in the bedroom? I'm going to take a bath and then lie down." Leah glanced around the room to measure the reaction. There was none.

After closing the bathroom door behind her, Leah undressed, folding her clothes into a pile on the toilet. She pulled a washcloth out of the cabinet under the sink and then climbed into the dry tub, closed the drain, and turned on the water. She shivered as the cold water swished around her naked body. When the water coming out of the faucet finally warmed up, her muscles relaxed. She let it run until the tub was filled to the top. After turning off the faucet, she slid down, dropping her head under water.

She wondered how long she would be able to hold her breath. It turned out that it wasn't very long before she popped back up, sputtering and gasping for breath.

She was exhausted and rested her head on the back of the tub. Leah had hoped that she would feel different back here at home. That she would feel more confident in herself, more in control of her emotions. But instead she felt neither. She pushed her wet hair back off of her face and then dropped her hands back down into the water, creating a small splash. She pulled them out and dopped them down again, causing a splash and a small wave that ricocheted from one end of the tub to the other. She rested one hand on her belly, exploring the softness of her own skin.

Coming home would be her chance to start over, she thought. She wanted to forget what she had done, to forget about her time at Lakeside. As those thoughts bounced around her head, she searched through the water for the washcloth and then rubbed it in circles across her stomach.

She hoped that being home would remind her that she should be grateful for her survival. She hoped to feel stronger. To feel a part of a family, of her own family. To be loved. She certainly hadn't found any of that while in the hospital.

She pushed and pulled the washcloth up and down her belly and from one side to the other.

She wanted to feel like she mattered.

The seal on the drain needed replacing, so the water had been slowly leaking out, eventually leaving Leah exposed in an emptying tub. She stopped scrubbing her stomach and draped the washcloth over the side of the tub. Her belly was red and chafed.

When the last of the water disappeared, she stepped out, wrapped a towel around herself, and made her way to the bed she shared with her husband. She climbed under the covers and let out a long sigh.

She didn't feel any different.

Chapter 40

December 1965

Cora looked in the bathroom mirror one last time. She straightened her collar and pushed a stray curl from her forehead. Then she reached for the lipstick off of the sink and carefully applied it, using her pinkie finger to straighten out the line on her lower lip. Then she smiled at her reflection.

She called out to her husband. "Robert? Are you ready? We need to get going."

"Coming," he called back.

Cora made her way to the living room where she had stacked the gifts she wanted to bring to Leah's. She was putting them in a large bag when Robert emerged ready to go. He was impeccably dressed, thanks to his years in the Navy. He wore dark grey trousers, the double pleats perfectly pressed, and a starched dress shirt. His shoes were perfectly polished, as they always were. And Cora's heart still skipped a beat when she saw him.

"Let me get that," he offered, giving her a quick kiss and reaching for the bag. She smiled up at him. She enjoyed her life with him. It was easy. It was uncomplicated. It was exactly what Cora sought. She considered herself lucky to have met him.

Cora had made the first move in their relationship after the Christmas fundraiser years ago. Why him? Cora caught the attention of many men over the years and really never accepted their advances. But Robert was different. After meeting Cora, he came into the restaurant with regular frequency. He later admitted that he periodically came in to see her, but at the time, no observer would ever have been able to tell. Including Cora. Which made him stand out.

So she took control.

She managed to catch him alone one day after he had lunch with other officers. He was the last one left, and he stood up to pull his jacket off the back of his chair.

"When do you think we should have lunch?" Cora asked without looking up at him as she picked up the check from his table.

"You want to have lunch with me?" he asked in surprise.

She smiled up at him. "Don't you think that's a good idea? I work tomorrow night, so I'm free for lunch."

He laughed as he slipped on his jacket, buttoning it down the front. "Yes. Let's do it. Do you like Chinese food? How about The Pagoda? I can meet you there tomorrow at 1. Will that work?"

"Cora? Can we get another round of drinks over here?" Another table called her over.

"Coming," she let them know. "And Robert? I'll see you for lunch tomorrow."

She flashed him a smile and left to check on her other customers.

Cora was surprised at herself for asking him to lunch. But she was more surprised Robert hadn't already asked her. She was glad she had done it though. Because now, she was glad she wasn't alone, she was glad for the opportunity to leave Portland, and she was grateful to travel the world, thanks to Robert's Navy career.

Over the years, Robert and Leah rarely interacted. Robert didn't have children of his own, and as made obvious by his distant relationship with Leah, he wasn't comfortable around children. It wasn't that he treated Leah badly. She was mostly invisible to him. And he was to her. Cora was aware of this, but she left it to Robert and Leah to figure out, which they weren't capable of or particularly interested in. But he always supported Cora and her relationship with Leah.

Robert opened the car door for Cora and then loaded the packages in the trunk before navigating the streets that were coated in a thin layer of snow that fell during the night. Since Cassie's birth, Leah insisted on hosting Christmas Day.

"Hello? We're here!" The front door was unlocked, so Cora and Robert let themselves in. "Hello?"

"Yes, yes, we're here!" Leah's voice found its way to the living room before she did. When she did show up, she was wiping her hands on her apron, and David was following her with a drink for himself and one for Robert.

"Should I unpack the gifts here? Put them under the tree?" Cora asked Leah as a greeting.

"That'll be fine. I need to get back to the kitchen. The potatoes should be about done," Leah responded.

"Where's Cassie?" Cora asked as she unpacked the bag she brought and placed the carefully wrapped gifts under the tree.

"She's in her room," Leah said as returned to the kitchen.

Once Cora emptied the bag, she excused herself from the men and sought out Cassie. She found the little girl upstairs in her bedroom, sitting on the floor in her underwear and scribbling in a coloring book with a green crayon. David and Leah had moved to this larger house a couple of years ago so that Cassie could have her own bedroom, and David could keep a home office.

"Merry Christmas, Sweetheart." Cora held her arms out, and Cassie stood up for the embrace. "Let's get you dressed. You wait right here." Cora hurried back out to the living room to fetch the box that contained a smocked blue corduroy dress for Cassie. It wasn't specifically for Christmas, but it would work.

Once she had her dressed, she picked up her granddaughter and carried her to the kitchen to find Leah, who was mashing potatoes. Cora couldn't understand why Leah didn't dress up a bit, even for Christmas. Or put on a little bit of makeup.

"Do you want me to take care of that for you while you finish getting ready?" She put Cassie down, and Cassie wandered off. "You look so pale. Maybe a little blush would help with that."

"I look pale? I haven't been feeling well. But I thought I just didn't get enough sleep last night. I haven't been sleeping well lately. But I'm fine. I can finish this."

Cora accepted her answer and joined the others in the living room. The men were sipping whiskey and discussing the Vietnam War. As a veteran of World War II, Robert always appreciated an audience willing to talk about what was happening overseas. Cassie sat near the tree, running her finger along the silky ribbon tied around a package wrapped in colorful paper. Cora had brought that package, so she encouraged Cassie to go ahead and open it. First, Cassie slipped the ribbon off. Then she searched for the paper's edge and carefully ran her finger under it to release the tape. Once she removed the paper, she opened the box, which contained two red velvet hair bows. She pulled them both out and, smiling, held them up to her grandma.

Cora pulled Cassie's hair back and braided it in silence. Robert and David had moved to the kitchen to do their best at carving the turkey. Cora pinned one of the bows at the top of the braid. She loved her granddaughter, but she also worried about her. She felt close to Cassie, for she had spent a lot of time with her when Leah was hospitalized. But now she was so quiet; she always kept to herself. But she also never complained. And she certainly didn't seem unhappy.

"Dinner's ready," Leah announced.

Cora took Cassie's hand, which she readily gave, and led her to the dining room.

"Cassie, go sit by your father. Robert, why don't you sit there? And Mother, you sit here, next to me," Leah instructed. "And everyone pass your plates to David, and he will serve the turkey."

Chapter 41

October 1968

"I want to thank you for taking the time to come in to speak with me today," said Mrs. Newberry, Cassie's third grade teacher. Leah was surprised when she got the call. Cassie had always been such a pleasant child, never causing any trouble for her teachers. Or anyone else for that matter. Leah couldn't imagine why she was asked to come in.

Leah considered calling the school that morning and cancelling. She didn't feel prepared to handle a problem with Cassie. She hesitated only because the two previous times that Mrs. Newberry had scheduled a conference with her, she had indeed cancelled at the last minute. But before she made a decision about whether to go or not, the phone rang. It was Mrs. Newberry calling to confirm before Leah had a chance to back out yet again.

They were scheduled to meet right after the bell rang at the end of the day. Leah was told to wait in the front office until Mrs. Newberry dismissed her students. She would escort Leah back to her classroom, where Cassie waited with the teacher aid.

"I'm sorry I had to cancel last time. It's just been so hard. I get these headaches all the time."

So went Leah's attempt at small talk as she and Mrs. Newberry navigated the hall filled with children eager to go home.

Mrs. Newberry and Leah entered Room 115; the teacher thanked the aid and excused her, wishing her a good weekend. Leah hadn't even noticed that Cassie was in the room until Mrs. Newberry spoke directly to her.

"Cassie, can you please get the chair from the front of the room and bring it right here in front of my desk? And Mrs. Evans, why don't you sit over here?" She motioned to a chair already positioned next to her desk.

Once the three took their assigned seats, Mrs. Newberry asked her student, "Cassie, how are you liking school this year?"

With hands in lap and chin lowered to avoid eye contact, Cassie shrugged her shoulders.

Mrs. Newberry continued, "Have you made any new friends? Is there anyone that you spend time with outside of school?"

Leah chimed in. "She has friends."

"I'm glad to hear that. Who are some of your friends, Cassie? Girls from class?"

Leah answered for Cassie again. "I don't know if they're in this class, but she has friends. There's the girl that lives down the street, right Cassie? What's her name? Sarah? Sasha? Something like that. You play with her sometimes."

"Cassie," Mrs. Newman interjected, "why don't you go wait in the hall for your mother. I'd like to talk with her for a minute. Is that ok?"

Cassie stood up, returned her chair to its original position, and left the room. When the door closed behind Cassie, Leah came to life.

"I'm sorry. Like I said, I get headaches. I suffer from migraines, and the doctor can't seem to find a way to stop them. I don't have a migraine today, thank goodness. Otherwise I never could've made it here. But I do have bad allergies today. In fact, could I have one of those tissues?" Leah pointed to a box on Mrs. Newberry's desk.

"I'm sorry to hear that, Mrs. Evans," the teacher began as she handed Leah the box. "But right now I really would like to talk to you about Cassie."

"Is she having trouble keeping up?"

"No, no. Not at all. She is a very smart girl. Actually, she's a model student. I wish I had more like her. But I'm concerned because she seems withdrawn. She doesn't participate in class, and she spends recess alone." Mrs. Newberry paused for a reaction from Leah.

But Leah had no comment. So Mrs. Newberry continued.

"You know, I asked Miss Jackson, her second grade teacher, about how Cassie did last year in her class. Do you remember Miss Jackson from last year?"

'Miss Jackson? Uh. No. She was her second grade teacher?" Leah's voice wandered off.

"Yes, and she couldn't tell me much about Cassie. She couldn't remember how she did in her class last year. Does that worry you?"

"I imagine they can't remember everybody." Leah shrugged and winced at the pain the movement caused.

Chapter 42

June 1971

As the years passed, David worked his way up in the established structure of his firm. Leah ran the household, and Cassie attended school. When school was out for the summer, she accompanied her mother on her errands.

The two stopped at Woolworths to pick up laundry detergent but also to share a slice of pecan pie at the counter. The pie was part of their routine whenever Leah had an appointment with her allergist. Her asthma had flared up, and she often had to retreat from her responsibilities to get her breathing in check. Eventually, she was prescribed once-a-week shots for a variety of allergies that even she couldn't keep track of. Leah would drag Cassie to the doctor's downtown office, where she had the opportunity to witness her mother perfect the role of sufferer.

The two sat at the counter, Cassie swiveling back and forth on the bar stool and her mother sighing with resignation.

"I've been going to this doctor for five years, and I've not gotten any better," Leah told Cassie.

Cassie took a bite of pie.

Her mother continued. "Right here," she said, pointing to her forearm. "See this right here?"

Cassie ignored her. And Leah ignored that she was being ignored.

"Something's wrong. It hurts right here. I don't know what the doctor did, but it's all red. Do you see that?"

"Excuse me, ma'am?" The man behind the counter was wiping up where another patron had managed to leave half his slice of toast in crumbs. He had mistakenly thought Leah was talking to him.

"Oh no," she said, waving him off. "I was just saying that my doctor might have burst a blood vessel in my arm today. See this?"

She may have found an audience. She held out her arm for the man to inspect it. Cassie took advantage of her mother's distraction to scoop up the last bite of pie and jump down from her stool.

"Oh yes, ma'am. I do see that," he humored her.

"I knew it. I have to go to the doctor every week. He gives me a shot for my allergies and sometimes tests for any new allergies. I asked him last week to check for grass. You think that's what this is? An allergic reaction to grass? I've heard that people can be allergic to grass, and we have a backyard full of grass? Or is it a burst blood vessel?"

"I have no idea, ma'am," he responded.

Cassie wandered over to the aisle with the troll and Barbie knock-off display.

"It's so hard having to go every week. Can you imagine?" The man now had his back to her and scraped the grill.

"Excuse me," she whispered. Through trial and error, she learned that lowering her voice brought people in closer.

He pulled their bill out of his apron, placed it next to her empty plate, and walked off in one fluid motion that provided no room for further conversation.

Leah dug out $1.25 from her purse and laid it next to the bill. She climbed down from the bar stool and walked to the entrance of the store. Cassie put a troll back on the shelf, and in a well-coordinated ballet, without a word, the two ended up at the door together and walked home.

Chapter 43

September 1978

Leah pulled the envelope out of the mailbox. It was addressed to Mom and Dad Evans. Cassie managed to finish high school and left for her freshman year a month ago. The college was about three hours from home. Leah wasn't surprised her daughter wanted to attend college. It seemed that was what everyone was doing these days. But she had no idea what Cassie's plans were. They had never talked about what she wanted to study, what kind of career she wanted, or any of that. Cassie never volunteered any of that information.

Leah had mailed Cassie a couple of cards to ask how classes were going and to let her know about the crown that her father needed on one of his back teeth (It had been giving him terrible pain.) and about Mrs. O'Reily's death (It was quite sad.). Mrs. O'Reilly lived down the street. She was a nice lady. And she died quickly after being diagnosed with brain cancer. Her husband? Devastated. She wasn't sure if Cassie knew the couple or not. She also wrote about how much her knee had been bothering her. The doctor told her it was arthritis, which would only get worse, he forewarned.

Leah had a hard time communicating with Cassie. She was intimidated by her uncaring eyes. After she left for college, Leah avoided calling her so she wouldn't have to hear the distance in Cassie's voice. She had no idea how to bring her daughter's eyes to life or to bring her voice close. She couldn't understand what she had done to deserve indifference. She mailed cards to avoid confronting the answer.

But this was the first letter she and David had received from their daughter. Leah placed it unopened on the counter and poured the hot water from the kettle into a teacup, holding the little square of paper at the end of the string so it didn't get swooped into the boiling water. She took both the tea and the letter into the living room, savoring the fact that her daughter had actually written her. Or the two of them.

Most teenagers push against the boundaries or rebel against constraints, but Cassie retreated. She had been retreating since the moment she was born.

Leah believed she valiantly worked to connect to Cassie, to keep Cassie's retreat at bay. But the problem was that Leah had only one tool in her arsenal. And like a captain on a sinking ship, she refused to abandon that tool.

Years ago, Leah's nine-month stay at Lakeside created a void between the two that Leah just hadn't been able to navigate since then. She forgave herself for this because she still wasn't well. After all, the doctors told her so, and her husband treated her as such. So she believed it and lived it.

Then there was the asthma. There were the accidents: the falls, the dislocated shoulder, the twisted ankle, the broken arm. There was the chronic pain, the "phantom pain," as more than one doctor over the years would record in her medical records.

A vague memory, more of a feeling than of a vision, was buried in her heart of a time as a little girl when she felt affection. She longed to recreate that feeling. She didn't exactly remember that time, but her instinct told her how to behave. Her instinct told her that if people were worried about her health, they would pay attention. But it was a tool that never proved effective. Regardless, Leah continued to up the ante in the only game she knew: waiting for Cassie, or anyone, to notice.

Once settled in her chair with her tea, Leah slipped her finger under the flap of the envelope and slowly pulled it across, savoring the anticipation. Cassie's letter turned out to be a generic recitation of banal events, but no matter. Cassie had written her. That's what mattered. Leah folded it up and placed it back in the envelope. She set it on the

Chapter 43

coffee table. Her thoughts moved to her knee, which was throbbing. She pulled the heating pad out from under some magazines stacked on the table. It was already plugged in. She flipped the switch to "high" and placed it on her leg.

Chapter 44

March 1979

"Is this Leah Evans?"

"Yes it is. Who's this?"

"This is a neighbor of your mother's. Your mother was helping me put together Easter gift baskets for my church, and, I'm so sorry to say this. But she tripped on the stairs to the rec room, and she hit her head."

"Wait, what?"

Leah had never heard her mother mention any neighbors. Or going to a church.

"They're taking her to Cook County Hospital now. The doctors will see her there. But I wanted to let you know."

"Is it serious?"

"Yes, I think you should get over there as soon as you can. She hit her head pretty hard."

In the complete silence, Cora struggled to focus. All she could see were shadowy shapes hovering over her. She felt nauseous and closed her eyes in hopes the feeling would disappear. It didn't. Then a voice broke through.

"Cora, are you all right? Can you hear me? Open your eyes, Cora."

And then another voice: "Someone call an ambulance."

"Who needs an ambulance?" she wondered.

The next time she struggled to open her eyes, the surrounding sounds were thunderous. A siren. Beeping. Shouting. Honks. She tried to lift her hand. Where was Robert? She wanted Robert's hand. To feel his squeeze. But she couldn't move. A young man leaned over her, and she thought she heard him say, "Your mom said you fell down and tore up your arm."

"Jimmy K.?" she asked. She remembered picking off the scabs. Jimmy K. didn't like that.

"Just lie back. We'll be there soon," came the reply.

Cora's head pounded.

The next thing she remembered was lying in a bed, her head elevated. She heard voices at the foot of her bed. Two women. She couldn't understand what they were saying, but the tone of their voices had her worried. Was the baby ok? Did Mr. Peterson find out and come looking for her? She gasped and then squeaked out, "No," causing the voices to momentarily halt. No one could find out. No one. Her mother would be devastated. Who knows what Charles would do. The sisters would know she lied. And Mr. Peterson was a dangerous man. He might try to kill the baby. No! She was desperate. No one can know.

She felt a prick in her arm. She was too tired to open her eyes, but she heard a man at her side say, "This doesn't look good."

It was a Saturday, so Leah asked David, who wasn't working, to drive her to the hospital. He agreed and dropped her off outside the emergency room entrance. He would run an errand and then return for her in an hour.

"I'm here to see Cora O'Toole. I'm her daughter," Leah informed the receptionist.

"Take a seat," the voice from behind the partition directed.

But before she had a chance to take a seat, an ICU nurse who had been expecting her escorted Leah to her mother's bedside, doing her best to delicately explain her mother's condition.

"The doctor made the decision to sedate your mother. Her injury has resulted in significant swelling of her brain, and we want to do everything we can to ensure her recovery. I just want to prepare you for

Chapter 44

what you are going to see when we get to her room. She is on a ventilator and an IV, and we are monitoring her vitals, so there will be a lot of machines taking readings."

"Thanks for warning me," Leah said. "This is all so new to me."

"I understand. This sort of thing is never easy," the nurse sympathized with her patient's daughter.

As they made their way through the winding hallways of the vast hospital, Leah groaned.

"I'm not feeling so great," she told the nurse as she slowed down to rub her head.

"This must be very upsetting," the nurse acknowledged.

"No, that isn't what I mean. I get migraines, and I can feel one coming on. I have Tylenol in my purse. Can I sit here for a minute?"

"Certainly. Let me go get you a glass of water. Can I get you anything else?" the nurse offered.

"No, no. I don't want to be any bother."

"No bother at all. Wait here. I'll be right back." The nurse disappeared around the corner.

Leah dug around in her purse and pulled out the bottle of Tylenol. She struggled to open it. She never seemed to be able to work these child-proof bottles.

"Here you are," the nurse said as she held out a glass of water.

"Can you help me with this? I can't get this bottle open."

The nurse took the bottle and popped the top off of it. "If you always have trouble with these, did you know that you can special order bottles without the child-proof caps?"

"No! I didn't know that. How do I do that?" Leah brightened.

"Just ask the pharmacist when you fill your prescription; he can give you a different bottle that is easier to open."

Leah took a sip of water and followed it with two Tylenol, swallowing it all in one gulp. Then she stood up, ready to continue.

The nurse led her to Cora's room, opened the door, and stepped back so Leah could enter. Leah mouthed to the nurse, "Thank you," before walking in.

She hesitated right inside the door to let her eyes adjust. The drapes were pulled closed, and the room was dark. Then her mother came into focus, immobile and stretched out in the bed. Had she ever seen her mother asleep? Not that she was actually asleep right now. But her mother had always been on the move, a whirlwind of activity without time to inspect or investigate. This was a rare opportunity. An empty chair was on the other side of the bed, so Leah quietly took a seat to observe her mother.

Bip … Bip … Bip.

Leah rocked ever-so-slightly back and forth to the rhythm of the heart monitor.

Bip … Bip … Bip.

Her mother had already had surgery, so a white gauze bandage covered her head. What happened to the thick black hair that she took such pride in? Leah supposed it had been shaved off. At least she couldn't see any remnants of her hair poking out from the bandages. She followed the line of her left arm down to where an IV pumped fluids into the back of her hand. Her mother still wore her wedding ring. Robert had died a couple of years ago. Thanks to Cora and his years in the Navy, his sendoff was filled with pomp and circumstance. But her fingers had swelled, and Leah figured that maybe she couldn't get the ring off.

She seemed so small. So frail. So exposed.

The nurse came back into the room to check. She asked Leah if she was feeling better. She managed to let her know that she was, but unexpectedly, the nurse's presence triggered a reaction, and Leah cried into her hands. The nurse apologized for disturbing her and quietly left the room. Alone again with her unconscious mother, Leah was able to regain control, and the tears dried up.

Seeing her like this, Leah decided that it would have been better for everyone if her mother had just died from the fall. As soon as that thought formed, she was horrified. She had made the same decision about her own life years ago. That it would have been better if she had died. What a cruel instinct it is—to fight for this life.

Her mother was in good hands. The nurse seemed nice; surely she was responsible too. But it would still be another half hour before David would return to pick her up.

A cup of tea, she thought. That's what I need. As she made her way to the cafeteria, she wandered into a little gift shop. Inside, she found a sentimental "Thinking of You" card. She bought the card and while she sipped her tea in the cafeteria, she signed the card and wrote a quick note to Cassie about her despair at her mother's fall. Cassie ought to know what happened.

And it was only two weeks later that a fading Cora disappeared completely. Leah bought a sympathy card to break the news to Cassie, who was immersed in midterms. She anguished over just the right words, the words to convey the right tone. She couldn't quite figure out how to express the emotions of the moment. Was she heartbroken? Grief-stricken? Saddened? Anguished? Anxious? Grateful that her suffering had ended?

Abandoned.

Leah ended the card by informing Cassie of her grandmother's burial at Oakdale Cemetery on the outskirts of the city. There would be no funeral or memorial. As an afterthought, she explained that she made the decision that her mother would not be buried at the cemetery where Robert was buried. Leah had a better place for her. Robert wasn't actually family, anyway. Leah wished Cassie good luck on her tests and signed the card "Mom."

The next day, the funeral home picked up the body from the hospital and delivered it to the cemetery in a coffin that Leah choose from a catalog. The same catalog contained pages and pages of grave markers. Leah had no idea what to choose.

"Can I help you out?" the funeral director saw her struggling to make a decision. "Tell me a little about your mother. Maybe I can help you find something," he offered.

Leah listed mundane facts about her mother: parents from Ireland, husband in Navy, only child.

As she spoke, the director flipped through the catalog until a large stone Irish cross caught his eye. It was one of the largest grave markers they offered. And it was expensive.

"How about this one?" he asked. "Isn't it gorgeous? That would really stand out. And it honors your mother's heritage."

"Isn't that a cross? My mother wasn't religious. I don't think she would want that," Leah replied. Then she remembered that she fell while at church. What was she doing at church?

"Oh, she wasn't? Oh, ok. I just assumed, since she was Irish. But we have other stones. What about this one, the one with the Irish trinity knot, the triquetra?" he asked.

Judging by the photo, the stone was larger than life.

"I think it represents the life cycle," he continued. "Let me see. Yes, here it is. The catalog says it 'signifies the Triple Moon Goddess, which encompasses the maiden, the mother, and the crone, and the connectedness of all things.' Does that sound like something she might like?" the man asked.

It did, thought Leah. She would buy that one.

"Beautiful choice. Beautiful," the funeral director praised her as he filled out the bill of sale.

Two days later, the only witness to the conclusion of Cora's story was a gravedigger.

Chapter 45

March 1981

Cassie,

I have been trying to get hold of you, but every time I call, Gail tells me you're out. We need to talk. I haven't talked to you since Gail told me that you're pregnant. You didn't even tell me. I'm concerned about what you are going to do. Or not do.

Look, I'm in no position to have a baby. I graduate in a couple of months and already have a job set up in New York City. I can't give that up and stay here after all the work I've done. I just can't. I'm sorry. Besides, we hardly know each other. It's not like we are in a relationship. But I also don't think I'm comfortable knowing that a child of mine is out in the world. Plus, my parents would kill me if they were to find out about this.

I can help you out if you need money. I don't know how much it would cost, but I have some money saved, so that wouldn't be a problem. I can also go with you if you want me to. Please let me know what you need. But you have to let me know what is going on. Please. Call me.

Scott

Part IV

Chapter 46

August 1982

Cassie made Leah nervous. She desperately wanted Cassie to see her, to understand her, but she hadn't figured out how to get the reaction she craved. It was easier when Cassie was at college, and she could communicate without having to actually interact with her. But Cassie still hadn't found a job. After graduation, she moved back into her old bedroom. Here they were, once again, so that whenever Leah tried to talk to her daughter, Cassie's blank face just stared back at her.

It was a Saturday. Cassie had been locked up in her room all day. Leah wondered what she could possibly be doing. But she tried to put that thought aside as she continued to go through the motions of her own day. She cleaned dishes, carried laundry down to the basement, swept the kitchen. But she kept coming back to the closed door. One time as she passed she pressed her hand up against the door, the closest she could come to touching Cassie. Another time, she pressed her ear up to it to see if she could hear what might be happening in there. A third, she held up her fist as if to knock but instead retreated to the kitchen. She made a sandwich. And then she made a second.

"Cassie! You want a sandwich?" she called out from the kitchen to no response. "Cassie?" She tried again. Nothing.

After cutting the second sandwich diagonally, the way she did when she made sandwiches for Cassie's lunch box back when she was in elementary school, she placed it on a plate with a dill pickle and a handful of potato chips and walked down the hall to present it to her daughter and stood outside the door.

"Cassie? I made a sandwich for you. Can I come in?" Without waiting for an answer, she opened the door.

Cassie sat at the desk she set up in her room. At her mother's interruption, she put down her pen and leaned back in the chair. Leah placed the plate on the desk.

"Here. I made you, well, I was making myself a sandwich. I was getting hungry. And I thought, well, um, I thought that you might want one too. A sandwich. Are you, are you getting hungry?"

Why was she so nervous bringing her daughter a sandwich? Cassie watched her mother as she mumbled her way through the offer. Cassie showed neither gratitude nor annoyance.

Leah turned to leave but then turned back and said, "Ok. I'm going to leave you to whatever you're doing."

But she didn't leave.

"You know," she added seemingly as an afterthought, but it was actually a well-played out conversation she had practiced in her head. "Grandpa Robert is not my father."

Leah launched the news into the room hoping its impact would land like a grenade while Cassie fiddled with her blouse, eyes downcast. Leah took a step further into the room and stood up straighter. She hoped that perhaps genuine curiosity and maybe even compassion might look back at her this time.

"That's the thing. I don't know who my real father is." Leah felt empowered, her statements delivered fluidly and with an air of haughtiness. "Your grandfather adopted me when I was eight."

She wondered what Cassie would think about that. She hoped Cassie would say, "It couldn't have been easy growing up not knowing who your real father is." Or that maybe she would say, "You must have had it pretty hard."

Leah continued. "I don't remember ever meeting my dad, and my mother refused to talk about him or about what happened. I asked her a couple of times and learned very quickly to never bring it up again. So I didn't. And now she's dead."

Cassie concentrated on a hangnail she found on her right middle finger. She worked at tearing it off without leaving a raw, exposed strip of pink skin.

Leah paused. Was Cassie even listening to her? She pressed on.

"I was hoping to find out the name of my real dad on my birth certificate, but the document's been changed. Instead it lists Robert as my father. But that's simply not true. It's all been very difficult for me," she concluded.

Her story over, she left the room. Cassie was left sitting at her desk with a stack of resumes and a sandwich. Leah returned to the kitchen, satisfied that this news might improve her relationship with her daughter. At the very least, maybe now her daughter would show her some compassion.

Chapter 47

July 1985

In the past three years, Cassie had graduated from the University of Illinois with a degree in history, began work at the Chicago Historical Foundation, and moved out of her parents' home. Her mother rarely heard from her. This hurt Leah's feelings, but it didn't motivate her enough to pick up the phone and call her daughter herself. Cassie should want to call her, shouldn't she? Leah had called her own mother every day. But Leah never conveyed this expectation to Cassie. She didn't think she had to.

The two never fought; they never even disagreed. They simply didn't have much to say. Cassie would call occasionally, but when Leah hung up after yet another conversation filled with awkward silences and fits and starts, she felt exhausted. And disregarded. So eventually, Leah stopped picking up the phone or even picking up the extension. She left David to take the calls.

One morning, after David left for work, Leah took a seat in the living room, picked up the phone extension on the side table and called her daughter, all on her own. She couldn't remember the last time she had taken the initiative to call Cassie, which made her increasingly nervous. But she had an idea. It occurred to her that Cassie still knew very little about her. If she knew more, she might want to talk to her more often. What story could she tell her? Leah had already told her that she didn't know who her real father was. That was important information. That can really mess with a person. And Leah would know. But she was surprised that Cassie didn't have more questions about that. Leah would not have had any answers. But still.

Today, she would reveal something she had never told anyone, not even David. She wanted her daughter to understand, to really understand, that things had not been easy for her.

"Um. Hi. Cassie? Yeah, hi," she stumbled through the greeting. "It's your mom."

Silence followed as Cassie waited for her mother to proceed. Leah mustered up the courage to broach the subject on her mind.

"Hello? Are you still there? Uh, I can't hear you," she faltered, stalling as she summoned up the emotional energy she promised herself last night she would find to begin this conversation.

After a few more moments of silence, Leah finally delivered the information, with little finesse or grace. With no lead up or chit chat but with plenty of verbal fillers.

"Um. Hmmm. Did you, um, know that one time I tried to divorce, uh, your father?"

Cassie had nothing to say. Leah couldn't understand why she wasn't capable of eliciting any reaction from her.

"When you were a baby, after your grandparents were killed," she began. She had found her voice. There were no more of those stuttering "ums" punctuating every sentence in an effort to not really say anything but still say something. Here, in seeking sympathy, was a place she was comfortable. Stories of her difficulties were told with the bravado of a superhero relating his triumphs against the villains. Nervous filler words never showed up in these stories. She spoke with confidence and clarity, as if reciting a monologue from a script that had been carefully rehearsed, specifically for this performance. She was in full character.

"Your father was never home. He was always at work and always out of town, sometimes weeks, even months at a time. We were living separate lives, he traveling the country while you and I sat at home. I was basically a single mom. I simply had no support."

Leah paused, giving Cassie a moment to interject, which she failed

Chapter 47

to do.

"I decided to leave him, your father. I packed a small suitcase, put together some things for the baby—that would be you—and found a lawyer in the Yellow Pages. The secretary politely showed me into his office. He invited me to sit down opposite the large oak desk that separated us. It was a lot like that desk your father used to have in his home office. Do you remember that desk?"

Her mother pushed on, no longer waiting for a response, despite asking the question.

"That lawyer wanted to know why I was there. And the way he asked? I felt foolish. But I went ahead and told him that my husband was never home, that I wanted a divorce."

Leah paused, not because she lost her nerve in this moment of vulnerability, but for dramatic effect. It would be the shining moment of her story.

Then the punchline: "The lawyer? He laughed at me."

The dramatic pause.

She continued. "The lawyer said that having a husband who worked a lot was not an acceptable reason for a divorce. He suggested I take my bag and my baby and go back home. So I did. I picked both up, thanked the secretary, walked out, and took the train back home. Your father has no idea I ever did that."

Leah held her breath at the end of the last sentence. She wasn't sure what she sought. She just wanted something. Anything. Perhaps a note of empathy, a tinge of understanding, or just a feeling of connection.

A connection. That was it. However, Leah didn't attempt to forge a connection with Cassie. No. This was an attempt to manipulate Cassie to make a connection with her. But Leah never learned the lesson that these things can't be forced.

She would just have to try harder next time.

Chapter 48

June 1994

Kevin met Cassie on the El of all places. The Red Line. He was on his way home from the University of Chicago, finishing up a semester doing battle with freshman, searching for the elusive evidence that they might actually find value in studying early twentieth century American history. Sometimes he would catch a glimmer of interest; more often he didn't. But according to his student evaluations, "Mr. Brighton sure is passionate about history." And that he was.

A woman squeezed her way into the crowded train car at the Clark/Division station. She blew in like the newly warmed summer air that was everywhere in the city this time of year. It swirled through the car but went unnoticed by the heads buried in books and newspapers, and it failed to rouse those lost in their own thoughts.

But Kevin noticed. There was something familiar about her, he thought. And comfortable. She was everyone. She was no one. A phantom. An apparition.

He stood up and offered his seat. She took it without acknowledgement. And she sunk in, dissolving into her surroundings and nearly disappearing. He continued to watch her as the train left the station. She was stunning, he decided, but not in a typical way. It wasn't the dark, silky hair against the blue eyes or the slightly upturned nose. It was the simple naturalness of her beauty and her casual disregard for her looks. Most women, he found, worked to highlight their assets, so to speak. This woman seemed unaware of her beauty. But it was also the detached face of deep concentration. What was she thinking about? What was on her mind?

At the next station, the seat next to Cassie opened up, and Kevin took the liberty of sitting back down just as the train wheels screeched and the curve of the track knocked them off balance. Their shoulders touched. When she turned her head to indicate "Sorry," he caught her eye. He got in a smile before she turned away.

Ever since he was a little boy, people accused him of being "as curious as a cat." He didn't understand the wonder with which people pointed this out. Wasn't everybody curious? Only cats?

His childhood consisted of endless questions: Why do we have eyebrows? Do spiders have eyebrows? Did you have spiders at your house when you were growing up? How do they learn to make the patterns for their webs? Do you think any spiders crawled into a rocket going to the moon? What happens to spiders when they die? Do they go to heaven?"

It was his toughest struggle as a professor. Too many students had been trained to simply consume material fed to them so that they could regurgitate it on tests and in essays.

"Will this part be on the test?"

"How many points is it worth?"

"How long should it be?"

"Are we supposed to argue that the Industrial Revolution was a good thing in this research paper?"

Instead it was his own curiosity that kept him engaged in the classroom. He sought topics that *he* wondered about. And he structured his classes around *his* questions. So it was no surprise that Kevin found himself curious about this enigmatic woman who seemed invisible to all but him.

He was single, but not for a lack of trying. He had dated a number of women. There was the colleague from the university, the neighbor in his apartment building, the friend of a friend that he met at a barbeque. And the young woman from his mother's church that his mother

Chapter 48

insisted would be perfect for him.

But they had all seemed interchangeable, a thought that embarrassed him. Sometimes he felt the same about his students, and he had to consciously fight that tendency. But very few of them wanted to stand out, to be unique, to have a contrary opinion. He had spent enough time studying history to know that it was the people willing to stand up and stand out who made a difference in the world. It saddened him to come across so much predictability.

And the women he had dated were predictable. They were all in the market for husbands who were already established in their careers. They had uneventful middle-class childhoods growing up in the Chicago suburbs. Their stories were all the same. They weren't passionate about what they currently did and didn't display curiosity about the world around them, let alone curiosity about him beyond "name, rank, and serial number."

He preferred the less obvious. He enjoyed discovering what others ignored. That was where the really interesting material lived. That was also where he differentiated himself from the rest of academics. It was all so obvious that his colleagues found interest in only the current trend. After all, that was the safest way to win grant money and notoriety. Few forged their own path.

A week after first seeing Cassie on the train, Kevin returned to his office at the university to clean out the last of the files he needed for his research over the summer. And he saw her again, aboard the same train home. Same scenario. This time she acknowledged him with a nod of the head as a thanks when he again offered his seat. But then he lost her after a crowd of boarding passengers pushed him to the front of the packed car.

It was only two weeks later that he ran into her yet again. But this time, it wasn't on the train. Kevin had been anxiously awaiting the end of the semester so that he could get to work on his next book. That's where his passion truly lived. In writing. He dreamt of one day making a living off his books.

His latest project was set in 1915 when the SS Eastland capsized on the Chicago River, killing 844 passengers, most of whom were under 25 years old. They were headed to a day-long outing for workers of the

Western Electric Company and their families. It was a horrific, and criminal, tragedy that he felt hadn't been given enough attention.

The first step in researching the book was to call on the Chicago Historical Foundation. Their library contained the largest collection of documents about the sinking. So Kevin made an appointment to browse through what they had. He looked forward to a summer pouring through articles, manuscripts, and reports in their basement.

On his first visit to the foundation, a young man led him downstairs to the corner of the library where he would be able to work in private. On the stairs, a woman in a hurry breezed past them. She looked familiar. But he couldn't place where he might have known her. The gentleman leading him around left him with a stack of boxes to wade through, and like a flash, he remembered. The woman from the train. He wondered if she worked there. And then he chuckled to himself. A badge was dangling from her neck. The next time he saw her, he pledged, he would speak to her.

It took two more trips to the foundation's library before he ran into her again. By this time, he had his own badge and was permitted to visit the library stacks by himself. And there she was. Gliding up the steps as unobtrusive as a whisper.

"Hello!" he blurted out before she could float right past him.

She came to a quick stop.

"From the train. The Red Line. Remember?" Kevin added.

It took a moment as she ran through memories, but yes, she had actually remembered.

Kevin properly introduced himself, as did she. They exchanged pleasantries, and Cassie bowed out, needing to get back to work. But Kevin took action. Who could explain that? He asked for her number. She rattled it off. Kevin had the sense that she didn't really mean to give him her number but that she was accustomed to doing as asked without thinking. He hoped that wasn't the case and that she genuinely wanted him to call. Then the two of them continued on their separate ways to finish the day's work.

Kevin wasn't interested in waiting a day or two to call. No need to play those kinds of games. He called her that night and asked her to dinner Friday evening. He invited her to a little hole-in-the-wall trattoria

Chapter 48

in Lincoln Park tucked underneath a brownstone that went mostly unnoticed by tourists but was beloved by locals. Cassie had never heard of it but agreed to meet him there.

At dinner, he found Cassie to be not only attractive and intelligent, but an enigma. At the end of the date and before they departed to their respective apartments, Kevin asked her out again, for Sunday. She agreed, and then she acquiesced to a goodnight kiss. It was a respectable kiss, but a kiss nonetheless. Kevin replayed the entire conversation on the way home. By the time he walked through his front door, he realized that she had actually revealed very little about herself. He had done most of the talking. He regretted that. It's an occupational hazard. He was used to lecturing. When students asked questions, he provided answers. Very thorough answers.

On Sunday, he wanted to take Cassie to a movie, maybe after an early dinner, but no movies currently playing interested him in the slightest. He suggested a trip over to Lincoln Park. They could visit the zoo, the beach, or wherever she'd prefer.

And as it turned out, Sunday could not have been more perfect: temperature in the low 70s, a slight breeze rippling across the surface of the lake, cottony clouds dotting the cerulean sky. They met at the Conservatory, a place neither had ever visited. Kevin always enjoyed exploring new places, ideas, people. He hoped Cassie did too.

He once again fell to monopolizing the conversation. He didn't mean to. But every time he asked her a question, she expertly maneuvered the conversation so he ended up being the one answering.

As they walked along a path in the orchid room of the glass house, he took her hand and asked the generic, "So tell me about you." He knew better than that. After all, his job consisted of eliciting thoughtful responses from his students who usually had little to say. Not surprisingly, his directive did not elicit much information.

"Tell me everything," Kevin tried again. This was still admittedly clumsy. As a writer and professor, he knew better. These vague, general requests do little to extract any more than vague, general responses.

Cassie provided the standard rundown: born and raised in Chicago, parents still married, mother recuperating after a fall, dad retired, no siblings, history degree from University of Illinois, job at the Chicago

Historical Foundation, as he already knew, and her recent promotion to associate curator.

When they left the Conservatory, they wandered the garden until they came across an empty park bench and took a seat. He took the opportunity to ask about her interest in history. He had been particularly curious about her interest in history since that was clearly something they had in common. But the question seemed to stump her. She hadn't really thought about why she studied history, she admitted, appearing a bit lost in that realization. By now, Kevin could see that it was the logical choice for her. He guessed that she found it easier to live in the stories of others rather than to create her own. He understood the draw of that. He also understood the danger of that. He was inclined to get lost in the stories he researched and had to make a conscious effort to create a life outside of the library. And he hoped that meeting Cassie would be a step in that direction.

Kevin realized it would take a careful excavation to uncover the real story, which he knew was buried in there somewhere.

He shook his head. Did he really just use the word excavation? He did love excavating. It was his life's work. He excavated when he gave voice to the individuals who had been lost to history. He found that in all his research, the study of history is typically divided into the good guys and the bad guys of the political theater and industrialist speculation. What is lost are the stories of average people who live at the mercy of the good guys and bad guys, distinctions that constantly shift. Kevin was driven to bring the voiceless back to life.

His obsession began with a faded photo of his great-grandparents that was displayed in a mother-of-pearl frame on a shelf in his family's living room. It had been simply part of the background noise as he grew up until one day when a neighbor asked his mother about the photo. He was ten. His mother mentioned something about World War I, which got his attention. After all, a set of little iron soldiers stood in formation in his bedroom, and he spent hours mapping out complicated battle plans when he should have been sleeping. He pushed the neighbor aside, much to his mother's horror, to see what photo she could possibly have been talking about. And there he was. His mother's grandfather, Private Thomas D. Martin, standing at ease in his army uniform with his arm around a slight, teenaged girl in a flowered dress.

The two had met in Batchtown, located on the other side of the state between the Illinois and Mississippi Rivers, his mother further explained, right before he left to fight in World War I. The young girl was heartsick at his departure, and the story goes that she wrote him daily. The letters, unfortunately, didn't survive. Little did from that time. He was home on leave for Christmas in 1917, and the two of them snuck off to spend some time alone.

He returned to the front.

She came up pregnant.

He was killed in the Second Battle of the Somme.

She died in childbirth.

That led to Kevin's first novel, *Fighting on All Fronts*. He sought to uncover not only their story but stories of others like them, stories lost to time, people lost to memory.

He dug through unexamined primary sources that illuminated the lives of people never considered. And when he wasn't digging, he was writing their stories, or rather he wrote his best version of their stories.

So the less Cassie revealed, the more interested in her Kevin became. He didn't have the sense that she purposely hid information from him. Rather, he sensed that she felt she had nothing worthwhile to share. She made no apologies for it and swore she had led a fairly uneventful life, nothing like the characters Kevin wrote about in his books or academic journals. But he knew that wasn't true.

She was a story to conquer.

Chapter 49

November 1994

Kevin introduced Cassie to his family pretty early on. They lived on the west side, and he visited his family quite often. It was only natural to bring her with him one of those times. She was unnecessarily nervous to meet them. He had a large family, two sisters and three brothers. And seven nieces and nephews. It was a bit chaotic, and that could be intimidating, he supposed. But they welcomed just about anybody into the fold. Not that Cassie was just about anybody.

His family thought she was lovely, in a very general sense. They would get to know her just as he was starting to. She just needed time.

Once he had welcomed her into his family, he was anxious to meet hers. She rarely talked about her own mother or father and seemed to rarely spend time with them. And he had never heard her mention any extended family. No cousins or aunts or uncles.

He knew that her mother had recently been put in a nursing home; she had been admitted after a failed surgery on her knee. She would wait there until doctors could reschedule the procedure. Cassie didn't expand beyond that.

But Kevin gently pushed. He hoped meeting her mother would give him some insight into Cassie. He knew from his research that within families lie the secrets to the future. Not that history is destiny. He didn't believe that. But he was well aware that people create a persona to show the world while underneath, storms rage unattended. None of us can escape that.

Cassie finally gave in to his playful appeals to meet her mother, and as a result, her father. The agreed-upon day was a rainy one full of downpours followed by periods of light mist. Cassie was a mixture of nervous chatter followed by long bouts of silence.

They took the train and then a bus before walking the final five blocks to reach the house where she grew up and where Kevin would meet Cassie's father for the first time. Cassie looked up at Kevin for reassurance before they walked up the sidewalk to the front door, and she let him take her hand; he gave it a little squeeze to remind her that he was right there with her. He rang the doorbell, and when they heard the deadbolt unlock and saw the doorknob turn, she dropped his hand.

The door opened, and a small, reticent man, reminiscent of another time, of the people and the times Kevin often wrote about, stood staring at them. Something about the stoic, unemotional man, robotically going through the motions of life intrigued Kevin. There was much more to him, whether Cassie realized it or not. He had experienced love and hate, fear and pride, thought Kevin, even if he was an expert at squashing all evidence of such. And there are so many others just like him, not only today, but throughout history: nameless, faceless cogs in a machine they have no control over and, seemingly, no opinion about.

"Kevin, this is my dad," Cassie said.

"David," her father responded, his arm outstretched for a handshake. "Nice to meet you. We need to get going. Your mother is expecting us," he added.

The rain, which had taken a short break, started to fall again. Cassie's father did not invite them in, but holding keys in one hand and zipping his jacket closed with the other, he hurried them out to the car parked in the street. Kevin was disappointed. He had hoped to see Cassie's old bedroom, to sit at the table where she ate dinner every night. To poke fun at photos from her childhood hung on walls and propped up on shelves. To scrutinize a collection of dusty books filling a bookcase. But that door was closed on him.

"Is your dad always so affable?" Kevin whispered jokingly to Cassie as they followed him down the walkway.

Chapter 49

Cassie had no answer for that.

She offered Kevin the front seat and slipped into the back. The half-hour ride to the nursing home was punctuated with small talk between Kevin and David: What do you do for a living? Where do you work? Where did you grow up? Are your parents still alive? Where does your father work? The usual.

Once at the nursing home, the two followed her father into the front door, past the reception area, where he silently nodded to the woman seated at a desk who hadn't bothered to stop working on her crossword puzzle, and through a series of halls. He made a wrong turn at one point that left them at a dead end, but a staff member soon redirected the trio.

When the three of them arrived at the room, two nurses stood at the bedside. One read Leah's blood pressure while another gossiped about John and Marlena finally making love aboard John's private jet. Leah had been following *Days of Our Lives* for years and was delighted to find someone here who would dissect the intimate details of the lives of its fictional characters with her. When Leah spotted them in the doorway, she excitedly exclaimed, "You're here! Come in, come in!"

She patted her bed, inviting someone to sit with her while the one nurse removed the blood pressure cuff. Leah assured the other nurse that they could catch up on the aftermath of the affair tomorrow, and the two ladies left as Leah laughed and thanked them. This was not the mother Cassie had described to Kevin. She commanded the room.

But as soon as the nurses left, Leah fell back into her bed. Her eyes turned black, and her eyelids formed two frowns closing down over them. Her voice dropped to a tinny whisper. It was quite the transformation. Kevin glanced over at Cassie and David. If they had noticed the change, neither gave any indication of such.

"My blood pressure keeps dropping," Leah explained as an answer to a question that was never asked.

Then commenced a discussion between husband and wife about blood pressure that Cassie and Kevin silently stood witness to. Once that discussion was completed, Kevin introduced himself since it appeared no one else planned to. Cassie's mother tried to hold out her hand to shake Kevin's, but she was stopped short. The tubes of the IV got tangled under her arm. She apologized as she pulled the tubing out from under her, giving her more range of movement. They all politely waited for her to finish fiddling with the tubing so she could meekly shake his hand.

"Are you going to sit down?" Leah asked. No one sat on the end of the bed with her, but Cassie took one of the only two chairs and motioned to Kevin to take the other. He instead offered it to her father.

Cassie's mother and father supported most of the conversation although Leah did periodically interrupt their discussion to ask Kevin the same questions he had been asked on the ride over about his job, his family, and where he grew up. They hadn't been there long, maybe a half hour, when Cassie's father announced it was time to leave. They said their goodbyes. Leah pressed David on when he would return. David didn't commit. Once out of the room, Kevin glanced down the hall. An old man sat slumped in his wheelchair; he appeared to have fallen asleep and been forgotten.

Kevin had looked forward to meeting Cassie's parents, hopeful that meeting them would answer some questions. Instead, meeting them only generated more.

Chapter 50

March 1995

The funeral director had brought the coffin into the church in the morning, positioning it in the middle of the sparse alter before anyone else arrived.

Leah spent the last seven months lying immobile in a bed in the basement of an institution someone else checked her into. While there, she sank into the familiar feeling of abandonment. Her husband had attended to her at home for the previous couple of years, but the physical care she required had long ago surpassed his abilities. The emotional care that she required had never been addressed.

She spent those last months trapped in a mental reenactment of her time at Lakeside. She couldn't shake the feeling of being forgotten.

The longer she stayed, the more unsettled she grew, her mind convincing her she was at other times in her life, in other places. In her decreasing times of clarity, she thought about her father, whomever he might be, wherever he might be. Certainly, he left because of her. It was the only explanation she ever seriously considered. It made sense considering her own mother's lack of interest in her. She mourned her husband's distance and her daughter's indifference.

Her growing desperation drove everyone from her. But she couldn't help herself. She had been born seeking recognition and spent a lifetime begging for it. Yet here she was, exactly where she feared most:

invisible, irrelevant. Inconsequential.

Death didn't come when she begged for it. Instead, it came calling thirty years later. Were those thirty years a blessing? Or a curse? Who could say?

A white board on the wall behind the nurse's station listed the current patients at the home, patients who day after day, bided their time, existing as barely a ripple in a little pond. When Leah died in her sleep, the staff erased her. They had forgotten her before a new patient was moved into her bed.

The funeral was held at a local church that Leah sometimes attended after Cassie had moved out and her own mother had passed away. The community there provided her with some structure. David rarely joined her, but Leah didn't mind going alone.

But since she entered the nursing home, many changes had taken place in the church, including the installment of a new minister, who had previously met with David to collect a check from him and to finalize the arrangements. David had assumed that this minister, Reverend Baske, knew Leah from her time attending, but he had never heard of her. With so little information about the deceased, he relied on his pile of worn manila folders and pieced together sentences from past services he had performed.

The reverend had an annoying habit of patting down his comb-over and brushing off phantom dandruff flakes from his shoulder. He placed his notes on the pulpit, pressing his hands on the paper to straighten out the wrinkles. The two volunteer ushers arrived next, and Rev. Baske directed them to the entryway to greet family and friends. Soon after, the great oak doors in the back opened and in walked the husband (Rev. Baske checked his notes—ah yes, David) and the deceased's daughter (He couldn't find her name. Why wasn't her name here?). He jogged down from the alter and up the aisle to greet the family, both hands on top of his head holding down his hair. He waved the ushers aside, introduced himself, and led them to the first pew before returning to wait at the pulpit. Behind the husband and daughter, the ushers greeted a handful of the husband's family who had travelled in from Wisconsin for the service. The church was eerily silent other than the padding of feet shuffling to the pews.

Chapter 50

"Cassie, I have arranged for someone else to do the eulogy for your mother," David leaned in to whisper to his daughter.

The information didn't register on Cassie's face, but she balled up the paper in her hand and slipped it into her jacket pocket. And then a stranger sat down at the organ and broke the silence with a loud, unexpected, ominous chord before continuing with Pachelbel's Canon in D Major.

The minister opened the service: "I did not know Leah, but her husband has told me a great deal about her, and that when she was well, I have been told, she was very active in this church." He recounted a life in platitudes and clichés. A neighbor was called to the alter to deliver the eulogy that described someone who could have been anyone but as a result was no one.

There was no official ceremony at the gravesite, so Leah was lowered into the ground alone. A week later, once the grave marker had been installed, David called Cassie to join him to inspect the plot. The cemetery was outside the city, at least an hour drive. Tucked into a clearing, it was surrounded on three sides by what could only be called small forests. The road ran along the fourth side. The two parked on the street, for the site wasn't accessible by car, and they walked the well-worn path through the entrance and around the headstones.

Cassie's father pushed forward to his wife's plot. David had arranged for his wife to be buried beside her mother. As the only family Leah ever had, he thought this most appropriate. Cassie struggled to keep up. She had never been here before; she had never visited her grandmother's gravesite.

Abruptly, he stopped under the branches of an ancient oak. The large headstone to his left marked Cora O'Toole's grave. And in front of him lay the flat marker that displayed the name Leah Evans. David brushed away twigs and small rocks scattered atop her gravesite, not realizing he was tossing them onto Cora's grave.

Eventually, he announced, "So there it is. Ok. Let's go."

Chapter 51

September 1995

In the months since Leah's death, Kevin and Cassie spent more and more time together. So when the lease at her apartment expired in August, they moved in together. Kevin's apartment was the obvious choice; it was larger, and he had a lot more furniture than she did. Her place was still pretty sparse. She hadn't dedicated the time or money to buy much beyond the basics.

Kevin finished his research at the history foundation over the summer and was back at the university teaching, adjusting to being back in the classroom and on someone else's schedule. He hoped his manuscript would be ready for the publishers by December.

Tonight Kevin and Cassie were to attend a department dinner to celebrate the publication of a book written by one of his colleagues. They had held a similar congratulatory dinner on his behalf when he finished his book *Fighting on All Fronts*, so he felt obligated to attend.

Brrring, brrring.

Cassie was in the shower.

Brrring, brrring.

He was sitting at the kitchen table and checked over the notes for his current book while she showered.

Brrring, brrring.

Click.

The answering machine picked up.

"Hi. You've reached Cassie and Kevin. Please leave a message."

Kevin smiled hearing their names together. They had just changed the message a few days ago.

"Hello, Miss Evans. This is Sunset Estates, and I am calling about your father. We have just brought him in."

Kevin jumped up and ran to the phone.

"Hello? Hello. Hello, yes? You're calling for Cassie Evans? Can I help you?"

"Oh yes, certainly. We just admitted her father, Mr. David Evans, into our hospice program earlier today, and she is listed as his emergency contact."

"Ok, great. Let me get the address, and can I also have your phone number? I will have her call you back."

Kevin jotted down the information.

"Yes, his colon cancer is pretty advanced, so we don't see him being here for too long. But we want to assure you that we will do everything we can to keep him comfortable," the assistant at Sunset Estates assured him before hanging up.

Colon cancer. Cassie had never mentioned that he had cancer.

The water in the shower abruptly shut off. Kevin would have to break the news to Cassie.

Still in her robe and with a towel wrapped around her wet hair, Cassie dialed the number Kevin had written down, her hand shaking, for her father had never said anything about having cancer. Kevin stood at her side as she waited for someone to answer.

"Yes, I am returning a call from, from, uh, Claire? She called about my father, who was admitted today? … Yes, that's him … Ok … I don't understand. How could things have progressed so quickly? … Ok. Yes, can I come by tomorrow? … I can do that … Thank you."

Cassie hung up, walked right past Kevin, and returned to the bathroom, closing the door behind her.

Chapter 52

September 19, 1995

Journal Entry:

I packed an overnight bag so that I could stay at my parents' empty house for a couple of days to begin the process of sorting through a lifetime of belongings. It seems that this will be a journey backward as well as a launch forward.

When I pushed open the front door, what can only be described as a gust of wind from inside the house rushed past me and dissipated outside. I feel different already. I carried my suitcase upstairs into what used to be my bedroom. Nothing in the room signaled that a little girl once lived here. Did I actually live here? It is hard for me to imagine.

One of the arguments Kevin and I repeat is the question about my childhood. No, they aren't arguments. That isn't a fair assessment. He genuinely wants to get to know me. To understand me. And that means lots of questions. Questions that I never seem to have the answers to. I simply don't remember much from growing up, which surprises me. I had never really thought about it before Kevin started digging.

He encouraged me to start this journal. He thought it might help me get my thoughts together. It might jog my memory. I'm not sure it has. Will I be able to find the answers here, in the home I grew up in? I don't recognize it. But at the same time, I can't really explain what is different.

I opened up my suitcase and then pulled open the drawers of my dresser, one by one. Empty. All of them. Same with my old desk. The thin middle drawer contains only a few stray paperclips and a couple of pushpins that rattled around when I jerked the drawer open.

After unpacking into the emptiness, I crossed the hall to the master bedroom. The room is immaculate, with zero nonessentials. Atop the only side table is a small lamp and a thick book, *The Last Lion*. I flipped through the book, and a bookmark slipped out. I quickly returned the book to the table and stuffed the bookmark in randomly, glancing around to make sure no one saw. Of course, no one saw. The house is empty. The dresser top is bare. The closet is filled with my dad's clothes. Where are my mother's clothes? On the floor, a pair of sneakers and a pair of men's dress shoes. Not a pair of women's shoes in sight.

As I stood in the living room, I realized that the house is a shell of the home it had been. Only the requisite furniture remain: couch, chair, coffee table. Nothing superfluous. The pictures on the walls are gone. So are the ferns that sat in the windows. The books and souvenirs that lined the bookcases too. And other little touches have disappeared: the teapot on the stove, the throw rugs in the hallway, the album collection.

My father must have sold, donated, or thrown away pretty much everything after my mom died.

What he left was paperwork. A lot of paperwork. Nothing left of the contents of her overflowing china cabinet. No Waterford crystal, homespun Hummel characters. No jewelry, no silver. No childhood toys. Just charts and spreadsheets telling the story of our lives in numbers and columns.

I thought maybe he packed everything up and put it in the basement. I

Chapter 52

flipped on the light and made my way down the rickety steps, only to find empty shelves, discarded boxes, an overflowing garbage can, and an ashtray filled with cigarette butts.

Some broken-down boxes were stacked next to the garbage bin. And stacks of snapshots lined the bottom of the bin. Why would he throw pictures away? I dug them all out, tossing them into an empty shoebox, which I took upstairs so I could go through them.

Once upstairs, I dumped the photos onto the coffee table in the living room and ran my hands across them. The images moved from black and white to color, marking first days of school, birthday celebrations, and Christmas trees. The photos captured uneventful lives moving through time. They'd crystalized the mundane. One black and white photo from the 1950s jumped out as if a magician had willed the card to pop out of a deck. It's a photo I had never seen before, of a stranger I recognize.

The woman in the photo stands in a doorway frame, leaning against one of the door jambs. She isn't posing. She has been caught in what may have been the most honest moment of her life. She leans forward, one arm around her own waist. And her head bends back. Her black hair provides a stark contrast to her porcelain skin. And she laughs. The laugh is spontaneous and unconscious. And true.

This was my mother before she knew what life would hold for her.

There was little to do. It appeared my father had done most of the work before he died. I suppose I should be grateful. But there's also a part of me that resents his decision to wipe the house clean. I called an estate sale planner to handle what remained, basically the furniture and a few kitchen items. I will meet them here tomorrow. All that was left to do was to throw away any toiletries left in the bathrooms.

I found the car keys on the kitchen counter and went out to the garage. The car started right up, and I considered keeping it, but I quickly dismissed that idea. A car is an expense I can do without. I'll take it over to the local Chrysler dealer to see what they can offer me. As I went to flip off the light before leaving the garage, I spotted a box up in the rafters. Just one box, nothing else. I couldn't find a ladder and had to knock on the neighbor's door, neighbors who had lived in their house since I was a child, to borrow one. They expressed sympathy and mentioned that they hadn't seen my father in a while. Apparently he hadn't left the house in months.

They lent me a ladder, and I successfully retrieved the box, which I carried into the living room. On the outside in Sharpie are written the words "Mother's things." That's my mom's handwriting. On the side, faded letters spell out "Important Papers" written in a different hand.

Before facing that box, I'm going to make a quick trip to the grocery store to pick up a frozen pizza and bottle of wine. It is going to be a long night.

*****

The pizza was sausage and mushroom. The wine was a merlot. Kevin introduced me to merlot. The box contained family papers. I covered the coffee table and the floor around me with records from those who would have been my great-grandparents back in Ireland. Birth certificates of people I never heard of. A couple of death certificates. An honorable discharge from the US Navy. A marriage declaration of one Elizabeth Coughlin to Patrick Murray. A birth certificate listing the birth of Leah O'Toole.

Grandpa O'Toole was my mom's stepfather, so she would have had a different last name when she was born. But he did adopt her. My mother told me about this. And sure enough, there was his name on the line for FATHER. The birth certificate had indeed been changed. She was born in New York City. I didn't know that. Wasn't she from Portland? And she was born at St. Anne's Maternity Hospital. Maternity Hospital? What does that even mean?

One faded black and white photo highlighted a man holding a baby in his arms. The baby wears a bonnet and a big smile. The man is turned

Chapter 52

away from the camera, so his face is obscured. The photo is encircled by a scalloped border with the year 1935 printed in the middle of all four sides. The year my mother was born.

Is that my mother? Is that her father?

A small jewelry box held a chain with a harp charm dangling from it. A woman, maybe a mermaid, serves as the harp's column. It had tarnished over the years and is covered in a black coating, but it's clearly beautiful. I'll have to clean that.

A small rectangular wooden case was locked. After failing to find the key, I settled on breaking it open. It took a bit of work, but I succeeded. Inside was a stack of unopened letters. Five of them. All addressed to Cora Coughlin.

Cora was the name of my grandmother, but her last name was O'Toole. I had seen the name Coughlin somewhere in all this paperwork. I dug around. There it was. Coughlin. Cora Coughlin is the name on the marriage certificate. It must have been my grandmother's maiden name. The return address on one of the letters lists Florence Nicolo, and the rest are from Florence Davis, all from New York addresses.

My grandmother had obviously received the letters, but she locked them up unopened.

I poured another glass of wine. There was no question. I would read the letters. I organized them by date, from the earliest to the most recent, as listed on the postmarks. They had been sent over five years, the first in 1936, and all on the same date: February 9, my mother's birthday.

February 9, 1936

My dearest Cora,

    I have been thinking about you ever since I left St. Anne's. I hope you don't mind that the Sisters of Charitable Works gave me your address so I could contact you.

You might be surprised to hear that I left the same day you did. I have a cousin who lives outside the city. We hadn't seen each other since we were in diapers, but she welcomed me with a love I could not have imagined. She has invited me to stay with her family until I can find some work and my own place. The country is in such turmoil right now. So many people are out of work. I don't like depending on the kindness of people who, although family, barely know me. But I am grateful for them beyond comprehension.

I'm writing to thank you. Meeting you gave me the strength to finally leave St. Anne's. For too long, I was paralyzed by my own wounds and by the sisters who lacked any compassion. But I can't be too harsh. The place did serve me when I needed it. And when you needed it too. It provided shelter during a very difficult time, a time when your mother kicked you out, and you found yourself alone. And with child. So I am grateful to St. Anne's for being a beacon of hope for a lot of hopeless women, including both of us. But just as you had to leave to move on with your life, so did I. I didn't realize any of that until I faced my own past, my own pain, by sharing my story with you.

I am so proud of you. You kept your baby despite the unrelenting pressure to give her up, especially since you were all alone. Most of those young girls had their own mothers supporting them. They had families who could help out even if that meant pretending the baby was actually the grandmother's or a sister's or an older cousin's, someone who was already married and had agreed to the deception. But you had nobody. Nobody fighting for you or for your darling daughter. It was only you, fighting the social stigma and the demands to make the only moral choice to put both your life and your baby's life on course.

But it wasn't only that. You also freed me. From my own confinement. I don't know your story. I don't know how you came to find yourself young, pregnant, and alone. And I didn't need to know. It was clearly a story filled with anguish. A story

Chapter 52

you held close to your heart.

And this is the true reason I write to you today.

In your eyes, I saw myself reflected back. For my story had caused me merciless torment. So I buried it. But in weak moments, the memories pushed their way into my consciousness.

Memories are relentless like that. As much as I pushed them down, the truth still resided there, hidden in the shadows, lurking in the recesses of my body, ready to spring forth at the first sign of vulnerability. And I saw all of that in your eyes. Whatever happened to you preyed upon you.

That's why I confessed to you what I had been hiding from the world for years. And that confession set me free. It's true. Expose the Devil to the light of day. It's the only way to defeat Him. And it defeats Him every time.

That night, as we sat in the chapel at St. Anne's, and you cradled new life, innocent life, beautiful life, in your arms, you gave me the gift of being my confessor. A confessor devoid of judgement. There was no penance to be had, no sins to atone for, no threats of eternal punishment, no repentance needed, no begging for mercy. What greeted me was simply a loving heart, a heart that had likewise suffered terribly in this imperfect world.

I no longer need to hide myself and my shame within St. Anne's, a place that had buried my secrets even deeper. And I shed the persona I had built there, Louisa, a woman with no past who sought to erase Florence.

You set me free. I can only hope the same for you. I hope you have found freedom. You have nothing to hide.

I send you all the love I can muster to rain down upon you and your little girl on her first birthday. She is pure love, and she is your salvation.

Love always,
Florence

February 9, 1937

My dearest Cora,

Your precious daughter celebrates her second birthday today. And I send my wishes for blissful happiness to both you and to her. Please give her an extra little squeeze from a woman she doesn't know but who loves her contribution to this earth immeasurably.

I met a gentleman last year. He is wonderful: loving, strong, forgiving, and of course handsome! He feels like home. He knows everything about me and loves me unconditionally.

We married in December and moved out of the city. But not before visiting St. Anne's one last time. I am an old woman, 37 this year. And he is of the same age. But he has been a bachelor all these years. And the abortion my mother inflicted on me left me unable to ever have children of my own. So he granted me the grandest gift a man could have given me.

Imagine Sister Rosella's shock when I strolled into the hospital with Mr. Andrew Davis on my arm! I still giggle at it. I told her I wanted to adopt a baby, but that I would do so on my terms. I would interview the girls residing there and find the one who had no doubts about giving up her baby. I didn't wait for an answer. I led Andy to the nursery where five babies napped. According to the folder on the nursery desk, which I helped myself to, there were two little ones who had not yet found adoptive parents: one a boy and the other a girl.

I told Sister Rosella to direct me to the mothers of those two babies, one at a time. She was quick to obey my commands (I certainly got a kick out of that!). She said she would fetch them and bring them to meet us in the parlor.

Can you imagine how surreal it was for me to be sitting on the other side of this process, in the arms of a wonderful man, waiting in the parlor?

The first girl walked in, clearly frightened. As you know, adoptive parents were never to meet with the real mothers. I assured her that I wasn't there to take her baby from her. I told her about my years working at St. Anne's and that helped drop

Chapter 52

the barrier she naturally built between herself and the rest of the world. After talking for a little bit, I left her and Andy while I went to the office to seek the file cabinet. I knew where all the paperwork was in that place. Nothing would have changed. And I was right.

I found the form the young mothers can sign that forbids St. Anne's from adopting out a baby. And I brought it back for her to sign. Sister Rosella spotted me and confronted me in the parlor. She wanted me to leave these girls alone. But I know her secrets, the ones she never wants to leave this building. I had observed too much and overheard too much. So her threats were hollow.

The young girl signed the paper and embraced me with a relieved hug. I told her, in earshot of Sister Rosella of course, that I would be following up to make sure no one would take her baby from her. I told Sister Rosella to bring in the other woman, which she did.

This second woman could have not been more different than the first. She felt completely put upon to be required to come speak with Andy and me. She made it perfectly clear that she did not want to have anything to do with her baby. She had been forced to lay with a man, she told us unemotionally, and she wanted to finish her time here so she could forget everything about what had happened.

I would have loved to have spent time counseling her about her anger, but at least she was honest about what had happened to her. That was the first step toward her healing. But right then, I simply wanted to save that baby. I thanked her and told her she was free to leave.

I had found the baby I would be taking home. And I would be doing so that very day. Sister Rosella protested, as you can imagine, until she realized I wasn't going anywhere without that baby. She walked out to retrieve the paperwork. Andy and I laughed when we realized that we didn't even know which baby was hers, the boy or the girl. Sister Rosella returned with the paperwork, which the two of us quickly signed.

> As we approached the front entryway, a sister I didn't recognize held a beautiful baby boy in her arms. He was swaddled in a scratchy blanket and clearly uncomfortable. I took the baby in my arms and thanked God for the path that led me here.
>
> So I am now the proud mother of a darling boy! Andrew Davis II. We call him Drew. And I couldn't be happier.
>
> I wanted to share my happiness with you. Hope you got a kick out of me being able to put Sister Rosella in her place. That was fun!
>
> I hope you have found some peace in your life.
>
> Love always,
> Florence

I put the rest of the letters down and emptied my glass, savoring the flavors rolling across my tongue.

St. Anne's. I recognized the name. I dug through the papers spread out around me. There it was: my mother's birth certificate. She was born at St. Anne's Maternity Hospital in New York City. Florence must have worked there and met my grandmother there.

I poured another glass of wine and swirled the liquid like I've watched Kevin do countless times before taking a sip.

Why would she have been there? "Fallen" women? It sounded like a place for unwed mothers. Then it hit me. Oh my god. My grandmother was an unwed mother. That explains why my mom didn't know who her father was. Did her father even knew my grandmother was pregnant? She wouldn't be the only one in this family to keep that information from a father.

What was that about having experienced something horrific? What had Florence written? I searched for the phrase. "A story filled with anguish." This didn't sound like a couple of teenagers who let their

Chapter 52

hormones get the best of them. Had her family disowned her as a result of whatever happened? That would explain why my mother wasn't allowed to ask about her real father and why I've never met anyone from my grandma's side of the family.

And Florence wrote that my grandmother kept her baby. That baby must have been my mother. And she cradled her baby, my mother, in the chapel. It sounds so beautiful and full of love. But was it? It sounds like my grandmother put up the fight of her life for my mom. I can't believe it. She must have loved her deeply, at least in the beginning. What happened?

I glanced at the return addresses. The return address on the first one must be her cousin's house. The address on the others must have been where she lived with her husband and where they raised their baby boy.

Chapter 53

September 20, 1995

Journal Entry:

I fell asleep on the living room floor. When I woke up, the sun was already high in the sky. The last time I remember looking at the clock, it was 4 AM. I woke to an annoying pounding deep in my head. I found bottle of aspirin in the master bedroom medicine cabinet, but I dropped that and a couple of other things still in the cabinet into the trash and settled for a large glass of water as a remedy.

I had spent the night trying to make sense of what I found in that box. My father must not have known about it. Or maybe he forgot about it. Otherwise I imagine he would have purged it with everything else. I like to think this was a clue my grandmother left, left for me actually, to finally reveal what couldn't be faced. What not even my mother could face, for she also left these letters unopened and hidden. I laughed out loud trying to imagine how my mother could have possibly gotten the box up in the rafters without my dad's help. It was a laugh I never would have afforded her when she was alive. If I had to guess, I'd say she had never climbed a ladder in her life. But I'm learning.

On top of my list of things to do was to call the crematorium that picked up my father's remains from the hospice. They told me that they would deliver him to Hillside Cemetery today. They let me know that he had already made all the arrangements. I thanked them and hung up.

Hillside Cemetery. Where is that? And why there? My grandmother and mother were buried at Oakdale. I was already concerned that my grandmother wasn't buried with her husband, and instead, she had been alone for all those years before my mother joined her.

But now it turns out that my father will not be interred with his wife. He is going to Hillside Cemetery.

A knock on the door startled me. It was the neighbors who had loaned me the ladder. As soon as I saw them out the window standing at the door, I remembered that I hadn't returned it. I apologized before they had a chance to say anything. But they weren't worried about it. They wanted to know the plans for the memorial.

There would be no memorial.

My father had explicitly and repeatedly stated that he didn't want any type of memorial or ceremony. He had made this announcement when my mom died. I protested, but my voice went unheard. However, I heard him.

I called Kevin. He was glad I made so much progress. I told him I didn't need to stay another night. Pretty much everything is done here. He told me he loves me. I whispered back that I love him too. And I really do.

The doorbell rang again. The people conducting the estate sale had arrived to negotiate a price to empty my parents' house. The whole thing felt cold and calculating, which it was, but we easily came to an agreement. I told them I would leave the key under the front doormat. They could let themselves in over the weekend so that they could price items for the coming sale.

Chapter 53

I want nothing to do with any of it. I included in my negotiations that I would like them to arrange for anything that doesn't sell to go to Goodwill or the Salvation Army or Vietnam Vets or wherever. The next time I'm here, I want the house to be empty so I can replace the carpet, bring in painters, and put it up for sale.

They glanced around; there wasn't much, mostly standard furniture, none of the knickknacks, framed pictures, artwork, books, or china that fill most homes. But one of the gentleman spotted the two tea tins from Queen Elizabeth's coronation that I had left out on the coffee table last night when going through the box.

Back when Princess Di married Charles, my mother reminisced about living with my grandmother and grandfather in London during the coronation of Queen Elizabeth. As a child, she stood among the throngs lining the streets and waving the Union Jack. They bundled up for hours on the Mall awaiting the procession and a glimpse of the Queen. She lit up when she retold the story, immersing herself in the memory. There weren't many stories that lit her up.

"Those right there might be worth something. They're in great shape," I was told.

"No, I'm keeping those," I responded, to their disappointment.

These marked a day of happiness that I want to hold onto. Because I'm getting a sense there weren't enough of those days.

We shook hands, and they left. I'm exhausted from glimpsing into lives I didn't know.

I separated the things that I wanted to take with me. The shoebox full of the photos I dug out from the garbage, the harp necklace, the letters, and the family documents. The coronation tins. And a folder of the important financial papers I would need: the mortgage, the title to the car, a list of bank and brokerage accounts, pension details, and a variety of statements from bills I would need to cancel.

I put the box in the trunk of my car. I went back inside one more time, to say goodbye, I guess. A real estate agent would handle the sale of the house. A handyman could come in and do some minor repairs before the carpet was replaced and the walls repainted to make the house sell-ready, but I wasn't interested in any major renovations in order to squeeze as much as I could out of the place. I wanted the break to be clean and easy.

As I was about to close the door, the phone rang. Reminder: cancel the phone. But I ran back inside to answer it. It was Hillsdale Cemetery. They had received my father's remains yesterday afternoon and wanted to inform me that they entombed the ashes in a columbarium on their grounds that morning. The gentleman on the other end of the line assured me that they took care of everything. He read me the coordinates of my father's resting place and wished me a good day, an odd sendoff considering the circumstances. But before he hung up, I asked if he could give me the address of the cemetery.

"You don't have that?" he asked. I heard the surprise in his voice.

He read off the address. I also asked for directions so I would be able to find it on my map. He gave me the general area. It was about an hour south of here. He finished with "Ok then," and he hung up. I hurried out to the car to grab a pen from my purse so I could quickly write the address down before forgetting it. I chanted it to myself on the way out: 15 Hillsdale Road, 15 Hillsdale Road, 15 Hillsdale Road.

I walked back up to the front door, locked the deadbolt before slipping the key under the doormat, and took one last look before I climbed into my father's car. All personal touches, all indications that a family had once lived here, all evidence of warmth had been stripped from the place. Maybe the house never had those things, and I am only seeing that for the first time. My mother tried to make a home. She surrounded us with the accruements of a home. But she never felt at home either.

Chapter 53

I lost the fight to hold back the tears. Those were strange tears. I wouldn't say I was crying. I wasn't. I was perfectly calm, and nothing in my body or in my expression would indicate to an onlooker what I felt. But the tears spilled out as a river gently overflows its banks, the water washing over the land. Surface material washes away, floating downstream. But those were temporary inhabitants that were only passing through anyway: rocks, leaves, sticks, plants. The larger elements hold on tighter: trees, people, houses. But with a big enough wash, even they will be rinsed away, leaving only the foundation. The land remains while it lets everything else go without a fight and without mourning. And after patiently waiting for the water to recede, the land rebuilds, without bitterness or sense of loss.

No, it's not about this house. The house was washed away long ago.

Then, I threw up. I actually threw up. It came on so quick. All I could do was open the car door and vomit right there in the street. But I instantly felt better.

Since it was still early, I located Hillsdale Cemetery on my map and drove south.

Hillsdale Cemetery is a huge expanse of land with tombstones extending beyond the horizon. A map near the entrance shows that the columbarium is all the way in the back of the property. So I wound my way across a hundred and fifty acres of buried bodies. I was able to pull my car right up to the spot. I could see the compartment where my father's ashes had been placed. The plaque glinted in the sun, obviously newly installed, and it was inscribed with my father's name, birth date, and date of death. I guess he planned that too.

So here I sit. I don't feel compelled to get out of the car. I wish I knew what to say to him, but I come up blank.

It's time to go home. To Kevin.

Chapter 54

October 13, 1995

Journal Entry:

Kevin is as fascinated about what I found in the box at my parents' house as I am. That's his thing. Stories.

It was his idea. To visit the addresses on the envelopes and try to find Florence or her son. The cousin's house where she had stayed for a bit after leaving St. Anne's was in Brooklyn, and Florence's later address was in New Rochelle.

Do I really want to do this? According to her age in the second letter, this Florence would be in her nineties. It's unlikely she would still be alive. But Kevin said, "No matter." And he wanted to go with me. It would be a great adventure, he promised. He likes to think of himself as a cunning detective, a modern day Sherlock Holmes. But I suppose that is what he has dedicated his life's work to. Unraveling the mysteries of the silent casualties of history. He has spent incalculable hours reading letters, diaries, court papers, census records, and other documents in an attempt to uncover the daily lives of ordinary people. What he has continuously found is that there are no ordinary people and no ordinary lives. So my finding those letters lit his curiosity kindling on fire.

And I am starting to think this trip might be important for me too. Maybe I can get some answers. I can say I never really knew my mother. I certainly didn't know my grandmother. And has anyone ever really known me? Do I know me? It's a question I keep asking. So often I struggle to find memories, and I fight to discover whether I have anything to say.

This journal has helped me though. Thoughts I didn't even know I had have spilled onto these blank pages. I'm learning there is more to me than I ever understood.

I write this from the window seat on our flight to JFK. I've never been to New York City, so even if we find nothing, it will be a nice escape for the two of us.

Maybe we can even visit St. Anne's. If it still exists.

Chapter 55

October 1995

Kevin was as eager to find out about Cassie's family as she was. Maybe even more so. He only met her mother the one time when she was in the nursing home. She died not too long after that. He had sensed that there must be more to her story than Cassie had ever been privy to. And it now appeared he was right.

This was Cassie's first time to New York City. Kevin had been many times, so he treated her to a day filled with all the required tourist attractions. They visited Times Square, ate dollar pizza slices, enjoyed a sidewalk cafe, and rode bikes in Central Park. He was of the belief that everyone had to go to these places at least once in their life.

They also explored the New York Historical Museum, which was hosting an exhibition about Prohibition in New York. Kevin already sent his completed manuscript on the SS Eastland disaster to the publisher. For his next project, he was considering uncovering the hidden stories buried in one of the old, abandoned moonshine towns. That meant he was currently interested in all things Prohibition. Cassie was kind enough to indulge him.

"Tony?"

Kevin stopped when he heard Cassie call out to someone, but he didn't recognize the man. The man didn't respond.

Cassie tried again. "Tony? Is that you?"

The gentleman, whose eyes signaled that he was close to their age but whose full, untamed beard made him come across as years older, heard her this time.

"I haven't seen you since grad school!" she said.

"I'm sorry?" he responded. "Grad school? At Northwestern?"

"Yes, Cassie Evans? We were in that Cultural Heritages Collections seminar together."

"Cassie! Yes, you always sat at the back corner near the bust of Louis Sullivan."

She laughed. That was true. That's where she sat. She noticed the NY Historical Museum badge hanging from his suit pocket.

"You're working here? That's great!"

"I am. Got the job right out of school. How have you been? Are you living here in New York too?"

"No, no. I'm still in Chicago." She motioned for Kevin to join her. "This is Kevin. We're here visiting. Hoping to see some, see some …." She looked up at Kevin as she searched for the word she wanted. Then she found it, and she finished her sentence. "Some family. And Kevin is working on a book about Prohibition, so he really wanted to see what was here."

After that, Kevin and Tony launched into a conversation about the exhibit, an exhibit that Tony was largely responsible for. Kevin was salivating over the documents the museum might have that could be useful. They all exchanged information, and Kevin promised to return to peruse items in storage that didn't make it out to the public areas.

Then it was time to get to the business of why they had come to the city in the first place.

The first stop was Lexington Avenue. St. Anne's no longer existed. The building was still there, but it had long ago been converted into apartments. The return address on Florence's last letter was the next stop, the house where she and her husband had most likely lived.

After two trains and a ten-minute walk, they arrived. The lawn had long ago died, and a few newspapers collected on the steps leading up to the front door. Cassie picked up the papers and knocked on the door. Kevin liked this side of her. Taking charge. And not checking with him for approval or support. It was showing itself more and more often.

Chapter 55

The two of them held their breath and listened for signs of movement. There was nothing. Until a car pulled up and parked right in front of the house.

"Can I help you?" A woman about Cassie's age stepped out of the car and approached them.

"Yes," Cassie offered. "We're looking for someone who used to live here. Florence Davis? Did you happen to know her?"

The woman smiled as she brushed past to unlock the front door. "Yes. That's my grandma. How do you know her?"

Cassie and Kevin exchanged shocked glances. It couldn't possibly be this easy. Could it?

"I'm sorry," Cassie said as she held out her hand. "I'm Cassie. My grandmother may have been friends with your grandmother. I found some letters Florence Davis wrote to her using this return address." She held out the letters for the woman to see.

The woman motioned for them to come inside. "I'm Debra. Nice to meet you both. And I can take those from you," she said, offering to take the old newspapers from Cassie.

Debra dropped her purse, her jacket, and the papers on a chair in the entryway. She invited them to join her in the living room and readied herself for what these two strangers might have to share about her grandmother.

But first, Debra revealed that Florence was indeed still alive. And 95 years old. "But a few months ago, we had to shoo her out of this house and move her to an assisted-living facility. She had been doing so great until one day when she forgot she had turned on the stove to heat up some soup. She simply forgot. The liquid boiled down to nothing. I happened to come over that day, and as soon as I walked in, the smell overwhelmed me. It was pure chance that she didn't burn the place down. We had been worried about her living alone, but we didn't have evidence of her struggling. Until that day. So I've been coming by as much as possible to pick up the mail, make sure everything is ok here. My brother and I haven't decided whether to sell the place or not."

Cassie ran her finger across the letters in her hand. Kevin let the silence fill the room. He knew Cassie needed to handle this.

"Do you know that your grandma worked at a maternity hospital in the city, one called St. Anne's?" Cassie finally asked.

"I do! It was because of her years there that she adopted my dad, right there from St. Anne's. And why my parents adopted both me and my brother."

Cassie leafed through the handful of letters. "That's where she met my grandmother. At least as far as I can tell from these letters."

Yes, Debra knew all about her grandmother's time at St. Anne's and about what brought her there in the first place: her stepfather, the abortion, the death of her mother. It was a story Debra doesn't remember having been told because it was simply a part of their family history, nothing to be ashamed of, nothing to bury in the cellar, nothing to deny. It was a story they shared.

The truth explained her father's adoption and even her own. People handle the news that they are adopted in many different ways; some ways are healthy, and some are not. Many adopted children grow up feeling betrayed or lied to. They feel abandoned. They feel rejected. But Kevin was in awe seeing that Debra experienced only gratitude. She understood how the experiences of the people she called family led her directly to them.

"Is your grandma still alive?" Debra asked Cassie.

"No, she died a long time ago. I think I spent a lot of time with her when I was young, but I don't remember much about her."

"I'm so sorry to hear that. I have always been close to my grandma. It hasn't always been easy for her, but she has had an amazing life," Debra said.

"I don't think it was easy for my grandma either, but I'm also not sure whether she had an amazing life. She and my mom weren't close. I never understood why. But now I'm realizing that she was born in a maternity hospital, with no father. Or family."

Debra jumped up.

"Let's go visit my grandmother. Maybe she has some answers for you. And if not, it'll still be worth the trip. She loves to have visitors!"

Kevin and Cassie had no need to consult each other. They followed Debra out the door and into her car. The car ride was filled with the small talk that often occupies the space between virtual strangers. When they arrived, they followed Debra into the assisted-living facility, and she was greeted by a staff who was clearly used to seeing her there. No one had to direct her to her grandma's room. In fact, Kevin and Cassie struggled to keep up with her as she navigated her way purposefully through the building.

Chapter 56

October 15, 1995

Journal Entry:

A strange mixture of nervousness, fear, curiosity, and guilt brewed in my core as we approached the facility to meet Florence. Kevin held one hand. My other hand grasped the stack of letters.

When we entered her room, Florence was listening to the radio. Debra flew into her grandmother's arms, and the two erupted in laughter. It was like watching two children who lack the scars of the suffering that life brings embrace love itself.

"And who are these nice people you brought, Deb-do?" This must be her pet name.

Debra pulled Kevin and me deep into the room and introduced us to her grandmother.

I hesitated. But with help from the pressure of Kevin's hand on my back, I stepped forward and took the empty chair at the small bistro table. Florence switched off the radio, which had been playing at a volume not conducive to a conversation.

"Gram, Cassie thinks she knows someone from your past," Debra said.

Florence ran her fingers across the table until she found one of my hands, and she squeezed it lightly.

I studied her, searching for a sign of the shocking story Debra shared of how she ended up at St. Anne's. But it wasn't there. Her eyes danced. Then I realized that she was studying me, and it felt like she could see right into my soul. I willfully absorbed her spirit and lost myself in the grey-blue orbs glinting in the light and floating in the filmy whites of her eyes, parts of which were obscured by folds of skin that encroached on the openings, much like curtains pulled over windows late in the day.

"I brought some letters you wrote to my grandmother. Her name was Cora Coughlin."

A cloud parted from her eyes, and she dropped my hand. She remembered. And I braced for what she might tell me.

She reached out to cup my face with both of her trembling hands, which calmed when connected with my cheeks.

"My dear, you are a miracle. I feel blessed to be looking in the eyes of Cora's granddaughter. Yes, I knew your grandmother. For a very brief time in her life. A very painful time in her life. I met your mother too. The day she was born."

"I think something terrible may have happened to my grandmother," I told my confessor.

Florence confirmed my fears. Something horrible indeed had happened to her. But more importantly, she advised me, "Don't fear the truth, no matter how upsetting. It is that fear which causes us to retreat rather than to charge forth in life."

But my grandma, Cora, perhaps in her own fear of the truth, never

Chapter 56

disclosed her story to Florence. Florence concluded that she may have been raped. Especially since she never had any visitors or mail; it appeared she had been abandoned by everyone who at one time may have loved her, including her own mother. Hundreds of girls made their way through St. Anne's. And Florence said she could quickly tell the difference between the girls who had tempted fate by laying with their beaus and those who found themselves pregnant through more odious means. And despite her protestations, my poor grandmother clearly qualified for the second group.

I placed the stack of letters on the table between us. Florence picked up the first one and smiled at the familiar writing on the envelope from so many years ago. I felt obligated to tell her that when I found them, they had never been opened.

Florence wasn't surprised. But she was saddened.

"It didn't have to be that way," she said. "It was Cora," she paused, "who changed my life and to whom I will forever be indebted." Florence pulled the memory from deep within. "Right after Cora's baby was born, I asked her to meet me in the little chapel at St. Anne's." Florence rested a moment to gather her thoughts before finishing. In the chapel, Florence confessed her secret to Cora, my grandmother, a secret she had previously sworn to take to her grave.

"I hoped I could provide Cora with the courage to confess her battle," she added.

To her dismay, Cora responded by locking her secret up even tighter. But for Florence, her own release gave her hope for a different life. She left St. Anne's the same day my grandma left, married the love of her life, adopted a baby boy, and lived long enough to meet her adopted grandchildren. They were open adoptions, so the children would know the names of their biological mothers. What they did with that information was up to them. But no secrets, Florence emphasized.

It appears that St. Anne's was in the business of forcing the adoption of the babies born to women who lacked the "righteous morals" required to raise a child. And it was my grandma that led Florence to stop believing in that business. And despite the pressure that the sisters put on her, Florence had convinced my grandmother to keep her baby, the baby who would grow up to be my mother. Florence had always wondered if that was the right decision for Cora. But with me, Cora's granddaughter, sitting next to her, she could see that it had always been the right decision.

Florence explained that she believed the road to redemption required facing what had happened. She wrote to my grandma with the hope that the two of them would become close, and Cora would finally face whatever it was that happened to her. But eventually her letters were returned, and Florence lost track of Cora.

For a moment, Florence sat in silence. Debra got up from her chair and went over to check on her. I had forgotten anyone else was in the room. But then I caught a glint of something around Debra's neck.

"Your necklace. Can I see it?" I asked Debra.

Debra's free hand grasped the charm that dangled from the chain around her neck and held it out for me to see. I immediately recognized it. It was the same Irish harp that was in my grandmother's things. With the same mermaid holding up the pillar of the harp.

Florence explained. "That day in the chapel? Your grandmother noticed my necklace. Turns out that both our mothers had given us this same harp charm. It was meant to serve as a reminder of our ability to bring forth life from the clutches of death," Florence closed her eyes as she visualized the past. "But your grandmother lost hers. So I gave her mine. I thought she needed it more than I did." She pointed to Debra's necklace. "This one isn't exactly the same, but while on a trip to Ireland years ago, I found that one for Debra."

Chapter 56

"I think I have your necklace," Cassie realized. "I found it in my mother's things."

"Oh isn't that wonderful!" Florence was tickled with the news. "That is her gift to you then."

Both Kevin and I thanked the two of them for their willingness to share the day and their lives with us. And I am forever grateful. I feel like creating gratitude has been instrumental in Florence's life. And she has passed that legacy on to her granddaughter.

I placed Florence's letters on the table to leave with her.

But before we left the room, Florence called to us one more time. "What did Cora name that sweet little girl?"

Leah. She named her Leah.

Chapter 57

October 18, 1995

Journal Entry:

I've had a few days to digest the trip to New York. I love that Kevin and I were able to spend some uninterrupted time together, something we too often forget to make room for. And I love that we were able to meet Florence. Remarkable. I can't help but wonder if her attitude helped her live for decades longer than not only my grandmother but also my mother.

Last night, I sorted through the folder of paperwork that I brought from the house. I pulled out the information I needed regarding my father's pension and IRA plus his bank account number. But there were other papers as well. A yellowed newspaper article with the headline, "Mr. and Mrs. Evans Killed in Tragic Accident" dated April 3, 1961. A year after I was born. Was this about my father's parents? The ones who died when I was a baby? I skim through the article. They were killed by a drunk driver. I had never heard that. No one ever talked about it or about them. And I never asked. I didn't even know to ask.

There's more. My birth certificate. Dog tags: O'Toole. Robert T. My mom's passport. A discharge receipt from a mental hospital: Lakeside

Institute. May 10, 1961-February 1, 1962. Mrs. Leah Evans.

I didn't know. I was only a baby then. My heart hurts.

The little box holding the harp pendant had been sitting unopened on my dresser since I brought it home. But after meeting Florence, I was anxious for another look. Years of exposure left the delicate features of the harp and the mermaid that embraces it badly tarnished.

I found a jeweler that's close to the foundation. I tucked the necklace into my purse and took it to the jeweler on my next lunch break.

I could see an old man behind a counter through the dirty window, but the door to his store was locked. I assumed he saw me, but he waddled off and disappeared. Then I heard a buzz. He had buzzed me in. I quickly pulled open the door and slipped inside.

"What can I do ya' for?" he asked in a voice that sounded like his mouth was filled with gemstones.

I laid the necklace on the counter. He waddled over, his body a sturdy barrel supported by two thin legs that looked like they could snap at any moment. He bent over to inspect the piece, and I found myself staring at the top of his head, where wisps of hair danced around as if he had barely escaped being swept up into a tornado. He reached under the counter and pulled out a loupe to get a closer look.

"I was wondering how I clean this. If it even can be cleaned," I said to disrupt the silence. And it worked. He came alive.

"Most definitely. This tarnish is only a thin layer on top of the silver," he began. "It's all actually quite brilliant. It works like this." He became lost to the wonder of the process, like a professor so completely engrossed in explaining the War of 1812 that he forgets his lecture is not supposed to be for his own benefit but that it should be for the benefit of the students. I have a feeling Kevin might do the same when he stands in front of a classroom. I smiled at the thought, admiring the jeweler's passion.

"This piece is sterling silver. That's what you want. You wouldn't want this to be made of pure silver. It's much too soft. It would never withstand the bumps and bruises that come from hanging around someone's neck. But that also means that there are other metals mixed in, primarily copper. It's the copper that is responsible for the tarnish."

He ran his stubby fingers over my harp. I couldn't imagine how those hands could work with the delicate pieces displayed in the cabinet.

"Here's the thing with jewelry. It is meant to be worn! That's what I always say. It's not meant to be kept hidden away in a box or a closet." His voice had risen angrily. "But," he warned, "that also means it will be exposed, exposed to the harshness of the world, the pollutants, all of it. But the copper, ah, the copper. It knows what to do. It doesn't retreat from the world. Oh no. It fights back. And it protects the vulnerable silver by creating this cover, this layer of armor."

So I learned that the ugly tarnish that covers jewelry, silverware, and tea sets actually serves as a protective measure. I had just assumed the black goop was a destructive agent. But no, it doesn't destroy what is inside. The heart of the piece always remains.

During a pause in his lecture, I asked, "How can I stop it from tarni…"

"You can't," the jeweler interrupted, perturbed that I would suggest such a thing. "Not if you ever expect to wear it."

He's right. It was a dumb question. I can see that the tarnish isn't a result of disuse, of inaction. No, it's an inevitable part of existence in the world, of contact with the harsh pollutants in the air, of exposure to life.

And the result is a dull piece of jewelry that has lost its ability to radiate its light.

Cassandra's Daughter

He finished his speech and shifted to the role of businessman. He flashed a smarmy smile as he offered to clean the harp for me for a "discounted" price. But I want to do it myself, if possible. I understand that the cleansing will leave it vulnerable to the same elements that caused the protective reaction in the first place. But I finally understand the value of that vulnerability. That is where the beauty lies. And now that I know, I can clean it as soon as I see hints of discoloration, long before it is completely hidden by tarnish again.

Chapter 58

January 29, 1996

Journal Entry:

It's 4 AM, and I can't sleep. I had a dream. A dream? No, that's not quite right. A dream sounds lovely, benign. This wasn't a dream. But it wasn't a nightmare either, full of terror and frights. A haunting. That's it. It was a haunting. In sleep, the baby that wasn't meant to be came to me; she wanted me to know I shouldn't worry. She's ok. I felt her love. But my heart hurt, and I woke up abruptly. What am I supposed to do with that? Oh God. None of it's ok.

The baby was a girl? I did love her. I did. Or rather, I should say that I *do* love her.

I couldn't bring forth this beautiful girl. I feel like it's my fault. I killed her. I simply wasn't enough. I didn't have what was needed to save her. She never had a chance.

But she loves me. How can that be? How?

I miss her. Is that even possible? How can I miss her?

But I do.

So now I am writing in this journal and sipping a cup of tea at the kitchen table while waiting for the sun to rise. I'm scared she will visit me again if I go back to sleep. But what am I scared of? She can't do anything to me. She just wants me to see her. And I do. I see her.

I will tell the story of what happened to her. She deserves it to be told. Maybe I deserve to remember. I've never told anyone. Or even thought about her since. It's been easier to just pretend it never happened.

I didn't spend much time mourning after I lost her. What an odd turn of phrase. Did I "lose" the baby? That makes it sound like I somehow misplaced her. That's not at all what happened. The baby expelled itself from my womb. The little head, the arms, the heart—it all ended up in the toilet.

I wasn't very far along. Eight weeks? Maybe nine? The doctor said it's very common. That struck me as odd also. It's common? Common to simply quit? To reject life?

It was a one-night stand. I honestly don't even remember the night. Some guy was in my roommate's stats class, and he came over to study. But it was college. So it wasn't long before some of his friends showed up with beers. And we were all drinking. I didn't pay him any attention in particular. But each time I was handed a beer, I drank it. My next memory was of him on top of me in bed. I remember thinking, "Really? That's what we're doing?" I let him finish his business. Then he climbed off of me and gave me a passionate kiss and a hasty goodbye. That's embarrassing to admit now. I wasn't embarrassed then. I simply didn't care. His name was Scott. He was a decent-looking guy. A year older than me, he was a senior, graduating and moving to New York City in a few months. He certainly was not interested in anything more than a one-night stand, let alone a baby.

My roommate broke the news to him. I really had no intention of letting him know. He wanted me to have an abortion. I couldn't decide what I wanted to do. But as it turned out, it didn't matter.

A day came when cramps gripped my back. The pressure grew increasingly sharp, but an unrelenting urge to go to the bathroom distracted me from the pain. Once in the bathroom, I let out an uncontrolled groan before plopping down on the toilet. It didn't take long to figure out what was happening. The toilet filled with bright red blood, parts of it in clumps. I stood up and, without thinking, I flushed.

The doctor said that's common too. Out of sheer force of habit, this is what we do. We stand. And we flush.

I never told Scott what happened. This had nothing to do with him. But I will need to tell Kevin. Because this has everything to do with me.

Am I ready for that?

Chapter 59

February 1996

I actually got the job. Kevin isn't surprised, but I'm stunned. Last month, Tony called. The New York Historical Museum is hiring a Curator of American History Exhibitions, and Tony put my name in for consideration; he thinks I will be a great fit for the job.

I didn't know how to broach the subject with Kevin. Or if I wanted to broach the subject at all. But it didn't matter. Tony and Kevin had also been talking regularly and sharing their interest in Prohibition. Kevin encouraged me to interview for the position. I was surprised. Did he want me to move to New York? I listened to his reasoning, which centered mostly on his opinion that I have spent too long at the Chicago Historical Foundation, that I am not stretching myself, that I am being taken advantage of. But do I even want to stretch myself?

I had never considered leaving Chicago. I never really considered working somewhere else. And what about Kevin? Where would he fit in all this?

I flew up to New York for a formal interview and was offered the job. Kevin has cooked me dinner to celebrate my new adventure, the new adventure I haven't yet decided I want to embark on.

He pours us each a glass of merlot. I pick up my glass to see how this new vintage compares to the glass we had before dinner. But before I have a chance to sample it, Kevin asks to make a toast. Reflexively, I hold out my glass.

"To new opportunities and to new possibilities." He lifts his glass to mine. We each take a sip. Wonderful. This is so much smoother than the earlier glass.

Then Kevin drops to one knee.

"I can write anywhere. I can move to New York with you. Or I can stay here in Chicago. I only want to be with you. I want us to write our own story. And I think we can write a great story. So Cassie, will you marry me?"

I hadn't thought about any future, with or without Kevin. I'd been going through the motions for a long time, not directing my path toward any particular destination but instead letting my path direct me. He watches as the thoughts ricochet through my mind. He loves me, doesn't he? He loves *me*. He anticipates exactly what I need in that moment, and he takes me in his arms.

"Yes. Of course, yes," I answer. But it doesn't need to be said.

The wedding will be here in Chicago before we move to New York. And Kevin will commit himself full time to the book on abandoned Prohibition towns. The wedding will be a simple affair, for our priority is on life after the wedding. I am all that is left of my family. But Kevin has a big family, and they have embraced me as part of their circle. I love feeling part of such a supportive community. It is one of the things that draws me to Kevin. They trust Kevin and his decisions, and so they trust that choosing me is a good decision. Isn't that what we all desire?

Chapter 60

September 1996

The widow who lives across the street came to my door today with a basket filled with rattles and bibs and bottles and a cassette tape of lullabies. We aren't close, but she has taken a sudden interest in me now that I'm pregnant. Her husband died thirty years ago, and her children long ago moved away.

Kevin's rhythmic snores indicate he doesn't suffer from the same sleeplessness I can't seem to conquer. Rather than continue to toss and turn, I crawl out of bed and sneak into the nursery, or what will soon be the nursery. It needs a lot of work still. But right now, it has a dresser, a rocking chair, and the gift basket. The rocking chair belonged to my grandmother. I'm not sure how it ended up with me, but I've had it since I first moved out of my parents' house, back when I was accepting any and all donations to fill my apartment. I'm glad it did follow me. I changed the seat from a plastic covered gold rayon to a generic light green cotton to match the curtains in this room. We want the sex of the baby to be a surprise. Hence, the green.

I rock slowly in silence.

More nights than not, I sneak out of bed, cross the hall to the baby's room, and sit in the dark spending time with both my babies, the one I carry and the one watching over us.

Surely my mother felt this way when she was pregnant with me.

Didn't she?

I reach over to pick up the small frame that holds one of the old black and white photos I pulled out of the garbage when I was cleaning out my parents' house. In it, my mother sits up straight with stiffly good posture on the edge of a couch decorated with a long doily delicately running along its back. She wears a two-strand pearl necklace and a dark, short-sleeved top with a high neckline. Her hair is perfectly coifed in the beehive that was popular at the time, with a few curls carefully pulled down to frame her forehead. Her head is slightly tilted, and she smiles up at the camera. One hand rests on her hip, her elbow jutting out to the side. The other holds a sleeping infant. That's me. She's carefully posed. And in her arm, I am staged as a mere prop for a requisite post-birth photo.

I search the photo, search for the love she must have felt for me. Or my love for her. I have searched this photo so many times. But tonight, for the first time, I stare into her eyes and notice a sparkle. It isn't obvious with a cursory glance. But yes, a sparkle. I see it. I feel it.

I put the frame back on the dresser and then dig through the basket of gifts. I find what I am looking for: the tape of lullabies. I pop it into the cassette player on the floor next to me. The moonlight shines through the split in the curtains, stars visible in the clear night. And I rock in preparation for the rhythm of the music to come.

I am addicted to this time deep in the night in the privacy of the nursery, accompanied by music that transforms the love I feel into melodies and harmonies and complex chords and dancing lyrics.

> *Well the sun is slowly sinking down.*
> *But the moon is slowly rising.*
> *So this old world must still be spinning round,*
> *And I still love you.*

I lift my pajama top and watch my skin bump and roll as the baby maneuvers inside me.

> *So close your eyes.*
> *You can close your eyes,*

Chapter 60

It's all right.
I don't know no love songs,
And I can't sing the blues any more.
But I can sing this song.
And you can sing this song, when I'm gone.

I place my hands under my belly to cradle my baby. I resume rocking, the two of us in rhythm with each other and the music, and I imagine easing its fears and comforting its troubles.

It won't be long before another day.
We're going to have a good time.
And no one's going to take that time away.
You can stay as long as you like.

I repeat, "I love you. I love you." My cheeks are coated like a windshield in the rain; a salty tear makes its way to the corner of my lip.

So close your eyes.
You can close your eyes,
It's all right.
I don't know no love songs,
And I can't sing the blues any more.
But I can sing this song.
And you can sing this song, when I'm gone.

Chapter 61

November 1996

We dawdle in bed on a lazy Sunday morning. I'm miserable, and Kevin rubs my back as I lie on my side, seeking any relief. The baby is due next week. But I am also in awe at the responsibility I have facing me. I think about the generations of women before me who anticipated the arrival of their first child. Their backs must have also been wracked with cramps. They also must have feared the pain of the birth, worried about the health of their little one, lay awake concerned about whether they were up to the job. I wonder, are we worthy of the obligation? Do we possess enough love to bathe our children in it?

I close my eyes and transport myself to my mother's body as she awaited my birth. To imagine how she felt. I do the same with my grandmother as she carried my mother in her womb, alone and abandoned. I can only imagine they felt the same fears, anxieties, and love that I feel. Yes, that I *really* feel.

"Kevin?" I brace myself. It's time. I need to tell him a story. A story about me.

Kevin pulls his hand from my back and sits up, nervous at the tremor in my voice. "What's wrong?"

I roll onto my back and hold out my hand. I want to feel his flesh. My other hand grasps the harp that rests on my neck, and I rub it between my fingers. I am ready to tell him, despite my shame and heartache, my guilt and horror.

"I had a miscarriage."

I say it. Out loud. And strengthen at the release. Kevin takes me in his arms, saddened that I am only now feeling able to confide in him. But I'm not sad. The confession is a victory.

He wants to know everything. He wants to feel as if he experienced the event with me. He wants the story to be part of his story with me.

I share with him, sharing more than I had remembered myself. I'd punctured its hiding place and let it bleed all over. We dwell in the silence of our own thoughts. Until we're interrupted by a wail.

Kevin shoots up. I curl down. Another wail.

It comes from me.

Chapter 62

December 1996

The labor room has been decorated to mimic a private bedroom, complete with dark wood bedside tables, a leather easy chair, and box pleat curtains that match the comforter and throw pillows. An anesthesiologist rolls me on my side and inserts the epidural catheter so he can administer the numbing medication. Soon after, two nurses wheel me out and into the delivery room. I won't be allowed to deliver here. They lock the wheels and then extend two thin sections jutting out from each side of the bed, much like a cross. They then stretch out both of my arms and strap them down to those sections.

I feel a twinge of claustrophobia. Something about having my arms strapped down. The feeling echoes through my bones.

Soon all four limbs are restrained, and the most vulnerable parts of my body are exposed. I'm numb from the waist down, and my head is clouded. Some primitive part of me fights like hell. It takes all my energy to keep from screaming. I imagine I am a hapless patient in some dystopian movie where the powerful conduct masochistic experiments on the powerless.

The nurses finally let Kevin in, which calms me. He pulls down his mask to give me a quick kiss but is quickly admonished and directed to take a seat. He sits near my head and lays his hand on my arm.

A hush sweeps through the room as the door opens and in walks the doctor.

My arms frantically pull against the straps, and my heart pounds hard against my chest. The more I pull against them, the more I panic.

A nurse hurries to my side. "Are you in pain?"

No, I'm not in pain. I'm sufficiently numb, so I won't feel the knife slicing through my skin, fat, and uterus.

But I'm scared.

Yes. I'm scared. I'm scared of how my life will change after today. I'm scared of the unknown and the unknowable. I'm scared of failing this baby. I'm scared of failing Kevin. I'm scared of what we will endure together. I'm scared of being honest. I'm scared.

A tug. No pain.

Another tug. And nothing. Oh no. I feel nothing. No pain. No relief. No change. Nothing. This is what I am most scared of.

"It's a girl!" comes the exclamation from a nurse. "You ready to meet your little girl?" she asks.

Before I answer, she holds the newborn's little face, eyes blinking slowly, right up to mine.

The numbness I held in my body and in my heart dissolves. The hidden shame of my grandmother. The deafening desperation of my mother. They are gone.

"Hi Chloe," I whisper.

Epilogue

April 2000

Rays of light explode across the horizon as the sun demands that my attention be focused on this moment. And I acknowledge its authority.

Oakdale is an old, private cemetery that appears to have surrendered to nature. What were once saplings now provide a canopy of cool shade. Wildflowers haphazardly dot the land as if Mother Nature playfully scattered a handful of seeds. A deer grazes nearby until it senses me and freezes, except for the twisting and turning of its ears. It concludes that I'm not a threat and carries on. An American flag staked at the side of a veteran's marker etched with the words "US Army, WWII, Bronze Star, Purple Heart recipient" is so faded and frayed as to be hardly recognizable.

I know not what death holds. I don't know if the dead have any awareness of what they have left behind or of the experiences of their loved ones who are still alive. I hope not. Wouldn't being aware of their suffering put us not in heaven but rather in hell?

We instinctively mumble "Rest in Peace," when we hear of a death. We etch RIP into tombstones. But how can one rest in peace when their lives have been lies, when the truth of who they are, their uniqueness in this world, their story, lies buried with them? Where is the peace in that?

I now have the tools to help my mother and my grandmother find eternal peace. I bring with me letters I have written to each, revealing their secrets to each other, exposing the stories they buried. They need to be told. My grandmother shaped my mother's life in ways my mother never understood, ways that left her desperate and lonely. She believed something was wrong with her. But there wasn't. I'm sorry she didn't know that. I'm sorry I didn't know that either. But I'll set her straight.

I recognize the spot where my mother and my grandmother rest, the sites indistinguishably intermingled under my feet. Where does one end? Where does the other begin? Where do I fit?

A branch from an errant bush landed on the marker and covers my mother's name. I move it off and clear some of the debris that has settled in the area.

I glance around at the community that keeps my mother company here. She lacked such a community while she lived in cruel mortality. My stomach sharply clenches. I know this strangling of my insides well. For I had also not provided my mother with what she craved. I don't feel guilty. I wasn't capable of helping her. But I feel badly.

Typically, I avoid stepping right on top of gravesites out of respect for those buried there, but today, much too late to be of any comfort to her, I drop to my knees in front of the stone that bears her name.

The sun has risen enough to be visible, and it blankets my back in a life-giving hug. A slight breeze tickles my arms, sending goosebumps across my skin. It only lasts a moment before a violent jolt unexpectedly hits my body. In defense, I double over, and in protection, I roll to the ground, legs tucked into my chest, like a startled armadillo.

Two butterflies calm me as they flit about. I stretch out in an embrace of the land while they flutter erratically, collide, and fly off. I follow their path until my eyes land on the grave of my grandmother.

Her headstone is one of the more ornate in the cemetery. But it feels appropriate; my few memories paint her as bigger than life, an imposing figure.

I push myself up to my feet and move towards it.

I place my hand on the cold, unforgiving stone and bend to trace her name with my fingers. She has no power. I feel guilty at the truth of that. She left this earth satisfied that she was the sole arbiter of her own story, a story skillfully plotted and disseminated. She had been a

Epilogue

masterful magician, pulling rabbits out of empty hats and making coins disappear into thin air. But it was only slight of hand.

I am her storyteller now. With a strength I didn't know I had, I ripped her story up through the dirt and the rocks and the roots, and I exposed it to the light of day.

What would she think if she knew? If she knew it had all been exposed? I can't concern myself with that. This story was necessary for my own survival. For the survival of …

My thoughts are interrupted by the splash of water.

"Mama!"

The little voice rings across the field, bouncing off headstones and birthing a tear of remembrance to every mother buried there.

I melt at the sound of the voice, a voice so consumed by the moment that it embraces life, unconcerned for the setting or the people buried there.

"Chloe!" I laugh, watching her father scold her from the side of the pond where our daughter has decided to splash around.

I don't remember running to greet her. But Chloe laughs out loud at my clumsy steps. She bounces out of the pond and leaps into my arms, nearly knocking me down, even as small as she is.

"I picked flowers. For your mom," she announces, holding out soaked and droopy daisies.

"Come with me. Let's give them to her. She would like that."

I put her down next to me and hold her hand as I guide her to my mother's gravesite. Chloe drops my hand and plops down, right on top of where her grandmother is buried. That is exactly where she should sit. She finds a little stick, which she uses to dig a hole, a little earthen vase for the flowers. She places the daisies in the makeshift vase, and they immediately fall to the side, but Chloe pays it no mind. Something has caught her eye.

"Oh! Hi Daddy," she says as Kevin joins them.

He had assisted Chloe in her search for "the most prettiest flowers" at the cemetery's entrance to give me a moment alone with my mother. But I am grateful he is here now. He walks up behind Chloe and gently puts his hand on her shoulder. He gifts me with a smile and then mouths, "Sorry," apologizing for the wet daughter between us. But there's no need to apologize. Let her explore, I think. Let her play.

"Is that your mother?" Chloe asks me, pointing to the name on the marker in front of her.

"Yes," I tell her. "It is."

Chloe jumps up. And with the innocence and curiosity of a child, she asks the question at the heart of everything.

"Can you tell me a story about her?"

To the Reader

Thank you so much for reading *Cassandra's Daughter*! If you enjoyed this book, please tell your friends and leave a review on Amazon, Goodreads, and anywhere else you might share books that you've read. Be sure to also recommend *Cassandra's Daughter* and share it on all your social media platforms.

My previous book, *Clara's Journal: And the Story of Two Pandemics*, a nonfiction story about life in rural South Dakota during the 1918 influenza pandemic told through the eyes of 18-year-old Clara Horen, is available as a paperback and an ebook on Amazon.

Sign up for my newsletter and blog to receive a free download of the first chapter of *Clara's Journal*. Simply visit my website, where you can stay up-to-date with me and my writing.

www.vickieoddino.com

Hope to see you there. And thanks for reading!

Acknowledgements

This book has been such a labor of love and has provided me with such joy in the writing. And I want to give a huge thanks to those who have supported me through this journey.

First, I want to thank my mother, Pat Horen, who passed away in 2013 and suffered from the secrets that her own mother kept from her. I wish she knew that she was a huge inspiration for this book.

I also want to thank my children, Emily and James, who have believed in me and in this project from the beginning. They were the first two to read a completed manuscript and both assured me that I had something of value here. That endorsement propelled me in my darkest hours. And even better, they both had incredibly helpful constructive criticism that made this book so much better.

Thanks to Robert Bidinotto, a great author in his own right, who provided the initial developmental edits and gave me invaluable feedback as well as enthusiastic encouragement.

My first readers each provided insightful feedback for which I am tremendously grateful: Marsha Enright, Dawn Heflin, and Lauren Keener. And of course, thanks to my advanced readers, who were the first to actually hold copies of the finished project. Their excitement to be involved in the process and to be among the first to read the novel gave me the persistence to complete the final steps of getting this book to market.

Finally, thanks to ebooklaunch.com for designing the cover, to Joseph Wallace for designing my website, and to Sue Colao of Purple Fish Creative for designing the interior graphics.

Book Club Discussion

Thank you for choosing *Cassandra's Daughter* for your book club! Having been in a book club for many years myself, I know how important the book choice is to the discussion as well as how important you all are to each other.

I am currently offering a free call-in to those book clubs that are reading *Cassandra's Daughter* to give members an opportunity to ask me any questions they might have about the book itself or about the writing process. I will do my best to coordinate my schedule to match yours. If interested, email information about your book club and possible dates to info@dobsonstpublishing.com, and someone will get back to you.

In the meantime, below is a list of some ideas you can use to kick off a conversation about the novel. Feel free to pick and choose those that are most appropriate for your group of friends.

Questions

1. What meaning do you take from the title of the novel?
2. The cover depicts a mother and daughter looking out at water. Typically, water symbolizes rebirth. How is water used as a symbol in this book?
3. Given that she has no family there anymore, why does Cora return to Portland after giving birth?
4. Most of the men in the novel aren't really given much of a voice. Why might the author have chosen to focus primarily on the women? Are men similarly impacted by secrets passed down in families?

5. Kevin is one male character who does have a voice in the novel. Why is his voice particularly important to include?
6. Are there any secrets in your own family that were revealed only after those involved in the secret had passed away? Did knowing the truth change your opinion of that person or of yourself and your own life? How did it feel to find out about the secret?
7. How does the birth experience impact each character, both giving birth and being born?
8. Do you know the story of your own birth? Did it have any particular impact on you or your mother? Have you given birth? How did that experience impact you and your child? Have you given birth more than once? How did the experiences differ? In the discussion, consider the role of the doctor, the midwife, the nurses, the child's father, other family members, any medication used, and the setting of the birth.
9. Would you consider Cora to be a good or a bad mother? Why?
10. Would you consider Leah to be a good or a bad mother? Why?
11. What is the significance of Cassie's first pregnancy ending in miscarriage?
12. Most of the story is told in limited third-person point of view (POV) with the perspective jumping around from character to character. However, Cassie's story is told a bit differently when it comes to POV. How is her story told? Why might the author have told Cassie's story differently? And does that change your perspective of her as compared to other characters?
13. Are there any situations that a character finds herself in that you would handle differently? What are they?
14. A dynamic character is one who undergoes an internal change as a result of events that occur in the novel. The opposite of that is a static character; he or she remains the same throughout the book, regardless of what occurs. When observing the main female characters—Bessie, Cora, Leah, Cassie, and Florence—are any of them dynamic? If so, what triggers their change? How would you describe the dynamic character(s) before and then after the change?
15. Consider that the definition of the theme of a book is the message that it tells us about the real world that we live in. What message

does *Cassandra's Daughter* give us about life? And there can certainly be multiple answers to this question!
16. What feelings did the book evoke? And why?
17. Are there any quotes, passages, or scenes you found particularly compelling? Why?

About the Author

Vickie Oddino is a writer, photographer, mother of two, and author of *Cassandra's Daughter*, a family saga spanning three generations of women that begins in Ireland and stretches from Portland, Maine, to New York City and then to Chicago. She is also the author of the 2021 nonfiction book *Clara's Journal: And the Story of Two Pandemics*, a glimpse at life in 1918 rural South Dakota through the eyes of an 18-year-old high school senior.

Vickie has a Bachelor of Journalism from the University of Missouri and a Master of Arts in English from California State University. As a professor, she taught college English for 25 years and wrote essays and narrative nonfiction for a variety of newspapers, magazines, and websites. More recently she has published most of her shorter essays on her blog. Her interest in family history and the extensive research she has done on her own family has driven many additional writing projects.

She has traveled the United States and the world, and she loves to document her trips through photography. Her passion is in street photography and capturing urban landscapes. Vickie is always searching for adventure and good stories, and she is fortunate to have plenty of family and friends who provide her with both. Currently, she lives in a very photogenic city, Chicago, with the family dog, Captain.

For more information, visit www.vickieoddino.com.

Made in United States
North Haven, CT
07 December 2022

28081925R10221